Katie Mettner wears the titl⟨...⟩
her leg after falling down ⟨...⟩
decorating her prosthetic leg to fit the season. She lives in
Northern Wisconsin with her own happily-ever-after and
spends the day writing romantic stories with her sweet
puppy by her side. Katie has an addiction to coffee and
dachshunds and a lessening aversion to Pinterest—now
that she's quit trying to make the things she pins.

Award-winning author **Kathleen Donnelly** is a K-9 handler
for a private narcotics dog detection company. She enjoys
using her K-9 experience to craft realism into her fictional
stories. Kathleen lives near the Colorado foothills with her
husband and her four-legged coworkers. Visit Kathleen
on her website at kathleendonnelly.com, on Facebook at
AuthorKathleenDonnelly, follow her on X @KatK9writer
or find her on Instagram @authorkathleendonnelly

Also by Katie Mettner

Secure Watch
Dark Web Investigation

Secure One
Going Rogue in Red Rye County
The Perfect Witness
The Red River Slayer
The Silent Setup
The Masquerading Twin
Holiday Under Wraps

TRACING HER STOLEN IDENTITY

KATIE METTNER

COLORADO K-9 RESCUE

KATHLEEN DONNELLY

MILLS & BOON

First Published in Great Britain 2025
by Mills & Boon, an imprint of HarperCollins*Publishers* Ltd
1 London Bridge Street, London, SE1 9GF

www.harpercollins.co.uk

HarperCollins*Publishers*
Macken House, 39/40 Mayor Street Upper,
Dublin 1, D01 C9W8, Ireland

Tracing Her Stolen Identity © 2025 Katie Mettner
Colorado K-9 Rescue © 2025 Kathleen Donnelly

ISBN: 978-0-263-39729-1

0925

TRACING HER
STOLEN IDENTITY

KATIE METTNER

For my Duluth friends.

Chapter One

Skylar Sullivan tapped her card against the screen at the pharmacy and waited while the card reader spun. The word *declined* popped up on the screen. She frowned. That was weird. Her seven-dollar prescription was not going to drain her bank account.

"Sorry," she said to the pharmacist, who was patiently waiting for her to pay. She realized they'd close soon, so Skylar hurried to find her cash. "I've been gone for two weeks and haven't used my debit card. The bank must have put a hold on it. I think I have cash."

"No problem, Skylar. I noticed you haven't been around. Were you on vacation?"

"A working one," she answered, digging in the bag under her wheelchair for her wallet. "I decided to get away from it all and drive to Grand Marais to work on my portfolio. The lake always inspires my nature mosaics, so I rented a little cabin on the shore."

"Well, that sounds like an idyllic place to work, if not a bit chilly for April."

"You could say that again." Skylar handed the woman a ten. "I was lucky the cabin had a great fireplace and lots of precut firewood. It was also accessible, which is rare these days."

The pharmacist smiled and handed her the receipt, change and bag. "I imagine that's always a consideration, but I'm glad you found a way to finish your work. You know I'm a huge fan."

"Thanks, Marguerite. I'm keeping my fingers crossed for a gallery showing soon."

"I'll cross mine, too!" Marguerite said, twining her fingers together before she waved goodbye. Skylar pushed the hand rims forward to the door, knowing she still had another stop before heading to her duplex in the middle of Duluth, Minnesota.

She'd lived in Duluth her entire life and had no plans to move—ever. Did it suck moving around the Northland in a wheelchair in the middle of January? Yes, but there was nowhere else she wanted to live. Seeing Lake Superior every time she drove down the street was her little piece of heaven. The city had everything she needed, including medical care and accessible housing. The art scene was also hopping, and she had her stained-glass mosaics placed in small galleries around the Northland. She sold out regularly, but they also brought in special orders that kept her afloat as a struggling artist. Her goal was to host an extensive gallery showing in the Twin Cities, but first, she had to have a portfolio to back her up. That was why she'd taken the time away to finish some of her tile mosaics. She needed diverse pieces to draw a crowd in a city the size of Minneapolis, where there were twice as many artists as in Duluth.

She could have stayed another two weeks in that little cabin by the lake working on nature pieces, but her friend needed it for her family. Truthfully, while she loved her time away to finish her work, she'd reached the level of solitude she could take. There was never any question that she was the outgoing one in her family. Unlike many artists, she needed human interaction to access her creativity. She'd strike up a conversation with anyone at any given time. That may have something to do with her disability and the fact that most people saw her chair but never saw *her*. Over the years, she'd learned that the chair melted away when she engaged them in conversation, and they'd see her for who she really was.

A smile tipped her lips as she transferred onto the truck seat and connected the hoist to her chair, using the remote to lift it into the pickup's bed. She could break the chair down and stow it in the front seat, but that was always a dirty and wet endeavor in the winter. Not only did the truck give her better traction in the snow for driving up and down the hills of Duluth, but the hoist saved her a ton of time, not to mention wear and tear on her chair.

After a quick stop to drop off some things at her friend's studio that she wouldn't need at the apartment, she headed toward the bridge, dusk gathering at the lake's edges to prepare them for bed after another successful day. Her aching back told her she'd be glad to get home and sleep in her own bed after a long time away.

Her laughter filled the truck as she exited and headed up the hill to her duplex. She was thirty-one, not eighty-one, but someone forgot to tell her paralyzed body that. Her accident had been fourteen years ago, and sitting in a wheelchair all day for that many years tended to be rough on the old vertebrae. Skylar noticed the billboard for her credit union, reminding her she needed to check her account as soon as she got home.

Once parked in the driveway, she hoisted her chair to the ground and did the same with her suitcase, using the chair hoist to catch the handle. Sometimes she wished she had a butler to help her move her things around. Then she'd laugh and remind herself to pack light, because a butler was not in the budget.

Happy to be home, she grabbed her bag and headed to the ramp leading to her duplex. Usually she parked in the garage, where she had a ramp to the house as well, but at the moment the garage was full of art supplies. She would have to bug a friend to help her load and unload them at his studio across town.

A mail truck drove by, reminding her to get online and start her mail delivery again, too. There were so many things to do, but her first order of business was the bank.

She unlocked the door and pushed it inward, surprised when she met with resistance. Nothing should be blocking the door. She'd held her packages and mail, and no one was even checking on the place. Her next-door neighbor, Mrs. Valentine, had a key, but she was unlikely to go in unless there had been a problem in her unit. She certainly would have called Skylar if that were the case, since she was Mrs. Valentine's landlord.

Determined, she pushed harder until the door opened far enough for her to roll in. Once she crossed the threshold, what she saw drew a gasp from her lips. The entire living room had been upended, her belongings broken and ripped apart, and her glass art statues shattered on the floor. She realized a table had been moved in front of the front door to block it, making it difficult to get in far enough to close it behind her.

"I have to call the police," she whispered, reaching for the phone as a text came in.

Still in shock, she opened the text, glancing at it for barely a moment before her eye was drawn back to the living room, where her beautiful art pieces lay in shattered dreams across the hardwood floor. She loved this duplex because of its hardwood floors and easy accessibility in her chair, but the destruction before her turned that love into hate.

The strangeness of the text filtered through her shock, and she glanced at it again. It had come from an unknown caller and was nothing more than a link she didn't recognize. Her finger on the delete button, she hesitated. In light of the carnage around her, she clicked the link. The worst thing that would happen was that her phone would get a virus, but in light of the destruction of her home and its timely arrival, she was afraid to delete it before she checked the link. Her next call would be to the police.

When the webpage loaded, a video started. An Anonymous mask filled the screen, with zeroes and ones scrolling in the background. What sent shivers down her spine was the computerized voice when it spoke. "Hello, Skylar. I'm Binate. It's so nice to meet you. We do hope you enjoy the redecorating we did in your absence. You've been on quite the tear lately with your vandalism, so treating your home with the same love and affection only seemed right. Naughty, naughty what you've done to those poor, unsuspecting art galleries. I bet you're sitting there in your bright white chair, starkly terrified by the trauma around you, not to mention this message I've sent. Good. I hope you suffer the same way you've made others suffer. I bet your finger is on speed dial for 911, but I wouldn't do that if I were you. It will be hard to prove that you own that house or that Skylar Sullivan exists anymore. I want you to feel the kind of pain that you've caused others. I'm coming for you, and the chase starts now, Skylar. Run as fast as you can— Oh, wait, you can't run! That will make this that much more fun." The voice broke out into evil laughter until it cut off sharply, the screen going black.

Skylar let out a breath, the phone heavy in her hand. She

had to call the police but couldn't bring herself to punch in the numbers. Not until she verified that what the text said was true. With a flick of her wrist, she locked the front door, rested the phone on her leg and pushed her chair forward, careful of the glass on the floor as she wheeled to the kitchen to check the back door. When she tugged on the knob, it was locked, which meant whoever had trashed the place had locked up after themselves. A shudder went through her at the thought of someone she didn't know in her home, touching her things and destroying her heirlooms.

Anger filled her. What did he mean by vandalism and pain and trauma to art galleries? Glancing around her kitchen, where every plate, bowl and glass she owned was smashed in a pile on the floor, she imagined the hatred someone must have to do so much damage. From what she saw, the only person suffering pain and trauma was herself.

Remembering what Binate said about proving who she was, she left the kitchen and wheeled down the hallway toward her bedroom. A glance to her left told her that the guest bathroom had received the same treatment as the living room. She brought the chair to a halt at the entrance to her bedroom and sucked in a deep breath at the sight before her. The room looked like a tornado had gone through it. Nothing was where it belonged, and the mattress was slashed open, as were the pillows, feathers strewn everywhere.

Fear rocketed through her, but she pushed the chair inside and went to her safe, her mouth falling open when she saw the door hanging half off the hinges. She felt around inside but found nothing. All her paperwork was gone—her Social Security card and everything she'd need to prove her identity. At least she still had her driver's license. She fumbled with the phone and opened her banking app. What she saw dropped her heart to her stomach.

"No, no. This can't be," Skylar whispered, refreshing the page only to get the same result.

Skylar lifted her head and blinked back the tears threatening to fall. She pushed in 911, but a little voice inside told her to stop, think and analyze the situation. It didn't take long for the complete picture to form, and once she understood the gravity of the situation, she opened the phone app and called the only man who could help her.

Chapter Two

A chime rang through Reece Palmer's house, and he looked at his phone as he chewed his Grape-Nuts. They crunched under his teeth like rocks, rattling his brain until he dumped the bowl in the sink. Chalk another nope up to the health gurus on the internet. So much for breakfast for supper. After he swiped the notification open, he almost choked on those Grape-Nuts when he read the Google Alert.

An arrest warrant had been issued for Skylar Sullivan? No, it had to be a different Skylar Sullivan, he thought as he walked to his desk. Reece sat at his computer and shook the mouse, waking the beast he used for his remote work for Secure Watch, a company out of northern Minnesota that offered physical protection of properties and digital protection of company assets. Reece used to be the muscle, but his boss, Mina Jacobs, had lured him to the dark side with cookies and the promise that he'd likely get shot at less frequently if he worked behind a screen.

She'd been right, too. Reece had been working for Secure Watch for the last two years and hadn't been shot at once, unlike his time working security, which often put them in some pretty interesting situations. Cybersecurity had been his first love when he went to college to study criminal justice. Still, it wasn't until Secure Watch came along that he'd found a home as a cybersecurity specialist.

He clicked the link included with the Google Alert and it took him to a page with a list of arrest warrants issued over the last week. Skylar Sullivan, thirty-one, was wanted for vandalism of several art galleries in the area. Reece opened a tab and googled the art galleries, reading the stories about the vandalism, including graffiti and breaking glass doors and windows. This had to be a different Skylar, the same age or not. The Skylar Sullivan he knew was the gentlest soul alive, not to mention she used a wheelchair and was incapable of tagging buildings with graffiti six feet off the ground.

Reece closed the window and sighed with relief. He'd known Skylar his entire life, and even though he hadn't seen her since he graduated from college, he'd kept tabs on her as best he could. She was a talented artist, and he followed her career even if she could never know it. He shook the mouse back and forth a few times before he grabbed his Secure Watch phone and dialed Mina's number.

"Secure Watch, Whiskey," she answered.

"Secure Watch, Riker," he responded, letting her know it was safe to talk freely.

"What's up, Reece?" Mina asked. "Did you finish that job I sent you?"

"Just about," he said, still wondering what he was doing. "You should have the report in a few. While I'm finishing that, would you do me a favor?" Mina used to work for the FBI, so she had channels that even he could never access when it came to finding information.

"I'll try," she said, as though she could hear his indecision about asking.

"A Google Alert came through for a friend of mine. Skylar Sullivan, thirty-one," he explained. "It's an arrest warrant from Duluth PD for vandalism of art galleries."

"Do you know Skylar Sullivan?" Mina asked, and he could hear her pen tapping on the faithful legal pad alongside her, always waiting for her to scratch out notes.

"I do—did," he said, quickly changing to the past tense. "We went to school together. She's an artist, and I set up an alert to keep an eye on her career."

"An artist is accused of vandalizing art galleries? That doesn't make a lot of sense, Reece."

"That's why I called. When I checked the news stories about the vandalism, I found that some of the graffiti on the buildings was six feet off the ground. The Skylar I know has been in a wheelchair since she was seventeen."

Mina was silent momentarily before saying, "I see" in a way only Mina could say it. She always made you feel like she knew all your secrets. She had probably honed that skill in the FBI.

"That's why I'm thinking it can't be her. My Skylar is thirty-one, born and raised in Duluth, and her parents are Mary and Joseph." No joke, her parents were named Mary and Joseph. He still chuckled every time he had to say their names together. "She had one brother, named Silas, but he's probably dead. No one has been able to find him for years, ever since he left home." He replayed the sentence in his head, and he stuttered. "Not *my* Skylar, but the Skylar I'm talking about."

Mina snorted but didn't respond. "Understood. Does the Skylar, who isn't yours, still live in Duluth?"

"Last I heard, but, oddly, they haven't arrested her yet. The last address I had for her was 1776 West Quince Street."

"Duluth Heights area. Got it. Give me ten. Whiskey, out."

Reece hung up and transferred the files and report Mina

needed into a zip file, then sent it electronically via their direct server. No sooner had he closed it than his personal phone rang, so he grabbed it, surprised to see a local number, though one unknown to him.

"Reece Palmer."

"Ra—Reece?" A woman's soft but terrified voice filled the line. "Reece Palmer from Duluth Denfield High School?"

"Yes," he said slowly, wondering who would call him and reference that. The thought had barely crossed his mind when the answer came to him. "Skylar?"

Her quiet gasp told him he'd nailed it. "I—I need help."

"Tell me what's going on," he said, waiting for her to explain the reason for her call. He didn't know why she'd be calling him, but hearing her voice again sent him places he didn't want to go at the moment.

"I was out of town working on my portfolio for a few weeks, and when I returned today and stopped for a prescription, my card was declined. When I got home, my duplex had been completely ransacked, and, Reece, they took all my documents like my Social Security card and everything that proves who I am."

"Who are *they*?" Reece jumped up and grabbed his wallet, jamming it in his back pocket. He pulled on his anorak and swung his go-bag out of the closet. It didn't get used much anymore, but the habit of always keeping one packed when he worked for Cal at Secure One was hard to break. He'd known it would come in handy one day, and today was that day. He hadn't expected that one day to involve the woman he'd grown up with and had once thought would be his, though. At the last second, he darted back to the desk to grab his Secure Watch phone and portable laptop.

"I don't know!" she exclaimed with frustration. "My bank

accounts are empty or, at least, they don't exist anymore, and I got a text from someone named Binate who said I shouldn't call the police because I've been a bad girl. Reece, I don't know what's happening, but I'm terrified."

Reece froze in place, his heart sinking the more she explained. "Where are you now, Sky?" He accidentally referred to her by the nickname he'd used all her life but didn't take the time to correct himself. "Are you safe?"

"I don't know!" she exclaimed again. "I locked myself in my duplex because I didn't know what else to do. I don't have any money or paperwork proving who I am other than my driver's license."

"Okay, stay put until I get there. What's your address?" he asked as though he didn't already know.

"It's the same place I've always been. You don't have to come. I can meet you somewhere."

"I'd rather you stay put until I get there. I'm only ten minutes away."

"You'll see a truck in the driveway. It's mine. The garage is too full to park in."

"Okay. Don't unlock the door until I ring the bell. If anyone else shows up, hide. I'm on my way."

After a quick goodbye, he hung up the phone, slammed the door behind him and ran for his truck. Something was rotten in Duluth, and the woman he once thought he'd marry was in the middle of it.

As soon as the truck roared to life, he threw it in Reverse, then headed toward the Duluth Heights neighborhood. They'd grown up there, and her address was the same as it had been her entire life, which meant she must have bought the house from her parents when they moved to Florida.

He blew out a breath and used voice to text to call Mina again. When she answered, he didn't let her speak. "Skylar just called me. Her duplex has been vandalized and all her bank accounts have disappeared."

"That's not all that's gone," Mina said, her voice even, but he could sense her underlying nerves. "Her entire life has been wiped away, Reece. She's in trouble."

Those three words had him jamming his foot down harder on the gas pedal as a sense of doom filled him. He'd let Skylar down once; there was no way he would do it again.

Chapter Three

The doorbell rang in eight minutes, which meant Reece had either broken some laws or was closer to their old neighborhood than he'd thought. Skylar rolled to the door and grabbed the handle, taking a steeling breath before opening it. She hadn't seen him since he'd graduated from college and left for a job elsewhere. She had attended the University of Wisconsin Superior across the bridge for a degree in art, but she had promptly dropped out after a year when she discovered making money as an artist had nothing to do with a degree.

While he'd attended college, Reece had lived at home, which was next door to her house. They'd grown up that way, spending most of their waking hours together as kids, but their social time had become less and less as he made new friends in college and his high school relationships became less important to him. When *she* became less important to him, but she'd wanted it that way, hadn't she? Skylar had told him in no uncertain terms they would never be more than friends, even though he had made it clear several times that he wanted to date her. She'd had her reasons back then. Reasons that didn't seem nearly as important to her anymore.

"Skylar!" He pounded on the door, drawing her from her thoughts as she jumped and yanked on the handle.

The man standing on her ramp took her breath away. "Back up," he said, his words clipped. Once she was clear, he closed the door behind him as he assessed the front room. "Holy hell." The two words were said in one breath before he knelt to make eye contact. "Are you okay?"

"Shaken but not hurt," she answered, inhaling his scent. He still wore Stetson cologne on his body and a Stetson hat on his head, but everything else about him, besides the color of his eyes, was bigger, stronger and sexier than she wanted to face right now.

As he gazed at her from under the brim of that black hat, his one blue eye and one gray eye sparked with the same kind of familiarity she was sure was in her own. Their childhood years ran through her mind as she came face-to-face with the boy who was now a man. Reece, the boy she had called Land because he called her Sky, had always been tall, but even squatting, he could meet her eyes in the chair. His curly blond hair peeked out from under the hat and nearly touched his collar. It was either a sign that he liked it long or hadn't had time to get it cut recently. She remembered how she used to play with his hair, twirling the curls around her fingers, when she was a little girl. She wanted to do it again and then let her fingers travel to his face to touch the shaped, tightly trimmed goatee that cupped his chin. She wouldn't do that, though, because they weren't friends anymore.

"Thank you for coming. I didn't know what else to do until I remembered you were back in town."

"I suppose everyone knew I was back in town after the Red River Slayer case ended."

"That, but also, your mom told my mom, who told me."

"Does anyone else live here?" he asked, and she could tell the idea that more people might be mixed up in this made him nervous.

"No, I live alone, other than while renting the other half to Mrs. Valentine. I don't know what's going on, but I'm the only one involved as far as I know."

"Good. Well, that's not good, but I'm glad we only have to worry about your safety right now. Let's get your things and get out of here."

"What? No. I can't leave my house like this!" She flung her hand around at the mess behind him, but he was already walking toward the bedrooms, the ones he knew well, considering he'd spent half of his childhood here.

Reece spun on the heel of what she noticed to be a pair of black snakeskin boots. "You can and you will. We don't have time to clean it up right now. Besides, my friends from Secure One will come in, look around and see what they can find."

"Don't you want to know what's happened?"

"Not here," he said with a tight shake of his head as he mouthed *bugs*. "We need to get out of here. Where's your phone?"

Without thinking, she dug it out of the bag under her chair. As he walked back over, she handed it to him. Did he think someone had bugged her house? A glance behind him at the destruction in her living room made her admit it was possible. The computerized voice started again, and she dragged her gaze to his, his brow up as he listened to the message. A shudder ran down her spine at the laughter. Would she hear that in her nightmares for the rest of her life? The idea worried her, but she bit back the whimper and straightened in her chair. When the video ended,

Reece grabbed a pen and paper from the table drawer near the couch and turned back to her.

Passcode, he mouthed, and she took the paper, scribbling the numbers down before handing it back to him. If he realized the significance of them, he didn't say. Instead, he tore the paper off the pad and tossed the phone and the paper into the drawer.

"I'll let my guys know where to find it, and they'll take it to my boss."

"Mina Jacobs?" Skylar asked, not surprised when he lifted a brow. That was always his "explain" action when they were kids. "Secure One and Secure Watch have made the national news multiple times, Reece. I don't live in a cave. The Spiderweb site your friends pulled down still terrifies me when I think about it."

Last year, the company he worked for might have saved the world in a roundabout way. They were involved in a situation on the dark web where one bad actor wrote a program that would slowly give him control over every camera in the world and the ability to collect all that data. The idea of that information in one person's hands was terrifying, and she had looked at security cameras in a whole new light ever since.

"Fair. I suppose that's why you called me?"

"No." She glanced down at her lap rather than meet his eyes. The last thing Skylar wanted to see was his reaction to her following statement. "I called you because even though it's been a decade since we've seen each other, I still trust you."

In a blink, he was kneeling in front of her again, his hands on her wheels. "You can trust me, Sky." His gaze darted left and right, maybe out of nervousness about the situation or because he kept using her childhood nickname despite his apparent desire not to. "Tell me what you need and I'll gather it. I don't want you to roll over any glass and get it stuck in your wheels. Remember what happened that one time?"

Her palm burned at the memory, and she held it up—a long, jagged scar puckered the skin even now, nearly a dozen years later. Reece ran his finger across the scar, sending a shiver of familiarity through her. He had always done that to her, and she was disappointed to know he still could. She'd thought she had Reece Palmer out of her head forever, but it turned out to be more of an out-of-sight, out-of-mind thing. "I suppose a trip to the emergency room for stitches would be inconvenient." Her wink told him she was teasing when she dropped her hand to her lap. "That suitcase is packed," she explained, pointing at the rolling suitcase in the hall-way. "I just got back from a trip, but I need more meds."

"Tell me where they are and I'll grab them."

"Lower kitchen cabinet to the left of the sink. But you don't know what I need."

Before she finished speaking, he was already walking to the kitchen. When he returned, he had a baggie full of pill bottles. He grabbed the one she'd set on top of the suitcase, stuffed it in and then unzipped the top of her bag to stash them. It wasn't orderly, but it got the job done.

"Stay here while I take the bag to my truck, then I'll re-turn for you."

"What if we're overreacting?" she asked, rolling aside so he could get to the door with her suitcase.

"Do you want to find out?" Slowly, he raised his brow again as he waited for her answer.

Binate's voice stuttered through her mind, and she shook her head as her heart rate picked up.

"I didn't think so. Wait right there."

Reece disappeared out the door, and she let out a breath

for the first time since he'd walked through it. She'd done many hard things in life, but spending the next few days with grown-up Reece Palmer would be the hardest thing she'd ever done.

Chapter Four

Reece slowed the truck and turned left into an area where the houses were separated by acres of land. Each property butted up to Paul Bunyan State Forest on one side and Leech Lake on the other. It was an area of anonymity if he'd ever seen one.

It had been a two-hour drive he'd done in near silence. A glance to his left told him Sky was still asleep. He'd pretended not to notice when she pulled straps from her bag and placed them around her thighs and calves. Without looking at him, she explained it kept her legs from falling open, which was uncomfortable on her hips, and then she'd promptly leaned against the window and gone to sleep. At least she pretended to, but she'd been awake for the first half hour. He knew, because he'd often notice her eyes pop open to see what he was doing.

It was probably the same thing she was doing: trying to forget all the time they'd spent together as kids but unable to stop the memories—both the good and bad. They had been thick as thieves growing up. Not only did they live next door to each other, but all four of their parents were coworkers at a large manufacturing firm in town. They ran, biked and played together. He was an only child, and Sky was the younger of two, but her brother, Silas, was already six by the time she was born, so they didn't have a lot in common.

Skylar was younger than Reece by three months and three days, but you'd never know it by how she bossed him around when they were kids. Her bossiness had always embarrassed her mom, but Reece loved it. He always said she wasn't bossy. She just knew what she wanted and how she would get it. There was something to be said about a girl with gumption, as far as he was concerned, and it had paid off for her. She had built an art empire, even if she didn't see it, and knowing Skylar the way he did, she didn't see it. She had always been driven to be better than she was the day before, which had kept her motivated to perfect her art.

Reece always thought it was strange that he'd had such a close relationship with Skylar as a kid. Their interests were so vastly different, but it never seemed to matter. Sky loved art—any art, from nature paintings to clay pottery. He loved playing cops and robbers, always fascinated by anything true crime-related. He loved comic books that told crime stories, and Sky, being who she was, loved to draw a choose-your-own-ending for the books just in case he didn't like how the original one ended. A smile lifted his lips at the memory. Everyone had always said they were as close as brother and sister, but Reece never agreed. His feelings for Sky had never been brotherly. They'd been something else. Something deeper that he couldn't explain. And then the accident happened, and everything changed.

Skylar had always been a sweet, beautiful, talented young girl, but now, she was a knockout. When he laid eyes on her holding that door open, her ice-blue eyes terrified, he'd lost the ability to breathe for a split second. At twenty-one, she had been thin and sickly, still recovering from the accident at seventeen, but the last decade had changed all of that. She had curves now, and he wanted to run his hands down them to feel her again. To connect with her again in a way that would settle his soul for the first time in a decade.

She wore her blond hair in a ponytail, swinging side to side as she moved the chair around. She had always worn her hair up, and the few times he'd seen her with it down as a teenager always did something to his lower half that gave him internal embarrassment. He shouldn't feel that way about the girl he'd grown up with, right? He'd asked himself that question almost daily in high school, but the answer had never been that simple.

A mailbox came into view, and Reece slowed the truck as he counted off the numbers until he found 1993 Cherry Hill Lane. 1993. That jogged his memory to earlier when she'd written down her phone passcode.

1 1 1993.

He'd been a New Year's baby as 1993 dawned, making his birthday January 1. He hadn't registered it then, but now the number hit him right in the gut. Did she purposely use his birthday as her passcode?

She shifted as though she knew he was thinking about her and blinked her eyes several times. "Where are we?"

"At a safe house owned by Secure Watch."

Her arms went up in the air as she stretched, and he forced his gaze away from how her chest jutted into his space. "How long have I been asleep?"

"About two hours," he answered, turning down the driveway and hitting a button on his truck console. "Secure Watch, Riker." They used the same greeting each time they made contact with each other. If they ever got a communication from a team member who didn't use the code greeting, they knew that the team member was under duress and to send help.

"Secure Watch, Whiskey."

"Mina, we're at the house."

"Garage in three, two, one," she said as the garage door opened. Reece couldn't hold in his laughter as he shook his head.

"Thanks, Mina. I'll be in touch as soon as we're settled." He hit the button again on the console to hang up and pulled into the darkened garage, his headlights illuminating the space around them.

"That's high-tech," Skylar said, glancing at him. "Is she going to shut it, too?"

He held up his finger until the overhead door slid back down behind the truck. "Yes," he answered with a wink. "The house has digital passcodes to lock and unlock the doors and open the garage. Mina has unlocked everything," he explained as he shut off the truck. "Once we're inside, she'll turn the passcode and security protocols over to me. If anyone breaches the security system or cameras, then Secure One takes control of the house to keep the occupants safe until they can get out."

"As I said, high-tech." She lifted a brow at him, and he shrugged.

"Secure One and Secure Watch are in the security business. It's what we do, and considering Secure One's track record with picking up cases that end up putting team members in danger, Cal stopped taking chances with his people. He now has places all over the area to stash people who need safekeeping."

"*Safekeeping.* That's a nice way of saying hiding out, I suppose." She worked at one of the Velcro straps holding her thighs together.

"Life is always about how you look at things, Sky." He winked. "Wait here while I grab your chair."

"Where am I going to go?" she asked, her head tipped sideways until he did a facepalm that brought laughter to her lips.

"Sorry, habit. I'll be right back."

Reece slid out of the truck and stretched his long legs for the first time in hours. The ride had been uneventful, and he hoped his time here at the safe house would be equally so. At least until Mina could tell them who this Binate person was. He'd do his own digging while they waited, and with any luck, he'd have Skylar back home and out of his life by tomorrow. Would that be his luck, though? He'd lived the last decade holding on to the occasional glimpses he'd get of her from a newspaper article or a clipping his mom would send him about her artwork. He'd always assumed that one day when his Google Alert went off about Skylar Sullivan, it would be because she had made it big. Not because she was wanted for vandalism. The thought struck him, and he grabbed his phone. After he opened the alert again, he checked the date of the warrant. It had been issued forty-eight hours ago. She was out of town then, so the police would have waited for her to return to the city. He tucked his phone back in his pocket and grabbed the wheelchair. As of forty-eight hours ago, Skylar Sullivan had still existed. That was an essential part of the timeline.

He lowered her wheelchair to the ground and pushed it to her side of the truck. His truck was twice the size and height as hers, so he'd had to lift her from her chair into the seat when they left. The sensation of having her in his arms again almost short-circuited his brain. She was soft, warm and smelled of lemons and tangerines. Whatever the scent was, it was a far cry from the overpowering perfume she wore in high school. This new scent fit her aura. She was always about nature and the soothing vibes it offered.

He'd noticed the soft, breezy linens in her home also reflected that. It was like Skylar Sullivan had come into her own while he'd been away, and it excited him to think he'd get the chance to know her again.

The door cracked open, and she peeked out. "Are you going to stand there all day?"

His daydream broken, he jumped and stepped forward, nearly tripping over the chair but righting himself at the last moment. "Sorry," he said, clearing his throat as though it would be as easy to clear his mind of thoughts of her. "I was checking something on my phone. I'll tell you about it once we're inside."

He moved in to scoop her up and noticed she'd unstrapped her legs while he was getting her chair. Guilt lanced him. It had been fourteen years, but he remembered every second of that night in slow motion. He relived those seconds in his dreams at least two or three times a week. If he was overtired or saw something that reminded him of her, he braced himself for the dreams to come. *The Friday night lights. The crowd loud and rowdy. The breeze on his face as he grabbed her waist, ready to lift her into the air.* He gave his head a shake and cleared his mind of those memories. She'd admitted she trusted him, and he wouldn't let her down this time.

He lifted her off the seat with a smile and cradled her against his chest. He'd been right. Her curves were soft, and when she'd thrown her arms around his neck, his chest tightened, reminding him that Skylar Sullivan still had a hold over him.

Wishing he didn't have to, but knowing he did, he lowered her into the custom manual wheelchair. It looked new and fit her like a glove. The seat reclined slightly, which he knew would make it easier for her to remain upright in the chair, since not all her abdominal muscles worked after the accident. Her legs were supported at the calves by a strap, and her footplate was tilted just enough to account for the tilt in the seat back. The custom backrest wrapped around her ribs to offer her support there, and the wheels were thin, black and, if he had to guess, fast. Sky always loved to go fast, whether on a bike or his go-cart. The frame and back of the seat were painted bright white, and he'd noticed on the way out to his truck earlier that the front rollerblade wheels lit up in rainbow colors with every turn. What he loved the most was the floral overlay on the frame. He ran his hand over the decoration, surprised when it was raised under his fingers.

"I painted it," she answered as though she knew his question. "That's why I went with a white frame. I needed a blank canvas to do my work. Otherwise, white would be a bad choice living in a city where it's impossible to keep it clean half the year," she added with a wink.

"Stunning work," he said, standing and slamming the truck door. "I thought it was a decal, but I should have known better."

Her laughter lit up the garage as though night had turned to day. "You really should have," she answered as she wheeled up the ramp.

Reece pushed the door open for her from behind the chair, and she wheeled into their home away from home. As he brought in their bags and shut the back door, he realized how true that statement was about too many things concerning Skylar Sullivan. He should have known better.

Chapter Five

Skylar studied the man who had dropped everything to run to her aid. It made her insides gel to accept that he was even more handsome now than in high school. It upended her a bit, since she never dreamed that was possible. She'd been wrong. He'd put years on, but those years had been kind. Age had changed him from the beautiful boy he'd once been into a ridiculously handsome man. Then there was the heterochromia iridum—a fancy way of saying two different-colored eyes. Fewer than one percent of humans had two different-colored eyes, and he'd always said that when he got old enough, he would buy a contact lens so that his eyes would finally match.

She couldn't help but smile at the memory of how mad she had gotten about that statement. After his suggestion, she'd given him the silent treatment for two days until he finally agreed never to wear a colored contact. From what she could tell, he hadn't broken his promise to her.

Speaking of the silent treatment, that's what he'd been giving her since they'd settled into the house. *Aloof* was a word that came to mind. He'd given her a necessary tour of the house, showing her the modifications that would help her and what to do if something happened to him. There was a basement, but that wasn't where she was to hide. There was a room behind a panel in the main bedroom closet. It wasn't large, but it was big enough for two people, including her chair. It also held the necessary computer equipment to access help if the situation arose. However, Reece had made it very clear that once she was in it, she wasn't getting out until someone opened it from the central control room when it was deemed safe. She supposed he'd told her that knowing about her claustrophobia, but in a life-or-death situation, she'd take being trapped in a small room over dying. Besides, it wasn't likely to come to that. Sure, whoever this Binate person was had tossed her place, but no attempts had been made on her life, and let's face it, she was easy enough to find. It wasn't like she could outrun anyone for very long. This house, and finding out there were several more around the state, not to mention the underground bunkers, had made it sink in how much danger she might be in. Secure One had battled sex traffickers, serial killers, mob bosses and everything in between. The fact that they had taken her on as a client without needing to be convinced told her she was in hot water. Sure, Reece had been her childhood friend, but if his team had thought for half a second that things weren't as bad as they were, they never would have given him the go-ahead to bring her here.

Reece acted like this was nothing but a job, but she knew the truth. He'd been acting like this since the night of the accident. One moment, he was warm, loving and laughing, and the next, he dropped a curtain of distance and pain between them. It might have had something to do with her pushing him away and telling him they could never be more than friends.

Staring at him now as he sat at the bank of computers pretending she didn't exist, she could still read him like a book. Spinning away from the sight of the man she'd always thought would be hers, she quickly searched the fridge. She was surprised it was stocked with eggs, Spam, cheese and fruit. Was she hungry? Not even a little bit, but Reece probably was, and cooking gave her something to do while he kept his head buried in the computer as though it had all the answers. It didn't, but she'd let him come to that conclusion all on his own.

She had an omelet going in no time despite the challenge of working from a chair in a kitchen that was made for someone much taller. She was used to it now, but in the beginning, cooking had terrified her. With the help of an encouraging occupational therapist who had the patience of a saint, she'd started to learn and believe that she could do anything. That included her art. She'd spent the first year after rehab doing nothing but drawing, believing that it would be too hard to be an artist in a wheelchair. Was it easy? No. But every time she finished a piece, it reminded her that it was worth the extra work and planning it took to complete. Stained glass and mosaics weren't lightweight or easy to move around. She was forever grateful to an "old and grizzled"—his words, not hers—artist in downtown Superior who let her work at his studio and helped her move her equipment around.

With a flip of the spatula, she turned the omelet and added some water to the pan before plopping a lid on the top to fluff it while she cut some apples and searched out plates. Of course, they were on the top shelf, because why not? That was normal for someone who could stand up and reach them. Her—not so much. Skylar flicked the burner off and moved the pan aside before she did what she never wanted to do: ask for help.

"Hey, Reece?" she called out, and he turned from where he sat at the bank of computers and other high-tech equipment that she was clueless about. "Could you help me grab a plate?"

He pushed himself out of the chair and strolled into the kitchen. "You can cook?" he asked with enough snark for her to know he was fully entrenched in his standoffish attitude, but she refused to take the bait.

"Surprisingly, I can do a lot of things." She made sure to make the sentence sound matter-of-fact and not sarcastic. He wouldn't make her feel small to avoid his feelings about the accident. "I wasn't sure when you last ate but figured you might be hungry."

Reece lowered two plates to the counter. "I could eat. You have the first one, and I'll make another for myself."

"I'm not hungry," she said, sliding the omelet onto his plate and adding the fruit next to it.

With a sigh, he dropped his hand onto his hip. "The first thing you need to learn about our situation is this. When you have a chance to eat, you eat. Our entire situation could change in ten minutes and we're moving again. It could be days before you can get a hot meal, so yes, you'll eat."

He split the eggs in half without asking and cut up more fruit. He dropped bread into the toaster and grabbed some jam from the fridge. Backing her chair up, she watched him work, appreciating how his black cargo pants accentuated his muscular thighs. Reece might work behind a computer all day, but he definitely stayed in shape.

The thought made her glance down at her body with a sigh. "In shape" was something she would never be again. At least not at the level Reece Palmer deserved. A T5 spinal cord injury left her with limited chest and trunk stability, which made working out difficult. The gym was great for keeping her upper body strong, but the years of sitting in a wheelchair had changed her shape in a way she couldn't deny. Seeing Reece again reinforced her decision to push him away all those years ago.

"When we're done eating, we're going to call in to Secure Watch and talk to the team," Reece explained as he put the toast on plates and carried it all to the small table in the corner of the room. "Does this work, or is it better to eat somewhere else?"

"It's fine as long as you don't mind that my elbows will be in the air."

Rather than answer, he spun and carried the plates into the main room, setting them on the coffee table. It was low, but that was less awkward than too high. He sat on the couch and shoveled the food in without another word, so she did the same. At least a few bites of everything to make it look like she was following his orders. They made sense, but after the trauma of the last few hours, her appetite was long gone.

The questions spun nonstop in her mind. Who would do this to her? Why had they picked her? Was it someone she knew? How would she get all her accounts and data back? How could she afford to hire Secure Watch? That was one question she could answer. One look around the room told her she couldn't afford them—not their digital work or their protection. Her fork fell to her plate when she realized that she would have to do this alone and had no idea how.

"My parents!" Her gasp was loud in the room, and Reece glanced up from his plate.

"They're fine," he said, his fork halfway to his lips. "Mina checked, and their digital footprint has not been erased."

"They need to know what's happening, though," Skylar said. "They should be warned in case this Binate guy decides to go after them."

"As soon as we finish talking with Mina, she will patch us through to them."

"I don't even know what to tell them, Reece. They're going to be so worried."

"Secure Watch will give them a rundown on what they should do to protect themselves until we figure out who is behind this. I'll be here when you talk to them and make it clear that you're safe and taken care of while we work through this."

Skylar was about to say she couldn't afford to keep working with them but bit her tongue. She would wait until she could talk to Mina and make it clear she didn't have the funds to pay them for this and never would. Reece would argue, but Mina wouldn't. Someone had to be watching the bottom line.

AFTER THE PLATES were cleared and loaded into the dishwasher, Reece checked the house's perimeter using infrared cameras. Satisfied that everything was quiet, he turned to Skylar, who was sitting in her chair staring at a book. Reading it wasn't an accurate description, as she hadn't flipped a page in ten minutes. She was despondent, and as much as he wanted to comfort her, he had to stay hands-off. Skylar was a dream of his that he couldn't shake even though he knew he could never have her. It had taken him years to understand that, even if he didn't fully accept it yet.

It was his penance, though, and he was glad she'd made him pay it. It was his fault she was in the chair. That was something he could never change. If he could get a redo on that night, he would, but that wasn't how life worked. It didn't let you see your mistakes and then allow you not to make them. You made them, lived the consequences and learned not to do them again. Only he wasn't the one living with the consequences of this particular mistake. Skylar was. That was the hardest part to accept. He should be in that chair, and he would trade places with her in a heart-beat if life worked that way.

"Ready to call Secure Watch?" he asked, leaning forward on his thighs.

The look on her face when she lifted her head gave him the answer. "Not until we talk about this."

"Talk about what?"

"This," she said, motioning between them. "You saying two words at a time to me and the grimace on your face every time you look at the chair."

"I'm worried about you. That's all," he answered, forcing himself not to react negatively to her observations. That would only prove her right.

"You're beating yourself up for an accident that was just that. An accident."

"I shouldn't have let you fall."

"Should have, could have, would have mean nothing in life, Reece."

With his lips held tightly together, he forced himself to hold her gaze, to let her see the shame he carried in his eyes for the things that had happened that night.

The air was electric as the cheer teams lined up on the sidelines. They'd made it to the finals, which meant everything had come down to one last routine. It was their senior year, the last year they could compete, and Skylar dreamed of going to a Big Ten school for cheer. Reece wanted to give her that. He grabbed her hand and ran onto the field, lining up with the rest of the team.

"We're in a position to play it safe," she yelled over the crowd. As the team captain, Skylar called the shots on the field after talking to the coach. "Let's do a double backflip lift into a cupie, transition into a scorpion and finish with a toe touch catch!"

Reece nodded. They had perfected that routine this year. He spread the word down the line so the bases and spotters knew what to do along with the other top girls. They'd been working on a new triple back flip into an extended lift followed by another flip to land it. He was glad she hadn't suggested that one. They hadn't perfected it yet, but Skylar never cared about perfect. She cared about wowing the crowd, so he was glad she was willing to keep it simple tonight. His arm was sore from the last few practices, and the last thing he wanted to do was pull a muscle and accidentally drop her.

The announcer called them out to the cheers of the crowd. They were always a favorite in the Northwood competitions and had supportive fans packing the stands. The music started, and the team moved into their positions, spotters in place as Skylar started her backflip. She hit the mark, and he lifted her into the cupie pose, where she preened for the crowd as they hooted and whistled, chanting her name. He took a step back and planted his foot, a sign that he was ready for her to move into the scorpion, where she'd bring her left foot up to her head and hold it—not an easy move on the ground, much less balanced on his hands. After hitting her mark, he pushed her up into the air, her legs coming out in a V as she touched her toes. His head was up and he was ready to catch her, his arms out with spotters on each side.

Then he sailed to the left, landing in a pile of bodies without the girl of his dreams in his arms. Screaming. Who was screaming?

"Reece!" Skylar's exclamation was sharp, and he snapped back to the present, blinking twice before he could even think about swallowing the saliva pooling in his mouth. She rolled the chair toward him. "Are you back?"

He wasn't sure he could speak, so he nodded and hoped she wouldn't notice that his hands shook where they sat on his lap. When she took one in her hands, he knew that hope had been dashed.

"Does that happen every time you think about the accident?"

"No," he said with a shake of his head. "Sometimes I scream your name until I wake up in a cold sweat." He smiled and winked as if that had been a joke, but it wasn't. The nightmares were less frequent now, which he was grateful for nearly fourteen years later.

"Have you talked to someone about it?" she asked, caressing his hand in a way that made him want to pull her into his arms. She was the one who had suffered an atrocity today and deserved to be comforted. Not him.

"Yeah, that's me after therapy," he answered with a lip tilt.

"Reece," she whispered, her gaze dropping to their joined hands. "You have to stop blaming yourself for the accident. There was no way you could have predicted what happened. Who would expect a golf cart to lose control and plow through the team, toppling everyone like dominoes? There wasn't a time that I ran out on the field when I didn't accept the risks I was about to take. Football players had helmets and pads to protect them. We had tennis shoes and miniskirts. We were never going to win against a golf cart."

"You had me!" His exclamation came along with a finger jab to his chest. "You had me to protect you, and I failed." The last sentence was whispered in shame. "I failed you, Sky. You were my sky, and when you fell, so did my world."

Chapter Six

Unable to sit still, he pushed his chair back and paced. All he wanted to do was figure out who was after Sky so he could get her out of his life again. Being with her was too hard. All he could think about was what could have been. What *they* could have been if she hadn't pushed him away. Fourteen years was a lifetime. It was forever ago and just yesterday. He wanted those fourteen years with her back, but he'd never get them. That was the hardest pill to swallow when the choice hadn't been his.

"I know life has never been the same for us, Land," she whispered, using the nickname she'd given him as a little boy. Reece had called her Sky and she had said, "If I'm your sky, then you're my land." And it had been that way every day after until that October night of their senior year. "But you have to promise me you'll stop blaming yourself for something you had no control over. If you can't do that, then I'm leaving now."

His laughter suggested they weren't in a life-or-death situation. "I don't think you're in a position to demand that, Sky."

"Maybe not, but it's time we clear the air once and for all, Reece."

"I'm not the one who pushed you away!" he exclaimed. "I'm not the one who said I couldn't be part of your life anymore!"

He turned back, and Sky spun her chair, blocking his way. He plopped down on the club chair and ran his hands over his face rather than make eye contact with the woman who had been the one to do those things.

"I know that, Land. That was me."

"Don't call me that," he said between clenched teeth.

"Do you think it hurts any less to hear you call me Sky? Do you think it doesn't destroy every part of me to know you've blamed yourself all this time or that you've dealt with PTSD all these years because of that night?"

"It's not PTSD," he said, shaking his head. "The guys I work with at Secure One, yes. Me. No."

"Denial isn't just a river, Reece. From what I just saw, you absolutely have PTSD about October 15, 2010."

Hard as he tried, he couldn't hide his sharp intake of breath when he heard the date. "Enough, Skylar." He didn't speak the words as much as he grunted them. "It's time to call Secure Watch."

"Oh, I get it now," she said slowly, her head nodding as she crossed her arms over her chest.

"Get what?"

"Get why you won't admit you have PTSD or talk to anyone about the accident. At least, I assume you don't, because you probably don't want the guys at Secure One to know, either. If they knew, they might tell you it wasn't your fault. It makes it harder for you to keep punishing yourself for my decisions whenever someone tells you that."

"That doesn't even make sense."

Her snort was loud in the silent room. "Only if you speak a language other than English. I've spent, what?"

She checked the watch on her wrist before glancing back at him. "A hair over six hours with you and already figured out that your big, bad, tough cybersecurity persona is an act. See, you try to temper the fact that you still blame yourself for me being in the chair with aloofness and fake aggravation, but your tells give you away. You can't look me in the eye. You can't touch my wheelchair without grimacing. You crack sarcastic comments to come off as uncaring when the truth is just the opposite."

"Okay, I care!" he exclaimed, unsure what she wanted him to say or do. When she took his hands in hers again, he was sure that wasn't it. "I don't know what you want me to say, Sky. I care you're sitting in that wheelchair because I didn't catch you. There. Is that what you needed to hear? Can we move on now?"

"No. We can't move on until you repeat after me." His huff did nothing to stop her. "Skylar uses a wheelchair." She paused and waited for him to repeat the words.

A hard eye roll escaped, but he answered. "Skylar uses a wheelchair."

"Because she broke her back during an accident that injured several members of her high school cheer team."

"Because she broke her back during an accident that injured several members of her high school cheer team."

"I couldn't have caught her from the ground with a broken wrist."

"I couldn't have caught her from the ground with a...no, wait," he said, rubbing his left wrist absently.

Rather than let him speak, she took his face in her hands. "Close your eyes. Let yourself see those last few moments of that night. You know I'm right, Land. You know none of us stood a chance."

This time, he met her gaze and held it. "I don't need to let myself see those last few moments. I see them every time I close my eyes. Yes, logically, I know none of us stood a chance that night. Emotionally, it is another story."

"And that's PTSD by definition, Reece. We can't make that part of it disappear, but I also can't sit here and watch you beat yourself up every second we're together. The only thing I can do is help you see that this wasn't your fault. Not when I knew the risk and agreed to it when I walked onto the field. Every game. Every practice. Every time I asked my body to do something that defied gravity, this was always a possibility," she said, motioning at the chair.

"I know that, too," he agreed, still holding her gaze.

"You were always my protector, Land. I loved you for it, but we're not little kids anymore."

"It looks to me like you still need my protection." He lifted his brow to challenge her, hoping she'd take the bait and get fired up. Anything to get her to stop forcing him to confront what he'd kept buried for fourteen years.

"I absolutely do," she agreed. Reece's shoulders deflated, knowing she wouldn't distance herself from him. "I'm scared to death, but I know if we can get past this and work together again, you'll protect me just like you used to. I've always trusted you, Reece, including that night in October when you held my hand and promised me everything would be okay even when I couldn't feel my legs. You were right that night. I'm okay. We're okay. Okay?"

"That's a lot of okays," he said, forcing back the emotion welling in his chest when she smiled that smile he had lived for back in the day. "I'll do my best to remember that we're both okay, the present situation notwithstanding."

"That's all I can ask for," she said, giving his hand one last squeeze before she backed up her chair. "Now, let's find this Binate so I can get my life back."

"Before we call Mina, I want to run down the situation with you so we're on the same page when we call in."

"I'm not even reading the same book," she said with a frown. "I have no idea why this has happened."

He held his hands up to calm her. "What I mean is, I want to give you all the facts so that you're not surprised by anything Mina might say."

There was no doubt Mina would bring up things she didn't want to hear about, and he wanted to give her the chance to ask questions when they weren't on camera. He ran down everything he knew, starting with the vandalism of the art galleries and ending with how, as of two days ago, she'd still existed in the world.

"Wait, you're saying there's an actual warrant out for my arrest and the cops didn't try to arrest me? That doesn't make sense. I'm not hard to find."

"That's what I'm saying. I also agree with you, which is why I think, more than anything, it was a way to drag your name through the mud for a hot second before they shut everything down to keep the cops from coming for you. You can't come for someone who doesn't exist."

Skylar waved her hand in the air. "Doesn't make sense. I do exist! The cops in Duluth know me, Reece. They know where I live."

He continued once he grasped her hand and lowered it to her lap. "I know you exist, and so does the Duluth PD. What I mean is the persona they were trying to sell the cops. The person-of-interest alert came out of Minneapolis. It would get filtered to Duluth and they would follow up. The police would come to your house and ask you to ride with them to the station to chat."

"They wouldn't because they know me," she said, motioning at the chair.

"My point is," he said, frustrated by her inability to hear what he was saying, "if the cops did come to your house, you were gone, which meant all they could do was keep trying until they found you at home or they changed it from a person of interest to suspect. Since it was only forty-eight hours ago, they may not have had a chance."

"Let's say that's the case. Eventually, I have to go home. So the question is, how do I prove who I am and that I didn't commit these crimes?"

Each word got louder until he grabbed her hands and squeezed. "Deep breath," he said, and he sucked one in, waiting for her to follow. Once she did, he nodded and spoke. "Remember, Secure Watch will help you, so don't let that fear paralyze you." He dropped his head. "I'm sorry."

"Don't be. I'd have made a joke about it any other day, but I'm not feeling it today."

"Understandable. What I was trying to say before I put my size twelve in my pie hole was to stay focused on the facts. Focus on the things we know are true about the situation. Those facts are that you didn't vandalize galleries, and you do exist. We also know someone out there has a vendetta against you for an unknown reason, but one that we'll uncover with time and investigation."

As though she deflated, her shoulders slumped forward and her head followed. "I know that, and you know that, but the galleries don't know that, Land. I've spent the last decade trying to get a full gallery showing in a city like Duluth or Minneapolis. This will make it all for naught."

"I don't believe that, Sky. Your reputation precedes you, which means anyone with a modicum of common sense will know you aren't physically capable of causing that damage to the galleries."

"I could have hired someone," she said, crossing her arms over her chest.

"You could have, but let me ask you this. Did you have any beefs with the galleries that have been vandalized?" He grabbed a sheet of paper and read off the names.

"Absolutely not," she said, shaking her head before he even finished reading them. "The Duluth one knows me well and would never believe I did it."

"You've made my point then. All I'm asking is you have faith in me and Secure Watch. We'll ensure your chances at a gallery show are still one hundred percent, okay?"

At her nod, Reece stood and walked to the computer console set up for precisely that purpose. All he had to do was keep his eye on the prize and off the woman he was supposed to be helping. Every minute that passed was another minute that Binate had control of her life, which meant Skylar had control of Reece's. While he dialed Secure Watch, he prayed they had gotten to the bottom of it, but one glance at Skylar told him that prayer would go unanswered.

"Reece," Mina said when her face flashed on the screen. "Did you find everything you need?"

"We're all good here," Reece agreed. "We had some dinner and I checked the perimeter. How about the other cameras?"

"Everything is quiet, according to the control room."

"Excellent, then official introductions are overdue. Mina Jacobs, this is Skylar Sullivan."

"Nice to officially meet you," Mina said as Skylar waved. "I'm glad we were able to help you out."

"Nice to meet you, too," Skylar said, nervously rubbing her hands on her thighs. "We've heard so much about you over the years. You're like an FBI legend."

Mina's laughter filled the house, and Skylar noticed it lifted Reece's lips for the first time all day. She was grateful to Mina for doing what she couldn't do right now. "I don't know about all that, but we're here to help, right, Reece?"

Before Reece could answer, Skylar jumped in. "About that," she said, lifting her chin. "I wasn't thinking earlier when I called Reece. I was scared and didn't know what to do, but I also didn't think about the fact that you guys employ Reece or that I didn't know how I was going to pa—"

"You're not going to pay," Mina said before she could finish.

"But, Mina, this house alone must need thousands to maintain every month. I can't even imagine what it would cost for people like Reece to do what they do."

Mina held up her hand to stop her. "The house is going to be there whether we use it or not, so it might as well be used, right?" She waited as though she expected an answer, so Skylar hesitantly nodded. "Then we use it. Make yourself comfortable and don't worry about the expense. What it costs us will be nothing compared to what it could cost you. Am I clear?"

"Yes, ma'am," Skylar agreed. There was no way she was crossing Mina Jacobs. Reece's smirk told her he knew it.

"Now that we have that settled," Reece said, still smirking, "do you have anything new? Skylar is worried about her parents."

Mina pointed at the camera and grabbed something next to the computer. "I spoke with them a few minutes ago, and they're awaiting your call. Once you speak to them, they will take a little vacation off the grid until this is squared away."

"You think this person might go after my parents?"

"We have to assume they will," she replied. "Whoever

this is, they know you, which means they know the people close to you."

"We'll call them as soon as we hang up," Reece said, reaching out to squeeze her hand. "What did the guys find at the duplex?"

"Nothing of much interest," Mina said, looking at the notebook in her hand. "At least in terms of evidence. Iris is working with her phone right now."

"Iris?" Skylar asked, glancing at Reece.

"She's one of our data recovery agents," Reece explained. "If anyone can figure out who sent that video and from where, it's Iris."

"In the meantime," Mina said. "I want you to list anyone who could be behind this."

"The list is going to be short," Skylar said. "I don't know that many people. Artists tend to live in their own little world."

"That just means fewer people we have to check out," Mina said with a wink. "But seriously, I'm talking about listing anyone you have ever had a cross word with. Did you have an issue with someone at the credit card company? Did you argue over a cup of coffee in the Starbucks a few weeks ago? Did you have a problem with a bank employee? That kind of thing. If you don't know their names, write down the companies or branches. We can run those things down easily but need a place to start." Reece looked like he was about to say something when Mina held up her finger and spoke to someone off-screen. "I have to go," she said, glancing back to the screen. "Get me that list ASAP. Whiskey, out."

Reece gave the screen a salute right before it went black. He spun toward her in the desk chair and lifted a brow.

"First, we call your parents. Once that's done, we need to talk about that list."

Skylar nodded but didn't say anything. She already knew who he thought should be at the top of it.

Chapter Seven

Reece stepped out onto the house's porch to give Skylar privacy while she spoke with her parents. At this point, there wasn't much she could tell them that would harm the case, so he didn't feel the need to be a voyeur, especially when he still had to talk to her about Silas. Her brother was always a sore subject in the family, and as much as it was a can of worms Reece did not want to open, there was little choice. All he could do was hope she'd forgive him for it.

A hand on his hip, he gazed out over the yard and sucked in a deep breath of the country air. Spring had arrived, but piles of snow still dotted the yard. Before long, they'd be gone, replaced by flowers and grass to mow. Cal had a company that came in to mow and keep the property looking like it had been lived in, even when it rarely saw occupants. He was grateful for it, because moving Skylar somewhere that wasn't accessible meant him being more hands-on with her, and that was something he didn't think he could do. Not if he wanted to walk away from her again once they'd restored her life.

His would never be restored. He'd always remember the feel of her skin against his. The warmth she offered when he didn't deserve comfort. She could believe there was nothing he could have done to help her that night, and maybe that was the truth of it, but that didn't change how he *felt*.

Pandemonium. Panic. Were they the same thing? As Reece untangled himself from his teammates, he decided they were. Screams penetrated the night air. Lights flashed. The sound of the crowd as it pressed in on them roared back to his ears, but what he didn't hear was his best friend.

"Sky!" he screamed, trying to push himself to his feet only to realize his left arm wasn't working properly. He glanced down at it and noticed it hung at an odd angle. "Sky!"

Why were there so many bodies on the ground? He looked left and then right until he heard a strangled cry. "Land!"

He spun, and behind him, on the fifty-three-yard line, was the girl he was supposed to catch. "Sky!" Reece screamed as he ran toward her, splinting his arm against his belly to stem the pain from each step. "Don't move!" Those were his first words as he slid beside her and grabbed her hand. "You're going to be okay."

"I can't move my legs," she whispered, tears sliding down her cheeks.

After a quick glance at her legs, he shook his head. "They don't look broken, but don't try to move them."

"No, Land, I can't—can't feel them."

Before she could say another word, he turned his head and bellowed for help, catching the attention of an EMT.

"You're going to be okay," he promised the girl he'd been in love with since he was old enough to know what that meant. "You're going to be okay. Just stay still. I love you, Sky. You're going to be okay."

Reece gasped and sucked in another lungful of the night air. He'd told her he loved her? He tried to focus his mind on that part of the night, but he couldn't grab the memory again. He'd lied to her earlier when he said he remembered those moments after the accident every night in his sleep. He never got that far. He always woke up screaming her name at the moment of impact. Did he have diagnosed PTSD after the incident? Yes. Had he told Sky that? No. He made sure no one but him and his therapist knew about that diagnosis. Was it shame that kept him from talking about it? No. It was fear, and his therapist agreed. He said Reece's brain woke him at that exact moment each time to protect him from the fear. No matter how hard they'd tried, they couldn't unlock the memory. And they'd tried for years. Then, he spent a few hours with Sky and her touch drew it out of him.

Even a solid shake of his head couldn't dislodge the rest of the memories flooding him. The surgery on his arm that they'd forced him to have even though he didn't want to leave Sky's side. Waking up to find out she was paralyzed for life and would never walk again. Learning that a golf cart had gone haywire and driven right into them as they did their routine on the field. Lying in a hospital bed, being told how half of the team had broken bones and were at hospitals all over the Northland. Ultimately, none of those injuries were as life-changing as Sky's. The settlement from the event had bankrupted the venue but set Sky up with enough money to provide for her immediate needs after the injury and for years to come.

Since his family was tight with hers, he knew that her parents had invested the money so that she got a monthly salary from the fund, and they'd set up another fund to help take care of the duplex with the rent her neighbor paid. He was glad they had done that, because that money was in a trust with a lawyer and not in her name. If they couldn't recover her accounts, at least she wasn't out all her trust money, too.

Reece closed his eyes and took stock of himself. Was he ready to put the past behind him and focus on the present now? Did he have a choice? No. If someone had told him when he woke up this morning that he would be taking care of Skylar Sullivan by day's end, he would have told them they'd lost their minds. His watch said she'd probably had enough time to finish the call, so he forced his feet forward and walked back into the ranch home, expecting to see her on the couch where he'd left her. Instead, she was nowhere to be found.

His heart pounding, he ran through the house, calling her name until he came to a halt in the hallway. His shouting had drowned out the sound that had always ripped him in two. Sky sobbing.

Gently, he rapped on the bathroom door. "Sky? Do you need help?"

"No," she said, but it was strangled. Reece could picture her sitting in her chair, head in her hands as the tears leaked between them. He'd seen it so many times after the accident, and his impotence in the situation flooded him every time. This time, he wasn't going to let it paralyze him. He was the only one here for her and had to step up.

"I'm coming in. Tell me if you aren't presentable."

When she said nothing, he pushed the door open. He'd thought he was prepared for the scene, but he wasn't. She was limp, with her upper body draped across the lowered sink as though she'd been trying to wash her face and had run out of strength.

"Oh, Sky," he whispered, walking to her and unbuckling her seat belt. "Everything's going to be okay. I promise. Is it okay if I carry you to the couch?"

Rather than answer, she gazed at him, dazed, until he put her arms around his neck and lifted her from the chair, supporting her back and knees. He'd done it so many times when she was first injured. She'd worn a plastic back brace that bit into his freshly repaired arm every time, but he'd never cared. All he wanted to do was comfort her. He hadn't been given that chance, so he would take this one and make sure she felt safe, if only for a few minutes of this wild, unexpected day.

Once they were settled on the couch, he held her, forcing himself to keep his lips closed and remind himself that this wasn't about him. This hadn't happened to him. Sky was the one whose entire life had been destroyed today, and there was no way for him to make that better for her other than to do his job. Right now, though, his job was to comfort her. She would need it for the conversation that was still to come.

The clock ticked off another fifteen minutes of her resting against his chest with her eyes closed as her breathing evened out. Reece wasn't sure if she'd fallen asleep, not that he could blame her. He hated having to wake her, but their work wasn't done for the day, so he had no choice. Holding her again reminded him of when they were kids and she would get mad or sad. She'd cry herself out, rest for a few minutes and then pop up, ready to go again as though nothing had happened.

When she sat up and swiped her hands under her eyes, Reece bit back a smile to know she hadn't changed. "Sorry about that meltdown. After I hung up with my parents, it hit me how hard my world had fallen apart today."

"Nothing to apologize for," he assured her. "After the day you've had, I don't blame you one bit for feeling like your world has fallen apart. How are Mary and Joe?"

"Scared for me," she said with a shrug. "Roman and Mina put a scare in them."

"They aren't a pair to mince words," he said with a shrug. "Frankly, I wouldn't want them to. We can't be too safe until we know who this is."

"Mom and Dad agreed. They've locked their accounts so no one can access them, which is about all they can do, and they're going out to an island with a friend for a few days. Dad got a burner like Roman instructed him to do, and we have that number so we can update them as necessary."

"Good. I'm sure your mom was frantic to think she couldn't race up here and protect you."

"You do know my mom," she said with a chuckle. "The only reason they aren't already in the car is because you're with me, she said. She knows you'll figure this out. Mom always called you her bonus son."

"Probably because I lived at your house half my life."

"Might have something to do with that," she agreed with a wink. "I need better support."

Selfishly, Reece didn't want to stop holding her, but he twisted to the side and propped her into the corner of the couch anyway with a pillow behind her back. Sky's core back and abdominal muscles were affected by the paralysis, so if she wasn't in her chair, she had to be adequately supported or she'd end up with a back spasm.

"Better?"

Her nod had him climbing up off the couch. "I'll get your chair and then I'll make some tea so we can talk."

"Oh boy. Tea and talking are not my favorite things. Wine and Netflix would be better."

Reece laughed. He couldn't help it. Sky was always witty and ready with a comeback to make him laugh. He was glad at least that much hadn't changed. "I would love to oblige, but life on the line and all that."

She bit her bottom lip as she nodded. "Fair enough. Okay,

how about coffee? You know I can't drink that swill you like so much."

"Coffee it is. We'll probably need the jolt of energy anyway. We've got a lot to talk about."

He didn't miss her exhaled breath and muttered words as he headed to the bathroom to grab her chair. "I was afraid of that."

Chapter Eight

Her head was pounding, and she could thank her crying jag for that. The worst part was they hadn't even gotten into the nitty-gritty regarding the list Mina wanted. She'd been thinking about it since Mina had brought it up, and there was only one guy she could think of who might have it out for her this badly.

Miles Bradshaw.

She'd run afoul of him without ever having met him in the beginning. He was another artist from the area who believed he should be the only artist. Miles didn't subscribe to the idea that there was room in this world for everyone's talents. He'd made sure she knew that at their last run-in a few months ago.

The sounds from the kitchen ceased, and Sky glanced up to see Reece walking toward her with a mug in each hand and a bag of cookies between his teeth. She couldn't help but smile at the look of domestication it gave him. The way he moved, even with a bag of chocolate chip cookies dangling from his lips, was like watching a lion stalk its prey. She remembered how he used to take flak at school for doing cheer instead of football. His response was always the same: He'd say running around the field and chasing a ball was a skill. Holding another human being over your head on one hand was a skill at a level they'd never achieve.

It made her smile every time she heard it. He wasn't wrong. Cheer was a sport, and it was a challenging sport that tested your endurance and skill in competition. Few understood that, but they had never cared what anyone else thought. It was a sport they could do together when everything else was separated by gender. Since the accident, people had asked her if she regretted it. Her answer was always the same: No. Nothing in life is guaranteed. When you take risks, sometimes you get big rewards. Sometimes you're disappointed. That's just life. She wouldn't give up all those memories they'd made together because of one night. Those were the terms she came to early on after her injury. Living in the past wasn't living, so she refused to do it.

Except when it came to Land. He was a part of her past she couldn't let go. The ghost of who they could have been haunted her every day of her life. They'd never gotten closure—about the accident or their relationship. Maybe they could have that now. Would she love to have him in her life? Yes. Would she allow it? Not unless he understood that she would never let them be more than friends. Skylar had accepted the reality of her world, but she would never ask Reece to sign up for it, too. That was why she'd pushed him away all those years ago. *You were always my land, but now I am your sky, so use me to be free.*

"Coffee, as you wish, madam," he said around the bag in his mouth as he set the cups down.

"I see you still don't like to make two trips." Sky winked with a smile, which brought one to his face when he took the cookie bag from his mouth.

"Not if I can help it," he replied, picking up her cup and handing it to her so she didn't have to lean forward to get it. He was always thoughtful that way, even before her accident. His friends teased him about waiting on her, but he would turn to them and say, "If you need lessons on how to treat a woman with respect, I have openings on Tuesdays and Thursdays." That memory brought a smile to her lips that she hid behind the cup's rim. Reece wore his confidence like a fine suit and never let anyone cut him down.

After they'd shared a few cookies, he grabbed a notepad and sat across from her. "It's time to make that list for Mina. Someone on the team will work on it overnight and update us with anything they may find in the morning. First, we have to give them somewhere to start."

Skylar watched him tap his pen on the notebook as though they were having a normal conversation about everyday life instead of making a list of people who hated her. Reece had always been strong, but he was never the silent type. She could see that had changed. He had changed. Some of it was growing up, but some parts seemed to come from a different place within him—from pain and anger, two things he still carried—and she could tell it was a heavy load.

"I've been thinking about it since Mina asked. The only serious aggravator in my life is Miles Bradshaw."

Reece wrote the name down on the pad. "Tell me about him."

"He's a local artist from Duluth. You're his competition if you color a picture on a restaurant placemat."

"One of those, eh?" he asked with a lip tilt. "Gotta love people with the ideology that the world isn't big enough for everyone."

"That's Miles to a T," she agreed, resting the coffee cup on her leg. Thankfully, he'd put it in a travel mug so it wouldn't spill.

"What is his exact beef with you?"

"We both do mosaics," she explained. "Miles would rather I didn't."

Reece rolled his eyes, bringing another smile to her lips. "I've seen some of your work. Your pieces are gorgeous, and they're always so colorful."

Her insides warmed for a moment before the meaning of the sentence struck her. "You've seen my work?" If that was true, that meant he had been keeping track of her all these years. When she gave him up, it had been so he would forget about her, not continue to look after her.

"Around the area," he said vaguely. "Shops and places. They always have the artist's name under each piece."

That fear seeped away a little but was quickly replaced with the gnawing regret she always had in the pit of her stomach. He wasn't seeking her out, which was what she wanted, so why did it feel so cutting to know the truth?

"That's probably Miles's biggest beef." She cleared her throat when she heard the sadness in her words. "He doesn't think my work should be in these shops. He feels it's deceptive to the customer, despite each display fully explaining how the piece is created."

"Because your mosaics are made from recycled glass?" he asked, and she nodded once. He must have noticed the surprise on her face. "I read the information near the display."

"Right, well, yes. He doesn't think I should be selling something made from 'junk,'" she said, putting junk in quotations.

"One man's junk is another man's treasure." She motioned at him with one hand as she sipped her coffee. "What does he make his mosaics from?"

"Glass, but his are more—" She waved her hand while searching for the right word. "Commercialized?"

"You tell me," he answered.

"It's a good word. There's nothing wrong with commercialized art, but that's not what people look for in the shops around this area."

"Which means yours sell because they are unique and his sit because they aren't."

"If you want to boil it down to one sentence, then yes, that's accurate. Miles's work is nice but doesn't stand out as unique. It doesn't scream, *hang me on your wall!* In fact, several of the galleries have stopped carrying his work altogether."

"If it doesn't sell, they're not going to give it shelf space," he agreed, tapping his pen on his paper.

"Correct. Especially when some of his art was proven to be manufactured."

"As in purchased and passed off as his own?" His brow went up, and she nodded. "This was confirmed?"

"By yours truly," she said with a grimace.

"Seriously?" When she nodded again, he leaned forward. "Has he confronted you about this?"

"Multiple times," she agreed, recalling the last time Miles had cornered her.

"Your expression just changed. Tell me about it."

"You always could read my expressions," she said, holding the empty mug out for him to take, which he did, setting it aside.

"Better than your own mother, she always used to say. When did you last tangle with this guy?"

Reece's words were stiff, and the question was asked through clenched teeth. He had always been her protector. Right or wrong, he'd stood between her and anyone who wanted to hurt her. He let her fight her own battles, but he made it known he was there to wade in if necessary. He didn't care if it was a teacher, friend or family member—no one who meant her harm was getting past him. This situation felt like a full circle that neither of them was prepared for emotionally. Binate hadn't given them a choice, though, and she had to remember it was Reece's literal job to protect her now, nothing else.

"He was the reason I went up the shore to finish my portfolio," she admitted. "He cornered me at a show around the end of February. He'd just learned another gallery planned to stop hosting his work, and he was angry. I get it. It's hard being a struggling artist, but as I explained to him, the galleries make their own choices. I wasn't even hosted in the gallery that dropped him, but he still blamed me. He said I was cheapening the art form by using junk and cheating the system by not paying for my supplies like everyone else had to. That I used my disability as a card to get special favors."

"I was waiting for that. He sounds like the kind of guy who would throw those words at you."

"And worse," Skylar agreed with an eye roll. "He has no filter and isn't afraid to be loud about it. The organizer caught on that I was not enjoying the conversation and kicked him out."

"*Out* out?" he asked with a lift of his brow.

With a nod and a head tilt, she continued. "There were two days left in the show, but he wasn't allowed back on the grounds. I haven't seen or heard from him since. Several more galleries dropped him after his tirade at the art show. The original one he was carrying on about?" she asked, and he nodded for her to continue. "They told me they hadn't simply dropped his work. They had to ban him from the premises as well. He was hard selling to customers on the weekends, and they were getting complaints."

"Do you go to the galleries to sell your work on the weekends?" Skylar could read his confusion in how his brow pulled down to his nose and the slight tip of his head.

"No. That's why the pieces are where they are—so the gallery can deal with the customer."

"Understandable why the galleries didn't want anything to do with him then."

"I'm almost positive most galleries and shops have dropped him completely now. Everyone talks in that community, and it would have been hard to miss the confrontation between us. Not that I had anything to do with it. I just took the brunt of it."

"So this guy," he said, practically spitting the words through his teeth, "has lost his income stream and wants someone to blame for it."

"And he picked me," she finished. "The gallery owner who started the whole thing by dropping him felt terrible and asked if he could host my work in a special showing. An evening with the artist where I would explain my process and why I find recycled and damaged glass perfect for the pieces I make and how I use it to express emotion in each piece."

"It sounds like an evening I would enjoy," he said with a smile. "As long as work doesn't keep me away, I'll be there."

There was a slight tap in her chest from a place in her heart that she'd shut down fourteen years ago. That one beat, a reminder that the old Skylar was still in there, made her want to cry. She wanted to cry for the kids they once were and the separate lives they were now forced to live. Skylar shook her head, forcing the tears away. She didn't have time for that right now. She was in a race for her livelihood.

"If we don't clear this up, it might not happen." Her voice was strangled, and she cleared her throat again.

"Secure Watch has you, Sky. I have you. No one will get

away with this, and we will get your life back. Miles looks like a good place to start."

"The gallery assured me there would be security the night of the event. There would be no way to keep it from Miles once they start advertising it, but they're worried for my safety and that of their patrons."

"I'm trying to figure out where your trip north came into play."

"To get away," she said with a shrug. "To concentrate on my art. The lake always centers me creatively. If I was going to do a private event, I would need a thick portfolio. The time up north gave me that peace where I didn't have to worry about Miles Bradshaw and his vendetta against me."

That word lifted his brow. "The fact that you used that word tells me how serious the last interaction with him was, Sky."

"It's not a word I'm afraid to use about him. Is Miles going to physically hurt me? Probably not. He's tall and lanky, but the only muscle he uses is his mouth." Reece snorted at that comment, and Skylar smiled as she shifted on the pillow. "I don't have him pegged as having the brains to conduct something like this either. He still uses a flip phone."

His grimace was comical, and she laughed until he spoke. "Trust me when I say that means nothing. Many very savvy tech guys know that flip phones are as low-tech as they come, making them hard to trace."

"I didn't think of that, but he doesn't give me the vibes of being the brains behind an operation like this. Could I see him having enough rage to destroy my house the way it was? Without a second thought. Could I see him trying to set me up by vandalizing art galleries? The fact that who-ever did it wasn't smart enough to spray the building at a level I could reach makes that a solid yes. I just can't get behind him knowing how to delete my life."

"Trust me, by the time Secure Watch is done with him, we'll know his IQ to the decimal point."

"I have no doubt," she said with a smirk. Smiling and laughing a little in light of the situation felt good. It released the stress and pressure building in her chest and let her take another breath. "Listen, I need to go to the bathroom and lie down. Can we take a break?"

After tossing the pad on the table, he opened his mouth as though he was going to say something. Before a word came out, he snapped it shut again, stood and held her chair while she transferred into it. "Sure. I'll contact Mina with this information, then turn security control over to Secure One and catch a few hours myself. Oh, I didn't think about it with how quickly we left the house. Do you have your catheter supplies?"

"I, um, don't do that anymore," she stuttered, suddenly wishing she were anywhere but there. "I couldn't deal with the constant infections, so when I turned twenty-one, they placed a suprapubic tube catheter. It goes through my abdomen into my bladder, allowing me to empty it throughout the day and use a bag at night in bed. I have that stuff in my suitcase."

His shoulders dropped a hair at the explanation, and she realized he'd been genuinely concerned for a moment. "I'm glad. I was worried I dropped the ball on that one. It's nice there are other options for you now to make life a bit easier."

"It simplifies my life," she agreed, staring at the floor.

"Do you need any help getting into bed?"

"No, I'm good," she answered quickly. There wasn't a chance on this side of the grave that she would let Reece Palmer help her into bed. "Thanks for everything today,

Land." She tipped her head up to meet his gaze. No longer was the man before her Reece Palmer, Secure Watch agent. He was Land, the boy who would have died for her on that field if he could have.

His eyes darkened when he leaned down and braced himself on her chair. "I should have stopped this guy before he became a problem. You can bet I'll be the one to make sure he no longer is, Sky."

Throat dry and her heart hammering in her chest, she forced words from her lips. "Land, we don't know if it's Miles." She used the nickname without hesitation. That's who she was talking to now.

"Maybe he isn't, but when he gets a visit from my friends at Secure One, he'll quickly understand that from now on, he's to cross the street when he sees you coming." He pressed his lips to her forehead in a way that surprised them both. "Get some sleep," he stuttered, pushing himself away from her chair. "Call me if you need anything."

Rather than speak, she nodded, turned her chair and rolled down the hallway to the sound of his heavy sigh, which she felt all the way to her soul.

Chapter Nine

A ding sounded, indicating an email had arrived, and Reece clicked over to his inbox. He'd sent Secure Watch the info on Miles Bradshaw so they could do the initial dive while he worked on other things. He hadn't expected them to return the information so quickly. His team was used to working under pressure and for high-stakes clients, so he shouldn't have been surprised, even as the clock ticked toward 2:00 a.m. He had sent the information and tried to sleep, but his brain wouldn't shut off. It just ran him around in circles over the woman sleeping in the other room.

Someone had been harassing her and she had just accepted it as normal. Nothing frustrated him more than her letting someone get away with that. The old Sky never would have. Then again, the old Sky could physically hold her own in a fight. This new Sky? The one who now depended on people more than she ever wanted to, he was sure, couldn't. It would take very little to harm her physically, something she was likely cognizant of at all times. It was easier to sit and take it until someone intervened than push back against the aggressor.

He clicked on the bolded email and began reading the report from his friend Iris. Mina had hired her a year ago when she met her at a doctor's office. She'd been inquiring whether they had any coding positions open and was dejected when she'd been told no. Mina had struck up a conversation with her, as Mina did, and learned she had a degree in cybersecurity but struggled to keep a position because of her traumatic brain injury. Working at Secure Watch was easier because she could work alone and at night, two things she needed to focus. Over the last year, she'd been an integral team member as they grew after the Spiderweb case landed at their door.

By the time they'd shut down the website someone had created to take control of every video camera in the world, they couldn't keep their name out of the news. Before they could take a breath, the phones were ringing off the hook and desperate people were hoping Secure Watch was the solution to their current nightmare. They'd hired several more techs and finally had a handle on things, but it was all hands on deck when big cases broke.

He scanned the body of the email. There was only one Miles Bradshaw who was an artist in Duluth. It hadn't taken Iris long to narrow things down and forward him the information. Reece spent the next hour clicking the links, reading articles and searching his background report. When he leaned back in his chair, he could do nothing but shake his head. The dude was a bit unhinged. After checking out his artwork, Reece agreed with Skylar that his work was good but highly commercialized and not what the art crowd in Duluth seemed to be looking for. There was no doubt that he was talented, but apparently, he wasn't a good listener or observer. If he had been, he might have changed his techniques and found a way to sell more art.

Clicking back to the other tab, he typed in the name of the person he was most interested in. Reece had planned to bring him up last night, but by the time they'd finished discussing Miles, Sky was done. He couldn't blame her. She'd had the rug pulled out from under her yesterday and a lot of information thrown at her. He'd talk to her about her brother after she rested and could look at things more objectively.

There was little objectivity in the Sullivan family regarding Silas Sullivan, but Reece didn't wear those blinders or rose-colored glasses. Working in law enforcement had taught him one thing: if an adult wanted to disappear, they'd either make it look like an accident or fall off the grid entirely to avoid being found. If their body wasn't discovered within a year, it rarely was. If they were still alive and off the grid, the chances of finding them after a year were equally slim.

Reece firmly believed that Silas had left of his own free will. Where he'd gone was still the burning question on everyone's minds. According to his mother, Sky's parents finally gave up on the private investigators and internet searches. They'd realized that if Silas left on his own without providing forwarding information, then he didn't want to be found. If he was dead, there was nothing they could do until his body was located. The police didn't believe a crime had been committed and wouldn't investigate, so there was little the family could do but wait to see if Silas contacted them. According to his parents, they'd given up looking for him years ago. Reece couldn't blame them. Silas's mental health was always unstable, and that only worsened after Sky's accident. Their parents had gotten him help and wanted him to attend college, but Silas was only dedicated to sleeping and playing video games.

After a few clicks, he was into a background program where he started looking for all Silas Sullivans. Did he expect to find him? No, but he had to start somewhere, and at least he'd have this much done by the time Sky was up and ready to talk about the elephant in the room.

"Reece?"

He snapped his attention away from the computer when he heard Skylar call from the bedroom. "Sky, are you okay?"

A quick look at the computer clock told him it had been four hours since he'd started researching Silas. It was almost 6:00 a.m., which surprised him. He minimized the programs and stood.

"I have a big problem."

Reece was in the room before she had finished speaking. "What's the matter?"

"Look." She pointed at her chair, which was listing to the left.

"Looks like you've sprung a leak, my lady." He pulled a chair over and tipped her chair onto its back before he pulled the wheel off. "The tube is popped."

"How?" she asked, stymied. "It's just been sitting there."

"If I had to guess," he said, lowering himself to the end of the bed. "A piece of glass from your house yesterday is the culprit."

"Land, I mean, Reece, I used the chair for hours after that."

"You did," he agreed, not commenting on her use of his nickname. He didn't care what she called him as long as she was safe. "But it could have taken that long of you rolling the chair over the spot on the tire before it nicked the tube." The tire was so flat that he could easily pull it off the rim, and, sure enough, a shard of glass fell out.

"There's a tube in my suitcase," she said as he showed her the split-open inner tube. "I always carry spares, but the tire is a problem."

"I don't think so," he said, running his thumb along the

inside of the tire until he found a small slit. "It cut the tire slightly, but that's easy enough to fix. There's some epoxy in the garage that I can use. Once I'm done, I'll return to help you get ready while the tire dries, but the chair will be out of commission for an hour."

"Sure, go ahead. I'll wait here," she said with a tight smile.

"I'll be right back," he promised, grabbing the tire and the old inner tube and heading for the door.

"Reece?" He paused by the door and turned back to her. "Thanks."

"I told you, we've got you. There's no need to thank me every time."

"That's where you're wrong," she said, resting her head on the pillow. "But you'd have to be in my shoes to understand why."

All he could do was nod once in understanding and head to the garage to MacGyver his ex–best friend's wheelchair tire so they could make a fast getaway if the need arose. All he could think was *Sometimes, life is weird.*

SETTLED ON THE couch after a breakfast of pancakes and coffee, Skylar watched Reece working in the kitchen as he cleaned up. His casual humming as he wiped down the counters and washed the dishes made it seem like any other morning in any American household, but that would never be them. Especially since they were hiding out in the middle of nowhere while trying to figure out who had imploded her life.

Sky inhaled a deep breath and noted the slight twinge in her chest. She'd cried herself to sleep last night, her face buried in a pillow so the man who had come to her rescue wouldn't hear her. The last thing she wanted was to end up in his arms again. Check that. She wanted to be in his arms, but she understood what a bad idea it would be if she wanted to get through this and go back to her life without him. Her life was already dull and lonely. When she returned to her duplex, it would feel nothing but desolate now. She'd already been considering a move to a bigger city but had vetoed it because accessibility was unaffordable for a starving artist.

Sure, she could use her settlement money to set herself up somewhere, but she wanted that money to last as long as possible, and her life in Duluth would allow for that. Maybe she just needed a change in scenery. When this was over and she could move around the world again as Skylar Sullivan, she'd buy a plane ticket and visit her parents in Florida. A little sunshine on her face would be welcome after all this.

"Can I get you anything?" Reece asked as he walked into the living room.

She glanced up, surprised by his presence. "Do you have a piece of paper? I thought of a design. I want to draw it out so I don't forget."

"There must be something here somewhere," he said, glancing around the computer setup. "Wait, I know. Be right back."

When he disappeared down the hallway, she pushed herself back into the couch and propped the pillows under her knees that had shifted. When she wasn't in her chair at home, she had a lift recliner that she sat in, which kept her trunk and back supported. Here, she had to improvise to keep herself from getting sore.

"I noticed this last night in my bedroom," he explained, handing her a sketch pad. "Charlotte must have left it here."

Skylar took the pad from his hand and flipped it open. It contained several sketches that looked like the start of a logo. "Charlotte was the one who killed the Red River Slayer, right?"

"Yeah, Charlotte Holbock," he said, sitting in the desk chair. "With her husband, Mack, they tracked him down and unexpectedly took him out. She won a presidential citizen medal for her involvement in the case."

"She's a great artist, too," Skylar said, pointing at some of the other drawings. She pulled a pencil from her pocket and opened a new page as he snorted. When she glanced up, he was smiling. "What?"

"You carry a pencil in your pocket."

"I'm an artist. Of course I carry a pencil in my pocket. There are also several in my chair bag and my truck, and sometimes I stick one in my hair just in case."

"Just in case all the rest desert you?"

"More like an emotional support pencil," she said, scratching out the image she'd pictured last night. "What exactly do you do for Secure Watch? Are you like a hacker or something?"

His laughter filled the room, and it lifted her lips, too. "No, I leave the hacking to Mina, Delilah and Kelsey. I'm what they call a digital forensic examiner. I get to solve mysteries."

"You always loved a good mystery book as a kid," she said with a smile, remembering all the choose-your-own-adventure books they used to read together.

"I love solving puzzles, and this job lets me do it day after day. When a company has a problem, I get the information from their devices and try to learn how the unauthorized person accessed the system. It's my job to follow the trail and gather all the evidence for trials and that kind of thing. It's rewarding work."

"It's the kind of work no one thinks about anyone doing,

to be honest. You assume you're safe online when that's anything but the truth. Case in point," she said, dropping her pencil to motion around the room.

"You nailed it. The cases we've been involved with over the years have unintentionally taught people that, I think. It's been hard for Cal. He went from being a small security group installing perimeter cameras to being thrust into the spotlight without being equipped to deal with the influx of business. He stepped up and kept evolving. That's all any of us can do in a world like this. What are you drawing?"

She turned it to face him. "We passed some sandhill cranes on the way here yesterday. They were standing there watching their baby waddle about. I've never done sandhill cranes before, but they inspired me."

"What are all the letters and arrows for?"

Lowering the pad to her lap, she pointed to the tallest crane. "Those are notations telling me what color glass to use or what technique to use on the glass to shade it."

"The way you do art has always fascinated me," he said, leaning forward and clasping his hands in front of him. "Listen, we need to talk."

She knew it was coming. They'd been awake for an hour and had made small talk but avoided the real reason they were there. They couldn't keep doing that if they were going to solve this problem so she could move on with her life.

"I know it's time, but I'm nervous."

"It would be weird if you weren't nervous," he promised. "That's normal, but remember you have an entire team behind you and they're working round the clock to find out who is behind this. Last night, while you were sleeping, Iris sent me the background information on Miles Bradshaw. Interesting guy, and not in a good way." She held her hand out to him as if to say, *Right?* "They're doing a deeper dive into him now that I highlighted some areas for them to focus on."

"What kind of areas?" she asked, setting the pad on the coffee table. Relaxing time was over. She needed to dig in and help Reece. People she didn't even know were trying to get to the bottom of this, so the least she could do was help.

"To start, his increasingly aggressive interactions with other artists and gallery owners. He also has some history of petty crimes and such. The team will ensure there aren't other accusations about more significant crimes against galleries or people."

"I still find it hard to believe that an artist would damage galleries just to get back at me," she said, her shoulders falling forward. "It's hard enough to keep art galleries open, so destroying them only makes it harder for everyone in the art community."

"I would say that I agree, and I do to a degree, but I've also worked with a lot of narcissistic individuals. Many believe that if they can't be involved in something, no one can. If that makes sense."

"It does," she said with a nod. "Miles certainly fits that bill. The amount of rage exhibited in my home yesterday makes me want to vomit, but it also tells me whoever did it was focused on my art."

"How so?"

Skylar pulled herself back up against the cushion to get comfortable. He must have noticed, because he moved beside her on the couch and braced her feet against his thigh so she wouldn't keep sliding down.

"Thanks," she said with a relieved smile. "It's hard to sit like this."

"I understand. I'll have your chair ready soon. The art?"

Her nod told him her head was back in the game. "What I

meant was, the house was tossed, but if you looked around, my art took the brunt of it. Every mosaic and glass piece was shattered. All the paintings or sketches were ripped apart and shredded."

Reece was quiet for a few moments before he nodded. "You're right. I was focused on the whole picture, but it's obvious when you break it down. That leads me to my next question."

"Which is?"

"Silas."

The name slammed into her like a thousand bullets that she wasn't sure she'd survive.

Chapter Ten

It was easy to be mad at him for bringing him up, but Skylar knew it was inevitable. You can't have a skeleton that size in your closet and not expect someone to want to take a peek. "We don't need to involve him. He's dead and gone, Reece."

"Gone? Yes. Dead? Maybe not."

"He's been gone for thirteen years, Reece. He's dead. A John Doe in someone's morgue or buried in a potter's field somewhere. Leave it alone."

"We have no evidence that he's dead," Reece argued. "When did your parents stop looking for him?"

Her shrug was jerky as she did the math in her head. "Probably nine or ten years ago? There wasn't much sense in paying someone to look for a kid who didn't want to be found. As parents, that was hard for them to accept, but let's not mince words here. Silas had problems. We can't and never did deny that was part of the situation." The following sentence would take him by surprise, but she had to tell him. "Silas didn't even graduate from high school."

"What? No, I remember that he did," Reece said, turning to face her better. "Your mom had a party and the whole thing."

"Silas walked the stage and there was a party, but that diploma case was empty. He had two credits he was supposed to finish that summer and then they'd mail him the diploma, but he never went to summer school, so he never got the diploma. That's why he worked low-wage jobs and just drifted around. My parents tried to help him. They found ways for him to get his diploma, but he refused to do any of them. Eventually they gave up, deciding he was an adult and had to make his own decisions."

"Which is why they stopped looking for him, too?"

She made the so-so hand motion. "In a way, yes. When Silas left home, we thought something bad had happened, but there was no evidence of that. The police could locate his car on traffic cameras throughout the state, but when he didn't return in a few months, Mom called the police again. They insisted there was no evidence of a crime or foul play, so they couldn't get involved. Private detectives came up empty-handed every time they hired one. Our family therapist finally sat everyone down and suggested that maybe Silas left because he wanted a fresh start. After my accident, life was difficult for a few years, and as an adult, he didn't have to stay there and live through it, too."

"He could have left a note," Reece said through clenched teeth.

"Silas could have done a lot of things he didn't do, Reece. That was the nature of the beast with him. It was hard for my parents to detach themselves enough to see their son for who he was. That's just being a parent. I never liked him, so that gave me clarity they didn't have. It was hard to hide my relief when he didn't return after a few weeks."

His shoulder tipped in agreement. "You know how I felt about him."

It released some tension in her chest when she laughed, which felt good considering the situation. "You never made it a secret that you'd like to take Silas to an island and leave him there."

That made him smile. "He wasn't my favorite guy, but I still believe we must do our due diligence where he's concerned. I don't need your permission, but I want us to discuss it so you're prepared for what we might find."

A heavy sigh escaped, and she tossed her head back on the pillow to avoid eye contact with him. "Do what you have to do regarding Silas. I'll continue to believe this has nothing to do with him. Even if he is alive, he doesn't have the base knowledge to pull off a quarter of what this Binate guy has done in the last twenty-four hours, but you do you."

"Thanks, I will," he said with a wink when she sat up again. "Now that we have that settled, we need to do a deep dive into your social media accounts."

"That's going to be difficult since I can't access them."

"You can't, but one Mina Jacobs can. She's working on it right now and will call me when she's in. While we wait, I'll fix your wheel so we're mobile should we need to be."

With a nod, he headed for the garage, and Skylar flopped her head back on the pillow again. There was no way Silas was behind this, right? She'd never had any illusions about who her brother was, even as a kid. He'd shown his true colors to her at an early age. Growing up, she had very few memories of her brother. He was always on the outer edge of their family. She could only describe it as he was there to cause problems and stir up resentment but emotionally checked out. Was it intentional to treat him as an outsider? It was for her. She was positive that if Land hadn't walked in on them one day when she was in the seventh grade, her brother would have crossed a line and done something that would have torn their family apart. Land may have been young, but he was loud. By the time he finished with Silas for touching her, Silas had a black eye, a busted lip, a concussion and a healthy respect for keeping his hands off his sister. Unfortunately, it also filled Silas with rage, which he carried for them for too many years. Skylar's parents had put Silas into therapy immediately and made sure their daughter was never alone with him again, but that only made matters worse for her.

The Sullivan household had always been tense, something she hadn't realized until Silas left home, but it got worse as soon as Silas hit puberty. That was why Skylar had gotten involved in cheer at such a young age. It gave her an escape she needed from the angry young man who often refused to leave his room for days, screamed at their parents and repeatedly got in trouble at school. Skylar always thought it was a case of any attention being good attention, but the weird part was that their parents were good parents. They loved them both equally and didn't play favorites. Silas didn't want love, though. He wanted power and control, at least if you listened to him. He took his hatred out on her for ruining the control he had over their parents for the first six years of his life.

The only reason she understood all this was due to the years of family counseling. Between the accident and Silas leaving, their family was in shambles. At the time, Reece's mom had gently reminded them that their work benefits covered therapists, so maybe it was time to visit one. Skylar had agreed immediately. Her father took a bit longer to convince, but eventually, they'd found a counselor who helped them see that what happened with Silas was no one's fault but his. They'd done their best to help him, but he'd refused all help and chosen to go it alone. Families fall apart all the time, and the only way to move forward is to accept that person's decision as their own and continue to live your life. If you don't and instead focus all your time and energy on someone who doesn't want or deserve it, your life is no longer your own.

It had taken her parents two more years to accept that, but everyone's lives improved once they did. They had retired from their jobs in Duluth and moved to Florida, where they'd invested money into a small marina. Her father had always loved boats and the water, and the new business allowed him to enjoy both at a slower pace. Her mom grieved the little boy she remembered, but she accepted that he was an adult now and that they couldn't change who he was.

The idea of letting Reece dig Silas back up after they'd buried him as a family rankled her. He didn't have the right to tell her she had blinders on when it came to her brother, because she didn't. She was fully aware of who and what her brother was. As in past tense, because whether he still sucked air or not, he was dead to her. He had been for most of her life. But she knew Reece. He wasn't going to let this go until he proved one way or the other whether Silas could somehow be involved in the destruction of her life. The implications of finding Silas alive hit her, and she groaned. She would have to tell Reece the truth about him, because if she knew one thing, it was this: Silas Sullivan had to remain dead, or their entire family was at risk.

REECE TAPPED HIS pen on the desk as he pored over the information about the nationwide network of crimes against art galleries. He'd be mad about it, but it was too laughable to think anyone would believe that Skylar was capable of something like this. She was so physically incapable of almost all the damage that he was starting to suspect that might be why the cops hadn't knocked on her door. It wouldn't take much underlying investigation to see she couldn't do this, and she was right when she said the cops in Duluth knew her. That might have been why they hadn't pulled her in yet.

They'd watched the original Binate video again after Mina sent a copy, but the voice was electronic and the figure behind the camera could have been his own father. Skylar couldn't say it was Miles Bradshaw, but she also couldn't say it wasn't, which was precisely what this person wanted. He wanted them to think everyone was a suspect so they could never narrow in on him. If Reece had to guess, Binate had been expecting Skylar to go to the police when she got that video, not the premier cybersecurity group in the nation. Maybe Binate should have done a little bit more research on who Skylar's friends were before he decided to take her on.

Were they friends, though? For the last fourteen years, he didn't know what they were. They weren't friends, but they also weren't frenemies. Reece couldn't speak for Skylar, but he could say with certainty that he had thought of her every single day since he'd last seen her. It was impossible not to when half of him was missing every second of the day. While he couldn't speak for her, since she was the one who pushed him away, he still considered them friends.

Sky had pointed out that whoever this was, they thought she was far more capable than she was. At first, he'd thought she was trying to explain why she'd pushed him away, but when he put that aside and listened—really listened—that wasn't what she was saying at all. She was saying that there was no way she could travel alone by car for long distances. She certainly couldn't fly and keep a low profile when she had to check her chair and be carried on and off the plane. She could not roll around these buildings, spray painting and breaking glass from a wheelchair without being noticed.

Short of hiring someone to do the crimes, it was unrealistic to believe Skylar was involved.

The sick soul that dreamed up this scheme either didn't know about her limitations or was hoping people would think she'd hired someone to do it and just wanted to ruin her reputation. It also made her a persona non grata within the art world. Unless they could prove this wasn't her, she'd never be invited to hold a gallery showing with these accusations hanging over her head. That's what made him lean toward Miles Bradshaw as the instigator. It seemed he'd do anything to sideline her career. The sticking point for him was that Miles knew her and could see her limitations, even if he didn't understand them. Then again, he didn't have to understand them to ruin her reputation. All he had to do was convince people she was behind it. On the other hand, Silas had taken off so early in Skylar's recovery that he might not know her limitations, but he also might not care.

"When is Mina calling?" Skylar asked as she rolled into the room, breaking him from his spiraling thoughts.

When Reece turned to face her, he couldn't help but drink her in. She would always be the girl next door, but she was also stunning in the simplicity of her style. She wore floral boho pants and a blue-green blouse that drew his eye to hers. Her eyes told him she was still terrified, but he also saw determination. When she gazed at him, he wanted to believe he saw desire in her eyes, but he couldn't let himself go there. She'd made it clear they could never be more than acquaintances, and once she was clear of Binate, he would have to let her go again.

Self-preservation had him turning away before he answered. "Mina will be calling any minute." An electronic tone rang out. "Speak of the devil. Are you ready? This won't be easy, but with any luck, she has the information we need to get your life back."

He waited, watching the fear, anger and determination roll across her face before she nodded. "I'm ready. It's time to end this so we can return to our lives."

As Reece pressed the button to respond to Mina, all he could think was that was the last thing he wanted to do.

Chapter Eleven

"We have a problem," Mina said as soon as Reece connected with her.

"Thanks, Captain Obvious," he said with a wink. Sky had wheeled beside him in front of the computer monitors, ready to sort through her social media posts.

Mina offered a rare grin that said she was amused. "My apologies. We have a new problem."

"Fantastic, because why not?" Sky asked, rolling her eyes.

"Enlighten us," Reece said, grabbing a pen and pad of paper. "How big of a problem is it?"

"He knows where you are."

"Impossible," Reece said, his heart rate ticking up at the thought. "It's been calm and quiet here all night."

Mina held up her finger and grabbed her tablet, tapping around on it while she kept one eye on the camera. "I was able to tap into her Facebook account. He's using it as a vlog of sorts."

"Whatever for, if no one can access it?" Sky asked, her head tipped in confusion.

"We'll get to that. But—" Mina flipped the tablet so they could see the screen. Binate was in front of the camera. Reece felt a shudder go through Sky, and he put his arm around her back to ground her. If Mina noticed, she didn't react. Instead, she pushed the play button, and Binate's electronic voice filled their space again.

"It's cute how you think I don't know where you went with that agent, Skylar. I know everything about you, including your address—1993 Cherry Hill Lane is so far out in the sticks that calling for help would be futile. I'd have you before the cops could even circle their wagons. Oh, sure, you think you're safe hiding there with an ex-cop, but I'm not afraid to hurt him to get to you. Bide your time, Skylar, I'm coming for you. It's too bad you'll never see this and know that. Then again, I do love a good surprise." The video ended with an electronic horror laugh that sent a shudder down his spine.

"My truck is clean," he said the moment Mina put the tablet down. "I have a device that tells me if any GPS was tacked to the truck."

"You might be clean, but I'm not entirely sure that Skylar is," Mina said, glancing at her. "You left your phone, but did you take anything else?"

"Just the things that were in my suitcase from my trip north and my chair."

Reece raised a brow at the camera, and Mina nodded. "I'll wand the chair." He jumped up and jogged to the garage, cursing himself the whole way. Why the hell hadn't he checked her chair before they left Duluth? They all carried wands to check for bugs and GPS clips. He knew the answer—he'd dropped his guard when he'd come face-to-face with Sky again. Big mistake. Big, big mistake. Mina would have words with him about this if they found a tracker. When he ran back in, he was already addressing the camera. "Rookie move, boss, I know. Dammit, I should have checked before we left."

"Relax, Reece. It was a situation that required you to get her out of there quickly, which doesn't always leave us time to think clearly. I also didn't think to remind you, so I'll share the blame if you find one."

Reece offered her a smile of appreciation. She was right, but that didn't make him feel any better about forgetting something so important.

"I think I'd know if it was in my chair. I'm never without it, and there aren't a lot of places to hide something where I wouldn't find it. How long do they even stay active?"

"Depends on the kind," Mina said. "Some are solar powered and can last up to thirty days."

After taking in the wheelchair, he knew. "The bag," he said, running the wand over it. Sure enough, the wand beeped.

Sky looked up. "The bag is always there. I have to carry things."

Reece ran it over the bag again several times, the beeping louder each time until he was right over it. He wanded the rest of the chair for completion's sake but got no other hits.

"Aren't you going to get rid of it or something?" Sky asked when he put the wand down.

"No." He shook his head as he took her hand. "It will stay where it is until we decide what happens next. Then, when we're ready to go, we'll put the entire bag beside the bed. If I lift the tracker out, he'll know we found it. We need to get out of here before he catches on."

Mina nodded, agreeing. "Leave everything in place and the lights on. Sky, can you duck low enough in the truck to not be seen?"

"I'd have to be on my side with my legs propped, but if he covered me with a blanket and it was dark, you wouldn't see me."

"Do that until you're clear of the place," Mina told Reece. "Can you hide the chair in the truck?"

He glanced at Sky for confirmation.

"If we take the wheels off and fold the back down, it would be lower than the back of the truck. A tarp would then hide it."

"To what end, boss?" Reece asked in confusion.

"If the perp is watching the house, he may approach if he sees you leave alone, with all the lights still on. It's worth a shot to see if he bites. If he gets into the house, I can trap him there until the police arrive."

"It's worth a shot," Reece said with a nod. "We need another place to go. Should I take the portable equipment so I can contact you?"

"Normally, yes, but it's time for you to come home. We have an empty cabin since Delilah and Lucas moved to Wisconsin. It's not perfectly accessible, but it will be better than a hotel room, and you'll have access to the equipment in the command center."

"I don't want to bring trouble to Secure Watch," Sky said, glancing between him and Mina. "I can't put all of you in danger, either."

His laughter filled the room, and he gently shoulder bumped her. "Sweetheart, that's the very last thing you need to worry about. Let Binate show up on Secure Watch's doorstep. It will be the last thing he does as a free man."

Mina shot him a finger gun and a wink. "Normally, I'd tell you to watch your tail, but in this case, I won't. If you bring along an unwanted pest, we'll swat him and take care of the problem by daybreak. Do be careful, though—the guy is unpredictable. Stay aware."

"You got it, boss. It will take us a few to get ready."

"Once you're in the truck, call in and I'll take control of

the house. See you in two hours. You can get some sleep and then go over the dupe I made of her Facebook page."

"You said we'd get to why he would put up videos that no one could watch," Sky said, glancing between Reece and Mina.

"You can look at that page as well." Mina nodded. "He's started a page on Facebook calling for your arrest for all the gallery crimes."

Reece paused what he was doing to tip his head at his boss. "The page is set up like a petition?"

"It's more like a hate page," Mina explained. "He's posting pictures of the galleries after the crimes."

"Listen," Sky said with a shake of her head. "I'm not a big name in the art world. Literally no one outside of Duluth even knows who I am."

"While that may be true, he's working hard to change that," Mina explained. "He's hanging out all the dirty laundry he can find about you. Whether any of it is true or not isn't what matters. What matters is convincing the public that it is."

"Is he having any luck with that?" Reece asked, anger filling his veins until his blood boiled and his ears turned hot.

"Not that I can see. As I said, we'll look at it when you get here. I can't convince Facebook to shut it down because he set it up as a business page using your personal page to do it, so to them, it looks legit."

"But it's my page!" Sky exclaimed, and Reece could tell she was holding back tears of anger and anguish.

"It is, but he changed the name and deleted all of your postings, so it doesn't look like it was ever your page."

"I don't understand how he could do that," Sky said, her tone telling Reece she was hitting the end of her ability to reason. Since he still had to get her to safety, he glanced at Mina, who nodded in agreement.

"I'll explain that on the way," Reece said. "We need to get out before we can't."

"I thought you said everything is quiet," Sky said, the words filled with nerves.

"It is," Mina said patiently. "And we want to keep it that way, so it's time to move. Will you be ready in ten?"

With a nod, Mina disconnected. Reece took Sky's hand to calm her. "I got you. Secure Watch is behind us, so don't be afraid."

"Too late," she whispered, her smile watery. "That ship sailed."

"I've let you down once, Sky. It won't happen again."

Not wanting to see the look in her eyes, he pulled her into him, his hand cradling her head as he held her to his chest. When she let out a shuddering sigh of relief, he silently vowed to protect her for life. All he had to do was convince her that she didn't need protection from him.

THE DARKNESS ENGULFED THEM, but Sky had never felt more exposed. With the blanket over her, just her nose and mouth stuck out. She couldn't see where they were going and had to trust the man behind the wheel to get her to safety. But then, she did trust him, or she wouldn't have called him, right? The truth came down to one thing, she realized. She trusted him with her life but not her heart. Call it a preemptive strike by not putting herself in the position to watch Reece walk away when he experienced how hard her life was. That would be easier than believing for a heartbeat that they could be more than old friends.

The way he'd held her earlier before they left the safe house told her that much. He was strong but gentle. Comforting but honest. He didn't dismiss her fears by telling her everything would be okay—an empty promise in this situation. Everything might not be okay, but he would be there to make sure she was physically safe. She'd accepted that she might have to start over with her career even though the very idea made her sick. She had worked so hard for so long to prove herself as an artist, but now, one man was systematically dismantling her work. If even one gallery owner decided she was guilty, trial or no trial, she might as well hang up her easel and find a new career.

"Hanging in there?" Reece asked, his mouth covered with his arm as though he were coughing. He had told her he couldn't talk to her, or it would be obvious he wasn't alone.

"Yes, but it's not easy in this position," she admitted. "How much farther?"

"Ten," he grunted as though coughing again.

Ten minutes or ten miles, she didn't know, but she could hang on that long if it meant they'd get to safety. The last thing she wanted was Reece to get hurt in all this mess—bodily or professionally. In her opinion, it was above and beyond for Mina to bring them to Secure Watch, but maybe that was how they did business. Skylar knew she could never repay them, but she vowed to try.

"When this is over, I'm going to talk to my parents and the lawyer about getting an advance from my settlement to pay Secure Watch," she said, knowing he couldn't respond. "I can't say I don't have the money when I do."

As expected, he said nothing but dropped his hand from the wheel and squeezed her shoulder, telling her without words that he had things to say about it. They rode in silence for what seemed like forever to her, his hand still on her and his breathing steady, though she knew he was wound tight and on watch for the slightest thing to be off. All she wanted to do was get to Secure Watch, find a comfortable position for the first time in days and fall asleep. Her body was starting to feel the effects of the last forty-eight hours. If she wasn't careful, she was going to require more medical attention than they could give her.

"You will not take money from your settlement account to pay Secure Watch," he said, his words clipped.

"That's what the money is for, Reece. To take care of my expenses."

"Your medical and daily living expenses, not this," he said, squeezing her shoulder. "If Secure Watch didn't want to help you, they wouldn't be, so please, don't insult everyone who is by insisting on paying."

"I'm disabled, not a charity case, Land," she said, anger rising in her chest.

"Did you hear me say you were?" he asked. Skylar couldn't see his face, but she could hear his exasperation loud and clear. Rather than distract him further, she sighed.

"Fine, I'll graciously accept the help of all of you at Secure Watch without bringing up payment. That said, you can't stop me from creating a special mosaic as a gift." She stressed the word *gift* so he didn't get his undies in a bundle about it.

Laughter rang out, making her smile, even though she didn't want to. "I certainly can't stop you from doing that, nor would I. Having a one-of-a-kind Skylar Sullivan mosaic is worth more than cash."

This time, Skylar's laughter filled the cab. "Land, you're smooth, but not smooth enough to make me forget that my name is mud right now in the art community, not that it was all that great to begin with. I was making gains, but now…" She didn't finish—she just shook her head under the blanket.

"Now, you'll come back stronger than ever once the real culprit of the gallery crimes is caught and revealed. You'll be hailed as the hero for helping apprehend and bring them to justice."

"By hiding out in a cabin in the woods?"

"It's all about the spin, Sky. Spin it right and not only does this not hurt your career, but it also helps it."

"That would send this Binate guy right over the edge."

"I like to aim high," he said, and she could picture that one gray eye of his winking the way he used to do when they were kids. "There's a rest stop ahead. There aren't any headlights behind me, so I'll pull over and help you get upright and better secured for the rest of the ride. We're driving into heavy deer country, and I don't want you to get hurt if I have to hit the brakes."

"You won't hear me argue. Another ten minutes and I won't be able to sit up."

"Why didn't you say something sooner?" She heard the anger in his words, which was another reminder that he didn't live in her world and never would.

"To what end, Reece? Getting out alive but sore was better than getting out dead in a body bag. Don't judge me when you haven't been a part of my life for years. I'm tougher than you think I am."

"You're right. I haven't been part of your life for years, but whose fault is that?" he asked softly. She suspected he didn't want her to hear the question at all, but she had, and it made her grimace internally. Before she could respond, the truck slowed and they took a turn to the right, rolling her gently into his side to remind her that she would never enjoy the comfort of his warm body ever again.

He left the truck idling when he got out and slammed the door. *Slammed* was the apt description, but she was too busy trying to throw the blanket off to worry about his mood. The faster she got upright, the better for her body and their mission. Lingering in one spot wasn't a good idea, and she wouldn't be the reason for it.

By the time Reece had her door open, his gentleness had returned. "Take it slow," he said, offering his hand for her to grab with one hand while she pushed herself up with the other.

Bright lights filled the truck as a vehicle came down the exit, illuminating Reece where he stood at the passenger door. Reece ducked as she heard a pop and then the sound of pinging metal.

"Stay down!" he yelled, dropping her hand, yanking his handgun from its holster and firing off a shot.

Chapter Twelve

"Where the hell did these guys come from?" Reece yelled as he aimed for the tires on the truck as it passed them. They'd drilled the back of his truck full of holes, and he owed them one. On a breath, he squeezed the trigger, the bullet finding its target and blowing apart the giant tire of the lifted truck. The operator lost control immediately. Before he could get off another shot, the truck went careening into the grass until it bounced off several trees and rolled, landing on its roof with the tires still spinning.

"Let's go!" Reece slammed the door and ran to the driver's side, throwing the truck into Reverse and slamming the pedal down as far as it would go, praying none of the bullets had hit any of his tires or the gas tank. The engine roared under him, but the gas gauge didn't budge, nor did the truck fishtail. His truck might now be ugly, but at least it would get them to Secure Watch.

"Reece! What if that was Binate? Shouldn't we check?"

He briefly cut his gaze to hers once they were on the road again. "I let my guard down again with you and look what happened. There isn't a chance in hell I'm doing it again by approaching that truck. That leaves you open and defenseless, which is all Binate needs to grab you. I'm not stopping this truck again, so push yourself up using my shoulder and buckle in. Use my arm if you need extra leverage." He held his arm out in a V for her to grab, and after a few attempts, she managed to get herself upright and belted in. Rather than belt her legs together, she leaned over and wrapped her arms over them to hold them.

"You can't ride that way for the next hour," he said, glancing at her.

"The way you're driving, we'll be there in ten minutes."

Her words made him laugh, and he eased off the gas a bit. "I don't know about you, but I wouldn't mind picking up a cop right about now. In the absence of an escort, I'll push this truck to its limit if it means less time on the road alone. I need to update Secure Watch."

He went through every second of their drive in his mind, from leaving the safe house until they took that exit. No one was in the rearview mirror, especially not a truck that big. Where had they come from?

"That truck came from the wrong direction, Land," she said, turning to look at him. "It came down the on-ramp."

Reece blinked, forcing his mind away from the bullets to the moment the headlights filled the truck. He let out a breath. "You're right, but how did they know we left?"

"I can't answer that, since we left the bag and the tracker at the house."

Frustrated, he used voice controls to contact Mina.

"Secure Watch, Whiskey."

"Secure Watch, Riker," he addressed his boss. "There's been a situation."

"This seems to be the theme of our calls lately. I can't say I like it," Mina responded. "Is anyone hurt?"

"Negative," he answered, glancing at Sky, who looked like she'd fallen asleep on her legs. The position was uncomfortable, but he suspected she was scared and didn't want to be visible in the windows. Honestly, that wasn't an unfounded fear. "A jacked-up truck tried to take us out at the rest stop on 371."

"I like the use of the word *tried*."

"They're upside down in the grass with only three tires. My truck is full of holes, but otherwise, it's fine. I didn't wait around to see if it was Binate. I couldn't leave Sky unprotected."

"You did the right thing," she agreed. "Why were you at the rest stop? You didn't leave too long ago."

"Sky needed to sit up. She can't lie in certain positions for long or she starts to cramp up. Mina, when I tell you there was no one around us, I'm positive of that. The headlights were insane on the thing when it roared at us. Sky realized they came down the on-ramp."

"They had to be watching the house. It wouldn't take long for them to figure out where you were going and set up a trap."

"That or I do have a tracker on my truck. I checked it before we left again and found nothing, but I suppose they could have hacked the GPS in the maps."

"Impossible," she said immediately. "I have full control of that. I'm inclined to believe that whoever this Binate guy is, he has friends who are willing to help him. In this case, they could kill two birds with one stone."

"Take me out and grab Sky?"

"Yep," she answered grimly. "You made the right decision. How far out are you now?"

"Sky says at the speed I'm going, less than ten minutes." His words dragged a laugh from his boss. "About an hour. Sky is a mess, though—physically, I mean."

"Get her here in one piece. The cabin has a nice accessible shower. She can soak in some hot water and then get some sleep. We can pick this nonsense up tomorrow. In the meantime, I'll send a team of guys out to the rest stop on 371 and see what's left, if anything."

"I'm sure the guys will be long gone. That truck is going to take some work to get out of there, though."

"That's what I'm hoping," she agreed with a snicker. "If our guys can take a gander through it, we might be able to track down a registration. Call if you need more backup."

"Will do. Riker, out."

He punched the speaker off and eyed his passenger again. Knowing she couldn't stay like that the rest of the ride, he pulled the truck to the side of the road and kept his foot on the brake while he helped her roll over onto the bench seat, using his lap as a pillow. He lifted her legs onto the seat and tucked the seat belt around them so she could rest on her back instead of her side. It wasn't perfect, but as he pushed the speedometer toward one hundred miles per hour, he hoped to cut thirty minutes off the drive.

Once they were on the road again, she snuggled her head into his thigh, dangerously close to his groin, and sighed. He might have made a mess of this night, but she was safe and under his protection. That was all he cared about. After the little stunt they'd just pulled, Reece vowed to be the one to take Binate down.

SKY WOKE SLOWLY, her tired mind needing a moment to remember where she was until she glanced to her left and saw the man who still haunted her dreams. Last night, when they arrived at Secure One, the team had a UTV waiting to take them to their cabin near the lake. It was dark, so she couldn't see much as they meandered their way to the back of the property, but something told her the view would be spectacular when the sun came up. She did notice the room was lightening, which meant another day had arrived. A day that they would begin with a meeting of the Secure Watch team at breakfast, according to Reece.

One thing Skylar had noticed last night was that the property was a fortress in itself. You weren't escaping their security measures unless someone could scale a fence while invisible. Appropriate since Secure One was a security company. Reece had explained the harrowing story of Mina's kidnapping from the compound when she arrived years ago and how Cal, the owner of Secure One, and her husband's brother, took it as a personal affront. Since then, he's ensured no one could attack him in his home again. Short of someone dropping something from a plane, no one was getting inside without an invite. Since Secure One and Secure Watch worked together under the same roof, it was nice to be in the one place that could get her out of this jam. She once again found herself grateful for the invite.

Once they were in the cabin, Reece had encouraged her to sit under the hot water to ease some of the tension in her back so she could get some sleep. She'd never been more grateful than to find the cabin had enough modifications to keep her independent even during the worst time of her life. The shower was a roll-in with a shower wheelchair, something she didn't have the luxury of at home. Once she'd showered and gotten ready for bed, she'd tried to convince Reece to let her sleep in the recliner so he could have the bed, but it had been a losing battle. He already had the bed set up and ready for her when she came out of the bathroom, including a heating pad for her back. Then he'd sat next to her and rubbed her forehead silently until she'd dropped off to sleep. To say she was surprised to see him in bed next to her wasn't true. There was no other option other than the recliner, but Land would defend her until his death, and there was no way he'd leave her vulnerable, even on a property that was monitored from all angles by his colleagues.

Reece wasn't wired that way. It was all or nothing for this man, and she had always loved that about him when they were kids. He never did anything halfway and didn't let anyone else get away with doing a job halfway, either. The Land-sized gulf she'd had inside her for the last fourteen years deepened, and a tear ran from her eye.

"Hey," he whispered, wiping it away gently. "Talk to me."

That was the last thing she was going to do. Opening up about that gulf of pain she carried regarding him would change their dynamics, and they couldn't afford to be anything but objective right now. It would be too easy for her to lose sight of why she'd pushed him away all those years ago.

"I refuse to drag you into this dumpster fire of my life," she whispered. When he lifted a brow, she sighed. "Okay, drag you any deeper into this dumpster fire I call life."

"I'm in it to win it, Sky," he promised, running his knuckle down her cheek to catch another tear. "A few tears won't scare me away if that's what you think."

"Tears never scared you away, Land."

"Sometimes they drove me to do stupid things, but I always came back," he said with a wink.

Until the time he didn't. She'd wanted it that way, though. She'd begged him to stay away from her and to get on with his life. When he had, she'd died inside, knowing she would never get to see him achieve all his dreams. They'd shared so much during their childhood, but it wasn't fair to hold him back when he could make his dreams come true.

"We're in the right place now to sort all of this out," he promised, brushing her hair off her forehead. "I have every tool at my disposal, and now that I don't have to worry about keeping you safe while trying to do my job, I hope we can resolve this even more quickly."

"That's good. The sooner I'm out of your hair, the better," she agreed, prepared to sit up and get the day started, but he grabbed her elbow and held her there.

"First, you aren't 'in my hair,'" he said, using air quotes with one hand. "I'm here because I want to be. Second, things aren't going to go back to the way they were before, Sky. I won't allow it."

Her heart hammered in her chest as he forced eye contact. His eyes told her everything he meant by that statement, but like a moth to a flame, she had to ask. "Back to the way they were before?"

"Both of us pretending the other doesn't exist," he said, his gaze holding hers. "There's no way I can go back to that way of life, so once we solve this problem, we're going to be friends again—the kind of friends who see each other and spend time together."

"No, Land—"

Before she could say more, his lips brushed hers. Sound and light disappeared when he did it again, this time letting his lips linger on hers. His warm breath met hers and she whimpered, wanting more but also afraid to want more. He solved that problem for her by pressing his lips to hers fully and sliding his fingers into her hair, holding her there as they breathed together in harmony for a split second. When he pulled back, he ran his thumb across her lips.

"It looks like it's time to start the day," he whispered, his thumb still grazing her overly sensitive skin. "The team will be waiting for us. Give me five minutes to clean up, and then the bathroom will be all yours."

Slowly, he pulled his fingers from her hair without breaking eye contact. The things she read in his eyes were dangerous to her way of life if she allowed him to touch her again. When he tossed the blanket off and climbed from the bed, her gaze followed him to the bathroom, his joggers low on his hips and his hard, muscular chest bare with just a smattering of blond hair. He was just as sculpted as in high school, but maturity looked good on him.

The moment the bathroom door clicked shut, she brought her hand to her lips. She'd been kissed before, but not like that. Not by someone's entire heart. And that was the only way she could describe it. It might have been the tamest kiss in history, but the action wasn't the point. The underlying emotions were the point. Hurt. Anger. Pain. Loss. Joy. Desire. Trust. She felt them all, and each one had pierced her heart and lodged there as an arrowed reminder of their past and why they couldn't have a future.

BREAKFAST HAD BEEN DELICIOUS. Reece had told her that their cook, Sadie, made a huge breakfast and dinner every night for the entire crew, which had to be a massive undertaking, from what Sky could see. Only part of the crew had been there, but the cafeteria was still full. According to Mina, Secure One and Secure Watch had more than doubled in size since she moved there with her husband, Roman. That wasn't even counting their remote operatives like Reece. She was starting to see the scope of who was helping her and how much power they had to make sure she rolled out of this alive. After last night, she didn't even care if she had a career to return to as long as she and Reece were still breathing at the end. As far as she was concerned, that was all that mattered anymore.

"You didn't eat much for breakfast," Reece said as they rolled into the conference room to decide the next move on the board. They didn't have many, but she had confidence that Mina had mapped them all and knew exactly what percentage each one had of working.

"I have a bit of a headache," she answered as he pulled a chair away from the large conference table so she could park her chair under it. Once her wheels were locked, she shifted in the chair to find a more comfortable position. The truth was, the ride to Secure Watch last night had left lasting effects. Her belly hurt from being hunched over for so long, but she wouldn't complain since she was alive to see the sunrise this morning. "I'll grab a snack later."

Once they were settled, Mina leaned in on the table. "I'm not going to lie—this has been a challenge. Binate knows what he's doing when it comes to hiding his footprints and your information. It's hard to stump me, but he's thwarted my every move."

"Mine as well," Reece agreed.

"That's why it's not Silas," Sky said, shaking her head. "He doesn't have the skill set to do this."

"He didn't when he left home, but that was nearly fifteen years ago," Mina gently said. "People change."

"Especially when driven by hatred or desire for revenge," Reece added.

Skylar adjusted herself in the chair again, partly to get more comfortable and partly to avoid spouting off at him about her brother. "I know you think I'm hindered by family alliance when it comes to Silas, but I'm not. I don't disagree that people change, but what you don't know is that Silas was diagnosed with schizophrenia when he was—"

"Nineteen," Reece finished before she could. "Why didn't you tell me?"

"My parents were adamant no one know," Sky said, averting her gaze from him and Mina.

"I'm lost," Mina said.

"When Sky was thirteen, I walked in on Silas attempting to assault her. Silas was nineteen at the time."

Mina's lips thinned. "My guess is that didn't go well."

"My brother was a waif," Skylar said. "Reece was bigger in height and weight, even six years younger. After Silas got out of the ER, my parents put him into therapy, where he was eventually diagnosed through a psychiatrist. Mom and Dad tried to help him, but—"

"You can't help someone who doesn't want help," Mina finished, and Sky pointed at her as if to say, *Exactly.* "All that said, I'm still following him as a lead, but I'm also looking closely at Miles Bradshaw. His past tells me he's an angry man. What I don't know yet is if he's capable of such a sophisticated wipe of someone's life."

Skylar braced her elbow on the table and rested her head on her hand as Mina and Reece tossed ideas back and forth. She couldn't pretend she hadn't noticed the hurt in Reece's eyes when he learned of Silas's diagnosis, but it also hadn't been her choice not to tell him. She'd wanted to, but her mom said if she told Reece, he'd tell his parents. For a reason she wasn't privy to, they didn't want anyone else to know of Silas's problems. Maybe it was time to let that ghost out of the closet and bury it once and for all.

Mina and Reece were deep in conversation, but she needed to use the restroom. "I'll be right back," she said, pointing out the door. "I just need the facilities."

"Need help?" Reece asked, pausing their conversation, but she shook her head.

"I'm fine. Thanks, though."

Before he could say more, she wheeled out of the room and down the hallway toward the cafeteria. She had noticed a restroom on their way to the conference room. Once locked inside, she pulled her shirt up and uncoiled her catheter. She wondered if her bladder was full, which would explain her pain. Once she had it uncoiled and over the bowl, she uncapped it, but nothing happened.

There was a knock on the door. "Sky, are you okay?" Reece asked.

"No. I think I need help," she said without thinking, her head pounding as she tried to recap the catheter. Before she could coil it, the lock popped and Reece held the door open for a woman she didn't know, then followed her into the small space.

"My name is Selina. I'm the crew nurse," she explained, kneeling in front of her chair.

"I didn't think you looked right when you left," Reece explained.

Selina was already checking her pulse before Reece finished speaking. "Does your head hurt?"

"Yes. I can't even remember how to get the catheter to flow, but my stomach hurts," Skylar admitted.

"Med bay, now," Selina said to Reece, who scooped her from the chair and ran down the hallway. "I'm worried it's autonomic dysreflexia."

"That's bad, right?" Reece asked as he laid her on a stretcher in a room that could have been an emergency room cubicle. "I remember that was a worry when you first were injured."

"It's always a worry," Selina explained, hooking her to the blood pressure machine by the bed. "There are many reasons someone with a spinal cord injury can develop autonomic dysreflexia, but when it happens, it's hazardous to the heart."

Snapping on gloves, Selina checked around her catheter and palpated her abdomen. "Your bladder is very full, so now we know the culprit," she said, grabbing a urinal. "You don't free drain?"

"Only at night. Intermittent draining is normally not a problem, but I'm worried the positioning in the truck last night damaged something."

"She was bent over for quite a while," Reece explained, taking hold of her hand. She was too scared to pull away from him. The warmth of his skin grounded her and made her feel like she would be okay.

Selina glanced up at the monitor when the blood pressure cuff deflated. "Blood pressure is high, but not in the immediate danger zone. I vote to change the catheter rather than try to make this one drain. Are you okay with that?"

"You can do that here?"

Reece chuckled, though she could tell it was forced. "She could do open-heart surgery here if she had to."

"I wouldn't go that far," Selina said, snapping on gloves. "As for a catheter, that's a piece of cake. I need to lay you flat, so tell me if your headache worsens when I do that. We will change it fast, drain your bladder and then reassess your blood pressure."

"Will that fix it?" Reece asked as she gathered supplies.

"If we can't keep the urine flowing, then we'll need to do something else with the catheter or get her to a hospital. If we're lucky, it's just sediment blocking this one and a new tube will solve the issue. I want you at her head to call out the blood pressure numbers each time it deflates. Keep an eye on her skin. Tell me if she starts sweating or her face gets red and blotchy."

"It's just a headache right now," Skylar assured them. "And I'm a little warm."

Selina paused and offered her a smile as she pulled the gloves off and squeezed her hand. "I've got you. Where's your level of injury?"

"T5," Reece answered before she could.

"I can't feel my bladder at all," Skylar added. Selina nodded as she lowered the bed and immediately snapped on new gloves.

Reece held her face in his hands and her gaze with his. "You'll be okay. Selina is the best there is," he promised, dropping a kiss on her forehead. "She's right. She's warm."

"That's not unexpected, but watch for excessive sweating," Selina answered as she worked. In less than a minute, she heard the catheter start draining into the urinal.

"That was crazy fast," Skylar said, a laugh escaping before she coughed once. "It takes me ten minutes to change that catheter."

"Selina can remove a bullet while riding a skateboard," Reece said with a wink. "How's your head?"

"Still hurts, but the pounding has slowed."

"That's because your bladder is almost empty," Selina said. "Did you empty it this morning?"

"Of course," she answered defensively. "Only a small amount came out, but we went to bed late, so I didn't think too much of it."

"There was no way you could in that case," Selina agreed. "Reece, what are the blood pressure numbers?"

Reece turned his head, giving her a side profile that made her want to weep. He was so handsome. She'd never seen a man with blond facial hair, which made him look like a Norske hunter. "One forty over eighty."

Selina nodded. "Good, it's coming down."

"Isn't that normal?" Reece asked, turning his attention back to her.

"For someone without a spinal cord injury, yes. I would guess Skylar's runs lower than that."

"By a lot," she agreed. "I'd like to see if it keeps coming down before I take medication, though. That usually makes it drop too much."

"We can do that," Selina agreed. "I'm going to sit you up now, which will help, too. Then, we'll decide how best to approach the catheter situation. Reece, would you go down and update the team?"

"No, I don't want to leave her." He shook his head, refusing to look away from her long enough to address his friend.

Selina walked to the head of the bed and put her hand on his shoulder. "I know you don't, but I'll need to monitor her for a few hours. You can check on her, but those are hours wasted and you could be helping Mina sort this out so Skylar can get her life back. You can trust her with me."

"I trust you, Selina. But I—"

"I know," she promised with a wink, stopping him from saying whatever he planned to say. "Trust me with her for a little bit. She'll be all the better for it."

He glanced down and met her gaze. "Are you okay with me leaving? If you aren't, say the word."

"She's right," she said with a nod. "There's no sense in wasting time with me when you could be helping Mina."

"Being here with you is not wasting time," he said as she brushed her hand across his face. His beard was soft and smooth against her palm. Tears pricked her eyes when she thought about the life with this man she'd been forced to give up.

"I promise to call you if there's even a hint of a problem," Selina said when she moved to the head of the stretcher. "You go do what you do best and I'll do what I do best. Okay?"

Reece made eye contact with Selina momentarily before glancing down at her again. "I'd be mad, but I'm too relieved that you're okay. I'll chat with Mina for a few minutes and then check on you."

"I can live with that," she whispered when she realized

how truly terrified he was about what had happened. That was when she remembered this was the reason she'd let him go the first time.

Chapter Thirteen

The memories overwhelmed Reece until he fell backward and slid down the wall, his head in his hands and his breathing ragged in the quiet space. He squeezed his eyes shut to try and push the memories away, but it didn't work.

"My legs! I can't feel my legs!" Sky cried, terror ripping through him as he knelt on the turf next to her.

"Help is coming," Reece promised, holding her hand as tears streamed down her face. "Don't move."

"I can't move." She didn't scream or cry those three words. Instead, they were barely a whisper, as though the realization had dawned on her that life as they knew it was over.

"Riker!" The sharp tone snapped his head up, and he came face-to-face with Roman. He held his hand out until Reece took it and let Roman help him up. "You look like a man who needs a cup of coffee," he said.

Roman led him down to the cafeteria where Sadie kept hot, fresh coffee going 24-7. He poured them each a cup before they sat at a table to drink it.

"Thanks," Reece said, holding up the cup. "It's been a long few days."

"Filled with many tense, destructive memories," Roman

added. "I remember how hard it was not to be overwhelmed by the emotions when I saw Mina for the first time after searching for her for a year. To see how much pain they're in does something to you here," he said, pounding his chest.

"My problem seems to be here," Reece said, pointing at his head. "Always has been since the accident."

"I know what happened to Skylar from helping Mina on the case, but now I understand that the accident affected you far more than a broken wrist."

"It was my fault," Reece said, lowering the cup to the table. "It was the final routine for the event and we thought we had the first-place podium clinched, so we decided to do an easier stunt lift than we'd planned. There was no point in risking the medal by trying something too hard. The stunt was flawless until I found myself on the ground and Sky ten feet away, unable to move."

Roman sipped his coffee silently while Reece slumped over his coffee mug. "I'm still waiting to hear how it's your fault."

"I didn't catch her!" he exclaimed. "It's not hard, man."

Reece noticed Roman blink several times and then opened and closed his mouth twice. "How were you supposed to catch her when you'd been plowed over by a golf cart and had a broken arm?"

"With the other one," Reece growled.

Roman leaned over the table and folded his hands. "Listen, Reece. I've been where you are multiple times while serving in the army. I blamed myself for something I had no control over. Then I worked with Mina for eight years, and on that final day, I let her down. I wasn't there when she needed me. She was injured and suffered needlessly for an entire year because of my impotence. I've learned from my brothers here that it's normal to feel that way, especially when it's about the woman you love."

"Roman, no," he said with a shake of his head. "It's not like that. We were childhood best friends, that's it."

"Oh, yeah, that's totally what I see in front of me right now. A man worried about his childhood best friend."

Reece rolled his eyes. He couldn't stop it if he tried, because he had no defense when it came to Sky—never had.

"Is Skylar okay?" Roman asked when the silence stretched on.

"She will be, according to Selina. Her catheter was kinked and not draining, causing a dangerous elevation of her blood pressure. That was my fault, too. She had to ride in an awkward position last night after everything that happened. I should have thought of having Selina check her over when we arrived."

"Was Skylar concerned about it?"

"No. Sky told Selina that it was draining this morning. She just didn't realize it wasn't emptying fully."

"Then I don't think you can blame yourself for something Skylar controls. All you can do is get her help when she needs it and be there to support her. It seems to me that's exactly what you're doing."

"It's not enough, man," Reece said, shaking his head. "I'll spend the rest of my life knowing I didn't save her that night. That's why she pushed me away after high school."

"Are you sure about that, son?" Cal asked as he walked through the door.

"Hey, Cal. Sorry about the drama. I'll get back to work here." Anything to get away from these two men who were mentors, friends and wise beyond their years. He enjoyed nothing more than talking with them, but not when it was about *his* life.

"I'm not your boss, son. You don't have to apologize to me. Besides, the last time I checked, you've been doing your job 24-7 for the last few days. Take a break and a breath, or you'll be no good to anyone, especially the woman who needs you the most."

Roman motioned at him with his hand while nodding. "Exactly what I've been trying to tell him."

"Secure One, Sierra," they heard over Cal's walkie-talkie, and he grabbed it, pressing the button. "Secure two, Charlie."

"Let Reece know that Skylar's blood pressure is normal again and her headache has resolved. I need to keep her for at least another hour, but she's out of the woods."

Cal pushed the button and held it out for Reece to answer. "Thanks, Selina. I appreciate everything you do."

"Oh, hey, Reece. It's no problem. Skylar is napping now that everything has been resolved. The exhaustion isn't helping the situation, so I want to let her rest for as long as possible. Can you work without her?"

Cal handed him the device and, taking possession of the cold plastic box, straightened Reece's spine a notch. "Yes, and I'd prefer it that way. The less stress she's under, the better. Do you agree?"

"From a medical standpoint, absolutely. This is stressful, but if she can get some rest, she may be able to cope with it better."

"Ten-four," Reece said. "Keep me posted, but I'll stop in after I check with Mina."

"She's in good hands, Reece," Selina said, her voice dropping slightly. "I know you want to be her hero, and you are, from what she tells me, so just take a deep breath and do what you do best while I do what I do best. Okay?"

"Can do, Selina. Thank you." Reece handed the walkie

back to Cal and stood from the table. It was time to do what he did best and resolve this situation so he could put Skylar out of his mind again. Any idea that they could be together ended when he remembered he wasn't her hero. He was her nightmare.

WHEN SKYLAR WOKE, she buried her face in the pillow so she didn't have to face Selina immediately. All she could see was the look on Land's face when he'd carried her to the med bay and then the lancing guilt when he'd spotted the catheter. She moaned and regretted it instantly, as Selina was by her side before it ended.

"You're awake. How are you feeling?"

"Awful," she moaned, throwing her arm over her forehead to block the light from her eyes. "How did I let this happen?"

"You didn't let anything happen," Selina gently reminded her. "Life just happens sometimes. You've been under severe stress and unusual conditions that your body isn't used to. You have to expect a few hiccups along the way."

"I'm not talking about that," she whispered.

"You mean Reece." Her nod was enough of an answer. "I've kept him updated, and he's been down to check on you a few times. He's been working with Mina on your case."

Rather than try to explain further, Skylar just nodded as though that was the end of it. "How is the catheter draining now?"

"Excellent," Selina answered. "I'm going to change it again before you leave, though. If there was any sediment in your bladder from it being so full, I want to make sure we clear it out and then put in a new catheter. That's why I've been free draining it for the last few hours."

"Do you think I can go back to intermittent drainage? A

bag is going to be extremely inconvenient right now." *Not to mention embarrassing*, she thought.

"During the day? No problem. I would still free drain it at night."

"I always do," Skylar said. "Well, I always do at home. Lately, sleep has been few and far between."

"That's easy to understand. Hopefully now that you're here, you can rest better at night, which will help your body deal better during the day."

Selina gathered the supplies needed to change the catheter while Skylar looked around the med bay. "This place is intense for a private medical suite. Are you a doctor or something?"

"Or something," she said with a smile. "I'm an ex-cop turned search and rescue paramedic turned advanced practice paramedic when I had to start over in life. Cal hired me as an operative and paramedic, but I found my place here in the med bay. I do certain ops with the guys when they need a medical person and an extra agent, but after much self-reflection, I realized that my favorite thing to do is help people. That's when I decided to play to my strengths."

"It sounds like you've lived an interesting life," Skylar said with a smile. "I'm lucky you decided to play to your strengths, or I'd be dead."

Selina smiled as she snapped on gloves and started changing the catheter. "I'm lucky to do what I love with the person I love."

"Oh, your significant other works here, too?"

"Yep. My husband, Efren. He was a sharpshooter for the army and then worked as a bodyguard, which is how he came to work here for Secure One. Now, he's an operative on the security team. He's an above-knee amputee."

"Oh," Skylar said, not making eye contact. After all the

years of dealing with medical professionals, she was used to letting others take control of her body. She didn't like it, but she'd learned that it wasn't always worth fighting for independence regarding her health. Sure, she could change the catheter herself, but it was more difficult for her to do it. Allowing Selina to do the task meant the catheter wouldn't give her any more problems, which was crucial in her current situation.

"All done," Selina said, attaching the new catheter to the drain bag. "I'll let it drain until you're ready to go and then I'll cap it off and you can take control of it again. Reece brought your chair down and said he'd help you transfer when you were ready."

The sigh escaped before she could stop it, so she looked away from the woman who had been nothing but kind to her. "Maybe I'll just stay here forever."

Selina's laughter was soft as she walked back to the stretcher. "That never seems to be a good way to deal with our problems."

But Reece was a problem Skylar didn't know how to deal with.

"Maybe not." She wanted to say more, but she couldn't promise that if she did, she would be able to hold back the tears.

Selina took her hand and held it, offering a smile of understanding. "You're overwhelmed, tired, scared and angry. That's all understandable. When you toss in medical situations like you deal with, it's easier to pretend none of it is happening than face it head-on. There isn't a person in this building who doesn't understand that. You're among friends here. We want to help."

"I've never been more grateful," Skylar said, a shaky smile tipping her lips.

"But that's also part of the problem, right?" Selina asked, and Skylar tipped her head in confusion. "Reece."

"Oh." That was all she said, because saying anything more would have ended in tears. Once she started crying, she wasn't sure she could stop.

"He's really worried about you. Roman and Cal had to talk him down off the ledge after he left you here."

"He's always been my defender," she agreed, still not making eye contact. "He feels guilty for what happened to me, even though it wasn't his fault."

"There isn't a person in this building who doesn't understand that, too. We also understand pushing people away because we think it's in their best interest."

"It is," she assured the woman. "Now he knows it, too. If there's one thing this episode did, it taught him what my life is like and why he doesn't want to be part of it."

"But what if he does?"

Skylar shook her head wildly. "He doesn't. Not after what he saw today. The accident hasn't been kind."

"You're upset that he saw your stoma?"

"I'm upset that he saw it all," she whispered. "My parabelly, the stoma, my body's reaction to the situation." She shook her head against the pillow. "It doesn't matter. It doesn't matter."

"It feels kind of like it matters, Skylar. You're a woman. Understandably, you don't want your crush to see you like this."

"He's not my crush." The words were vehement even if they weren't true. "I didn't want him to see it because he'd just feel worse about the accident. It's bad enough I had to call him and ask for help. I knew he'd do it out of guilt, but I had nowhere else to turn."

"He's not helping you out of guilt, Skylar. He's helping you because he cares about you, whether you like it or not. Honestly, that's his right. You're a beautiful woman, para-belly, stoma and all. You can't blame him for being attracted to you."

"He's not. We're old friends in a strange situation."

"Okay, well, let's just say your para-belly and stoma are the least important part of who you are and Reece knows that. I'm not a therapist or a psychiatrist, but I do recommend that you talk to him about what happened. Be honest with him about how you're feeling so he can be honest about the same."

Selina patted her hand and then released it to take her blood pressure again. Skylar closed her eyes, but all she could see was the look of concern on his face. That was when she realized he had never taken his eyes off hers. Maybe he hadn't seen as much as she thought or didn't register it if he had. Did it matter? No. He should see it all. Let him see her sagging belly and the tube doing what she no longer could. Maybe it was the reality check he needed after that kiss this morning. She would cherish it forever as the one and only kiss she'd get from the only man she would ever love. That didn't mean she wanted him to stay with her. It meant that she loved him enough to let him go.

Chapter Fourteen

Mina walked into the conference room with her lips in a thin line. Cal and Iris Knowles followed her into the room. Iris was a member of the Secure Watch team and was second to none in her work, but she struggled with social situations, so Reece was surprised to see her here. He had no doubt what she was about to tell them was anything but good news.

The only good news he'd gotten today was when Selina called him an hour ago to say that Sky was ready to leave the med bay. He'd dropped what he was doing and run down there to help. Once she was back in her chair and he'd taken the information Selina had given him about what to watch for should the autonomic dysreflexia flare, they'd returned to the command center to work through the videos on her Facebook page. He wanted her to rest, but she insisted she was fine and wanted to resolve this sooner rather than later. He didn't blame her. He couldn't imagine what it must be like to be in her shoes and not know if she would get her life back. He'd worked with many people in the same situation during his career, but it was different when it was someone you were close to. He hated using the past tense when it came to Sky and prayed that he no longer had to when this was over. But the look on Mina's face told him they might be a step closer to answers.

"I have news," she said, setting the tablet down.

"It doesn't seem like good news, judging by the look on your face," Sky said from beside him. He smiled. She was never about mincing words.

"You could say that," Cal agreed, glancing at Mina. "We'll walk you through it."

Mina handed a sheet of paper to Reece. "An arrest warrant?" he asked, skimming it. "Wait. I don't understand. I thought the cops knew she didn't do this."

"That's what we thought as well," Cal said. "Then I heard from one of my contacts at the Duluth PD that they had no choice but to update the warrant and execute it."

"I'm confused," Skylar said. "How are they going to arrest someone who doesn't exist?"

"That's where things get interesting," Mina said, and Reece could see the wheels spinning in her head. She had found a thread to pull and was giddily unwinding it. "Skylar Sullivan once again exists in the world. Everything has been restored except for your social media pages. Binate is still controlling those."

"And your bank accounts have been restored but emptied," Cal added. Skylar gasped, but Cal held up his hand so he could finish. "Your accounts are protected, so we're gathering the proper information to send the bank so your balances can be restored once you're clear of this."

"And you think the sudden return to the living for Skylar Sullivan was for the purpose of the arrest warrant?" Reece asked Mina, who nodded.

"I believe that Binate finally forced their hand by causing damage to enough galleries that they didn't have a choice. Since Skylar is now 'missing—'" she added air quotes "—it looks like she ran."

"Pun not intended," Sky added, making his lips twitch.

"Rolled," Mina said, with the tip of her fake hat.

"It has to be Miles," Skylar said, her arms crossed over her chest in a tight embrace. "No one else I can think of would hate me enough to go through this much to set me up."

Reece could, and his name was Silas, but he knew better than to say it. Skylar was stressed enough, and tossing her brother into the mix wouldn't help matters. Instead, he gently tugged her arms off her chest and rested them on her lap. "Remember what Selina said about keeping your posture open and not tense for the rest of the day."

The scathing look she sent him would have made a weaker man cower. "Thank you, WebMD, for your insight into living in my body."

Mina snorted, and Reece sent her a glare that did nothing but make her grin wider.

"I'm still digging up dirt on Miles Bradshaw," Iris said, speaking for the first time. She stared at the table, not making eye contact with anyone, which wasn't unusual. She'd been in an accident as a child that left her with a traumatic brain injury. "He's a disgusting individual, I can tell you that." Iris finally looked up and met Sky's gaze for half a second before she dropped it again. "If there's a way to tie him to this, I'll find it."

"Thanks, Iris," Reece said with a smile, knowing she'd never see it but appreciating her nonetheless.

"No thanks needed. I'm doing the job that I'm paid to do." Cal cleared his throat, and Iris grimaced. "Sorry." She glanced at Sky again. "I had an accident when I was younger, too. It scrambled my brain and messed up the pathways that would have helped me in social situations. I apologize for my bluntness. It's not that I don't care. It's that I don't know how to show it."

"You're fine, Iris," Sky assured her. "I appreciate that you're here helping me. Honestly, bluntness is good, especially in this situation. Coddling isn't necessary when my life and livelihood are at stake."

Iris nodded once as though she agreed with everything Sky had said. "Miles Bradshaw is a boil on the backside of life," she said, jumping right back into the situation at hand.

"I couldn't have said that better myself," Sky agreed.

"I thought I was stunted socially, but this guy has zero filters and zero humility. If someone isn't stroking his ego and calling him pretty at all times, he takes it as a personal affront."

"It's like you've met him or something," Sky muttered. "Miles is all of those things."

"And more," Iris said, holding up her finger. "Turns out, he prides himself on being an aficionado when it comes to sussing out fake art."

"Spoiler alert," Sky said, "his art is the fake art."

"That is correct," she agreed. "Or, at the very least, it's copied art."

"Meaning?" Cal asked as he tried to follow the conversation.

"Meaning he may make the art, but he's using other artists' ideas. Maybe he changes the colors, but the designs are always a copy of someone else's work."

"Is this something I can have my police contact look at him for?" Cal asked, and Iris sat blinking at him in confusion.

"He means, is it something Miles can be arrested for," Reece clarified for her.

"Oh! No, I mean, not really. He changes it just enough to claim it's 'original,' even when the design is recycled.

It's kind of like fan fiction. It resembles the original story, but they change it enough so it's not obvious plagiarism."

Sky motioned at Iris. "Exactly that. And it's not illegal to use someone else's design—it's just lazy. If you look through his portfolio, you understand why no one wants to carry his work in their galleries. The galleries and shops around Duluth are looking for unique pieces. Even when he can convince someone to take his work—that's usually due to a hard guilt he lays on them—the art doesn't sell and they sever ties with him quickly. He can't take constructive criticism, either. And not about his art, because art is in the eye of the beholder, but about his propensity to push people away rather than engage. Miles doesn't have a future in the art world as it stands now. Maybe if he came up with something original, he could move to a different city and find a place for it. First, he'd have to change his entire personality. I don't see that happening."

Cal leaned toward Sky and Iris. "Personal opinion time. Do you think Miles is capable of vandalizing these galleries?"

"Yes," they said in unison, lifting his lips into a smile.

"Most especially because of his hatred for Skylar," Iris said. "I found some posts on a public forum board that were anything but complimentary."

Sky rolled her eyes as Iris handed out some papers to everyone. "All I could do was sort through and find some of the best ones. There was a lot to choose from. Sorry, Skylar, but he doesn't like you."

Sky's laughter filled the room. It lifted Reece's heart and brought him back to life. If Sky was laughing, she was going to be okay.

"Sweetheart, that is not information I didn't already have.

The last altercation we got into was in February. Long story short, he got mad when another art gallery dumped him."

"Tell them why," Reece encouraged her, wondering if this was the crux of the problem all along.

"I could prove that some of the art he sent them was manufactured."

The room was dead silent for a beat before Cal whistled. "That sounds like motive to me."

"He was so angry security had to remove him from the event, and the event planners banned him for the rest of time," Reece explained. "He claims that Sky's art is the problem because she uses recycled materials."

"That sounds like my kind of art," Iris said. "If I want manufactured pieces, I can go to the store. If I want unique, I'll look for an artist doing something unusual in the art form."

Sky nodded as she made eye contact with every person in the room. "I know who Miles Bradshaw is. This is not new, unexpected or distressing information. He was the first person I thought of when Mina told me to think of people who might have a beef with me. If he could make me go away without it blowing back on him, he would."

"Make you go away?" Cal asked with a lifted brow.

"He says I use my disability to get sympathy, which is why people buy my work."

"See line four," Iris said, shaking the paper.

Heads dipped as everyone read line four. Reece saw red. "'I'd like to drive that sorry excuse for an artist into Lake Superior. I'm so tired of her poor-pitiful-me routine at events. The only reason people buy her art is because they feel guilty that she uses a wheelchair.'"

"Wow," Mina said, lowering her own paper. "He really doesn't like you."

"Established," Sky said with an eye roll. "The thing is, I'm not sure he has the skills to do all of this."

"From what I can see, he doesn't," Iris agreed. "I'm still digging to see if he has friends who do."

"Miles has friends?" Skylar asked the question with such shock that Reece snorted.

"None I've found so far, but I'll keep looking."

Skylar froze and turned to Reece. "Camille Castillo."

"Who?" Mina asked, but Sky never took her eyes off Reece.

"Camille Castillo. They were tight, like two peas in a pod."

Reece noticed Mina patiently waiting for him to get the information for her and nodded. "Is Camille from Duluth, and is she as aggressive as Miles?"

"I don't know if she's from Duluth," Sky answered, turning to the rest of the team as though she had just remembered they were there. "But she's been part of the art scene for…" She tossed her head back and forth as though trying to sort things out. "At least a year now. She's always the first to come to Miles's defense, but when asked if they're together, she vehemently denies it."

"So they're friends but not lovers?" Mina asked.

Sky gave her the palms up. "I can't answer that, but I know they're friends. Iris jogged my memory on that, so thank you." Iris gave her a nod before she stared at the table again. "I'm not her favorite person, either." Sky gave him a cheeky smile, and he couldn't help but laugh. "That said, I haven't had the same hostile interactions with her that I've had with Miles. Camille does stained-glass art that's gorgeous and all original. She sells well in all the galleries, so I haven't figured out why she hangs with Miles. Not that I've spent too much energy thinking about it."

"Camille Castillo." Mina spelled the name aloud, and Sky nodded when she finished. "Do you know her age?"

"Not her exact age, but she's close to mine. There can't be that many Camille Castillos in Duluth."

"Iris," Mina said, "I'll hand you this to look at since you're digging on Miles."

"Yes, boss," Iris said, scratching on her pad of paper.

"She probably has nothing to do with this," Sky said, glancing between everyone while chewing on her lip. "I just thought maybe you could learn more about Miles through her."

Reece gently rubbed her neck. "She won't know we're looking into her. This is purely information gathering."

"That's correct," Mina said with a reassuring smile. "If they're friends, maybe he's staying at her house or working together on a project. It's important to check out the people close to him so we can eliminate them as part of the problem. Now, that brings us to the videos. Did you find anything, Iris?"

Iris shook her head. "As you know, it's nearly impossible to reverse engineer a voice like the one Binate is using."

"I don't understand," Skylar said, glancing around the table. "Reverse engineer it?"

"They're trying to decipher Binate's voice to see if you can recognize it," Reece explained.

"I tried everything, but as expected, I couldn't hear the original voice," Iris replied.

"That's another thing," Skylar said. "The fact that he uses 'Binate' rather than 'Binary' is telling. Miles would never use something so overly used as 'Binary.' He'd find something close that means the same thing."

"Wow, he really stretched himself going with 'Binate,'"

Iris said with an eye roll to which no one could hide their snort.

"That's Miles for ya," Skylar said.

"Well, I got this sound when I started playing with the recording. Do you recognize it?" Iris asked.

She held up her finger and then pressed a button on her computer. A sound filled the room, and Skylar glanced at Reece. "That's a ship's horn."

"A laker," Reece agreed. "He has to be somewhere by the lake to pick that up."

"Lakers honk going in and out of a harbor, right?" Cal asked.

"Yes, and occasionally if they pass another ship, but you'd be hard-pressed to hear that on the shore from the middle of a shipping lane, especially loud enough to be picked up on a recording."

"You're saying our best bet is to search areas around a harbor?" Mina asked, and Reece nodded.

"You can eliminate any harbor that can't accommodate the big lakers, but my bet would be on Duluth/Superior or Two Harbors. That said, I don't know how it helps."

"We'll look for any property owned by Miles or his family. If we find any, it's a place to investigate. In the meantime, I want you to take Skylar back to the cabin and comb through those videos," Mina said.

"What are we looking for?" Skylar asked.

"Anything that might give him away," she explained. "Something he might say that jogs your memory about a conversation you had with him or something you know about him. That kind of thing."

"I can do that," Skylar said with a nod. "Cal, will you get in trouble if the police find out I'm here? Or do they already know?"

"No and no," Cal said. "If they learn you're here, they'd need a warrant to enter the property. That said, there's no way they'll find out you're here. We all know you aren't responsible for the vandalizations. Even my cop friend knows that, but they're being pressured to find you."

"I can understand that," Skylar said, shaking her head sadly. "I'm just upset that anyone thinks I'd ever damage anything, much less an art gallery."

"What matters is that none of us here believe it," Reece said, squeezing her hand gently.

"What he said," Mina agreed. "Not only would it be physically impossible, but it doesn't make sense. Whoever thought this up isn't the brightest bulb in the pack."

"Miles." Iris coughed the word, bringing a smile to Reece's lips.

"I hate to agree with her, but I do," Skylar said. "As long as no one is going to get in trouble for me being here, we'll watch those videos repeatedly if it helps you guys figure this out."

"You're safe here," Cal said, squeezing her shoulder. "Considering the day you've had, I don't want you to worry about anything. This is a security company, and even if the cops suspect you're here, they'd have to prove it, and that's going to be hard when I don't have to let them on my property." He gave her a wink and then stood. "I need to touch base with the rest of the crew, but Mina, keep me posted on anything you need my help with."

"You got it, boss."

"Charlie, out," he said, leaving the room.

"I'll take my leave as well," Iris said. "I've got some other cases to get back to, but once those are caught up, I'll dig into Miles and his friend."

"Iris, wait," Mina said, standing, too. "The Miles angle

is urgent. Let's figure out who can take your other cases while you focus on this." She turned to Reece. "Take Skylar back to the cabin and let her rest while she listens to the videos. You can keep searching, too."

Reece nodded, knowing without her saying it whom he should keep searching for—Silas Sullivan.

Chapter Fifteen

It had been a long day, but it wasn't over yet. Thankfully, the recliner in the cabin was a comfortable place to sit and watch the videos from Binate while Reece worked on whatever Reece worked on. She had finally convinced him that it was wiser for her to watch the videos while he worked on finding more information on Miles to help Iris. He didn't know Miles, so he wouldn't catch something on the videos that would give him away. Only she could do that. If it was there to find, she would.

However, her focus was split, making it hard to concentrate on the videos. What had happened today at Secure One weighed on her—both the health and personal implications. Autonomic dysreflexia was a dangerous condition that could turn deadly. Her level of spinal cord injury made it more common, but the episodes she'd had so far were few and far between. It probably wasn't fair to compare anything she was going through right now to her day-to-day life. This was anything but that, the least of which was being in a tight space with Reece Palmer for days on end. While she thought about him every day, it was easier to pretend she didn't care about him when he wasn't protecting her—when he wasn't sleeping next to her in a buttery-soft, king-size bed.

Her body was…not attractive, to say the least. After years in a wheelchair, gravity had taken its toll, and while she was able to work out her upper body to a degree, there was nothing she could do for her paralyzed abdominal muscles. She didn't want to think about her legs. They used to be what she was most proud of. She'd had lean, strong, long legs that did everything she asked of them on the field without hesitation. They were still long, but they were also thin, weak and shriveled. The skin and bones reminded her every day of her choices, the good and the bad.

Reece walked into the room with two plates in his hands. "Sadie brought dinner. Selina suggested you stay put for the night, so she made us some to-go plates."

"That was so kind of her," Skylar said, setting the laptop aside so she could take the plate he held out. "Everyone here truly goes above and beyond."

Reece sat on the couch beside her chair and handed her silverware and a napkin. "It's that military mentality of leaving no man behind. They carried it over into their civilian work, and it's served them well so far. What Cal has built in this little town since he first moved here is nothing short of brilliant. He started as a mercenary and ended up running one of the most sought-after security companies in the nation."

"What's funny is that he doesn't act like he knows that."

"He knows, but he also knows that we got to where we are as a team. You'll never see him resting on his laurels. He's not wired that way."

"I can tell," she said with a chuckle. "Cal didn't have to be in that meeting today, but he wanted to keep his thumb on the pulse of what was developing, even if he left it in Mina's capable hands."

"You picked up on that, did you?" he asked with a wink.

"Does Sadie do freelance chef work? I could get behind homemade Swedish meatballs like these on a regular basis."

"I wish!" His laughter was easy for the first time all day. "It's always sad when I'm here for a week and then go home to my TV dinners and takeout."

"You've been single a long time and still don't cook?"

"I do, sometimes," he said with a shrug. "Honestly, it's more depressing to cook for one than to heat something up and eat it in front of the computer. It makes you feel less alone."

"I hear that," she agreed, not making eye contact. "Your computer is my easel, but it's the same concept. Since Mom and Dad moved to Florida, it's been difficult. I have friends and people I hang out with, but there are a lot of empty hours to fill."

"You didn't want to move to Florida?"

Dropping her fork, she set the plate aside on the end table. Sadie's meatballs were filling, and she didn't want to get sick after the day she'd had. "We talked about it, but it would have meant finding an accessible place there to accommodate my needs, which wasn't impossible, but it would have limited my parents when this was their time to make a new life. They had gone through enough and deserved the freedom to enjoy the life they'd worked hard for all those years. I didn't want to hold them back by wheeling around after them."

"I know your parents don't feel that way about it, Sky."

It was easier to stare at the opposite wall than to make eye contact with him when she talked about her family. "We went through a lot with my brother, Land. Stuff that you don't even know about. There were things I never told you because I knew you'd kill him if you knew."

He tipped his head to the side. "You're not wrong. Especially if it involved him touching you."

"That time you caught him? It wasn't the first," she admitted, shame filling her voice. She glanced at him and noticed the light go out in that gray eye while fire filled the blue one. They always said people with two different-colored eyes could see heaven and earth simultaneously. She was starting to wonder if that was true.

"So help me God, if I find that man alive, he won't be for long," Reece ground out, his plate clattering on the table as he tossed it aside to take her hand. "Why didn't you tell me? And don't say it's because I'd hurt Silas. You weren't bothered in the least when I beat him senseless in the seventh grade."

"I was ashamed, okay?" she asked, defense clear in her tone as she tried to pull away.

He held tight to her hand and breathed deeply through his nose. "How long, Sky?"

"A couple of years," she whispered, staring at their joined hands. "It wasn't all the time, and sometimes I wondered if I dreamed it."

"Sounds like something a victim would say." She could tell he was trying to be gentle but wanted to pound on something. Probably her brother's face. Reece wasn't a violent man except when it came to Silas. It was like he could see under her brother's skin to the monster he was when no one else could.

"I'm still mad they didn't kick him out the moment he turned eighteen," Reece said, holding her hand and leaning in as though he couldn't stand the distance between them. She knew that wasn't true. Not after what happened today, but having someone to talk to who cared about her felt nice. "I suppose by then it was clear that something was very wrong with Silas."

"My parents knew something was wrong, but Silas refused to go to therapy. After you beat him and I told them why, they insisted on getting him help. We were all scared out of our minds, and the worst part was I couldn't talk to anyone about it. After many years of therapy, I know it wasn't my fault. My parents did their best with the hand they'd been dealt. When my accident happened, everything fell apart with Silas."

"Why did your parents work so hard to find him after he left? If everything you said is true, weren't they happy he was out of their lives? He was twenty-three by then and could more than go it on his own."

"You're forgetting that he was their child. We don't have children, so it's easy for us to judge what they did or didn't do."

"Fair," Reece agreed. "I'm not judging them. I'm trying to understand their thinking."

He was more likely digging for an angle to help him find Silas, but she wouldn't bring that up. He could look all he wanted. Silas was dead.

"I asked my dad about it after the third private investigator couldn't find him. If I'm honest, his explanation gutted me."

"He felt guilty, right?"

Skylar made the so-so hand. "Guilty in the respect that he worried letting Silas out in the world unmanaged meant—"

"He might hurt someone."

She nodded for a long time before she spoke. "Silas had real issues, and leaving home wouldn't fix them. Staying on his meds and going to therapy would help him, but it's doubtful that happened."

"You always use past tense with Silas. Why?"

"Because whether he's alive or not, he's dead to me, Reece. We were never siblings. We were two people who lived in the same house. By the time I was born, he was way too old for us to bond with any meaningful kind of relationship."

"The age difference was there, but that can work in a family's favor sometimes," Reece pointed out.

"Sure, if everyone is mentally stable, but we both know Silas was never that. Now we know why. It was no one's fault, but we had to protect ourselves. The therapist finally convinced my parents that they weren't responsible for the choices Silas made once he left their house."

"But you think he's dead and buried?"

"Definitely dead. Don't know about buried. It's been thirteen years since he left, and we haven't heard anything from him. The fact that you're wasting time looking for him is like watching someone spin their wheels in the mud. Walk away, Reece. Not only is Silas not behind whatever is going on, but we're wasting time and energy that could be better used."

"Sweetheart, it's my job to cover every angle of a case. Pretending Silas is dead works for you, and that's okay, given the history you share, but it doesn't work in a case like this. We have to look under every rock for anyone who wants to do you harm."

"He's dead, Land. And even if he isn't, he—"

"Isn't capable of carrying out a plot like this. I know," he said, holding up his hand to her. "I want you to know I agree with you, but I have to do my job. The last thing I want to do is bring him back into your life, but we have to know if he has anything to do with this. Right?"

This time, she held his gaze, and what she saw in those

eyes of heaven and earth said he meant every word. His search for Silas wasn't to hurt her. It was to help her. "You're right," she admitted. "As much as I want to pretend that he's dead and buried, until we have proof of that, it would be foolish not to consider his involvement."

"Did you come up with anything on the videos to help us yet?" he asked, motioning at the laptop.

"No, but I'm not giving up. I will watch them ten times if I have to. Reading the comments on the petition page propped me up. There wasn't one comment that agreed with whoever this is about me being responsible for these gallery crimes."

Reece squeezed her hand and smiled. "Hang on to that. Remember that when you return to your normal life, you won't be shunned in the art world. No one believes you're responsible for this."

"It might be better if they did," she said slowly, her brow going up.

"I don't follow," he said, leaning back on the couch.

"Hear me out," she said, turning on her side a bit to see him better. "If Binate thinks people are buying his story, it might benefit us. If suddenly he sees the tide turning against me, he might ride that wave."

"Embolden this Binate guy to do or say something that tips us off to his real identity?" Reece asked, following her train of thought.

"That's what I'm starting to wonder, Land. Should we be feeding his ego rather than fighting it? Can we do that without him knowing it's a setup?"

"Fake comments on a Facebook page? Mina could do that in her sleep. It would have to be gradual, though, so he doesn't suspect it's a ruse. You might be on to something here, angel. Let's call Mina and get her opinion. If there's a way, she will know it."

Angel.

That new nickname was far more dangerous to her heart than *Sky* would ever be. Sky was a throwback to their childhood. It was easy and filled her with the warmth of yesteryear. *Angel* filled her with a different kind of warmth—the kind of warmth that she'd experienced this morning when his lips were on hers. It was also the kind of warmth that would break her heart night after night the moment she was alone again.

She couldn't help but wonder why now. Why tonight? After what he had witnessed this morning, he should have been walking away. Then again, maybe it had everything to do with what had happened this morning. He wasn't using it as a term of endearment as much as a way to coddle her now that he saw the truth about her fragility.

Her mind wandered back to the look in his eyes this morning when he held her face in his hands and kept her calm as Selina saved her life. That didn't feel like coddling. That felt like love.

Chapter Sixteen

The cursor sat blinking, a reminder that he hadn't found his man. How did a person live in the world for thirteen years without any identification? He glanced at the woman asleep in the recliner and sighed. He couldn't give up. Reece had never wanted to be a hero for anyone until today, when he was so hopelessly useless that he would have traded his life for hers. He couldn't do that physically, but he would work through the night if it meant finding the jerk who was tormenting her.

Frustrated, Reece flicked to the Facebook tab and checked the comments on the petition page. The first planted comment had arrived.

It takes no brainpower to believe Skylar Sullivan could commit these crimes or hire some flunky to do it. Lord knows she makes enough money on that garbage she passes off as art.

A smile lifted his lips. Mina had played to Miles's beliefs perfectly but in a way that didn't feel fake or forced. He left the tab open to hear when Binate replied to the comment—and he had no doubt he would. Mina had gotten behind the idea quickly. She could see they were at a stalemate until they lulled Binate into a sense that someone was on his side. While they couldn't stop the organic comments defending Sky, they could make sure to plant enough negative ones to start stroking the ego of a very fragile man. Maybe they couldn't prove it was Miles, but at this point, Reece didn't find it hard to believe he was involved in some way. His money was still on Silas, though.

Staring at the blinking cursor again, Reece ran down what he'd done so far to find Silas. Had he crossed every t and dotted every i? Was there a database he'd missed or a program he hadn't used? A quick consult with his list said he'd exhausted every avenue to find this guy. His gut burned with the knowledge that Silas had been abusing her for years and she'd told no one. He understood why—that was a common situation victims found themselves in, but it still made him feel as impotent as he'd been this morning when she was dying before his very eyes. The same way he'd felt that night on the field when all he could do was tell her it would be okay even though they both knew it wouldn't be. In just a hair over three days, Skylar Sullivan had consumed him again. When this was over and she was safe, he had zero idea how he would get her out of his system. Not that he'd had much success with that over the last decade, but he'd managed by simply ignoring the pain of having half of his soul torn away every morning when he woke up. He filled his life with endless jobs, conferences and degrees to hide how empty it had become.

Now that he'd had a little taste of being whole again and having tasted her, Reece was well aware he'd never return to that kind of life. When he'd brushed his lips against hers this morning, his soul fractured. An ache engulfed him, leaving him drowning in sorrow at the time they'd spent apart. At the same time, he rode a wave of pleasure and completeness at being connected to her that he had never experienced with anyone in his life. He'd been with women, but no one left him feeling so hopeful and hopeless with a simple kiss the way Sky had.

Then, in a dark moment, he'd taken her in his arms, and it had become clear that there was no way to return to the life he had led a week ago. When he glanced at the screen, it reminded him that a week ago, Sky had also been living a different kind of life, and if he didn't figure out who wanted to destroy her, a week from now, she could be sitting in a jail cell. He set his jaw and refused even to consider that possibility.

Focused again on the case before him, he reviewed everything, only to reach the same conclusion: Silas had fallen off the face of the earth the moment he drove out of Duluth. That was just a mirage, though. He gave Silas far more credit than Skylar did when it came to his level of intelligence, so there was only one explanation—he had to be using an alias. His gut told him that her brother was behind this, which meant he was very much alive and living as someone other than Silas Sullivan. Cracking the code on the alias was the problem.

Extended family. Always start with extended family.

He remembered the lesson from one of his first professors in college. Spine straight, he put his hands on the keyboard. The Nebraska grandparents were Skylar's mom's parents. What was her maiden name? He could ask Sky, but he didn't want to wake her if he didn't have to. She was exhausted after their day, and her body needed to recover. Also, after her soliloquy about the futility of looking for Silas, he didn't want to bring it up again until he had proof that her brother was alive and well. He was out there somewhere dressed as Anonymous and spewing hatred for a woman who didn't deserve any of this. Reece might not have been able to catch and protect her that night fourteen years ago, but he would do it this time if it killed him.

Pear Pickin' Farms, where the sweetness lasts year-round.

Tobias and Marlene Pear, he typed into the computer, remembering the long-ago tagline from their orchard. He'd never been there, but he and Sky would tease each other with that line for years. Funny the things you forgot until it was a matter of life and death.

The screen filled with information about the deaths of Tobias and Marlene ten years ago. They'd passed away together due to carbon monoxide poisoning. His gaze flew to Sky, who was still slumbering in the chair. He'd had no idea they'd passed, but such a tragic, preventable way made it that much harder. He couldn't help but wonder if her Grandma Barbara was alive, so he quickly googled her name, only to discover there were way too many Barbara Sullivans to weed through. His attention was back on Silas, and he opened one of his background programs. He typed in, Silas Pear, age thirty-seven United States. He hit Return and let it spin, not surprised when no one showed up. That would have been too easy. What was Silas's middle name? Joseph, which was his dad's name. No, he wouldn't make it that obvious. If he was trying to become someone else, he'd have to be far more subtle, or the detectives the family had hired would have found him. He removed the age, and again, nothing came up. Reece tried several combinations using his first initial, his grandfather's name and any other combination of his middle name but came up empty.

Maybe he wasn't using Pear as a last name, which made this a game of finding the needle in the haystack. A glance at the clock told him it was after midnight and he should get some sleep and tackle this again in the morning, but his mind was far too activated to sleep. Since Sky was comfortable, he'd keep working. His mind was tumbling with all the information he knew about Silas. He was older than them by enough years that he'd been a teenager when they were still in grade school. Their experiences were vastly different, but Reece forced his mind to calm and methodically think through the conversations he'd had with Silas. Once Silas became a teen, Reece and Sky had tried to avoid him as much as possible—especially after he beat the stuffing out of him.

Reece stood on the patio with a cold can of pop in his hand and watched Sky doing handstands and backflips in the yard while Silas yammered on about his video games. Whoopee, so some character in a video game had the same last name as him. What good did that do if you couldn't even play the game as that character? He didn't understand the fascination with video games. Sure, they're fun when it's raining or you're bored, but revolving your life around them was a bit much.

With a jolt, he opened a tab and googled video game characters with the last name Sullivan. Before he could take a breath, he had an entire page of results. The first one? Sergeant Tom Sullivan from *Call of Duty*. That was Silas's favorite game.

"Got you," he whispered as he returned to his program and typed in the name. There would be a lot of hits, but he could whittle them down quickly. Once it was down to the two dozen within the age range, he added an S as a middle initial just for grins. Bingo. That brought it down to six. *Why not go all the way?* He thought as he typed in Silas as the middle name. The boy he used to know had always thought he was the most cunning of video game players, and he wouldn't be able to resist mixing his name with the hero of his favorite fake war game.

Fingers crossed, he hit Enter and waited not so patiently while the program did its work. Then, before his very eyes, a thirty-five-year-old version of Silas Sullivan filled the screen. Without taking his eyes off the picture, he reached for his phone.

Chapter Seventeen

"Angel, I need you to wake up," Reece whispered in her ear.

Blinking, she glanced up into his face. Unable to resist, she smoothed her hand over his soft beard, and he smiled.

"I need to shave. It's been a busy few days."

"I like it," she said with a smile. "I still see you as the boy I used to know. This shows me the man you've become."

His blue eye darkened to navy as he gazed at her, drinking her in as though she wasn't a shell of a woman in a shriveled body. "I see you as the stunning woman you've become from that girl I used to know. You've left me breathless for days."

The eye roll happened, even though she knew it was rude. "Sorry, but, Reece, have you looked at me? I'm a hot mess, both physically and apparently in life. 'Stunning woman,'" she said, using air quotes, "is not this." She motioned down her body as he shook his head slowly.

"I understand why you feel that way, but it doesn't mean I do, Sky. We need to put that aside for now and get you to bed. Selina said the catheter should drain freely tonight to prevent issues."

"What time is it?" she asked, rubbing her eyes. "The last thing I remember was watching Facebook videos."

He chuckled and gave her a wink as he lifted the blanket

off her and folded it. "It's nearly 2:00 a.m. You fell asleep, so I covered you and let you get some rest while I worked. Now, it's time for both of us to be in bed. I'll carry you to the bedroom and return for your chair."

"Not necessary," she said immediately. "I only need help putting the recliner down." If there was one thing she hated about her disability, it was recliners. If they weren't powered, she couldn't push the footrest down to get out of the chair and always required help.

"It is necessary," he said, bending down and sliding his hands under her back and knees. "It's necessary for me to feel you in my arms again as a reminder that I didn't lose you this morning. Give me that, please?"

Never able to deny him anything when he asked with a pure and open heart, she nodded and allowed herself to be lifted and carried to the bedroom, where he lowered her to bed, which had already been prepared for the night. Once she rested comfortably on the pillows, she pointed to the bathroom without making eye contact. Shame filled her, but his need to carry her to the bed meant she had to open herself to embarrassment again.

"Would you get my drain bag? It's hanging in the bathroom."

"Nope, got it right here," he said, lifting the tubing for her to see before he lifted her shirt far enough to reveal the catheter taped to her abdomen. Selina had suggested she leave it taped at an angle rather than coil it to prevent it from kinking.

"What are you doing?" she asked, grabbing his hand to stop him. "I can do it. Please, get my chair."

"I'm connecting your catheter to the bag. Selina showed me how."

"I can do it, Land. Please," she begged.

He held up his hands and then motioned for her to do it. It was then that she realized she couldn't see the connections while lying flat.

Frustrated, she flopped her head back onto the pillow and sighed. "I can't see the connection. If you'll get my chair, I can transfer to that and do it."

"Or, I can connect it in five seconds to save you the effort required to transfer twice."

Finally, she nodded and let him carry out the process until it was connected, and she heard the catheter draining into the bag.

Reece lowered her shirt and covered her with the blanket before kneeling beside the bed. "It's okay to accept help sometimes, angel. It doesn't mean you're weak. It means someone cares about you enough to take that burden off your shoulders for a few moments."

With her eyes squeezed shut, she nodded, but mostly, she wanted him to leave long enough for her to fight back the tears. She knew she'd lost the battle when his finger trailed down her cheek to wipe one away. "Could you have picked something less gross to help me with?"

"Angel, there's nothing gross about what I just did. My God, I'd do it fifty times a day if it meant you never had to go through what you went through this morning. It's a basic human function that we all do. You do it differently. That doesn't mean it's gross or shameful. I think it's an amazing advancement for spinal cord injury patients. You don't have to do the intermittent catheterization that used to rule your life and make you sick. I know I don't live in your body or understand what it's like to do that, but I do want to learn how to help you."

"Why?" she asked, her voice barely above a whisper. The light was low in the room, and the darkness and shadows made her feel braver than she was as she wiped a tear from her face. "Why do you even care?"

"I've always cared about you, Sky, and I always will. We can't go back to pretending that the other person doesn't exist once this is over. At least I can't, so if I learn how to help you, at least I can be there for you as a friend, right?"

"I don't want to lose you as a friend again," she agreed with a whisper. It was her way of telling him that all they could be was friends, and the look in his eye told her he understood that.

"Then you won't," he promised, kissing her forehead. "I'm going to get your chair. Be right back."

Land stood and strode from the room, so she quickly wiped her face with the soft sheet. He wouldn't be gone long, and she wanted to get herself together before he returned. He wanted to help, and she'd allow it for now. It felt good to feel cared for, but once this was over, that was a different story. He had his own life, and staying in touch, while it sounded nice, would be far too painful to her heart when she couldn't have him in her life for all time.

Once he had the chair next to the bed for her, he climbed onto his side, keeping a sheet between them, and then covered himself with a spare blanket. He propped himself on his arm and slid the other across her chest to cup her shoulder.

"We need to talk."

"Can it wait until morning? We're both exhausted." The last thing she wanted to do was talk about their relationship, or lack thereof, at 2:00 a.m.

"I'm afraid not. I found Silas."

"What?" she asked, turning to meet his gaze. "How? Why? Where?" Her moan that followed the rapid questions said exactly how she felt about knowing he'd dug up part of her past. "I wanted him to stay buried."

"He is," Land said, raising his hand to stroke her cheek with his thumb. "He was using the alias Tom Sullivan."

"Oh, God, from that video game!" she exclaimed. "He was obsessed with that game. Why didn't I think of that all those years ago?"

"It probably didn't cross your mind that he'd use an alias. I'm surprised the private detectives never asked your parents."

"They may have, but I was pretty out of it for those first few years after he left. So, he's dead?"

"Yes," Land said with a sigh. "Once I found his alias, I could trace him to a death certificate in Colorado."

"Colorado? That's an odd state for him to pick."

Land opened his mouth as though he was about to say something, but paused. "There are a lot of places to hide in Colorado."

"When did he die? Did you find out anything else about him? What did he do for work?"

"According to the death certificate, he died three years ago. The cause of death was drowning. There wasn't a lot of information I could find about him regarding his life or work history. Iris will dig into it in the morning. I'm sorry, Sky. I hated to be the one to tell you this, but you had to know."

"I'm not upset, Land. I'm relieved, actually. It's like that weird ball of nerves that he might show up in our lives is gone. I always assumed he was dead, but with no proof, there was always a lingering worry. That's gone now. I can't thank you enough for that."

He kept stroking her cheek with his thumb, all his attention focused on her. "He was still your brother. It's okay to grieve the innocence that was lost."

"Trust me, that happened a long time ago. Seriously, I'm solidly relieved, Land. The only hard part will be telling my parents, but that can wait until this is all figured out and I can see them in person. Please, make sure no one from Secure Watch tells them."

"It has already been said," he assured her with a smile. "I'm proud of you."

"Why? Because I'm so inspirational?" Her eye roll was hard and practiced but also defensive. If she could keep him focused on her anger with life, he'd learn he didn't want any part of hers.

"I see through your defenses, angel. Your walls aren't hard for me to scale when I know you as well as I do, even fourteen years later. I'm proud of you for the way you're plowing through this situation. Losing your identity is difficult, but you're hanging in there and working through it with us. Not everyone can do that. I've dealt with people who curl up in a ball and shut out the world. We can solve this if you can hang in a bit longer."

"I want to be part of the solution. My life already involves enough situations where people have to do things for me. I can help with this and want to do that, so you don't have to treat me with kid gloves."

His laughter was soft when it filled the room. "Oh, that is the last thing I would ever do. There's never been a situation you haven't tackled head-on. We can do this together as long as we're honest with each other."

Land leaned down and planted a kiss on her forehead, his lips soft and warm as they hesitated there for a moment, as though he was thinking about doing so much more. Instead, he pulled back and shut off the small lamp on the bedside table, plunging the room into darkness. This was one time she was grateful for darkness. It gave her time to stuff all those feelings she had for this man back into the box where she kept them so she could live without crying every single day he was missing from her life.

Then he rolled over and cupped her shoulder, his face just inches from hers as he snuggled into his pillow. It felt like they were an old married couple who had slept this way for years. The tears leaked from her eyes, because he remembered how she liked to be touched. She could feel her shoulders and had told him early on that when she needed to feel human touch, that was the best place to hold her. He'd done it ever since. God, how she loved the sensation of his protective hand on her as he relaxed into sleep.

Carefully, she swiped at the tears while trying not to disturb him in his sleep. Those tears represented loss. Losing her future after the accident, losing Land and now, losing another piece of her family. However, she wasn't upset by Silas's loss. She was upset about losing the chance to face him again and tell him how he'd hurt her. Her therapist had told her that if she ever got that chance, she should take it. She needed to put all the negativity back on his shoulders to be free of them. That was no longer possible. She thought about the letter she'd written. Had they ever found him, she'd planned to mail it to him, but now, even that option was gone. When this was over, she'd fold it into a paper boat and set it free on Lake Superior, where it could disintegrate and sink to the depths, never to be seen again, just like Silas.

With a deep breath in, she knew that was the right decision. Then he feathered his thumb across her cheek to wipe a tear, shattering her heart into a million little pieces with that slight touch. Making the right decision about Land would be the hardest decision of her life.

Chapter Eighteen

Cal walked into the meeting with his jaw ticking. Immediately, Reece knew whatever he had to say wouldn't be good.

"Sorry to interrupt," Cal said to Mina, who motioned at him to take the floor. "There's been a development." He glanced down at the paper in his hand. "Around 2:00 a.m., a body was found on the Lakewalk in Duluth. When the police arrived, they identified the victim as Miles Bradshaw, age thirty-five."

Sky's gasp was loud in the quiet room. "No. No. That's not true—no. It can't be."

Sliding his arm around Sky's shoulders, Reece scooted closer to her chair, hating that the wheel got in the way of them connecting hip to hip. "My assumption is the cause of death wasn't natural."

"Not unless you call blunt-force trauma natural."

"Nope," Reece answered, popping the *P*. "No one saw anything?"

"Whoever left him there did so while avoiding all the cameras."

"Wait, left him there?" Reece asked with a brow raised.

"That was also my second question. My police contact says there wasn't enough blood or splatter when compared to his injuries for it to have happened there."

"What is going on?" Sky asked, mournful and angry. "Do you think this is connected to my case?" She was starting to recover from the shock, so he rubbed her back a bit before releasing her.

"It could be a coincidence," Cal said slowly.

"And you know what I say about coincidences," Mina said with a snort.

"Coincidences are easily manufactured," Iris, Cal and Reece said in unison, playing to Mina's mantra.

"She's right, though," Iris said. "There is no way his death isn't related to this whole mess."

"But there's no way Camille is capable of killing him," Sky insisted. "She's smaller than me, and Miles was a big guy."

"There is always a way," Cal said with a brow raised. "And one of those ways is to hire someone to do it for you. Not always the smartest regarding the trust factor, but it happens more than anyone thinks."

"What are the police saying? They can't possibly think Skylar had anything to do with this?" Reece asked.

"Even though there was a note in his wallet that said this?" Cal handed him the paper, and he read it while trying to keep it from Sky.

"'If I'm dead, Skylar Sullivan did it.'" Sky's eyes rolled so hard that Reece feared they'd never return to center. "Lord, he was so dramatic," she said between clenched teeth. "Tell me the cops don't believe that?"

"They have to investigate it, of course, but as of right now, they have no leads. Not only are you incapable of that kind of killing physically, but you couldn't transport him anywhere. Then we're back to the idea of hiring someone, which would be difficult for you right now, considering you're on the run from your other warrant."

"That's what the police think? That I'm 'on the run'?" she asked, using air quotes.

Cal shrugged in a way that told Reece he was holding back a smile. "Well, no. The police think you're hiding out at Secure One while we try to figure out who's setting you up. They're okay with pretending you're on the run for a bit longer since they can't find proof you have been in any of the cities with vandalized galleries or took out large sums of cash to pay someone else to do it."

"That's because I didn't," Sky said, her words tight. "Could they link Miles to any of them?"

"I don't believe they were trying," Cal answered.

"But we have been, and the answer is yes to several," Iris said. "That's what I wanted to bring to your attention today."

Skylar glanced between all of them. "Do you think with Miles's death the vandalism will stop?"

Cal lowered himself to a chair and leaned forward, clasping his hands together, his metal and plastic fingers clicking into place around his flesh and bones. Cal had lost half of his fingers on his right hand while in the service, but the prosthesis he wore was so perfectly fitted to him that he could use the prosthetic finger to pull a trigger with deadly aim.

"I'm going to be real with you here, Sky. Someone killed Miles, which means—"

"Someone else is pulling the strings." Reece felt her heavy sigh all the way to his bones. "I should have thought of that. Even if Miles was doing the vandalism, that doesn't mean the person behind his death won't keep doing it."

"Hey," Reece said, rubbing her neck again to calm her. "You've had a lot thrown at you in the last few hours."

"And you don't do this for a living," Mina added. "That's why you've got us."

"We've got you," Iris assured her, still not making eye

contact. "We may not know who is behind this yet, but we won't give up until we do."

"What she said," Cal said with a wink. "We aren't giving up. I was sorry to hear about your brother. I'm sure that wasn't the kind of news you expected to hear during this time."

"Thank you for your concern, but it's a relief to know he's dead and not out there hurting or abusing anyone else. My brother had problems, and he took a lot of them out on me. There was no love lost between us, and truthfully, I'm glad he's dead and buried. That's a part of my life I am happy to put behind me."

You could hear a pin drop in the room, and Reece kept his hand on her neck to let her know he supported her.

"I'm sorry, that was dirty laundry I didn't need to air."

"No need to apologize to us," Mina said with a shake of her head.

Cal turned to Mina. "Have there been any videos uploaded to the Facebook page today?"

"I haven't gotten any notifications," Reece said, pointing at his tablet. "I have it set up to alert me."

Mina held up her finger and clicked around on her screen. After a few moments of silence, she let out an oof and leaned back in her chair. "There were no videos, but look."

She clicked, and the screen on the wall mirroring hers lit up. It showed that the page's owner had responded to every negative comment. "Those responses started about five thirty this morning and went until nine thirty."

"Which means Miles wasn't running that page," Reece said.

"It doesn't appear so," Mina agreed.

"The IP address for the first few comments came up as overseas," Iris said. "I'll check these new comments to see if that's changed, but I'm sure they're using a VPN." Anyone capable of taking control of Sky's digital signature would certainly use a virtual private network to avoid detection.

"I agree." Reece glanced at everyone in the room. "I feel like whoever is behind this just sent us a checkmate message with Miles."

"From one security guy to the other, same," Cal said.

"Maybe Camille *is* behind this," Skylar insisted. "Miles was a puppy when it came to her. What's to say she didn't have other guys doing her bidding, too?"

"Trust me," Cal said, leaning back in his chair, "that's the working theory now. Someone is behind this, so all we can do is wait for another message or finally crack through the Facebook page to see who's behind it."

"I'm just afraid by the time we wait for another message to arrive, another gallery will be damaged, or someone else will be hurt," Skylar whispered, her gaze taking in all the comments on the board.

Reece was sure everyone else felt the same way, so when no one said anything, she snapped off the brakes on her chair and wheeled out of the room.

THE SUN WAS setting over the manufactured pond at the back of the property. Skylar couldn't get over how gorgeous the land was, and she truly appreciated the little bit of peace and quiet she got sitting there watching the sun sink below the horizon. Besides an arduous trek back to the cabin across the grass, she was safe. Since the meeting this morning, she'd tried to stay away from the case, but as night neared, she would have to face Reece again. He'd given her an update when she woke up from a nap earlier but hadn't pressured her to take part in the investigation or to try to focus her thoughts on the videos. Even if the person behind the mask was Miles, he was dead now. Dead because they were connected. They were missing something, but she couldn't figure it out. Then again, it was more like missing someone—a key player in the campaign to destroy Skylar Sullivan. The only person left whom she dealt with regularly with any hostility toward her wasn't capable of killing a grown man. Was she capable of hiring someone to do it? Well, Skylar couldn't deny the answer to that question was yes. Camille was gregarious and gorgeous. She could easily convince someone to do her bidding, and she sold high-priced art pieces, so she could afford to pay for it.

"I've been looking for you," Land said as he approached her from the direction of the cottage.

"Sorry, I wanted to sketch the sun as it set over the pond," she explained, motioning at her sketch pad.

"I don't blame you," he said, his hand to his head as he stared at the sinking orb. "I always make it a point to watch the sun rise or set at least once when I'm here. It's different than in the city."

"When this is all over, I want to make this into a stained-glass piece for the cafeteria," she explained. "It's not much, but it will come from my heart for what they've done for me."

Land squeezed her shoulder with a smile as he gazed down at her. "They'd be lucky to have an original Skylar Sullivan piece."

"Not if we don't find the person behind this," she sighed as she closed the book. "I'm sorry I checked out earlier. My brain couldn't take any more."

"Everyone understood," he promised, smoothing a hand down her cheek. "You hadn't even had time to deal with Silas's death when we dropped Miles on you. Did you get any rest?"

"Some," she answered, glancing up at him. "I haven't slept well the last few nights, so I needed it. I also wanted to let the catheter drain freely for a few hours. I always feel like we're a minute away from having to take off again."

"I'm sure you do, but we're safe here until we or the police sort out who's behind these threats against you."

"You mean against the galleries."

After kneeling next to her chair, he tipped his head to the side. "No, I mean against you. They have a vendetta against you. They're just using the galleries to escalate it."

"To what end, though?" she asked in frustration.

"I wish I could say," he whispered, gazing over the water. "I do feel like they'll reveal it soon enough. Killing Miles was a pretty strong escalation."

"What aren't you telling me, Land?" She turned in her chair and tipped his chin to face her. "Did something else happen today?"

"No," he promised while holding her gaze. She could tell by how his pupils didn't react that he was telling the truth. "I'm frustrated with all the dead ends we keep hitting when it comes to Camille Castillo. She's nearly as hard to investigate as Silas was. Sure, we have her name and know where she last lived, but it's like she's fallen off the face of the earth, too."

"Do you think Camille was an alias?"

"We're starting to think so, and now she's using a different one, or she's gone back to using her real name, neither of which we have."

"After dinner, I'll watch the Facebook videos again from the angle of Camille behind the mask. I'll think about my interactions with her while watching them, and maybe I'll pick up on something?"

Despite his skeptical expression, he nodded. "It can't hurt.

We've hit a stalemate with this until we get another video or they post something on the petition page."

"Am I wrong, or does it feel like the person behind this has been bolder about posting on the petition page?"

"It's not just you. Mina and Iris also agree. We're hoping that works to our benefit. Since it's a public page, if they want to send you a message, they could use that page to do it."

"Do you still believe they don't know we can see the page where they post the videos?"

"That's a bit murkier, and even Mina agrees with that. Facebook tells a person how many times their video has been watched. Technically, since we're using a dupe page, every time we watch the video, the count shouldn't change, but we can't be sure. Secretly, I hope they know we can see the page. If they know someone else is watching the videos, it might embolden them."

"I hope so, because my nerves can't take too many more days of this."

Land stood and put his hands on his hips. "Sadie sent dinner to the cabin. How about we share it and a movie? Take a little time to relax and think about something else?"

"I'd like that," she agreed with a smile. "It'll let me clear my head and get it back in the game."

While he helped push her back to the cabin, she wondered if she'd ever get back into the art game. If they didn't stop this soon, she would lose everything—including Reece Palmer.

DINNER HAD BEEN DELICIOUS, as always. Sadie's meals were the reason Reece found a way to hang out at Secure One at least once a month. She could cook and had honed her skills since marrying Eric and working full-time as a chef for Cal. She usually cared for Mina and Roman's daughter, Hannah Grace, when she wasn't cooking. He suspected the Secure One family might be growing, though. Earlier, while looking for a cup of coffee, he'd walked down to the cafeteria to find Sadie in the kitchen looking a bit green around the gills as she fried ground beef. He couldn't help but wonder if Sadie and Eric would have an announcement of their own to share soon.

He glanced at Sky, sitting next to him on the couch as they watched the latest mystery flick. She was as invested in it as he was, which was not at all. They'd shared a wonderful dinner, laughing and kidding the way they used to as kids. It was hard to remember their years apart now that they were together again. It was as though nothing had changed, since they could still finish each other's sentences.

"Why did you refuse to date me after we graduated?" he blurted out, groaning at the rough delivery. He'd been thinking about asking it for days and couldn't hold back a second longer.

"What?" she asked, clearly pretending she didn't understand the question when she most certainly did.

"Right after we graduated, I asked if you'd go on a date with me. You said no. You told me we could be friends but nothing more. Why?"

"You mean other than being paralyzed?" She pushed off his shoulder and sat up straight, grabbing the arm of the couch to steady herself.

"What did being paralyzed have to do with it? It was months after the accident when I asked. You were back to school and just doing outpatient therapy."

"Using a wheelchair every day for the rest of my life had everything to do with it," she said between clenched teeth. "In a split second on that October night, we became different people, Land. You remained you, but I became someone new. Someone even I didn't know yet. There was no way I would subject you to the kind of life I would lead. It was nonstop doctor and therapy appointments, expensive medical equipment, and procedure after procedure. That was not the kind of life I wanted for you."

"Wait, what are you saying?"

"I'm saying that I refused to date you to give you a better life. I didn't want to saddle you with my unexpected circumstances. You walked away from that accident and had a chance to do great things. There was no way I was going to drag you down with me. I wanted you to go out and live your dreams. I wanted you to find a woman who could do everything you loved to do and give you everything I couldn't."

"You're saying that you decided for me what I wanted out of life? What gave you that right?"

"This," she said, transferring into her chair and smacking the tires. "This gave me the right. You should thank me for it!"

"Thank you? I should thank you for deciding my future on my behalf without consulting me? How is that fair?" His questions got louder with each one until he sat on the edge of the couch, vibrating with anger.

"Fair? You want to talk to me about fair? You got a broken wrist. I got this!" She smacked the tires again. "Yes, I decided to go out there that night, and I accept that, but there's nothing fair about this!" Before he could react, she snapped the brakes off and wheeled around him.

"Where are you going?" he asked as she wheeled down the hallway.

"To bed! You're not welcome to join me. Enjoy the couch!"

The door slammed shut, and he growled, slapping a cushion in anger and frustration. Dammit, why did he have to go and open his big mouth? Flicking off the television, he stormed outside to pace on the small porch that held an old-fashioned rocking chair and a small table made from a tree stump.

"Everything okay over there?" Roman had walked out onto his cabin's porch and down the stairs.

"Fine," he growled, running his fingers through his hair.

"It didn't sound like it to me. I couldn't hear what was said, but the tone was loud and clear."

Reece rolled his eyes. "I figured Cal would have better insulation in these things."

"Well, when the windows are open, sound travels."

He'd forgotten about the windows. He'd opened them earlier to cool the house off after the heat of the day. "I totally forgot the windows were open. It's fine. We just had a bit of a disagreement."

Roman leaned against the railing, pulled a beer out of each jacket pocket and handed him one. They popped the tops off and clinked the necks together before taking a drink. The malty liquid turned his stomach when he swallowed, but it wasn't the beer as much as it was having upset the woman in the bedroom.

"Want to talk about it?"

"Not really," Reece said, lowering himself to the rocking chair and taking another swig of the beer.

"Will what just happened somehow interfere with resolving this situation she's in?"

"Probably," he agreed, hanging his head to stare at the porch floor rather than at his friend.

"Did you make an unwelcome advance?"

"Absolutely not!" he growled as he rose to a standing position. "That's not who I am."

Roman tipped his beer at him. "Agreed, so what else

would make her angry enough to lock herself in the bedroom?"

With a shoulder-sagging sigh, Reece sat again. "I finally found the courage to ask her why she refused to date me after graduation. She told me she decided I deserved to go out and live my life and not be saddled with someone in her situation."

Roman lifted his brow before he took another sip of his beer. "Yeah, that tracks."

"Excuse me?" Reece stood again, but this time, it was to pace.

"I remember the days right after Mina's amputation. She decided that I was better off without her. I could do so much better than her and deserved someone who could keep up with me physically."

"Those are the same words Sky used on me," Reece admitted, pausing his steps.

"If you give women time to think in that situation, that will always be the answer they arrive at." He shrugged as he took a drink from the bottle. "Hell, we might feel the same if the roles were reversed. Maybe not wanting to be a burden on someone is a human trait, not a gender trait."

With a soft chuckle, Reece shook his head. "The way you say *maybe* tells me it's not a maybe at all."

Roman shrugged again, but this time, it was a confirmation shrug. "You can't blame her for having a different view of life while sitting in a chair you weren't sitting in. She was young, injured, scared and probably embarrassed by what had happened to her body."

No doubt that was the truth. Reece still remembered how she had closed in on herself, refusing to talk to anyone for days while she did nothing but draw. Her parents and doctors told him that drawing was good therapy to help her deal with her injuries and a new way of life, but he hadn't thought so. He'd always thought it gave her too much time to think and not enough time to remember she was still the same person, even if she had to use a chair to get around. It was obvious to him now that he'd been correct.

"I'd venture to say that she's still scared and embarrassed by what has happened to her body. She's pushing you away equally as hard now to fight the attraction she still has for you."

That drew him from his ruminations of the past. "Come again?"

"Dude, if you can't see that girl still has feelings for you, you shouldn't be an investigator. Of course, if you think you're hiding your feelings for her, you're also wrong."

"We're friends, Roman, and barely that. Until four days ago, I hadn't seen her in nearly fourteen years."

"Yet the first person she called when she was in trouble was you."

Before Reece could object, Roman held up his hand and started for the cabin stairs. "I have to check on Hannah and make sure she fell asleep. Before you walk back into that cabin, I suggest you have a game plan for groveling. You're going to need one."

"Gee, thanks," Reece grunted as Roman laughed. He gave Reece a cheeky salute before disappearing inside and shutting the door.

Reece swiped the half-empty beer off the table and finished it in one swallow. Maybe he did need a game plan. Then again, he could always try honesty and see where that got him.

Determined to make things right, he walked inside, closed all the windows and drew a deep breath before knocking on the locked bedroom door.

Chapter Nineteen

There was a knock on the door, and Skylar forced herself not to say anything.

"Sky? Can I come in?"

Biting her tongue, she kept sketching on her pad, hoping he'd go away and leave her alone. She'd heard the front door slam shut and had hoped he would decide to work, but here he was, just fifteen minutes later, bugging her.

"I know you aren't sleeping. I can hear your pencil on the paper."

"How can you hear that?" His soft laughter came from the other side of the door, and she groaned. He'd been baiting her. "Go away, Reece. I'm tired."

"I'm sure you are, but I want to apologize. I'll do it through the door, but it would probably mean more if I didn't have to." She remained silent and, after thirty seconds, heard his sigh through the door. "I'll start by saying I was an insensitive oaf for bringing it up. My timing was never great."

Obviously, he was determined to have his say, so she closed her sketch pad and called out to him. "You can come in. I'm sure the neighbors would appreciate it."

A key slid into the lock before the handle turned, and in walked the man she couldn't stop thinking about—or crying about, for that matter. She swiped at her face with her shoulder just in case there were any stray tears. Not that she could conceal the splotchy red face from the tears she hadn't tried to hide when she was alone. Reece walked to the bed and sat as she fiddled with her pencil to avoid eye contact.

"I'm sorry," he said, swiping a piece of hair off her forehead before he let his finger trail down across her tearstained face. "Hang on."

Surprised, she waited while he ran the water in the bathroom before returning with a warm washcloth that he held to her face. He gently blotted her salty skin before handing it to her. She held it to her cheek, allowing the warmth to soak into her skin and soothe her.

"If I could take back the last thirty minutes, I would," he said, taking her other hand. "You're dealing with enough right now. You don't need to worry about the past."

"I shouldn't have overreacted," she said, staring at their hands linked together.

"And I should have considered your side of the situation before I got angry."

Her shrug was jerky as she tried to push back the tears. "We were both navigating adult situations without the benefit of adult maturity."

"You were in pain, scared, angry and—"

"Jealous." She'd rather say it than hear it from his lips.

"Jealous of me?"

Her nod made her lip tremble. The time had come to admit the truth to the man she had pushed away as a boy.

"You were jealous that I wasn't hurt in the accident that changed your life."

"That's not true!" Her vehement denial set him back a step. "You were hurt, and I don't just mean your arm. It was easy to see that the effects of the accident would always be with you. The jealousy was more about your dreams still being alive while mine were dead and buried. If that accident hadn't happened and you'd asked me to go on a date after graduation, the answer would have been a resounding yes. Instead, right or wrong, I chose—"

"Me," he said with a nod. "You set your wants and needs aside to give me a chance at the kind of life we'd always talked about having, even if you could no longer be part of it."

"And you did, so it was worth it." Her words were filled with sadness, but the idea that he was happy reminded her that she wanted nothing but good things for him.

Slowly, he lifted her hand to his lips and brushed a kiss across her knuckles. "Maybe I had the professional success we'd always talked about, but personally, I'm still that boy asking his best friend out on a date. After I graduated, I stayed in Duluth, hoping to catch a glimpse of you somewhere. Sometimes, I'd see you sketching on the Lakewalk, and I'd sit in my truck and watch you, thinking about what could have been. I set up Google Alerts for your name so I would get alerts when you were having a show somewhere. I'd go to as many as I could in disguise to see your work and maybe, just maybe, the beautiful blue eyes of the girl I couldn't stop thinking about no matter how many years passed."

"Seriously?"

In answer, he just brushed another kiss across her knuckles.

"I wanted you to go out, meet someone, marry, have babies. You deserve that, Reece."

"So do you, Sky. This," he said, motioning at the wheelchair, "doesn't mean you have to give up on all of your dreams."

"You were my dream, Land. The only dream that ever mattered to me." Before she could finish her thought, his lips were on hers, pressing her head back into the pillows.

With her eyes closed, she let the kiss happen, responding to his touch in a way that left no doubt in her mind that she would love this man forever, even if they would always be star-crossed lovers. When he slid his hand up her ribs to cup her breast, it took her by surprise. She moaned, only to immediately break the kiss and push his hand away.

"Land, stop," she said with a panted breath. "You can't touch me like that."

He moved his hand immediately. "Did I hurt you?"

"No," she said, shaking her head to keep the tears at bay. "You didn't hurt me. Having you touch me like that is all I've ever dreamed about, but it can't happen."

"Why not?" he asked, his forehead balanced on hers as he gazed into her eyes. It was hard to lie to his face, so she didn't.

"Because I'm a weak woman, and if it happens, I won't be able to give you up when this is over. The first time nearly killed me. I can't do it again."

"Who says you have to?"

"This," she said, motioning at the chair and around the room. "There's so much about my life that you don't see, Land."

"Maybe, but you didn't allow me to learn about you, either."

"You want to learn about me?" she asked, tugging on the blanket until he shifted so she could pull it off. "Fine. Let's start with my legs." Rather than meet his gaze, she just waved her hands at her legs. "Remember how strong they once were?" She lifted one with her hands, watching it fall to the bed in a tangle. "Noodles, Reece. They're like noodles." Before he could react, she lifted her shirt and lowered her panties. "Then there's this. Isn't this the sexiest thing you've ever seen? Oh, wait, you've seen the whole catheter debacle already. How could I forget? That means you've seen my beautiful para-belly, too. What's that? Well, it's the sagging and bagging of my paralyzed muscles being dragged down by my internal organs. I have to wear a binder during the day so I don't feel like my insides are falling out. Sexy, right? Should we keep going?"

Reece's hand touched hers, and he leaned over her until she was forced to meet his gaze. "Angel, stop. None of this is about your body."

"What is it about then, Land?" she whisper-asked. "This is my body, and there's no changing it."

"I wouldn't want to, Sky. Don't you see? This body has made you who you are today. You would not be the person you are today if that accident hadn't happened. You can look at that as a positive or a negative for sure, and I see both sides, but when I look at you, all I see is strength and determination. I can't sit here and listen to the girl I've cared about my entire life show me her body with tears in her eyes and anger in every word, as though she doesn't deserve to be cherished by someone because of something beyond her control. Let me be clear, Sky. That is false. You are beautiful, and any man would be lucky to spend his days with you."

When he broke eye contact, she sucked in a deep breath, still fighting back tears when he lowered his head to her left leg and kissed his way from her ankle to her thigh. He tenderly massaged her skin as he made his way north. She couldn't feel it as anything other than pressure, but watching him do it made those tears fall over her lashes. Land tenderly loved her other leg the same way before he positioned them again on the pillow. When he finished, he knelt on the floor and massaged her hip bones that jutted out on each side, the catheter dead center and still taped to her skin instead of coiled in her bag. His thumbs worked their way across her abdomen, stroking the skin on each side of the stoma. It was healed now to nothing more than a small hole the tube went through, and he leaned down, pressing a kiss to the skin just above it.

"Land, don't," she whispered, the tears falling at the idea of his tender touch that she couldn't feel.

"Why are you crying?" he asked, reaching up to wipe away a tear.

"I never wanted you to see me this way."

"Sweetheart, I can't tell you how much I wish you'd have talked to me. We could have worked through it together, because you are turning me on in a way I can't hide." She raised a surprised brow, and he shrugged, standing so she could see the outline of his maleness through his jeans. "My body doesn't lie, Sky."

He lowered his head again and kissed across her ribs, where there was still minimal sensation. "I can't feel you against my skin, and it's killing me," she whimpered.

In a heartbeat, he'd removed her T-shirt, pausing long enough to gaze at the lacy bra that hooked in the front. Land's growl was low and throaty when he unsnapped it and pulled it away. With all the patience and tenderness in the world, he kissed his way up to her left nipple before slipping it between his lips to tease with his tongue.

"Land!" she cried softly, arching her chest to get closer to him.

"You can feel that?" he asked, barely releasing her breast long enough to ask.

"It feels so good." She cried out again when he grasped

her other nipple between his fingers and rolled it gently while he lavished her other one with his tongue. To throw her off, he switched sides, and she couldn't stop the eruption of sensation that filled her. "Land," she whimpered as the waves flowed over her. "Don't stop, please," she begged, riding the sensations high up into the sky, where she lost track of her thoughts and anything but how good it felt to be loved by this man.

When she came back to earth, he was holding her in his arms, teasing her earlobe with his tongue and teeth. "That was unexpected," he whispered, kissing her behind the ear. "Are you okay?"

"Better than okay." Her laughter was soft when she answered. "I'm literally on cloud nine. Since I don't have a lot of sensation in my lower half…" She paused, unsure what she should tell him.

"Be honest with me, angel. I want to know everything," he whispered in her ear. The sensation sent a shiver down her shoulders and pooled at her nipples again, making them tingle.

"My erogenous zones are different than other women," she explained. "I can only orgasm through intercourse if I have direct G-spot stimulation. My breasts, on the other hand, are highly orgasmic."

His soft laughter in her ear made her smile, her tears long gone after his tender loving. "I noticed. I loved every second of it, too."

"You did?" She tried to position herself so she could see him. He propped a pillow behind her back and held her waist to steady her.

Rather than answer, he held her hand to the front of his jeans. "I did." When she rubbed her hand across his hardness, his eyes rolled back in his head, and he moaned. "Is this a dream, or are you touching me right now?"

"It's not a dream unless I'm in the same one," she whispered, sliding her hand under the waistband of his pants to feel his heat. His gasp was loud when he pressed himself against her hand, his eyes closed and his body vibrating with her touch. "We can't do this."

"Do what?" she asked, grasping him through his boxers and reveling in the way his breath hitched. This was the most unexpected moment of her life, and she wanted to memorize it for when they parted ways again.

"Make love," he whispered, thrusting against her hand. "We're not prepared."

"I'm on the pill, Land."

"Not that," he whispered, grasping her hand to still her. "I refuse to endanger you for my satisfaction. After some research, I know that for a woman with a spinal cord injury to enjoy making love, planning is required or—"

"I'll have another episode of autonomic dysreflexia?" His nod was enough for her to know he had done his research. "It's possible, but there are ways to prevent it and have a satisfying sex life."

When he took her lips, his kiss was hungry and demanding. When he finally broke for air, they were both panting. "I'm satisfied just being able to kiss and touch you, sweetheart. I don't need more right now. We can wait."

"Your body tells a different story," she whispered, squeezing his hard maleness. His moan told her she wasn't wrong.

"I just want to kiss you and hold you in my arms. It makes me feel like all the years that passed don't exist anymore."

"We can do that," she promised, unsnapping the button on his jeans without dropping his gaze. It was now or never if she wanted to show him that while a life with her might not be typical, that didn't mean it couldn't be enjoyable.

Check yourself, Skylar. There's no life with him. There's only tonight, because when the sun comes up tomorrow and reality comes floating back through those windows, nothing will have changed.

With all her might, she tried to ignore that voice of reason as she unzipped his pants, the chattering of the teeth sending a visible shiver through him. Just for tonight, she wanted to pretend she could have a life with this man.

"You're killing me, baby girl," he ground out, lifting his hips to lower his jeans and then his boxers.

She was holding him in a breath, his warm skin connected to hers in an elemental way that told her nothing would ever be the same between them again, and she didn't want it to be. She wanted him, and all of her reasoning about why she shouldn't went out the window the moment he throbbed against her. She stroked him, his hips thrusting as she did, and his moans long and low. She had no question that he was enjoying their time together. Then he cried out in pleasure, his desire throbbing rhythmically in her hand as she carried him up onto his own wave of pleasure. After his release, when he gazed down at her, she saw everything he couldn't say. She prayed her eyes told him the same story.

Chapter Twenty

Reece woke slowly, his gaze taking in the woman in his arms. Sky was still naked, as was he, and they were wrapped together in a blanket he'd pulled over them after she'd made him a very happy man. She was gorgeous, all of her, and it killed him to think she believed she wasn't. If she gave him the chance, he'd tell her she was beautiful every day for the rest of his life. He suspected that would be harder to do than to say. When this was over and she had her life back, he expected her to push him away again. This time, he wouldn't let that happen.

He noticed she was still clutching her charcoal pencil and the pad lay off to the side, having fallen from her lap in sleep. She must have woken up with an idea she didn't want to forget and sketched it out. He gingerly lifted the sketch pad and paused as he went to close the book. It wasn't a mosaic she'd been sketching. It was him. His jaw dropped slightly at the image in his hands. He was alive and vibrant, even in black and white. She'd managed to represent his two different-colored eyes using only shadows and light. Stroke by stroke, she'd built him as she saw him, half the boy she used to know and half the man he had become, and married them perfectly into what he embodied as a man today.

She had incredible talent, but she also had incredible insight into people and drew them from the inside out.

"Secure Watch, Whiskey." Mina's voice filled the room from his walkie-talkie, and he grabbed it carefully to avoid waking Sky. A check of the clock told him it was 2:00 a.m., which meant they'd been sleeping much longer than he'd realized.

"Secure Watch, Riker," he responded quietly.

"This is an all-call alert," Mina said. "I need you and Skylar here immediately."

"What's up?" he asked, eyeing the woman in his arms as she began to stir.

"We've got a new video. Things have escalated. Can you meet me in the conference room in ten?"

"We'll need twenty. We were sleeping, so Sky needs time to get ready."

"Ten-four."

He sat up and shifted a sleepy Sky to the pillows. "Mina doesn't do an all-call at this time of the night unless there's a massive change in the situation. We need to move."

Skylar grabbed his arm before he could leave the bed. "We need to talk, Land."

"When this is over," he said, praying the words didn't sound as harsh to her ears as they did to his. "Until you're free of this threat, that's where our concentration needs to be."

Without another word, she shifted her wheelchair and transferred into it. Watching her struggle to get her legs onto the footplate, he walked around the bed and tenderly lifted them down. She wouldn't meet his gaze, and he knew she'd heard the sharpness of his tone.

He leaned in on her wheels and forced eye contact. "Let me be clear—if I had a choice, I'd still be in that bed holding your warm body and kissing your sweet lips. First, it's my job to keep you safe and eliminate this threat. Don't misconstrue my shift in attitude to anything other than wanting to protect you and give you your life back. Got it?"

"I want the same thing, both your warm body and being free of this threat. I'll do whatever you tell me to do to make that happen."

"Good," he whispered, leaning in and stealing a kiss from her lips. "Because when this is over, we aren't going back to the lives we used to live. That's over. Fair warning."

Rather than answer, she gave him one nod and turned her chair, wheeling into the bathroom in a way that said she wasn't as convinced of that as he was. That was okay. He was a patient man. He'd waited fourteen years to be with her. He could wait a few more days.

When he and Sky arrived at the conference room, the team was assembled, meaning this video undoubtedly changed the game.

"Sorry to rouse you so early," Mina said as a greeting, "but we've got a situation."

"How bad is it?" Reece asked, pulling a chair away from the table so Sky could roll in.

"Explosively bad," Iris said without looking away from the table. "I was on duty when it came in on the Facebook page. Whoever it is, they know we can see the page."

"Can we see the video?" Sky asked, glancing at Mina and Cal.

"I've got it ready to show you," Mina said. "Fair warning. It's traumatic, and we will protect you no matter what."

Taking her hand, Reece held it tightly between his and then nodded at Mina for her to play the video. The screen across the room lit up with a building filmed in low light.

It was grainy, but they could make out a woman sitting in a wheelchair, strapped down with ropes, her mouth taped and wearing a vest. Skylar gasped.

"That's Camille Castillo!" she exclaimed.

Mina paused the video. "You're positive?"

Skylar nodded robotically. "No question. Why is she dressed like that?"

"The vest is full of explosives that can blow her and that building to kingdom come," Iris said before she grimaced. "Sorry. This is why I shouldn't talk to people."

"You're fine," Skylar said, though Reece could tell she was in shock. "I'm grateful that you tell it like it is. I can deal with that better than being lied to."

It was difficult, but Reece bit back the smile that threatened, because Sky was something else and he was glad to be the one to help her win this battle. Mina hit play again, and a familiar voice filled the room.

"Hello, Skylar. It's time we end this little tête-à-tête, don't you think? I'm sure you recognize our friend. I've been saving her for the finale." The video panned to the roof of a building with decorative brickwork.

"No," she cried. "That's the art gallery Taken for Granted. It's owned by a conglomerate of artists. We have to do something!" Skylar turned to Reece and grabbed the front of his shirt. "We have to stop him!"

While Reece tenderly grasped her hand on his shirt, Mina flicked the video back on so they could hear the rest of the message.

"I know how tight you are with this building. Last I heard, you were throwing some of that settlement money into it." The man in the mask shook his head as though he was disappointed, clucking his tongue. "Imagine how the other artists will feel if you're the reason the building comes tumbling down."

Mina paused the video again. "Is that true?"

"No," she whispered, her gaze glued to the screen. "I was asked to do a gallery showing there in a few months. I could become a partner if my work was accepted and the showing was strong. I wouldn't be using the settlement money, though. I'd use the money I saved for this reason—money that's now gone, I'm sure."

"But wait," Reece said, turning to Sky. "How many people in your life know about the settlement money?"

She tossed her head from side to side. "I suppose it wouldn't be hard to find the information online if you google the accident, but I haven't talked to anyone about the settlement money. Even when we first got the payout, we didn't discuss it. It wasn't something to celebrate or to brag about. I'd rather we hadn't needed it."

"So only people close to you know about the settlement?" Cal asked to clarify.

"Well, yeah, that or people who followed the case or were part of the accident themselves." She glanced at Reece. "Could this be one of the other accident victims?"

"Did everyone get a payout from the accident?" Cal asked, glancing at Mina with a grimace. Obviously, he had started to put things together, too.

"To a degree," Reece answered for her. "The amount depended on how serious the injury was and if the victim would have lifelong needs because of it."

"I am not a victim," Sky said between clenched teeth.

Reece pressed a kiss to her temple, not even caring what his boss thought about it. He noticed her smiling when he spoke again, though. "Not what I meant, Sky. Let me rephrase. Anyone who was injured got a payout, but it depended on their injuries. I had a broken wrist, so my bills were paid and that was it. It was the same for others who broke their arm or leg. For those who suffered traumatic brain injuries, they got a settlement that reflected the life-long care they would need."

"That must be nice," Iris muttered with an eye roll.

"Skylar, was anyone else injured as severely as you were?" Cal asked.

"No, most suffered broken bones or cuts and bruises. Because I was in the air when the team went down, my injuries reflected the height from which I fell."

Everyone in the room grimaced at the thought as Reece took her hand again. "She's correct that anyone from that time who followed the case or was part of it would know that she got a large settlement."

"That still narrows it down considerably," Cal said. "That's a path we can follow if need be."

"Let's finish the video. Then we can hash out a plan," Mina said, clicking the remote.

The creepy voice filled the room again. "It's not too late to save Camille and your beloved building. I'll trade them for you. That seems even. Be outside the loading doors of the gallery this morning at six, alone. No cops and no security guys. If I see anyone besides you, I will blow this building and all of you sky-high. See what I did there?" His creepy horror laugh sent a shiver down Reece's spine. "There'll be a phone waiting for you there on which you'll receive a call with further instructions. If you're not there at exactly six o'clock, well, boom! Ta-ta for now, Skylar. Tick tock, run, run…oh wait, wheel, wheel as fast as you can…"

The room went silent for a beat before everyone inhaled. "That's not happening," Reece said before anyone could speak.

"But it is," Skylar responded, turning to him. "A woman's life is on the line!"

"A woman who could be in on this!" he exclaimed in return. They stared at each other in a stalemate until Cal spoke.

"Unfortunately, we have no evidence whether Camille is or isn't in on it."

"Rather than call the police and ask for assistance," Mina said, "we tapped into the security systems around the building. We can see the side of the building where that would have been recorded, but there's no one there now."

"Am I the only one who thinks it's weird that he strapped a woman to a wheelchair, set her in front of a video camera and did a full video without anyone noticing?" Iris asked, making Reece turn toward her.

"You're right. I hadn't thought of that. It would be almost impossible to film something like that where the gallery is located in Duluth. He'd have to be quick, and I can't see that happening with a woman tied to a wheelchair like that."

"But I know that was Taken for Granted. I have no doubt," Skylar said, shock still filling her words. "And that was Camille."

"Could the video be altered?" Reece asked Mina, who nodded with a shrug.

"That's possible. The quality is low, which could be on purpose, and the shots of her were tight to the brick. He could have spliced them together to make them look like they were at Taken for Granted," Mina said.

"We could call the bomb squad to go in, but I'm afraid he's watching the building," Cal explained. "If he sees movement and the bomb is inside the building, a lot of people would get hurt."

"We can't risk it," Skylar said, shaking her head. "Whoever this is has an issue with me and no one else. I don't want anyone to get hurt because of me. We follow his directions and don't deviate. Camille, while not my favorite person, doesn't deserve to die, and neither does anyone else. If that building blows, many other businesses and people will get hurt."

"I ran the casualty report if the building goes," Iris said, grabbing a piece of paper. "Because the gallery is located so close to the residential section of the city and the hospital, we're talking easily a billion dollars in property damage and countless lives lost if the building explodes. It's old brick, and it will fly like stone bullets."

Reece swore, his chest tight as he imagined the implications of that. "She can't be out there alone, Cal. She has no way to defend herself."

"Agreed," he said, but Sky snorted.

"He said no cops and no security guys. If he blows that building when I'm sitting in front of it, I'm dead, too."

"That's why you've got us," Roman said as he walked through the door dressed in a Secure One uniform, followed by four guys dressed the same. It was the core team of Secure One operatives.

"Skylar, my name is Efren Brenna. I believe you met my wife, Selina. This is Mack, Eric and Lucas. With all due respect, we've infiltrated a mafia kingpin's home without his knowledge. We can stake out and protect the building in question in our sleep. We got you."

Reece nodded his agreement when she glanced at him. "The team will not let you down. You can put the same amount of trust in them that you've put in me. We won't let you or anyone else get hurt, but you have to follow directions and not go rogue."

The room erupted in snickers as they glanced at Mina, who was laughing harder than any of them. "What did I miss?" Skylar asked.

Reece waved a hand in the air. "I'll tell you on the way. It's a long story. For now, will you agree to listen to the plan I know Cal has already developed and is ready to implement?"

"I'll listen, but I think I should get a say in this, too. I don't want anyone else to get hurt because of me. If anyone is going to die, it will be me."

His pulse pounding in his ears, he tipped her chin around to face him. "And you don't think that going out there and getting yourself killed would hurt me? Don't you think that watching you nearly die once was enough? Now I have to do it again?" Reece felt a nose budge against his thigh, breaking his concentration on the woman before him. He glanced down at Haven, Lucas's PTSD dog, who wasn't afraid to come to the aid of others in the group who needed a reminder not to fall too deep down a hole that would only torture them. Instinctively, he stroked Haven's head while inhaling a deep breath. "I'm sorry, but I can't do it again. We can't be reckless with your life."

"And we won't be," Cal said, trying to gain control of the situation. "Both of you need to hear me out. We can adjust the plan once you've heard it, but until then, I want your lips zipped and your eyes on me. There are a lot of moving parts and we don't have much time with a 6:00 a.m. deadline in front of us. Emotions are charged between you right now. We all feel that, but if you both trust us," he said, emphasizing *both* while holding Reece's glare, "everyone will come out of this alive."

"You have the floor," Reece said to Cal's nod. When Cal turned his back to walk to the whiteboard, Skylar slipped her hand into his and squeezed.

It was the lifeline Reece needed to focus on the plan and get her out of this safely, even if that meant he had to give her up in the end.

Chapter Twenty-One

The sky was starting to lighten ever so much as 6:00 a.m. approached. Storms were rolling in, though, and by the looks of it, they'd made it to the Duluth airport in Cal's helicopter during the calm before the storm. The Secure One team was getting into position at the art gallery and she was sitting on the sidewalk near the hospital, which was well-lit and patrolled by security. The gallery was across the street and down a few blocks but close enough that she could wheel herself to it.

The team wanted her to arrive at the gallery at 5:58 a.m., giving them time to get into place and prevent this criminal from coming in hot before they were prepared. He was surely watching the building, but she had confidence the guys could still infiltrate it without him knowing. Who this was, she still didn't know. With Miles and Silas dead and Camille tied up in the chair, it had to be someone from her past that she wasn't aware had a grudge against her. The idea that someone would do all of this because of money was hard to swallow, even more so if it was someone from their cheer team. Reece had assured her that it wasn't her fault. This rested directly on the shoulders of the person behind the mask, and when he was caught—and they would catch him—he'd answer for his crimes to the fullest extent of the law.

Before they left, Iris had told them that the Facebook page, including all the videos and the petition page, had disappeared. That proved the person behind this knew what they were doing in the digital world and didn't want to leave a trail for the authorities to follow. Unfortunately for them, Secure Watch had multiple backups of all the videos and the petition page. Once this guy was unmasked, he wouldn't wiggle out of this one.

Nervous, Skylar shifted in her chair and checked her watch. It was time to get rolling if she would make her deadline. All she could see was the pain in Land's eyes when he lowered her to her chair when they arrived at the hospital parking ramp. His blue eye was filled with so much hope, while his gray eye was filled with pain, fear and worry. Her demand to do this had cut him deeply and made him bleed again, something she hated but couldn't prevent. Having him back in her life had been fantastic despite the circumstances, but he couldn't remain there. She never wanted to be the reason he hurt again.

You don't think shutting him out of your life again won't cut him deeply?

That voice was back at a time when she needed to hear it the least. To avoid focusing on that thought, she snapped her brakes off and pushed forward, the slight incline distracting her from thinking about anything other than making it to the gallery in time to answer the call from a lunatic she couldn't see and didn't know.

Headlights illuminated the street and nearly blinded her as they came around the corner toward the hospital at a high rate of speed. Someone must be in trouble. Sky turned her head to block the light as she pushed her rims, but she was suddenly snapped backward and flailing in the air. She landed hard on her side as a door slid shut. An engine gunned, and she rolled to the side until her head slammed up against metal to stop her.

"Well, well, who do we have here?" a voice asked. For the first time since all of this began, she recognized it, and her insides gelled.

"Riker in place," Reece said into his walkie.

"Ten-four," Cal answered. "We're in position. Everything is quiet here. We have confirmation on the phone waiting by the loading dock."

"What are the chances that when it rings, the place blows?"

"From what we can tell, there are no explosives inside the building. If there are, they're well hidden."

"It's more likely a bullet will be headed her way once she's in position," Reece ground out, his heart pounding. "I don't like this, Charlie. There are too many variables."

"None of us disagree," he responded. "You need to trust us as much as she trusts you, okay? Love and fear are equally powerful emotions, but you can't let either one take control of the situation."

"Don't believe love was ever mentioned in any context here, Charlie," Reece responded as he watched Sky from his position.

He heard Cal snort softly when he released the button on his walkie. "If you think it needed to be mentioned, then you're more delusional than I thought. You two make more googly eyes at each other than Roman and Mina, and we all thought they were bad. You two are insufferable."

"Charlie?" Reece asked, releasing the button.

"Yeah, Riker?"

"Shut up," he said, then released the button to hear several snickers.

"Secure Watch, Whiskey," Mina broke in. "I hate to break this up, but we have a situation." Mina had stayed at command central to run their coms and keep them abreast of any communication that may come in from this guy. "Charlie, your PD contact just called. They just got the DNA match back on the body thought to be Miles Bradshaw. It's not him."

"What?" Reece asked, leaning forward in the van seat. "I thought he'd already been identified."

"Only using the identification on the body. The face and hands suffered so much trauma they had to run DNA to be sure. The person they found is a known felon from the area who had been living on the streets."

"Dammit!" Reece growled as he noticed Sky snap the brakes off her chair. "The package is on the move. We've got to stop her. This is a trap! Miles has to be the one behind the mask."

"If we stop her, we can't predict what he will do," Cal said, and Reece heard the hesitation in his voice.

"She's cresting the hill," he said. "We don't have much time to decide." He'd barely finished the sentence when a van came around the corner going way too fast. It clipped the curb as it came to a stop, and before his eyes, the occupant pulled Sky from her wheelchair and dumped her into the van before rocketing down the hill.

"Oh, hell no!" he yelled, jamming the SUV into gear and screaming into the walkie-talkie a description of the van. "I'm in pursuit, but I need backup! They're headed to I-35!"

"Stay on them!" Cal yelled as Reece dropped the walkie to put both hands on the wheel. The van ran a yellow at the first set of lights, and he didn't brake. He ran the red, the screech of brakes filling his ears but not breaking his concentration. The next set of lights turned green just as the van reached it and roared through. Reece nearly caught up as they turned past Leif Erikson Park, but the van's brake lights lit up. Then it sailed to the right toward the park, barely missing the giant statute of Leif before it went airborne and soared into the park until it rolled twice and came to rest on the roof near the shore of Lake Superior.

Reece ran toward the van, screaming Sky's name as he drew his gun. The wheels of the van spun in the air as he aimed his gun at the passenger window, expecting to see crumpled bodies where there were none.

"Sky!" When he finally spotted her, she was crumpled against the side of the van on the driver's side. He pulled the sliding door open, the creak and groan of bent metal sending a shiver down his spine.

He caught motion from the side of his eye as someone barreled toward him. Reece raised his arm to block the guy, but he took a punch to his head, knocking him back a step. They tussled, but the other man was no match for Reece, who quickly subdued him after a bit of grappling. He had his knee in his back when Cal ran up with Mack and Eric. Cal slapped a pair of cuffs on the guy before he stood him up then Mack ripped his mask off.

Reece registered the face of Miles Bradshaw before he practically ripped the door off the van and crawled toward the woman he'd loved his entire life, now crumpled in a heap on the roof of the van. "Sky. Angel," he said, gently slapping her face. "Wake up, please. Don't do this to me again. You have to wake up. I love you. Wake up so I can see those beautiful blue eyes of yours fill with anger when I tell you that I love you and I'm never letting you out of my sight ever again. I don't care if that makes you mad. We were meant for each other, and it's time to stop pretending that's not true. Skylar, please." He checked her pulse as he pleaded with her, pleased when it was strong and steady.

"Reece, I need you to move so I can assess her," Selina said, crowding into the space next to him.

"No, I'm not leaving her."

"I didn't ask you to. I need you to move toward her head and hold it carefully to protect her neck while I check her vital signs."

Doing what she asked was easier said than done, but he finally managed to shift himself into the space between Sky's head and the back of the driver's seat. "Come on, angel. Wake up." He heard an ambulance in the distance, and a little of the tension in his belly was released. As if on command, her eyes fluttered open, and she gazed into his with a blank stare for several seconds.

After she blinked twice, she gasped. "Land."

"It's okay, Skylar," Selina said, holding her shoulder so she didn't try to move. "The ambulance is on its way, and they'll take you to the hospital to assess you. Does your neck hurt?"

"No," Skylar said, staring at him with big, round blue eyes. "My neck is fine. I swear the guy who pulled me into the van sounded just like Miles, but he's dead!"

"He's not," Reece said quickly. "His identification was planted on the body, but it wasn't him. We got him. He's cuffed and waiting for the cops."

Sky moaned when Selina pressed on her side. "Something hurts, but I can't tell you what." Selina lifted her hands off her body. "There were two guys. Miles was the one who tossed me inside, but there was a driver. The driver never spoke."

"I'm going to get the EMTs," Selina said, ducking out of the van and leaving Reece to hold Sky steady.

"How did the van crash?" he asked, holding her gaze. He couldn't help but notice her eyes were displaying signs of a concussion.

"I couldn't let them take me, Land. I was afraid if they got too far away, you'd never find me alive. Miles left me on the floor, thinking I couldn't move, and got in the front seat. I pulled myself forward with my arms and grabbed the wheel. We weren't going fast yet, so I thought it would be safe. I didn't realize we'd roll the way we did. I'm sorry. I'm sorry I didn't listen when you told me not to trust them. I should have trusted you."

"Shh," he soothed, kissing her forehead. "You're okay. We've got Miles. As soon as you're in the ambulance, I'll tell Cal about the driver and then meet you at the hospital. Okay? Just stay calm."

Shouting ensued as the EMTs arrived to transport her a few blocks to the hospital. Reece moved aside to give them room to work and pulled Cal aside.

"How's Skylar?"

"She's hurting, but she doesn't know where. It's probably her ribs, but she doesn't have full innervation, so that's making it easier for her to tolerate the pain. She was able to wrestle the wheel from them and crash the van, but the driver somehow got away before I got there."

"That girl has moxie," Cal said with a grin. "Do you think it was Camille?"

"She's the only player left in the game," he agreed. "I have to go to the hospital with her. She's a sitting duck if Camille shows up."

"Go. Don't let Skylar out of your sight. I'll update you about Camille once Miles squeals on his partner."

"If he squeals on her."

"He will," Cal assured him with a wink.

Motioning behind him, Reece sighed. "I hate to leave you with this mess to sort out."

"Go," he said, pointing to the ambulance with his robotic finger. You didn't argue with Cal when he gave a direct order with that finger. "This is child's play compared to the messes I've cleaned up over the last few years. I'll send some guys to the hospital once I can spare them. Keep me updated on your location."

"You got it, boss." He saluted and took off for the van, where they were pulling out the woman he loved on a backboard. He wanted to crumple at the memory of the same scene repeating itself from fourteen years ago, and he tripped, putting his arms out to break his fall when a strong hand grabbed him instead.

"Head in the game, Riker," Cal whispered. "She needs you to keep her calm and be her advocate right now. It'll be hard, but you can fall apart later. Push everything else aside and concentrate on the second chance you've been given."

He took a deep breath in and exhaled on four. "Thanks, Charlie."

Cal slapped him on the back and returned to the team while he headed toward his second chance.

Chapter Twenty-Two

The machines beeped in alternating rhythms and reminded Skylar of all the days and nights she'd spent in the hospital over the years. Today, though, they reminded her that she was a survivor and had saved herself.

She'd been paralyzed with fear when he threw her against the side of the van, but terror had ripped through her when she recognized Miles's voice. He was supposed to be dead, but there he was, taking her only God knew where, and she was the only person who could stop it. She'd used the momentum to slide forward on the cargo van floor toward the driver's seat as they flew down the hill. She'd had one chance to push herself up and grab the wheel. It was a risk and she could have died, but she'd hadn't known Reece was right behind her then, so she'd had no choice. Even lying in a hospital bed with broken ribs and a fractured pelvis, she didn't regret it. She was alive because she took a chance.

If only she could find the same courage to take a chance with Land. Until a few moments ago, he hadn't left her side since they'd pulled her from the van nearly six hours ago. He'd kept in contact with Cal and the team as they tried to find the driver, but so far, nothing. It didn't help that Miles wasn't talking about the identity of his companion. Even when the cops read the list of charges against him, including first-degree murder, he'd refused to answer any of their questions. That was his right, but it wouldn't end well for him. Then again, as far as she was concerned, that was fitting for a man like Miles Bradshaw.

Now that Land had stepped out of the room to take a call from Mina, she thought back to the first few moments in the van when she'd started to come around after the crash. He'd been begging her to wake up by telling her he loved her. He hadn't said it since she opened her eyes, and she wondered if it had just been a ploy to get her to wake up. The thing was, it had sounded sincere to her concussed ears. He'd also looked sincere when she opened her eyes and gazed into his, filled with worry and fear. That emotion she could never name before was also there, and that was the moment she'd realized she could name it. Love. It was love. Somehow, she had to find the courage to open up her soul and say the words back. Let him know she'd heard him and felt the same way.

Skylar had accepted one thing on the short ambulance ride to the hospital with Land holding her hand the whole way. She wanted a chance with him—deserved a chance with him—and nothing else mattered.

There was a knock on the door. "Phlebotomy," a voice said, and she called for them to come in. A man dressed in scrubs stepped inside the room wearing a surgical mask and carrying a tool kit.

"Are you sure you have the right room?" she asked when he set the tub on the bedside table. "Someone just drew my blood about thirty minutes ago."

"I'm positive I've got the right room," he said as he lowered his mask. The man before her had a giant bruise covering the left side of his face, but she didn't need to see that side to recognize him.

"Silas?"

"You act surprised, little sister." He frowned in an exaggerated, scary dipping of his lips. "Let me guess, our mutual friend found the article about my untimely death? I figured if anyone was going to uncover that little tidbit, it would be him. He always stuck his nose where it didn't belong."

This wasn't good. If her brother was in the room, that meant Land hadn't seen him come in or Silas had done something to him.

"Did you hurt Reece?"

Her brother made the same sarcastic snorting sound he'd made since they were kids. "No, I didn't touch a hair on his pretty little head. He was talking on the phone, completely ignoring your room. I'm sure he's tired of all your dramatics by now. God knows I am."

It looked like she would have to be her own hero again, but this time, it would be much harder to beat the man before her. She'd have to keep him talking until she figured out a plan.

"THANKS FOR ARRANGING their flights, Mina," Reece said from the lounge. He had a full view of Sky's door and was watching it, but he didn't want her to overhear him talking to Mina. "I know Sky's mom won't sleep until she has seen her with her own two eyes. We also want to tell them about Silas in person."

"Do you think they'll be surprised to learn he's dead?"

"Logically? No. Emotionally? Yes. They're his parents, regardless of everything that's happened. I think it's fair to say it will still be a gut punch."

"True," Mina agreed. "Lucas stayed behind with Haven. He's on his way to the hospital now to help you keep an eye on Sky's room. When it's time for their flight to arrive, he'll meet them at the airport and bring them to the hospital. We thought Haven might be a useful addition to the party."

Reece sighed and rubbed a hand over his face. "Tell Cal I'm fine."

"Haven is a calming presence when emotions are high and people are facing memories of the past, so we thought he'd be useful when they learned their son was dead. That said, the fact you felt the need to tell me you're fine concerns me."

He shook his head with a smile. "I had a moment after the accident, but Cal was there and set me back on the right path. I'm good now."

"Cal's good at that," she agreed.

"Tell Lucas we're on floor five West. If he texts me when he's in the parking garage, I'll run down and meet him."

"You won't do that. I don't want you to leave her there alone. I've already sent him her room number. He'll meet you there."

"Whatever you say, boss," he said with a smirk.

"Tell Sky we're all looking forward to the day when we can share dinner with her again. Sadie is itching to cook for her to help her heal."

"I'll tell her. Thanks for everything, Mina. You've all gone above and beyond for someone you had never met."

"We didn't need to meet her, Reece. She was yours, which made her ours. That's what makes us Secure One."

"I still feel fortunate to be part of this team." He noticed an orderly with a toolbox in his hand knock on Sky's door before he entered. "It looks like they're back for more blood on Sky. I better go check on her."

"Tell her we're rooting for her. Whiskey, out," she said, and the line went dead before he could respond.

Reece stood and stretched, his back sore from the hours

of sitting once the adrenaline had drained away. The CT scans on Sky had shown broken ribs and a fractured pelvis, not to mention the concussion, but she was going to be okay. They'd keep her in the hospital for at least a week to treat the fractures and prevent bed sores from developing. Once she was released to home, she'd need specially made cushions in her chair and bed that would prevent sores while she finished healing. Despite her osteoporosis, the doctors were confident the fractures would heal well if she took the new medication to promote bone healing and followed their orders. Knowing her injuries wouldn't give her any problems in the future was a relief to hear after the day they'd had.

The one elephant in the room that hadn't been addressed was his declaration of love inside the van. He couldn't be sure she'd heard him, so rather than say anything while she had a head injury and was in pain, he decided to wait until tomorrow—unless she said something today. Cowardly? Yes, but he wasn't ready to deal with Sky trying to push him away again. She would try, but he wouldn't allow it. He just needed a day to be with her without making her angry.

He stood to the side of the door and listened, not wanting to walk in and distract the person with a needle in her arm. They had just drawn blood a bit ago, so it was strange they were back, but in a hospital, you came to expect the unexpected.

"Why, Silas? Why do all this?" he heard Sky ask, and his blood ran cold. Silas? He was dead. Was she dreaming? Was the head injury worse than initially thought?

Ready to run in, he paused when a man spoke and he recognized the voice. "The answer is simple. Revenge. From the day you were born, I spent my childhood in your shadow, and I was the oldest," the man shouted, lowering his voice before he spoke again. "It was really annoying when that accident didn't kill you. I did take great pleasure in knowing you'd never have a normal life and, at the same time, I destroyed the life of Reece Palmer. Honestly, that was the only balm when you survived."

"Wait, you caused the accident that night on the field? How? You weren't driving the golf cart."

Reece pulled out his phone and sent a text with three letters: SOS. Then, he opened his recording app and hit Record before he pulled his gun from his holster.

"See, this is so typical. Everyone thinks I was too stupid to know basic things like how to cut the brake lines on a golf cart. That was child's play, little sis. Then you drug the person driving it and wait for the carnage to ensue."

"You're a monster," she said. Reece heard the sound of skin slapping, and then Sky gasped.

"I am a monster, and now is my chance to finish what I started fourteen years ago. Thank God, as I'm tired of this game."

"Who did you hire to obliterate me from the internet?" Sky asked.

"Again, I'm not as dumb as you all thought I was. You've heard about online classes now, right? They're easy to sign up for with a fake identification, and since you never have to show up to class, no one really knows who's behind that computer. In a matter of a year, I'd graduated with a degree in cybersecurity, just like your little lover boy." He said the words with so much venom it sent a shiver through Reece.

"Were you the one behind the mask in the videos?"

"Iconic, right?" Silas asked as though he should get an Oscar for his performances. "It was such fun. I wanted to make more but, alas, it's time to end this now."

Silas was right about one thing. It was time to end this.

"Stop right there, Silas," he said, swinging into the room with his gun pointed at the man holding a hypodermic needle.

Silas spun in surprise but didn't drop the needle in his hand. "Cripes. Not you again. I should have killed you before I put all this into motion. I never dreamed my baby sister would call you after shunning you for fourteen years, but what they say must be true. Our past always comes back to haunt us."

"Put the needle down and back away from the bed, Silas," he said, walking toward the man who'd grabbed Sky's intravenous line and held the needle near the port.

"I don't think you're in any position to give orders, Reece. Now, put the gun down on the floor and back up. This is between me and my sister. You've got no place here."

He had to think fast if he was going to keep him from injecting whatever was in that syringe into her vein.

"I mean it," Silas growled. "There's enough fentanyl in this needle to kill her three times. Put the gun down."

That was not the answer he wanted. Reece glanced at Sky, who nodded for him to do it, but he caught the way she flicked her gaze down and followed it, noting she had the call button in her hand, her thumb hovering over it. Whatever she was planning, between his SOS and her, maybe they'd get out of this alive. They just had to keep him talking.

"Okay," Reece said, lowering the gun to the floor and kicking it to the edge of her bed, his hands in the air. "You don't want to hurt anyone else here. Where's Camille?"

Silas rolled his eyes but lowered the syringe a hair with the motion. "Wasn't it Gordon Lightfoot who said the Lady of the Lake never gives up her dead?" His laughter was deranged before he spoke again. "She went overboard somewhere between Two Harbors and Grand Marais. The wheelchair and vest full of rocks probably didn't help her float."

"Were you going to kill Miles after he helped you get Sky?"

"Miles." He spat the name like it was poison. "Such a whiny crybaby." He motioned around in the air with the needle. "He was one of those guys who wanted all the credit for doing very little. I'm over here working hard to take care of my problems and he wants to cry about how my sister is better than him. It was sickening. I wish I'd had time to end him earlier, but of course, there you were to save the day again and I had to disappear. He won't last long in prison."

"Neither will you," Reece said, raising a brow. "Especially in the general population. Then again, maybe you'll end up in an institution for the criminally insane. Seeing as how you've killed four people now? At least?"

"Four?" Sky asked, glancing between them. "You mean two, right?"

"Two that we know of," Reece answered. "I'm betting that your grandparents' deaths in Nebraska weren't accidental."

"Well, look at the investigative cojones on Reece Palmer," Silas said, his words dripping with sarcasm. He scrunched up his nose for a moment. "It was almost too easy to knock those two off, but satisfying nonetheless. When I finish here, I'll have to pay Mommy and Daddy dearest a visit."

"You killed our grandparents?" Sky asked, her words dripping with shock and disdain.

"You weren't the one who had to suffer through multiple summers listening to that old windbag go on about how repenting to Jesus was the answer to all my problems. I made sure he met Jesus, that's all." Silas shrugged as though it was completely normal.

The curtain billowed back as a nurse walked in. "I'm here with your…"

The intrusion drew Silas's attention, and Reece took his chance, charging the man, head down, until he slammed into him. They went down to the floor, Reece trying to prevent Silas from stabbing him with the needle. The nurse was at the door screaming for security, and Sky kept screaming his name repeatedly while Silas grunted.

Reece swung at him with his right fist just as Silas moved, and the needle jabbed him between two tendons in his hand. "Night-night," Silas sang right before he hit the plunger. The last thing Reece remembered was the look of terror on Sky's face when she realized what had happened.

Chapter Twenty-Three

"Where's Reece?" Skylar had asked the same question for an hour and a half, but no one would answer. "Lucas!" she exclaimed in frustration as he stood guard at the door of her room.

Haven whined and nudged her hand with his nose until she smoothed a hand over his soft head, each stroke calming her. She drew a deep breath and let it out again, reminding herself it wasn't Secure One's fault that Reece got hurt. That was her fault.

Her room had turned into pandemonium when Silas stuck that needle into Reece's hand. Security had wrestled her brother off Reece while the nurse administered Narcan to the man she loved. EMTs ran in and hauled Reece away before she got a chance to see if Narcan had reversed the effect of the drug. It had been an excruciating ninety minutes waiting to hear if Reece was okay. Added to the worry was that no one could confirm if Camille was actually dead or if she was waiting in the wings for their final swan song.

There were voices in the hallway, and then Lucas spoke. "Haven, return." The dog gave her one last nose boop and then trotted to his handler before they disappeared out the door. Selina walked in with a smile on her face, which, in some way, gave Skylar hope that Land would be all right.

"Hi," Selina said, grabbing a chair and pulling it over to sit by her. "Has anyone given you an update on Reece?"

"No," she answered, her lip trembling. "I don't even know if he's alive."

"He's doing fine," Selina assured her immediately, patting her hand. "They need to observe him a bit longer in the ER before he can be with you. They're currently testing the syringe to see what the drug mixture was that Silas gave him. Narcan reversed it, so it was certainly an opioid, but they're often mixed with other things these days, and it's important to know what. Since it was injected into his hand, they're worried about abscesses or injury to the soft tissue. His hand will be wrapped to prevent infection until they know. I wanted to warn you, but it's just a precaution until they know what drugs Silas gave him."

"My brain is struggling to wrap itself around all of this," she admitted.

"It's probably the concussion," Selina said with a wink. "Bottom line—Reece will be fine in a few hours. He's in the ER yelling about getting back up here, so my medical opinion is he's out of the woods."

Her head was definitely sore after the number of times she'd smacked it on the metal of the cargo van, but that wasn't the problem. "My brother hated me so much that he caused trauma to an entire team of teenagers to get revenge. How do I live with that?"

"Don't forget he changed your life in irreparable ways when he hatched that plan," Selina added.

Forcing back an eye roll, Skylar huffed. "Gee, thanks for the reminder."

The woman beside her bed shrugged. "I like to keep it real, and this is about as real as it gets. You have to know this wasn't your fault, though, right? Your brother had serious mental health issues that caused him to hallucinate things that weren't true and then fixate on them."

"I know what schizophrenia does to the brain, Selina. That doesn't mean I don't feel responsible for every injury and death that's occurred since that day on the field."

"You shouldn't," Selina said firmly. "First of all, he's not your son. He's a sibling who abused you and caused you unbelievable pain and suffering throughout your childhood. Your parents failed you and your brother multiple times over the years, but even they aren't responsible for his choices once he was an adult. They got him help, right?"

"Yes," Skylar agreed. "The gamut, including a stint of inpatient therapy. Nothing seemed to help for very long."

"Not unusual," Selina agreed. "But here's the thing, Skylar. Everything that happened was the result of *his* choices, not yours."

"You're saying I've suffered enough and waging psychological warfare on myself about this is unjust?"

"Yep," she agreed with a wink. "You deserve a little bit of happiness in life. I hope you've found that now and never let it go."

If Selina was talking about Land, she had to be delusional. There was no way he was going to be with her after this. Not only had her family tried to kill him twice, but now everyone in this town would know what Silas had done and how many people he maimed and hurt. She moaned, throwing her hand over her eyes in despair.

"What is it? Are you in pain?" Selina asked, standing from the chair to check her machines.

"No." Skylar moaned the word more than she spoke it. "I realized there's no way I can stay in this town. There'll be a trial, and our skeletons will be paraded around for the world to see. No one will host or buy my art here ever again."

Selina squeezed her shoulder gently. "Maybe it's time for a new name and town then. Just keep an open mind. Remember, you didn't do this and don't carry any responsibility for it. You're the victim and Silas is the perpetrator. The public will see that's true once the trial begins."

Skylar nodded, but it was more for show than agreement. She wasn't sure Selina was right, but she meant well, and for that, she was grateful. "Thanks, Selina. I'll think about that. It sounds like I've got at least a week in this place, so I'll have plenty of time on my hands."

"All of us at Secure One and Secure Watch are proud of you for being your own hero when the chips were down. Not everyone would have been that strong or quick on their feet."

"Or, in this case, quick on their belly," Skylar said, laughter escaping her lips. "I couldn't let them win."

"Because you didn't want to die?"

Skylar tipped her head side to side for a few moments before answering. "Death is always coming for us, Selina. I didn't want to accept it before I had a chance at a life with Land. That's what drove me to grab that wheel. The chance that we could be something despite all the history between us. I might have made a different decision if I knew Silas was behind that mask and all the carnage he'd caused."

"No, you wouldn't have," Selina said, standing and squeezing her shoulder again. "Everyone deserves a chance at happiness in their life, Skylar. When Reece comes to you, please keep an open mind and remember that he doesn't blame you for what happened. You've always been his hero. Today, you reminded him of why. I'm going to check on him, and I'll send Lucas a text with how he is. You get some rest."

"Okay, thanks, Selina," Skylar whispered, waving as

the woman left her room and Lucas took his place outside her door.

Skylar gazed out the window at the lake beyond and sighed. Selina was right. It was time for a new name and town, but they wouldn't include Land. He had suffered enough because of her. Despite their lifelong connection, she couldn't let him throw the rest of his life away. Resolved, she closed her eyes and let the tears fall. They weren't the first ones she'd cried for Reece Palmer, and they wouldn't be the last, but she'd take the suffering if it meant he could be happy. After all these years, he deserved that more than anyone.

It was late when Reece returned to Sky's floor, but he paused at the end of the hallway to look down the hill and out over the lake. It was ironic that he could see the accident site from where he was, but he chose to focus on the thousand-foot laker that was headed into port. It was an iconic image of the Twin Ports and one he'd grown up with, but things were changing, and he had to be willing to change with them.

He pushed the door open to Sky's room and noticed only the small light to the side of her bed was on. It cast a glow across her that reminded him why he always called her his angel. Tonight, seeing her wearing a custom pelvic brace made at her bedside and connected to machines that beeped and hissed, he had never loved her more. From what Selina had told him, he'd have to work hard to prove that to her.

Her eyes were closed and her face was blotchy, and he expected when she opened those sweet blue eyes, they'd be bloodshot from tears. Tears she'd cried over losing him for the second time in her life. That wasn't going to happen. Not on his watch.

"Hi, angel," he whispered, kissing her temple. "I know you're awake, so open those beautiful eyes for me."

"I need to rest," she said, her voice raspy from the tears. "The doctors said I'll heal faster."

With a smile, he pulled a chair over and sat down. "Angel, look at me."

When she opened her eyes, she proved him right, and his gut clenched to know she'd been alone, in pain and crying. He should have been holding her. "Selina said you're going to be okay."

"I am," he agreed as he held up his hand. "The doctors bandaged it with some antibacterial wrap until they know what the drugs were in the needle. I feel fine, so I'm confident all will be well, but I'll wear this until the results return."

"I'm so sorry," she whispered, her chin and lips trembling as she gazed at his hand rather than make eye contact. "I'm so, so sorry."

He couldn't stand the guardrail between them, so he lowered it and slid his hand under hers to hold it loosely. "Sweetheart, stop apologizing. None of this was your fault. Silas is a disturbed individual. He's the very definition of the criminally insane. They've got him on twenty-four-hour suicide watch while they try to find someplace to send him that can handle his extensive needs."

"My parents," she whispered, tears falling from her cheeks. "They're going to be so torn apart by this."

Reece knew they'd be surprised, but more than likely, they'd be more angry than torn apart. Their son had killed his mother's parents. There would be animosity and anger, but Reece knew the love was already gone.

"Your parents are on their way here. I was returning to tell you that Mina had gotten them on a plane to Duluth when the Silas situation happened. They'll arrive in the morning and Lucas will bring them to you. I'll also be here to help answer questions."

"No, you won't be," she said, her voice breaking. "You have to go, Land. You have to go and live your life without me. You don't want any part of the trial that's about to happen, much less to associate with a Sullivan in this town."

This would be tougher than even he'd thought it would be. Once he'd raised the head of her bed, he got a washcloth and wiped her face, letting the warmth soak into her cheeks. After she'd settled again and he'd gotten her a drink of water, he sat on the edge of her bed and took her hand.

"There likely won't be a trial, Sky. It's doubtful they'd find a psychiatrist who would consider him mentally competent."

After taking a calming breath and clearing her throat, she finally held his gaze. "What will happen then? They can't let him go."

"No, Silas will never see freedom again. He'll be sent to a maximum-security hospital for the criminally insane, where he will stay until he's either fit to stand trial or dead."

"That makes me feel slightly better," she sighed. "I don't know that I'll ever get over all the hurt Silas caused, Land. What did I do to make him so angry?" she asked, poking herself in the chest.

"Nothing," he promised, wiping another tear. She'd been through so much the last week, and he just wanted to do anything to make it better for her. "Silas has been sick his entire life. There's no blame or fault to be had here. You have two choices. You can move forward and live your life doing as much good in the world as possible, or you can dwell on the past in a lonely, solitary world. I don't see any justice in the latter, do you?"

Her head shook, but her lips still trembled when she spoke. "No, I don't. The problem is that this will taint my future. No one will buy art from a Sullivan ever again. Not in this town or anywhere."

He tipped his head side to side while considering what she said. "I don't know if that's true or untrue. Some people probably wouldn't, but I would venture to guess that most people won't hesitate. That said, maybe it's time for a change in name and place."

"What, like using my mom's maiden name or something? I suppose I could do that, but finding a new living situation would be tough."

Fishing in his pocket, he pulled out a box. "I had a different name in mind." The box opened, and a diamond solitaire sparkled back at her. "I think Skylar Palmer has a nice ring to it. Always have."

"You— Is that an engagement ring?" she asked, her lips struggling to form the words.

"It is," he said, swiping another tear off her cheek with the bandage on his hand. "The diamond is a bit small, but it's what I could afford fourteen years ago when I bought it. We'll consider it a placeholder until you're well enough to go with me to pick out one you'd like."

"I'm so confused," she whispered. "How did you get a ring when you've been in the ER?"

"Friends," he said with a wink. "Once I explained to Cal how to find it, he was there and back in less time than it should take to get to my house from here."

"Sounds like Cal," she said, and this time her lips were smiling.

"Technically, I should wait until your dad is here to ask his permission, but since he gave that to me fourteen years ago, the same answer probably still applies."

"Wait, what? You were going to ask me to marry you after high school?"

"I was," Reece said with a nod. "See, I love you, Skylar Sullivan. I have for just about forever. That's why I'm sitting here at thirty-one, still single and holding out a ring I bought when I was eighteen. It seemed to me this was always where we'd end up. Then, now, it didn't matter—this was our destiny."

"You've kept the ring all this time?" she asked in awe, her gaze drifting to the box he held up again.

"And I'm glad I did, given where I sit tonight. Skylar Ann Sullivan, will you please marry me? I've wanted nothing more than to love and hold you every day for the last fourteen years. There's no reason to wait another day."

"But, Land, I have to leave town," she whispered, leaning forward slightly from the bed until she remembered her broken ribs. "As sad as it makes me, I can't stay here after all this."

"Well, I did accept a new job today. Okay, a new old job, but it does require me to relocate."

"To a little cabin behind a big security fence?" she asked, her lips tilted upward.

"At least for the foreseeable future," he agreed. "Imagine having a little studio in a place where inspiration is everywhere you turn."

"That's easy to imagine. So is a life with you, Land. Always has been, but I was too afraid that you'd give up opportunities in life because of my disability."

"Angel, I would give up any opportunity for you, because that's what love is. Ask yourself if you'd do the same for me."

"I don't need to ask myself that. The answer is yes. That's why I pushed you away all those years ago and planned to do it again tonight. I love you, Reece Palmer. I've loved you since the first day I met you, but it took me too long to understand that I deserved that kind of love."

"You, more than anyone I've ever known, deserve all the love in the world," he whispered, taking the ring from the box and sliding it onto her finger.

Her brow went up. "I haven't said yes."

"You did," he said, his heart pounding with joy and happiness to see that ring nestled on her finger. "You said, 'The answer is yes,' just a moment ago."

"I meant about if I'd give up the world for you."

"In my opinion, that answered my question."

Sky's smile grew as she gazed at the ring, the lights from above making it sparkle each time she moved her hand. "I like how it looks, but the way it feels is even better."

"How does it feel?" he asked, leaning in to steal a kiss from her lips but pausing so she could answer.

"Like love," she whispered, and he waited no longer to start the first kiss of the rest of their lives.

* * * * *

COLORADO K-9 RESCUE

KATHLEEN DONNELLY

To the love of my life, Jeff.

And in memory of my Mom. Mom, thank you for always encouraging me, helping my dreams take flight and most of all for all your love. I miss you, but I know you're looking down from heaven and you're proud.

Chapter One

The porch was secure. Or so she told herself.

Clouds drifted over the full moon, like curtains with a face peeking through. As Mckenna Parker sat on her back porch in her Victorian mountain house, the smell of one of her neighbors enjoying a fire on their patio wafted through the air.

The July night air was still and hot, almost constricting, although it wouldn't be much longer before temperatures dropped and the first flakes of snow appeared. Give it about six weeks and Mckenna would need a sweatshirt sitting out here—her happy place most of the time. But not tonight.

Next to Mckenna was her black Lab, Mocha, a crisis K-9 for the FBI. The Lab rested on his bed but periodically lifted his head to gaze at Mckenna, asking if she was okay. She let her arm drop and started petting him. Bear-resistant mesh screened in the porch, a dead bolt lock on the door was engaged and the security camera was on. All of it was supposed to make her feel better.

Safe.

But the reality was, even nine years later, the fear could still paralyze her, gripping her in its own way. Like the moon peeking through, Mckenna would try to push away the cloak of fear and peer through it. Often, she could make those around her feel like she had conquered her nightmares, that they no longer scared her, but deep down she knew the truth.

Her family had begged her to go tomorrow. There was a parole hearing for the man who had created this feeling. The man who had changed the course of her life forever and made sure she would never feel secure again. The reason she lied to her neighbors about why she installed the bear-resistant mesh—it would be harder for someone to saw through. Not impossible but harder, and the same reason the door had multiple locks and the camera sat strategically placed to catch anyone trying to break in.

He'd been in prison the last eight years, but it didn't matter that there were bars and guards and razor-top wire between them. People escaped from prison more than anyone wanted to admit. Mckenna knew. She'd joined her sister, Cassidy, at the Denver FBI Office as a victim specialist, and they were both aware of the reality. The kicker was, Mckenna had never been able to fully liberate herself from her own prison even though she was the one who was supposedly free.

That was why she'd become a victim specialist. Other victims needed support and she felt like she could help. She understood the emotions. In her family's opinion, unless Mckenna did what they wanted her to do—speak at the parole hearing and ask the board to make her captor serve the full sentence—she wouldn't feel safe. The thing was, for her, what was the difference between him being free now or in two years? Mckenna shivered and Mocha stood, putting his head in her lap, feeling the change in her. "I should go ask the board to make him serve the full sentence, shouldn't I?"

Mocha gave a little whine and put his front paws in her lap, climbing up so he could kiss her face.

"Thanks, buddy," Mckenna said, holding her dog.

Busy work schedules made it easy to avoid her sister for two weeks until Cassidy caught her in her office. Mckenna stared down her sister. Cassidy drummed her fingers on Mckenna's desk and didn't break her gaze. Of course, she never would, because Cassidy was tough as nails and one of Denver's top FBI agents and K-9 handlers for a reason.

"So, explain to me again why you decided to ditch us all at Toby Hanson's parole hearing?" Cassidy bent forward, getting closer to Mckenna. "We were all there to support you. Me. Mom. Dad. Everyone. But you didn't show. Maybe if you'd been there, he'd still be sitting in prison and not out free, where he can commit the same crime again."

Mckenna leaned back in her chair. She was the younger sister and Cassidy had always been protective. It was worse now. She heard the thumping of a tail and gazed down into Mocha's brown eyes. Mckenna couldn't imagine life without him. In fact, in her mind, he was the only guy she needed. He was handsome and never complained about having the same dinner every night. He wasn't upset that she didn't attend a parole hearing and he loved her no matter what. There were no guys out there like that. Mocha smacked a paw on Mckenna's arm, and she answered Cassidy.

"Toby Hanson is a part of my past. I've moved on from what happened."

Even as Mckenna spoke, a shiver went down her spine. Had she moved on? That night changed the direction of her life, creating a before and after for her at only eighteen years old.

"Thank you all for going there, for being there for me," Mckenna said. "But I need to get on with my life and sitting in a parole hearing wouldn't have helped with that. Plus, didn't you say that Toby has a great probation officer? The guy will be so on top of Toby, he won't even be able to use the bathroom without the PO knowing. Or something like that?"

Cassidy rolled her eyes. "Yes, he was assigned Keith Warren and he's good."

"Warren? Didn't he grow up in our town?"

"Yeah, he left in middle school. I heard his parents moved, but he eventually came back to Colorado."

"Well, then I have nothing to worry about," Mckenna said, trying to figure out how to get her sister to leave so she could get back to her work and move on from this event. *I should have gone and given a statement at the hearing. Now my nightmare is out, walking around, all because I let fear overcome me.*

She was getting ready to tell Cassidy that she needed to buckle down and get some paperwork done when a cry of "Parker!" came from outside her office.

Mckenna and Cassidy glanced at each other.

"Which one of us is being summoned by him?" Cassidy asked just as Mckenna noticed that Mocha had gone AWOL.

"Crap. Me."

Mckenna leaped out of her chair and darted outside her office. She heard another yell of "Come get your dog."

Sprinting down the hall, she slid around the corner to find Mocha proudly licking his lips in the office of an agent who'd been recently transferred—Agent Evan Knox.

Agent Knox had been the talk of the office. First, it was because he was ruggedly handsome, with his perfectly disheveled blond hair and eyes the color of the Colorado blue sky. Every female was ogling him. Then, though, the talk had turned to the fact that he was difficult to work with, gruff, and kind of a lone wolf.

He worked long hours and Mckenna could tell he'd even stayed at the office to pull all-nighters at times. He also had recently told her that he didn't think the victim team was very helpful and only stood in the way of his work. Mckenna had told him that someday, he would eat his words. She'd gone home furious that night; no matter how handsome the guy was, he was a jerk and she hoped she never had to work with him.

Ever.

Mocha seemed to have missed this recent memo analyzing the new agent. He sat on his hindquarters and stared hopefully into Agent Knox's flushed red face.

"Your dog ate my sandwich."

Mckenna stifled a laugh and worked on appearing serious. "What? Is this a federal offense? Are you going to arrest him? Do we need a lawyer?"

Agent Knox stared at her. She was making a joke out of this, and he didn't look like he appreciated it. "You're not taking this very seriously, are you? You really need to work on your dog's training."

With a sigh, Mckenna pulled a ten-dollar bill out of her pocket. "Here. I'm sorry. He snuck out of my office. Does this cover the cost of your late lunch? Dinner? Whatever it is?"

Knox shrugged.

"I'll make sure it doesn't happen again. I can go get you another sandwich if you'd like."

"No, I don't need another sandwich, but you better hope this never happens again. And find someone to help you train him."

Now Mckenna was annoyed.

"What makes you the expert on dog training?" she fired back.

"My father was a K-9 handler for the local police where I grew up. He taught me everything he knew."

"And you never had a dog misbehave or have a moment where they stole food? Your dogs were always perfect?"

Knox put his hands on his hips. "Just keep a better eye on your dog."

"Can't answer that, can you? I'm sure your dogs messed up. And don't worry, I will keep a better eye on Mocha. I've been a bit...a bit distracted." Mckenna glanced down at the carpet, thinking about Toby walking free. The only way she knew how to cope was to continue with her life. Her work—helping other victims. If she didn't know better, she could have sworn that Agent Knox's face softened a little bit. But it didn't matter. She could see the edge that kept everyone away from him. God help her if she was assigned a case where she had to work with him.

Chapter Two

Agent Evan Knox watched Mckenna and Mocha leave. He was annoyed about his sandwich—it had been a long day, and he hadn't had much to eat—but luckily there wasn't anything on it that would be poisonous to Mocha, like onions. He knew he'd snapped at Mckenna, and felt bad about that. It would only add to his reputation. One he knew he'd earned, but at this point he didn't care.

The other day, he'd heard the water cooler gossip where other agents and a few secretaries were discussing how hard he was to work with. Evan didn't want to be that difficult, but after what had happened to him in his previous field office, he didn't trust anyone. He didn't want to get burned again. What had happened before could have cost him his job, and without his job he was nothing.

He caught Mckenna talking with her sister, Cassidy, and they both gazed his way. He shuffled some papers on his desk to look busy and then picked up the ten-dollar bill Mckenna had given him.

What kind of person are you, Knox? It's not like you can't afford another sandwich. She's a nice person. You know that. You've seen her enough around the office.

He'd give the money back later.

He glanced again toward the two women. There was

something about the victim specialist that made him look twice. She had a vulnerability but at the same time was strong, like she'd overcome something in her past. He'd seen the same traits in other victims he'd worked with. There was a power unique to someone who had overcome trauma. And Mckenna had that power. That and those gorgeous sea blue eyes that stood out against her dark, almost black hair.

"Don't go down that road," he muttered to himself. "Just focus on your job, solve some big cases and work toward the promotion you've always wanted."

A few minutes later, Mckenna came back out of her office with Mocha, waving at other agents in the office and saying good-night. He stared a second longer than he should have, and she caught him looking at her. Agent Parker, her sister, was the classic beauty, but Evan couldn't help studying Mckenna for a little bit longer.

She wasn't an agent and in fact he wasn't sure he believed in her job or the job her dog was meant to do. The FBI wasn't touchy-feely. They were there to solve crimes, but the strength and determination on Mckenna's face made him wonder what she had overcome. What was her past? Had something happened that pushed her down the career path of a victim specialist? He wanted to know more and as she and her Lab headed out the door, he couldn't help but see how perfect her body was—at least to him.

He hadn't felt that in a while, but the last thing he needed was a female in his life. Or anyone else for that matter. He just needed to keep his head down, work hard, solve cases and put the bad guys away.

Maybe if he did that long enough, he'd accomplish his goals. He'd wrapped up some cases this week, and for once, he might get out of the office early. Then what? His work was his life. Maybe a run in the foothills and then dinner, since he had missed his late lunch. After that, home to an empty, barely decorated house. Maybe he'd call one of his sisters or something, although they'd lecture him about getting a life. *I'm not in the mood.*

Evan's phone rang. It was his boss, and he was being summoned to his office.

Hopefully, Mckenna hadn't complained about him. That was all he needed.

EVAN COULD TELL by the look on his boss's face that he wasn't going on a run anytime soon. His boss, Adam Clark, the special agent in charge or SAC, was on the phone and waved at him to come in. Evan leaned against the wall, arms crossed, and waited for his boss to get off the phone. After a few more "yeahs" and "I'll send Special Agent Knox tonight," Adam hung up. Evan waited to be filled in. It looked like his plans for the evening would be all work. He didn't mind. He'd rather work.

"That was Sheriff Charlotte Stewart. There are two girls that have gone missing in her jurisdiction. She has a large mountain county but a small department. They don't usually deal with anything like this and the girls have been gone about forty-eight hours now, so the chances of finding them alive are diminishing. I told her you'd go up there tonight and help. We will provide her department any resources we can. I'm also calling in our victim unit and sending Mckenna Parker and her K-9 to help with the families…"

"Sir, if I can say something," Evan interjected.

"Yes?"

"I don't know if it's a good idea to have Mckenna Parker and her K-9 meet with the families until I can talk with them."

"Agent Knox, you're talented, you're driven, you're everything the FBI wants, but think outside the box. The victim services response team has grown. There's almost three hundred people on that team now, including former agents. Why? Because the FBI has learned that it helps. They are an important piece to helping families out, and if we can offer support, they will be better witnesses. We have a greater chance of convicting people like human traffickers. For all we know, it's scum like that who took these girls. Get over it and do your job. Mckenna Parker will do hers. And maybe we'll get lucky and find these girls alive."

"Yes, sir," Evan said, as Adam handed him the address of the sheriff's department. It wasn't that he minded a victim specialist helping. Then why had he argued?

Admit it. It's this particular one that's the problem. She bothers you in a way that you can't handle.

It was going to be a long night.

Mckenna and Mocha had arrived home when her work phone rang. She answered quickly. It was her boss, Marcia Jackson, the Administrative Assistant Special Agent in Charge, giving her orders for a new assignment. Mckenna wasted no time loading Mocha back into the car to get to work. All cases were important, but this one even more so. This one felt personal.

A little while later, after navigating the back mountain roads, they pulled up to a large mountain home with a deck that overlooked a breathtaking view to the west. Mount Blue Sky sat above the other peaks. She'd never driven on the highest paved road in North America to the top of the fourteener, but that was on her bucket list. She'd seen pictures of the shaggy white mountain goats that lived up there and would love to capture some pictures of them too. In reality, she knew she wouldn't go—especially now that her captor walked free. Hiking on her own was not a good idea and only created more crippling fear. *I have to get over feeling apprehensive, but I don't know how. One of these days, I'll make myself go on my own and start hiking without worrying.*

It's not as if he's really out there waiting for me...but what if he is?

Taking a deep breath and focusing back on why she was at this house, Mckenna wrapped her fingers around Mocha's leather leash. She reached over and straightened his vest that identified him as a crisis K-9 for the FBI. Her family's ranch wasn't too far from here—a ten-minute drive. While she loved the mountains and lived in Idaho Springs, another small mountain town about twenty minutes from Denver, she didn't like coming to this area that was once home. It only brought up memories. This case would make it near impossible to block her thoughts about Toby Hanson walking free.

Is there any way he had taken these young ladies? Probably not.

Unfortunately, there was a good chance that someone had been grooming the girls and managed to kidnap them for human trafficking. That tragedy was happening more and more often. Even young adults could fall victim.

That was why she was here. She understood. Mckenna's experience not only made her resilient, but it was also why she was doing this work. With her own case, she'd been assigned a victim advocate who helped her learn her rights, including speaking in court and gaining access to reports. Mckenna knew what it was like seeing law enforcement move onto their next case while the victim dealt with what happened to them for the rest of their lives.

Now she was doing the same thing after going to school

and working her way into the FBI victim services response team program. Mckenna loved the feeling of giving back and helping victims have the epiphany that they could overcome what happened to them. Mocha sat next to her and gazed at her longingly. He'd been requested because the families of the two girls loved dogs. Her boss thought Mocha could help with the situation. Mckenna agreed. In her mind, her dog was a superstar and the best employee in the Denver office.

Even if he did eat an agent's sandwich.

Chapter Three

She'd been given orders to wait for Agent Knox and the sheriff to arrive. She and Mocha stayed outside enjoying the cooler air rolling in as the sun started to set behind the mountains, casting rays up onto the clouds and creating an orange hue. Mckenna turned toward the light and closed her eyes, enjoying the heat across her face. Something so simple, and yet something she never took for granted anymore.

Tires crunching on gravel made Mckenna open her eyes and turn around. The sheriff's vehicle parked next to hers followed by the stereotypical black SUV, or "bu-car," as she'd heard the agents call it, with Agent Knox inside. Mocha gave a happy whine and wagged his tail.

"Be cool," Mckenna said. "You may not be forgiven yet. What got into you today?"

Mocha tilted his head and Mckenna massaged his floppy black ears, receiving a happy sigh in response. The newly elected sheriff stepped out of her vehicle and Mckenna waved. She didn't know Charlotte or "Charlie" well, but she'd heard good things.

The other sheriff had overseen Mckenna's case, and she always suspected that he'd only wanted the limelight. He loved nothing more than giving press conferences and telling everyone how *he'd* solved Mckenna's kidnapping. Something about him always rubbed her the wrong way and she hated it when she had to speak to him about her case.

Agent Knox took off his sunglasses and stared at her for a moment. Mckenna did her best not to lock gazes, but then decided why not? She wasn't going to back down. An FBI agent didn't scare her. Not after what she'd been through in her life. Putting a hand on her hip, Mckenna gazed back, vowing to make him break eye contact first. She hated to admit it, but it wasn't hard to keep looking at him. "Rugged good looks" was one description that crossed her mind.

She would bet money that he was ripped and in good shape. Probably worked out every day. Nope, he wasn't hard to look at, and for a second today, he'd seemed almost nice. Maybe there was more to him than everyone thought. Or maybe not. She'd heard he was unshakable when defense attorneys grilled him in court and that he'd closed some good cases, but there was supposedly one that went wrong. That was the case that preceded his transfer to the Denver office. That could explain his tough-guy persona.

Agent Knox strolled toward them, and Mocha started wagging his tail. Was that a small smile on Knox's face? It only happened for a fleeting second, but Mckenna could have sworn that the tough-guy exterior broke for a moment. To her surprise, Agent Knox came up to her, "Parker."

"Knox."

"Sorry I yelled at you and your dog earlier. Here's your ten bucks back. I appreciate your thought, but you were right, he was being a dog. Typical Lab trying to eat everything. You might need your ten bucks to replace other things he eats."

Mckenna didn't know what to say, but she took the money and shoved it into her front pants pocket. "Thanks."

They all headed up to the front of the house. Before they could ring the doorbell, a pale, thin woman opened the door.

"Hi, Ms. Hendrix," the sheriff said. "Thank you for meeting us tonight. I know this is hard, but this is Agent Knox and he's going to be helping with this case. We're fortunate he's involved. The FBI's resources will be a big help."

"Thank you," Ms. Hendrix said, stepping inside. "Please come in and just call me Brenda. I'm Lily's mother. Autumn's parents and little sisters are inside. Autumn is Lily's best friend, so we're all like family. We've known each other since the girls were in grade school together."

Mckenna would guess that she was normally quite attractive, but the stress of the situation was already taking its toll. And this was the beginning. Mckenna's mom had told her about not being able to sleep, the worry, the crying and the anger—the strain on the entire family.

They all sat down, and Autumn's two younger sisters asked to pet Mocha. Mckenna gave them permission and they squealed with delight as he licked their faces. For a moment they could forget that their sister and her friend might not be coming home.

She heard Agent Knox take the lead in asking questions, but one of the fathers interrupted. "I want to hear from her. I want to know what she thinks."

Mckenna realized that he was pointing in her direction. Everyone was staring at her, and she froze. What did he mean he wanted to hear from her?

"Sir, I don't understand," said Agent Knox.

"I don't either," said Mckenna. "What do you want to know from me?"

"You're, you're that girl who was kidnapped, but you came home. You survived. My daughter can survive, right?"

Mckenna swallowed hard…memories of her own night-mare, when she had become a victim, came flooding back.

I had been to a party. Drank hard, had a good time, had been saying goodbye to my high school years before I was about to go to college. Getting Cassidy to cover for me at home with Mom and Dad, the big sister telling me to be careful, but have fun.

Then nothing.

Until I woke up and didn't know where I was. My shoes and jacket were gone. I was in an old building. I could hear a creek and there was a terrible smell—like rotten eggs. I huddled in the corner, shaking, wondering when my parents would realize I wasn't home. Would Cassidy be in trouble for covering for me? She didn't really know where I was going. I only told her about a party. But I left out the part about it being a secret party that only a few kids knew about.

He came into the room where I was. I was already crying, but the fear made me start sobbing. He'd come over and crouched down, a mask over his face. He'd taken a finger and wiped away my tears. Then he'd said, "Don't worry, sweetheart. I'm going to let you go. I promise. There's nothing better than a good game of catch and release."

There was a water bottle that he left behind. I drank some of the water and fell asleep again. When I woke up it was early morning and there was a window. I took an old chair in the room and hit the window until it broke.

I shimmied out and gashed my side, but I didn't care. I'd run track in high school and at this moment, I knew I had to run hard and fast—this was the race for my life. There were weird trees, but I couldn't stop to comprehend what made them odd. My feet pounded and I heard laughing. I think he was on an ATV, shooting and coming after me. I slipped and then changed direction. I didn't know where I was going but I knew if I had any hope of surviving, I had to hide until he gave up looking.

But who was she to say if their daughter would or wouldn't come home? How could anyone answer that question?

"We have no idea if your daughter's case is like mine," Mckenna gently answered. She could see the fear in his eyes. The waves of anxiousness sweeping through his body. Brenda cried and folded her hands in her lap. They wanted to hear an answer Mckenna couldn't guarantee. The other girl's parents stared blankly. When a trauma occurred, reactions were so different for everyone.

The father spoke again, "We want to know what your experience was like. What are they going through right now? How scared are they? We need answers. Your kidnapper was just released. Do you think it could be him?"

"Sir." Mckenna gathered her wits and found the deep spot inside her where she had discovered strength before. "I can't answer those questions. This isn't about me. This is about your daughters—" she glanced at her notes "—Lily and Autumn. This is about bringing them home. You need to let the sheriff and Agent Knox interview you and your family. I'm here as a victim specialist. I'm here to help you with resources so you can learn more about your rights. I'm not here to tell you about my personal experience. Please, let Agent Knox ask you some questions."

Mckenna thought the man would argue, but he nodded and turned and waited for Agent Knox to speak. Silence filled the air and then Agent Knox cleared his throat. Mckenna caught him staring at her again, only this time there was a look of curiosity on his face. That's the way it always was with guys.

They became curious when they found out that she was

"that girl" from a *Dateline* or *20/20* episode. She'd discovered the hard way that the interest in her wasn't about her as a person, but rather to have an inside look at a terrible story. It was almost odd to Mckenna that she had gained celebrity status for a while. She'd worked hard to "disappear" and not be hounded by the media.

Agent Knox now gazed at her as if he recognized Mckenna. She didn't like it and, apparently, Knox was no different from everyone else. To them she was a specimen to be studied rather than a human being.

He thought of her as another case. One he could learn from or something. She'd encountered that too. Law enforcement always wanted to use her case to "teach" officers better response tactics. Mckenna was sick of it and vowed she would have very little to do with the agent once this case was over.

For now, she was stuck with him.

Chapter Four

Evan had to tear his eyes off Mckenna and focus back on the investigation and the questions he needed answered. From what the sheriff had told him, he doubted the families knew much about the abduction, but anything he could learn about the two girls would help. The sheriff had mentioned the girls had grown up in the community, graduated from the local high school with honors and completed their first year of college. They were home for the summer and getting ready to leave in a couple of days to go back to school for the fall semester.

But what was all this about Mckenna Parker being kidnapped? He never was into office gossip, but this time he regretted it. Maybe if he opened up more, he would know more about Mckenna. He found himself intrigued. This revelation explained so much about her. He forced himself to get back to the interview.

He flipped open his memo book and started with the usual questions. When did they last see the girls? Where were they going? What were they doing? Did they know of anyone contacting them through social media? Had they ever run away before?

The families gave the usual answers. They were good

kids and students. Autumn was a great older sister. She and Lily didn't stay out too late and all that jazz. Evan had heard it all before and, unfortunately, he knew from experience that once he started digging, there was always something the family didn't know. There could be someone grooming them on social media, or they could be dating someone who had ulterior motives. Usually, the victims went from low-risk "good girls" to higher-risk "we didn't know our daughters were doing that."

He just had to dig.

As Evan and the sheriff finished up their questions, he saw the younger siblings had become tired and were now lying with Mocha on the floor. The black Lab had curled up next to them and even had a paw softly resting on one child's arm. Evan resisted smiling; he needed to keep up his "agent face" as he called it, but Mocha reminded him of his childhood Lab. The dog was loyal and would have followed him anywhere. Evan's father had taught him skills like tracking and finding narcotics with the Lab. Evan had loved every moment of it. And while Mocha wasn't a working dog but rather a service dog, he still brought back good memories.

They headed out into the night. The sun had disappeared behind the mountains, but rays of light still illuminated the peaks. Evan had never seen the West or the mountains until his dad and sisters moved to Colorado. The scenery still filled him with awe. Leaning up against his vehicle, he waited for Mckenna and Mocha to come out. He wanted to know more about her and her past. Did the vulnerability mixed with strength he sensed come from her experience? Or was she just like that? There were so many questions he had.

She stepped out of the doorway, closing it behind her,

and walked with Mocha down the stairs to where the cars were parked. She seemed lost in thought and then looked startled, seeing him still standing there.

"I didn't know you were still here," Mckenna said. "I figured you'd be off on the next interview saving the world or whatever it is you do."

Evan let out a small laugh and then stifled it. He didn't know what was wrong with him. Mckenna brought out a different side of him. Something that hadn't existed for a long time. Part of him liked it and part of him didn't.

"I wanted to ask you about your experience. This kidnapping deal. Tell me more."

The smile and twinkle in her eyes instantly disappeared and her expression darkened.

"I thought maybe it would help this case to know more, that's all," Evan said, stumbling over his words. He usually felt like he was tough and in charge, but she made him question that. "I want to know more about you."

"This kidnapping deal." Such an ignorant thing to say. Mckenna ignored him and strode to her vehicle, pulling out portable stairs and helping Mocha load into the crate in the back. She closed the tailgate and started the car while standing outside her vehicle so she could turn on the air-conditioning for Mocha. Even though the night was cooling off, it was still August, and the car could get too warm. Evan admired how well she took care of her dog. Minus the sandwich incident of course.

"Agent Knox, I don't know why you want to know more about my past and what happened to me, but I'm used to it. Everyone wants to know the gory details. What was it like escaping? What was it like running for your life while someone was shooting at you? How did you dodge the bullets? I've answered those questions enough for television. I shouldn't have given them any interviews. I've sat through hours of law enforcement interviews. My past is that, it's my past. My future is helping others because when you're done with this case and it goes through court, you'll already be working on the next case. There will always be a next case for you. My job is to help the family because there is no next case for them. For them, their lives have permanently changed, and right now, those parents in there don't know how drastically it will change, even if their daughters come home alive."

"I'm sorry, I didn't mean…" Evan started to say, but Mckenna cut him off.

"We both know the probability of those girls coming home alive is low. It doesn't happen often. There's not too many of 'us' and our cases are rare, but no matter what, life as the family or the victim knows it is shattered. They must pick up the pieces one by one and start putting their lives back together. There's a chance those pieces will get shattered over and over again. My past doesn't play into that. My past won't help them other than the fact I understand them. But my job and Mocha's job is to be there every time those pieces get shattered again. Have a good night."

Mckenna turned and climbed into the front seat of her vehicle. Evan watched her drive away. For once in his life, he was speechless, which was good, because her reaction was right—what he'd said had been stupid and insensitive. He rubbed his face with his hands. Everything about Mckenna piqued his interest. He wanted to know more. He wanted to spend time with her.

And that was the last thing he needed.

There was a reason his job was his life. There wasn't room for anyone else, not after everything that had happened. She was right. He needed to investigate this, help the sheriff, figure out who took these girls and then move on to the next case after someone was arrested. If someone was arrested.

But he couldn't get Mckenna Parker out of his mind.

Chapter Five

It was late, but Evan headed back to the office rather than home. He wouldn't be able to sleep, and the things Mckenna said had resonated with him. Whatever happened with this case, he'd be assigned another one. Not that there were cases where you didn't work tirelessly seeking a resolution, but there was always, unfortunately, another case. For the victim of a crime, there was only their case. He hadn't thought about it that way before.

He was also curious about Mckenna and why one of the victims' father had asked if her kidnapper might be the one who took his daughter. Evan parked and went into the building. It was quiet, which was the way he liked it. Getting to his office, Evan booted up his computer and let his thoughts about the case wander while he waited for the screen to come to life.

Finding out more about Mckenna and her kidnapper was his intent. Maybe he was wasting time, but the victim's father wanted to know if a guy convicted of kidnapping out on parole could be on the hunt again. Evan sought an answer to the same question. As of now, there were no suspects, but the jaded side of him thought that offenders often repeated their crimes.

And he was curious about Mckenna and her past. He should have let it go with her, but he couldn't.

The screen came to life and Evan started searching for Mckenna's case. It wasn't hard to find on the internet. He could get the case files too, but for now he wanted to know the basics.

There were headlines about her being found alive. A good Samaritan had seen her running down a road and stopped to help. She'd been bleeding and dehydrated, but otherwise, considering she'd been kidnapped and was missing for three days, she wasn't in bad shape. He continued scrolling. The sheriff zeroed in on Toby Hanson quickly after an anonymous tip led to Mckenna's jacket and some other belongings being found in his vehicle. After a lengthy interrogation, Hanson had confessed.

He'd been sentenced to eleven years in prison and now he was out in eight for good behavior. There were pictures of the man being released a couple of weeks ago, walking out of prison.

Evan sat back in his chair feeling for Mckenna and the terror she must have suffered. Today was incredibly hard for her and he'd treated her callously. In fairness to him, he hadn't known about her past, but still, like the office gossipers pointed out, he could be a little nicer.

Rubbing his eyes, Evan flipped open his memo book and readthrough the notes on the current kidnapping. He took out a pad of notepaper and started reworking the notes. Evan was a big believer in victimology. The more he could figure out about the victims of the crime, the easier it often was to zero in on a suspect. Hopefully, these girls hadn't been trafficked. If that were the case, they might not ever be seen again. Or if they were found, they would never be the same.

He'd tried to force out the memories of going undercover to help bust a trafficking ring, but there were things in life he couldn't unsee. Those memories gave him both daymares and nightmares. He had to find these girls before it was too late.

Lily and Autumn. Evan preferred to call the victims by their names. It made it more personal, which was great when cases were solved, although harder when they weren't. He scribbled down a list of questions on his notepad.

Could the suspect be someone they know? Could they have been drugged? Groomed online? Followed? Will there be a ransom? And the last question Evan circled, *How were they forced or talked into complying?*

Taking one person by force was tougher than television ever portrayed it. In real life you didn't just grab someone very easily unless that person was outnumbered or incapacitated. Even though Evan thought of the victims as girls, they were adults. Not small children. For two girls that would mean several suspects, or they were drugged. Depending on what was used, it would be hard to lift them both and move limp bodies from point A to point B, but if there were drugs that would make it possible.

Evan circled the question about being drugged.

Could they have known their attacker? Was there any chance the girls did just take off somewhere even though their parents denied it? No, Evan didn't believe that based on the evidence. The sheriff might run a department that was smaller, but she knew her stuff. He had to agree, it did appear to be a kidnapping. Back to the trafficking possibility, which meant he needed access to all their social media and their posts prior to being taken.

He couldn't do anymore tonight. Should he even bother going home? Or should he catch some sleep on the break-room couch like he'd done other nights? Evan elected the break-room couch. Home at this moment would only seem cold and empty.

EVAN STIRRED EARLY the next morning and rolled off the couch. No one had arrived yet and he needed coffee. Starting a pot, he went to his office to see if he had a fresh shirt. He didn't. There were two more dirty shirts hanging on a coatrack behind his desk. He supposed he better go home at some point. Or take these shirts to the dry cleaners.

Hearing the coffeepot chime that it was done brewing, he poured himself a cup that said "G-man." One of his sisters had bought it for him when he'd been accepted into Quantico.

Sipping on the hot coffee and letting the caffeine hit his system, he started a to-do list for the morning. He'd put in a request with their tech person to start getting information off the girls' phones and social media. Then he typed up a warrant and shot it off to a judge hoping that the judge was an early riser and overachiever too.

Was Evan an overachiever? Or did he just not have a life? Or was he just avoiding his family and friends like his sisters all claimed? Those were questions he didn't want to think about. He headed back to the break room to get his coffee when he heard the door open and close. The jangling of dog tags told Evan who was coming in and he felt a sudden urge to go say hello and offer Mckenna a cup of coffee. *What's wrong with me?*

He figured it was better if he stuck with his MO—stay at his desk working and pretend like he didn't know anyone else was there. That would have worked in theory, except he peered up and sitting by his door was Mocha wagging his tail.

"Looking for another sandwich?" Evan asked. "I don't have any food this morning."

Mocha thumped his tail on the ground and then lay down, rolled over and exposed his tummy to be rubbed. Evan glanced around and didn't see Mckenna or anyone else. He set his coffee down, went over to the dog and then crouched down and complied with Mocha's request for a belly rub. Mckenna came around the corner, catching the two of them.

"Looks like you two made up," she said with a laugh. Then her face straightened again.

She's still upset over our conversation last night.

Evan shrugged and tried to focus on Mocha. Mckenna smelled like a mixture of shampoo and bodywash. He liked it when she laughed rather than her serious face. Becoming aware of that only concerned him more. He really needed to get a grip.

Just get promoted and then get out of this office. You know how relationships end, from your own parents. You have no time to mess around. Look how Mom hurt Dad and all of us kids. Being a lifetime bachelor with a few flings here and there and no commitment is not a bad thing.

And yet, he found himself hoping she might stick around and talk a little bit.

"Here," Mckenna said, holding out a brown paper bag in one hand and a cup in another. "I appreciate you giving me my cash back, but Mocha did eat your sandwich yesterday. We bought you a breakfast sandwich and coffee. I don't know if you like lattes, but that's what that is. Forgiven?"

"Forgiven," Evan said, standing up straight. "Thank you. You didn't have to do that."

Mckenna waved him off and gave a low whistle. Mocha jumped to his feet and went to her side.

"Look, uh," Evan stuttered. Why couldn't he talk to her?

You're an FBI agent. You've interrogated dangerous criminals. Get your act together.

He'd been around plenty of beautiful women, and many had hoped to earn their Mrs. title with him. But his career came first and none of his past girlfriends had stuck around with his job and hours. Plus, after his mom left his dad, he knew there was no such thing as real love. But he wouldn't mind talking with Mckenna. Learning more about her. He heard himself saying, "I'm sorry about yesterday, about asking you about your uh, experience. If this case is tough for you, I understand. Just let me know what you need from me."

Mckenna tilted her head, her dark hair touching one side of her shoulder. What would it be like to touch her cheek? Run his fingers through her hair? Wrap his arms around her and then run his fingers under her shirt. *Good grief, get a grip. She thinks you're a jerk and isn't even interested.*

"Thanks. I appreciate that," she said. "Well, I better get to work. Let me know if you need us today for anything. By the way, if you're going to spend the night here, you should bring extra shirts. You're a bit wrinkled this morning."

Slightly annoyed, Evan put his hands on his hips. This was another reason he didn't need a female in his life. But then he noticed that she had a glimmer of a grin and when she laughed again, he realized she was teasing him. "Good point."

"I'm just giving you a hard time. I know how it is when you can't sleep," Mckenna said. Then her expression became more serious, "I hope you can find out more about those girls today. I'm scared for them."

This is where you could say something nice, Knox. Instead, Evan heard himself answering, "I'm going to head back up to the sheriff's office today and interview their friends. I'll keep you posted."

I'll keep you posted? Where did that come from? Yes, they were working together on this case, but telling someone he'd keep them posted wasn't his style. Evan's phone rang and he saw it was the sheriff calling. Answering, he turned away from Mckenna slightly, and when the sheriff filled him in, his blood went cold. His plans for the day drastically changed.

Chapter Six

When Agent Knox's phone rang, Mckenna was going to head to her office, but his expression changed to concern. She hesitated, thinking about her interaction with him. After cooling off last night, she had decided she was being too hard on him. He didn't seem so bad. Maybe a bit serious, and he hadn't realized she was kidding him about the shirt. Mckenna knew that he seemed to crash on the couch in the break room more than he went home, but that wasn't any of her business.

And the apology for the incident yesterday with Mocha? Maybe there was a nicer side to the office grouch. But right now, she could tell that whoever was on the phone was delivering tough news. Agent Knox hung up and snatched his keys off his desk.

"What's going on?" Mckenna asked, knowing that most of the casework the agents did wasn't any of her business, but she could tell that Agent Knox was bothered.

At first, she didn't think he was going to answer, but then he said softly, "They found the girls…"

Mckenna sucked in her breath. "And? Are they okay?"

He shook his head. "One is okay, but one girl is deceased."

Heart dropping, Mckenna stared at the floor and balled

up her fists, her chest constricting. She wouldn't cry in front of him, but the emotions hit her hard. Mocha, sensing the change in his handler, came over and leaned against her. She crouched down and hugged Mocha, allowing him to lick her face a couple of times while her heart raced. What had happened? How much did the surviving girl know? Which one survived? Did it matter? One girl was gone. Forever.

"Do you know which girl is deceased?" Mckenna asked. "I will go help with the notification. Mocha can help too."

Agent Knox shook his head, "I'll have to go to the scene and find out. The sheriff said that they found the girls together. The one girl was trying to resuscitate the other. I need to get going."

The change in tone took Mckenna back, but the devastation across his face made her realize that he was being abrupt because he too was upset. She knew what it was like to try to shove away emotions. That never turned out well. "I can help. I can go with you and Mocha can help the survivor."

Agent Knox stopped and turned back to Mckenna. "I don't need your help. This is now my investigation with the sheriff's office. You can go talk to the families, but don't ask them anything. Just do whatever it is you do."

"Whatever it is I do? That's nice," she snapped.

"I can't have someone interfering with my investigation. I need to do my job."

Anger started building in Mckenna and she was already changing her mind about thinking that there was a nice-guy side to Agent Knox. "Okay, fine. You do your job and I'll do mine, but at the end of the day we're all in this together and we all want the same thing."

"And what is it that you think we all want?"

"Justice. That's what I want. Nothing will bring back the

young woman who lost her life, but if the asshole who did this goes to prison, then the family can start moving forward. To figure out who did this, though, you're going to need the survivor to talk to you and I guarantee that she's going to be so traumatized that getting anything out of her is going to be difficult. Mocha can help. When you need us, I'll try not to say, 'I told you so.'"

Agent Knox opened his mouth and closed it again. Then he muttered that he needed to go and stomped out of the office. He passed Cassidy on his way to the exit and brushed up against her. He apologized brusquely and kept going. Mckenna stared at his retreating back, daring him to turn around. So much for her earlier thoughts about him not being a jerk. He'd just proved her wrong. And why did she have to be so damn attracted to him? It was like she wanted to slap him and then kiss him. But who would want to be with her? Especially some agent who was completely out of her league in looks and made her spitting mad. She was destined to be a spinster with dogs.

"Being single with dogs isn't so bad, is it, Mocha?" Mckenna asked. Mocha gave a soft whine and nudged her hand with his head. She petted him as Cassidy approached.

"Everything okay?" Cassidy asked.

"Yeah, it's fine," Mckenna said, letting out a sigh.

Cassidy peered at her, tilting her head slightly in a way that reminded Mckenna of Mocha. Cassidy was analyzing her.

"You like him, don't you?"

"What?" Mckenna said.

"You like him. I mean, I agree, he's not hard to look at, but a little bit of sisterly advice—he's a disaster waiting to happen. He has baggage. Or so I've heard. Just ignore him. What did he say?"

Mckenna filled Cassidy in on the return of the girls and what had happened. "He said I should do my job and he needed to do his," Mckenna finished.

"He does kind of have a point," Cassidy said. "I mean your job is different. Very important, but it's not investigative."

"I know that, but he's going to need an interview from the survivor, and I know what she feels like. I know how hard this is going to be. She knows she's home, but she won't know who to trust. And then, the second part of her nightmare will begin. There will be interviews, TV crews, social media. Some people will blame her for being kidnapped and her friend dying. Others will be sympathetic. If Agent Knox wants to get information from her, he needs someone who understands what she's going through. And Mocha. Mocha could help just with his presence."

Cassidy crossed her arms. "Are you sure you're not too close to this case? Maybe you need to excuse yourself."

"No, it's fine. I'll admit this case is a tough one, but I'll be okay. I just need time to myself. And quit worrying about me and being the bossy, overprotective older sister."

"Is that so bad?"

"No," Mckenna said, "but it feels like you can't let go either. You're so worried about everything with me because you feel guilty about covering for me at that party where I was taken."

"Yeah, wouldn't you feel some guilt if you were in my shoes?"

"I guess, but at some point, we all need to move on."

"Then maybe this is the case to help you with that," Cassidy said. "But don't forget my sisterly advice—stay away from Agent Knox. He may be attractive, but he's trouble."

"What is the baggage that everyone keeps talking about anyway?"

"I don't know for sure. I heard he was working undercover and then some sort of office love-triangle thing started. He was sleeping with his partner or something and her boyfriend, another agent, found out and blew his cover. Somehow Knox kept his job and so did the female agent, but the boyfriend lost his job. That's probably why he doesn't want to work with anyone here or share case information unless he has to."

"Huh," Mckenna answered. "All right, I need to start doing my job. I came in early to do paperwork. I'll catch you later."

"Mckenna?"

"Yeah?"

"I might be an overprotective sister, but it's because I love you."

"I know that," Mckenna said, softening a bit. She was probably being too hard on Cassidy.

"If you need anything, let me know."

"Thanks, sis."

Cassidy headed on out. Mckenna watched her leave. Her sister's career choice had been a result of Mckenna's kidnapping. That experience had changed her entire family's life. Now she needed to go help two families whose lives would never be the same. She would do everything she could to help these families and the survivor through their ordeal. Nobody would stop her from doing that—especially Agent Knox.

Chapter Seven

Evan pulled up on the shoulder of a dirt road and parked, taking in the scene around him. While it was difficult, there was always an adrenaline rush too with a crime like this one. He wanted to solve this and—Mckenna was right—he wanted justice. Nothing felt better than the moment he put handcuffs on a suspect. It made the long hours, no friends, and barely going home worth it.

What was hard was the emotional toll. Those were the times he wanted someone to go home to and talk about things, but between his parents' disastrous marriage and his previous partner, he didn't know how he'd ever have a relationship he could trust.

Which was why he needed to stay as far away from Mckenna Parker as possible.

He felt bad that he'd snapped at her again, but she seemed to see through the wall he put up and understand him in a way no one else did. He didn't know what to do with that or how to handle it. The last thing he needed right now was to fall for someone—especially someone in his office. As if the gossip wasn't bad enough.

Just get to work and figure out this case. Forget Mckenna. You do your thing, and she can do hers. The last thing I need is her interfering with this case.

Evan stepped out of his vehicle and walked over to the crime scene tape. He checked in with the person securing the scene so they could log him in and then stepped under the yellow tape flapping in the breeze.

The yellow tape seemed so out of place here in the mountains where other than the sounds of officers working the crime scene, there was silence. Sometimes a Steller's jay or magpie squawked in the distance, but a big piece of the beauty for Evan was the quiet. It was like heaven to him. He'd love to live in the mountains. When he'd moved to Colorado he'd bought a house in the foothills near Morrison, but there were still neighbors and too much noise. He flashed his badge to another deputy as he approached a young woman on an ambulance gurney. They were about to load her in, and he stopped the EMTs.

He recognized Lily Hendrix from the picture her parents had provided. Blond hair framed her face that had dirt smudges and enough blotchiness for Evan to know she'd been crying…probably sobbing. His heart went out to this young woman who also happened to be his only witness right now. How could such a horrible crime be committed when he was surrounded by such a beautiful setting? It didn't seem right. He hated to ask her, but he had to try to see if Lily could remember anything.

"Lily? I'm Agent Evan Knox. Are you up for a few questions?"

No answer. Lily's eyes stared off toward the mountains behind him.

"Lily?"

"Hey, man," one of the EMTs finally interrupted. "She hasn't been responsive for any of us. We need to get her to the hospital so she can be checked out."

"Okay," Evan said, stepping back. "Lily, I know this is

hard. I'll find you later at the hospital. Maybe we can talk then."

Lily's eyelids opened and closed, but that was the only reaction. The EMTs loaded her up and closed the doors. He'd find out for sure, but they'd probably take her down to Denver General.

It was crazy that in a short drive they could be in the heart of the busy city versus the rugged terrain and open wilderness that surrounded him. As much as he loved the mountains, he wished this crime had happened in the city. There were no cameras out here. No witnesses. None of the possible investigative tools that came with the city. He sighed as he watched the ambulance negotiate the dirt road, dust billowing up behind it.

"Agent Knox?"

Evan turned around and found the sheriff behind him.

"Our other victim is over here." She nodded in the direction of a coroner's truck and a couple of deputies watching. No one would touch the scene until the coroner gave permission.

Evan walked with her toward the scene. Her face said it all—the look they all had when they saw something they didn't want to. A young woman, her life gone. It kept it real and motivated him to find the son of a bitch who did this. Evan shuddered as he approached the scene. Just another thing to add to the list of things he couldn't unsee.

Time to get to work.

"If you'd like, I can check into getting some of our ERT folks out here," Evan offered to the sheriff, referencing the FBI's Evidence Response Team or their version of CSI.

"I'd appreciate that," the sheriff said. "Thank you. I hope you don't mind, I also called in the CBI."

"No, that's good. The more help we can get processing the scene, the quicker we might be able to figure out a suspect."

"Agreed."

Evan took in the still body of the young woman. The coroner carefully moved Autumn to prepare bagging up her body. Evan noticed an injury on her upper arm.

"That looks like a gunshot wound. If it went through her bone and entered her body, she might have bled out," Evan said.

"That could be what happened. If that's the case, then maybe we'll get lucky and find a bullet for evidence. Hopefully, we'll know more after the coroner examines her."

"Who found them?"

The sheriff nodded in the direction of a couple standing near a picnic area. "They were coming up for the day to get out of the city and have a picnic. Weekday, so they figured it would be quiet. Retired couple. They said that Lily was doing CPR on Autumn and screaming for help. Once they were able to get a text out to 911, they realized Autumn was deceased, but Lily wouldn't stop chest compressions. When the EMTs arrived, she held Autumn and wouldn't let go. Once they convinced her that Autumn couldn't be revived she shut down and quit talking."

Evan nodded. There was nothing to say. He'd need to talk to the couple. Even rule them out although he highly doubted they had anything to do with the kidnapping. "I'm glad they were here to help."

"Me too. Although I think the wife is about ready to pass out. I've talked to them. I have their information. Mind if I tell them they can go? They want to get home, and I don't blame them."

"No, I don't mind. If you've talked with them and have a statement, we will follow up."

"Okay," Sheriff Stewart said. "I'll go and tell them they can leave."

Evan watched the sheriff head over to the couple, his mind shifting back to the morning and what Mckenna had told him. Her words flipped through his mind. She put out a strong facade, but underneath it all she too was still trying to move forward from what happened to her. Did she know that Lily wouldn't want to talk because she'd been the same way? How was she doing knowing that the man who took her was now out free at the same time this case was going on? There were so many things he wanted to ask her, but he didn't dare.

Unfortunately, he had to admit, she was going to get to say, "I told you so," because if Lily didn't want to talk, the best bet was to bring in Mocha and see if he could help her through the trauma. Evan knew how much dogs could help, not only from his own experience. He'd heard of crisis K-9s at mass shootings around the country and how they'd helped victims give their statements. One person was even able to say what happened only when the dogs showed up and he was able to walk with the K-9 through the scene of the crime telling the dog what had happened.

Yes, Mckenna was going to get the ultimate *I told you so*.

Chapter Eight

Evan drove to his house. Coming home at two in the morning only made everything seem even more desolate. Everyone else on the street was asleep, lights off. He showered, crashed for a while in bed and rested fitfully until the alarm went off at 5:00 a.m. Smacking the off button, he rolled out of bed, drank some coffee and went for a quick run, which took him back to the shower. His closet resembled something out of the *Men In Black* movies—white shirts, boring ties and dark jackets. Not like there wasn't a dress code in the FBI, but there was a lack of day-off clothes or go-hiking clothes or go-out-with-friends clothes. Minus jogging shorts and T-shirts, his wardrobe was all about his job.

He shut the closet door and tried to ignore the nagging feeling that there was something missing in his life even though he'd achieved his dream of becoming an agent. There must be something more to life. More than just crimes, suspects and victims.

He'd heard through the sheriff that Mckenna had done a wonderful job helping her break the awful news to Autumn's parents. If *wonderful* was the right word. But the sheriff had mentioned that Mckenna knew what to say and how to talk to the parents. When they insisted on seeing their daughter, it was Mckenna who helped them understand that while they would need to identify Autumn's remains, they also needed to remember her the way she was before the kidnapping and her death. Memories would make this difficult time easier.

Evan hadn't been excited about a victim specialist helping, but he could see the benefit. Now he admitted, only to himself, that the reason he was short with her and didn't want to see her had nothing to do with work.

Grabbing his keys and heading toward the hospital, Evan forced thoughts of Mckenna out of his mind. But as he sat at a red light, he couldn't help thinking about the way her face lit up when she smiled. The way she looked at Mocha and the love she had for her dog. He enjoyed being around her, but he couldn't go there. Not now. He had his sights on a promotion to assistant special agent in charge or ASAC, but his previous field office assignment had put an obstacle in his way to that advancement.

What a mess that had been. He'd agreed to work undercover, and his partner, Melissa Anderson, had helped him. They had been friends too outside of the office, but nothing more. Melissa had confided in Evan that she wasn't into guys but didn't want anyone to know. Not yet. He had kept her secret.

The problem was there was another agent who had the hots for his partner and the guy didn't seem to get that she wasn't into him for several reasons. The guy had blown Evan's cover with the investigation to get back at Evan for his friendship with Melissa. Then he'd spread rumors about Evan and his partner sleeping together.

Evan was suspended without pay while the whole situation was investigated and he was eventually cleared. Melissa had been furious, especially since it forced her to come out about her girlfriend. She hadn't been ready to tell everyone that she had a girlfriend. However, Evan had heard they were now married, and he was happy for his partner.

But the rumors had been harsh and the special agent in charge at that field office had sent him to Denver to try to ease the situation. Evan didn't mind, since his dad and sisters all lived in Colorado, although they were spread out over the state. He'd decided when he arrived in Denver that he would not share much with anyone unless he had to, he would work hard, try to let the gossip die down and then put in for an ASAC position.

Then he'd met Mckenna.

The more he was around her, the more attracted he was. At least she wasn't another agent, but even if he only had a friendship with her, he was certain the rumors would flare up again.

No, he had to quit thinking about Mckenna for many reasons. Evan parked at the hospital and found his way to the nurses station. One of the nurses took him to Lily's room but mentioned that she hadn't spoken at all.

"She just stares out the window at nothing," the nurse told him as they approached Lily's room. "I don't know how much I can share with you, though."

Evan hesitated outside the door. "Lily's parents gave me permission to have access to her records. You can find it in her files. How are her vitals? Did she have any injuries?"

The nurse peered at Lily's chart. Evan saw her double-check the note allowing him to receive medical information.

"No, vitals are good," she answered. "They did a CT scan and there's no brain trauma. Overall, she's in good health, but won't speak, eat, and has barely slept. The doctor has ordered a psych eval. That should happen in the next hour or so."

"Did the doctor pull blood for a tox screen?"

"He did. It's been sent to the lab already, but it may take a couple of days to get results even with a rush."

"Thanks," Evan said, wishing he had contacts to pull strings and get the tox screen done faster. As he stepped into the room, the first thing he noticed was untouched food on the overbed table. Like the nurse mentioned, Lily was staring out the window in a fugue-type state. Her parents sat next to her bed holding hands. Evan reintroduced himself to them as the nurse left.

"If it's okay, I'd like to try to talk to her," Evan said.

Lily's mom, Brenda, spoke up, "It's fine, but she hasn't said a word to anyone."

"Okay," Evan said. He went over and pulled up a chair to sit down next to Lily, taking in the view that seemed to completely occupy her. The city bustled below, and buildings blocked any view of the mountains. "Lily? I'm Agent Evan Knox. I met you yesterday. I need to ask you some questions. Is that okay?"

No answer. Evan continued.

"I'm here to help you, Lily. You can talk when you're ready. No hurry. I want to catch the person who did this to you. I want justice for Autumn, and I know you do too."

Lily blinked a couple times and Evan leaned forward hopefully. If she could even just give him something to go on, that would be helpful. Instead, Evan watched tears start streaming down her face.

"I'm sorry, Lily," he whispered to her. He pulled a Kleenex out of a box and started dabbing her cheek. Brenda leaned in and took over with the Kleenex as Evan stood and backed out of the way, keeping his frustration in check. He could ask the tech person if they'd been able to get anything off Autumn and Lily's phones, but his best bet was getting Lily to talk. He could try again after the psych evaluation. Maybe there was something they could give her to help.

Evan heard the words again—*I told you so.* Mckenna. *Mocha.* It was worth a shot. Did Lily even like dogs? Evan asked her father, and he answered with a very enthusiastic yes. Pulling his cell phone out, Evan stepped out into the hall. He hesitated before hitting the contact he'd created for Mckenna. The call rang and rang as he paced back and forth.

Good grief, I'm nervous to talk to her. It's like being in high school and asking a girl to the prom.

Just when Evan thought the call would go to voice mail, Mckenna answered. He was tongue-tied for a moment hearing her say "Hello" again.

"Uh, Mckenna?"

"Agent Knox?"

"Yes. You know how you said you'd be able to say, 'I told you so?' Well, you're going to get to tell me that. Could you come to the hospital? With Mocha? To see if he can help me with Lily?"

"Mocha will always help, especially with Lily," Mckenna said. "Text me her room number. I can be there in about forty minutes."

"Thanks," Evan said.

"I'd say you're welcome, but I want to make it clear that Mocha and I are coming for Lily. Not for you. That's what I was trying to get across to you. This is why I get to say, 'I told you so.' See you soon."

Mckenna hung up and Evan was left once again speechless. *You deserved that. She had every right to speak to you that way. I guess I was hoping for a warmer reception, but why would I think that would happen after the way I've been?* Plus, why would he even think she would like him like *that*? No one else in the office seemed to like him. And the thing was, that never bothered him—until now.

Chapter Nine

Mckenna locked the door to her house and loaded Mocha into her SUV. She'd saved for a long time and her parents had helped her with the down payment so that she could live in a house that was in the mountains and made her feel safe. There was too much activity in the city and the sound of emergency vehicles, people yelling or even laughing after a late night out and everything else that went with city life set Mckenna on edge.

Instead, she loved her home in Idaho Springs—a small town that attracted many tourists through the summer and winter months. The commute to Denver wasn't bad; the wintertime drive could be dicey, but there were plenty of things she could do for her job remotely on the days that I-70 was snowy, slick and nasty. It was all worth it to escape the city and breathe in crisp mountain air.

I wonder if Lily will eventually feel the same way. Or will she be the opposite and want the safety of people around her?

After closing the rear door, she grabbed her large mug of coffee off the hood of her car and climbed in to drive to the hospital. Mckenna hadn't slept the previous night. Memories of her kidnapping had kept cropping up—like a slideshow. She knew she'd been drugged so many of the memories had been lost, but occasionally she could remember something new.

She'd taken out her journal and jotted down what she could.

Why am I doing that? It's not like they didn't catch the guy. Maybe if I can regain my memories, I can regain a piece of myself that I lost. But I never did see my kidnapper. That's always bothered me.

Mckenna merged onto I-70 toward Denver, the trees blurring by as she approached Floyd Hill and all the signs flashing yellow lights warning truckers they weren't down yet and there were steep grades ahead. A runaway truck ramp was on her right with fresh tire marks in the deep gravel. Hopefully, she'd never witness the horrific sight of an out-of-control semi. She shifted her thoughts back to her kidnapping and how she could help approach Lily with Mocha. It would help him figure out who did this.

But what if she's like me? What if she didn't see him? How can someone be sure they're prosecuting the right person if I never saw him?

Mckenna hated it when those thoughts crept into her head, but even though she was still at the beginning of her career, she'd been doing her job long enough to know innocent people were prosecuted and sent to prison. The Innocence Project existed for a reason. They'd helped over 240 wrongly convicted people get out of prison. Was Toby innocent? Or was he the monster the previous sheriff had made him out to be?

She may have skipped his parole hearing, but she'd watched his trial. He'd kept a poker face, staring down at the table in front of him, barely acknowledging his lawyer.

Everyone said it was because he was guilty, but Mckenna always thought it was because he seemed broken.

The sheriff at the time had said Toby confessed. Her jacket and some other belongings were in his vehicle. The crime scene investigators had found some sort of drug in his truck that they suspected had been used on her, but a tox screen had never been done. Why, she didn't know. Nor had anyone followed up on the anonymous phone call made to the sheriff's office stating the person had seen these items in Toby's truck. Why not? There were enough whys that Mckenna had never felt completely convinced Toby was guilty.

Why am I going through this? Do I really think Toby is innocent? No, there was enough evidence. And he did plead guilty. Just look at your scars on the side of your body and be reminded of Toby's guilt.

Mckenna gripped the wheel, glad to be coming into Denver, getting closer to where she could quit thinking about her case and focus on Mocha helping Lily solve her kidnapping and Autumn's homicide. If anyone could work some magic and help Lily, it would be Mocha. He'd helped her personally, and Mckenna was glad he'd flunked out of the FBI Doggy Academy as she called it.

Mocha had been destined to be a tracking and bomb dog with Cassidy, but he would start tracking and then lie down and refuse to move. He did the same thing when she asked Mocha to search for bomb odors. He would check one or two vehicles and then flop to the ground, pretending to be exhausted. He wasn't enjoying the work.

Cassidy and Mckenna worked together to see if they could motivate him to at least track by Mckenna being "lost." Mocha would find her with joy, but as soon as Cassidy asked Mocha to find a different person, he'd quit. He only wanted to find Mckenna. The FBI decided that if he couldn't make the cut as a K-9, then maybe Mckenna could take him on as a crisis K-9. Mocha passed those tests with flying colors and came to live with Mckenna. Cassidy had trained another dog, a yellow Lab named Cooper, who had been much better at working than Mocha.

Mocha had helped Mckenna move forward even though she still experienced anxiety. For a while she had felt like she'd been followed, but her family told her it was just her imagination or the media. For a while, the media would camp out on the roads near their house, waiting like vultures. "Talk to them or don't," Mckenna had advised the families of Lily and Autumn. "It's up to you, but don't think that the media will play fair or help in anyway."

Now that feeling of being followed hit Mckenna again.

Stop it. It's only because of this case. It's only because you told the families yesterday about the possibility of someone following you.

Mckenna turned and could see the hospital down the road when she glanced in her rearview mirror. There was a blue Jeep behind her. She could have sworn it had been behind her since Floyd Hill, even when she was in the slow lane, shifting down and driving cautiously. Most people went around her because she drove too slowly.

"You're seeing things. Stop imagining things. Be in the moment," Mckenna said aloud.

Mocha suddenly let out sharp barks startling Mckenna. She weaved slightly into the other lane, receiving a honk and an unfriendly finger wave from the other driver, but Mckenna didn't care. The Jeep was still behind her. She made an extra turn just to see if it would follow.

It did.

Her hands started to shake. What if it followed her into

the parking garage? She could call Agent Knox. He'd come and meet her.

No. I won't do that. I can take care of myself. If this vehicle follows me in, I'll drive back out and call 911.

With her plan clear in her head, Mckenna pulled into the hospital parking garage only to see the Jeep drive by.

"See? I'm being silly," Mckenna said to Mocha. "And what was up with the barking? Cat? Squirrel? We might need to work on that, so you don't make me drive off the road."

Mocha gave a little whine in response and then sighed.

"Okay, we need to get inside. You have work to do, big guy."

MCKENNA AND MOCHA made their way to Lily's room. As Mocha trotted along, doctors, nurses and other hospital team members turned and smiled at the happy black Lab. Mckenna knew that Mocha brought joy to everyone around him, which delighted her. She was glad he hadn't made it through K-9 training—he was doing what he was meant to in life, just like her.

Agent Knox stood outside Lily's room, arms crossed and appearing frustrated. When he turned and saw the pair coming, Mckenna could have sworn something changed in him. A slight smile, his face relaxing. Or was she imagining that? Her heart picked up a beat and Mckenna scolded herself for feeling this way. Plus, he hadn't exactly been friendly with her yesterday. And why would he be interested in her? Cassidy was the one all the guys wanted. Once they were done with this case, she would be happy to work with another agent.

"Hey, there," Agent Knox said.

Mckenna decided formal was best. She meant what she

had said—Mocha was here to help Lily with her trauma. If
that helped to gather more information for the investigation,
then that was a bonus. "Hello, Agent Knox."

To her surprise, she received a smile and it transformed
everything about him. *Stop it*, she told herself again. *He's
being nice because now he knows he needs you. Otherwise,
he never would have called.*

"Please, just call me Evan."

"I'll stick with Agent Knox."

"Fine."

"Good," Mckenna said. "Mocha is ready to go be with
Lily. Make sure you follow my lead."

"Follow your lead?" Evan's face changed back to his
dark, serious look. "Just remember who the investigative
agent is here."

Mckenna locked eyes with him and said, "If anyone can
help, it's Mocha. Right now, your job is on hold."

Evan muttered an agreement and opened the door to
Lily's room. Mocha edged his way in first. Mckenna allowed him to have a slightly longer leash and he went over
by Lily and sat on his haunches, perking up his floppy ears
and then letting them droop back down.

Lily stared out the window with no reaction.

Mckenna drew in a deep breath. She'd had a tough time
talking about her experience, but this was worse than she
thought.

I'll have to let Mocha help her and see if she responds.

"Hello, Lily," Mckenna said, softly, taking a seat near
Mocha, who continued to watch the young woman. "I'm
Mckenna Parker and I'm a victim services response team
member. I'm here to help you. More importantly, this is
Mocha. He's a special dog that works for the FBI. If you'd

like to pet him, you can. Mocha is great at comforting peo-ple in a time of need."

No reaction.

Mocha stood and took a couple of steps closer. He gen-tly laid his head on Lily's arm, giving it a couple licks and then staying quiet.

"Are you okay with him doing that?" Mckenna asked. "If not, let me know. You don't have to say anything. You could tap a finger or blink twice."

No reaction.

"Okay, I'm going to let him sit with you for a little while. You don't have to say anything to any of us until you're ready."

Mckenna heard Evan clear his throat like he was going to say something. She shook her head no. Evan opened his mouth to argue and Mckenna shot him a glare. "Stay quiet," she mouthed at him.

She understood him better than he thought. Having a sis-ter as an agent helped with that: Mckenna knew that Cas-sidy would want to run this investigation her way. Evan was even worse about it given his "outgoing" personality. His lips tightened and cheeks flushed a little red, but he didn't speak. Mckenna needed him to back off right now. Give Lily space—something he didn't seem to understand.

Lily's parents stood in the corner, staring at their daugh-ter. Mckenna motioned for them to sit down. She could feel the pressure in the room, and it was getting to her. She could only imagine how much it was affecting Lily.

Taking in the hospital room brought back memories for Mckenna.

I had been sedated at first because the panic was over-whelming. I remembered slicing myself open escaping through the window. I couldn't even remember how many days I'd been missing, but I hated the sound of the hospital with the beeps and cords coming out of me. My parents and Cassidy had stared at me like I had been broken.

Like I was a science experiment. Mckenna rubbed her side where she could still feel the scars. She'd covered them up with a tattoo. She loved the design, but ultimately the scars were still there. They always would be. She noticed Evan watching her with curiosity and she dropped her hand back down.

They waited.

The clock ticked. Each second lasting longer and longer.

Mocha continued to leave his head on Lily's arm, closing his eyes like he was going to enjoy a nap. He took a deep breath and Mckenna heard Lily do the same. Mocha responded by putting a big paw on her arm and leaving it there.

Her dog had more patience than any human.

Staring out the same window as Lily, Mckenna watched the treetops sway in the breeze. Sun glinted off the windows of city buildings. She didn't know the city well, but at times it could be pretty too. Nothing like the mountains, though. The mountains were still her escape. Growing up on her parents' ranch, Mckenna had learned to love open spaces, cloudless nights where the stars could be seen for miles and the high mountain peaks dotted with snow. That was her special place. Would she ever have anyone to share it with?

A slight noise came from Lily and Mckenna turned back to the young woman. Mocha still had his head and paw resting on her arm. Tears were streaming down Lily's face. Mocha sensed the change and, paw by paw, climbed onto the bed with her. Mckenna was thinking about asking him to get off when sobs came from Lily, and she wrapped her arms around Mocha. Mocha licked her face.

"I killed her."

Mckenna didn't know if she had heard that right. But Lily was speaking so she didn't want to say anything. Evan took a step closer.

Lily turned and her eyes locked onto Mckenna's. "I killed her. Autumn is dead because of me."

Sobs took over Lily's body as she held Mocha tight.

Chapter Ten

Lily continued to sob and Mckenna leaned forward in her chair. Why did Lily think she had killed her friend? Evan sat down near them and Mckenna worked to not think about the smell of his cologne and how close he was to her. She could reach out and run her fingers down his chest. Good God, where did *that* thought come from? Sweat beaded up on her palms and she scooted her chair a little bit away from him. He gave her a questioning look, but she ignored it even though she wanted to gaze back and lose herself in those blue eyes. She had to focus on Lily and Mocha. That was her job right now.

"Lily, I don't believe you killed Autumn. You were both victims," Evan said. "Take your time. Tell me what happened."

Annoyed, Mckenna shot Evan another look. *Just give her time. You don't need your answers immediately.* Lily shook her head and more tears streamed down her face. Mocha remained by her side, every now and then giving Lily kisses on her cheek, wiping away her tears.

"You don't have to say anything until you're ready," Evan said.

Mckenna appreciated Evan changing his tactic slightly and not pressuring Lily. Mckenna forced herself to take a deep breath and calm down. The previous sheriff hadn't been so nice to Mckenna during her own case. He had told her that she needed to tell him everything. *"Now."* Mckenna had struggled through that, but somehow managed to answer his questions—although she had barely remembered much at the time. *Probably why I'm so touchy with Agent Knox. I hated law enforcement for not having any patience. At least he's trying to be nice. Is that why he said I could call him Evan? Is that his way of being nicer? Or is he messing with me somehow?*

Stop thinking about Evan and your own case. Help Lily. But I do like seeing this softer side to Evan. Maybe everyone needs to give him a chance. Or, maybe, I just want to get to know this softer side. I need to stop all these thoughts and focus on Mocha and our work.

"I'm ready to talk, but I don't want my parents here," Lily said, breaking Mckenna's thoughts.

Mckenna saw Lily's parents start to disagree, so she stood and headed in their direction. She knew they never wanted to leave their daughter's side. Her parents, especially her mother, wouldn't leave Mckenna alone for a long time after her kidnapping. She had to eventually tell her mom that she needed space. She needed to talk to therapists. She needed to figure out who she was now. It had been rough on her parents, but it was the best thing for her.

"I'll be in here with Agent Knox," Mckenna said to Lily's parents. "As you both know, I'm a survivor myself and I understand what Lily is going through. I can tell you that it's going to be hard to say what happened, especially around her family. There's lots of feelings like shame and you also want to protect those you love from knowing what you went through. I'll give you some great resources and therapists for Lily, but also for both of you. You're victims too. Right now, though, we need to speak with Lily so that Agent Knox and the sheriff can move forward with the investigation."

"Okay," Lily's mother said as her father nodded. They both stood up to leave and paused at the door. "We'll be outside."

"I'll come get you when Lily is ready," Mckenna said, closing the door behind them. She sat back down over by Evan, trying to close her mind to anything about her experience. Mocha picked his head up and stared at her and then flopped it back down near Lily's shoulder. The girl continued to keep him in a tight hold, but Mckenna figured Mocha would let them know if he was uncomfortable.

"There's no rush," Evan told Lily. "Just start when you're ready. Maybe think about before you went missing. What were you doing?"

Lily took a deep breath and just when Mckenna thought she wasn't going to speak, Lily started in with her story. "We'd had a great summer back home and we were excited to get back to college. There was one final bash of the season. It's kind of a secret party and it's out in a more remote area at a house where the cops don't go very often. I'd always wanted to go. Autumn couldn't have cared less about it. She wasn't as into partying as I was, but I talked her into it…"

As Lily trailed off, Mckenna was struck by how similar Lily's story was to hers.

I attended a secret party too. Same kind of thing. The person who threw it only chose "special" people to come and we were all sworn to secrecy.

Silence filled the room and Mckenna was glad that Evan waited for Lily to speak again, not pressuring her.

"We were drinking," Lily finally continued. "And dancing and having fun. Then everything is kind of hazy. I vaguely remember being out in the woods, but no one was forcing me out there. I don't even remember how I got there. Then things are fuzzy, but when they become clear again, Autumn and I were in an old building. I don't know where it is. It smelled weird, like rotten eggs mixed with dust and we could hear critters scurrying around. Trees would brush up on the building and make a scraping noise."

Mckenna shivered. Her memory was similar. *Stop thinking about your experience. Focus on Lily. But rotten eggs? I smelled that too. I was in an old building. Not a barn or a cabin, but whatever it was, it was old. I don't remember how I got there either. Things are fuzzy, just like Lily said, between the party and waking up in a strange location.*

Clasping her hands together, Mckenna worked to not shiver or shake. Lily's experience couldn't be Mckenna's. Or could it? Toby had been out just long enough that he could have done this. She caught Evan glancing at her, seeming to notice how she gripped her hands. Mckenna stared at Lily, ignoring Evan.

"What do you remember next?" Evan asked.

"There were letters carved into the side of the wall."

"Do you remember if they spelled a word? Maybe initials?" Evan said.

I carved my initials into the wall. I wanted there to be a trace of where I was because I figured he was going to kill me.

Mckenna started shaking harder. *Stop it. Just listen to Lily. You're making connections in a way you shouldn't. Your kidnapper was caught. But he was released...*

"I don't remember if it spelled anything," Lily said. "In fact, I can't even remember what the letters were because that's when he spoke."

"Your kidnapper," Evan said.

"Yes."

"What did he say?"

Lily started crying again. "He said if we behaved, he'd let us out alive. He didn't want to kill us. This was just a game to him—his version of catch and release. But rather than fishing catch and release, he liked to hunt and release humans. It made the game much more fun. Then he gave us water and we blacked out again. I don't remember much until we woke up."

Mckenna stopped listening. Nausea swept over her, and she fought to hold down her coffee and breakfast. Her entire body started to shake. Evan stared at her again.

"Are you okay?" he whispered to her.

It was all Mckenna could do to squeak out a *yes*, because she wasn't fine. Everything Lily said brought back the same memory—including the "catch and release" phrase.

Toby. Her kidnapper. It must be Toby. He's done it again. If only I'd gone to the parole hearing. If only I'd spoken up, we wouldn't be here today.

"When we woke up again, I think it was the middle of the night," Lily said. "I told Autumn we had to try to escape. I think it's what he wanted, because we found a hole in the side of the wall. We barely fit but managed to squeeze through and there was a broken window. Autumn took her shirt off and finished breaking the glass. I was so scared that he was waiting for us, but Autumn said we had to get out the window. She put her shirt on the bottom of the window to help protect us and helped me get through first. She'd been a gymnast, and she was able to jump and push herself up and through. We started sprinting and all of a sudden there was a loud, popping noise and a tree trunk next to us shattered into pieces. We realized he was shooting at us, so we ran into the thicker trees to make it harder to see us. Autumn screamed in pain because a bullet had hit her arm, but she told me she was okay. She said to keep going.

"There was a creek running nearby and I told Autumn we needed to follow it. Maybe if we followed the water, it would lead to a road. We were running so hard and when I turned to see if anyone was following us, I saw a lone tree up on the hill."

A lone tree that seemed like a ghost, Mckenna thought, continuing to shudder. *There were other trees too. They were weird in shape. I remember a creek, but I ran the other way because he was also shooting at me and I started to run a zigzag pattern to make myself a difficult target. I was in good shape from running track and I managed to get away even with my side bleeding. I was lucky to find the road. I was lucky that a good Samaritan stopped, because he was close behind.*

"We found a road, but a truck came along, and it was him, so we hid behind some bushes, huddled together. I was so scared that he'd see us."

"How do you know it was him?" Evan asked.

"He had the window down and was cursing. I don't think we were supposed to get away that quickly. I don't know. He also had like a spotlight and was searching for us. He never saw us, and we stayed there until morning. Autumn started to say she wasn't feeling good." Lily started to cry again. "I don't know how long we were there, but the sun started to rise. I saw a car come along and Autumn wasn't right. She quit breathing. I waved them down and then started CPR, but nothing seemed to work. The couple called 911 and I continued CPR until the first deputy arrived. He kept telling me there was nothing more we could do, but I didn't want to stop. Someone made me stop, but I killed my friend. If we hadn't gone to that party, she'd still be alive."

Chapter Eleven

The room closed in around Mckenna. Everything Lily said was pretty much the same as her experience. The only difference was that a door had opened for Mckenna to go through after a couple of days. That was when she'd seen the opportunity and taken it, not caring how bloody she was, or how she escaped. The kidnapper also had taken her shoes when she'd been drugged, so she was running in bare feet. It didn't matter. She was in a race for her life.

Later, Mckenna realized that was what he'd had in mind all along. He'd wanted to watch her scramble out and to see if she could get away just like catch and release fishing, where the fisherman took pictures of his trophy and then let it go just before it was too late. Only he wanted to catch Mckenna again and probably had no intention of allowing her to live.

Dizziness washed over her, and Mocha, sensing the change, climbed off the bed as Lily and Evan continued to talk. He came over and put his head in Mckenna's lap, big brown eyes staring at her in concern. Mckenna tried to pet him, but her hands shook too violently. Mocha placed his head on her hands as if he knew she needed them to be held.

The party. I never did say who threw the party. I pretended not to know. If only I had, this wouldn't have happened. Toby. It had to be him. He couldn't control his compulsion and obsession. Why didn't I go to that hearing? Why didn't I give a victim statement?

A hand lightly touched Mckenna's shoulder, and she jerked away.

"Are you okay?" Evan asked.

Mckenna glanced back and forth between Evan and Lily. She needed to leave. Now.

"No, I think I ate something that's not settling well," Mckenna lied. "I'm sorry, Lily. Mocha and I need to leave now."

"Can I see him again? Soon?" Lily asked.

"Sure. We'll come back for another visit."

Mckenna forced herself to her feet, swaying back and forth, trying to make herself leave.

"Let me help you," Evan said.

He was instantly by her side, softly touching her and supporting her.

"No. No, I'm fine. I just need to get some fresh air."

"You don't look fine."

"Keep talking to Lily. I'll be fine," Mckenna said.

She and Mocha managed to get out of the room. Lily's parents were waiting outside the door, but she couldn't say anything to them. She had to get somewhere with no people. Somewhere she could think.

A sign down the hall said Chapel.

"Perfect," Mckenna muttered.

Mocha led the way, and she followed the remaining signs until she was in the small replica of a church, complete with stained glass. She managed to sit down and then leaned forward, her breathing harsh and irregular, heart pounding.

Maybe if she'd gone to the parole hearing, Autumn would be alive. Then she started sobbing, letting feelings she'd hidden for years finally escape.

EVAN FOUGHT THE urge to rush out of the room after Mckenna. What had happened? One minute she appeared bright, chipper, and happy to put him in his place. The next minute she had turned pale and seemed like she saw a ghost. Lily's case must have brought back memories for her. Tough ones.

"Thank you, Lily, for everything you told me. If you think of anything else, will you call me?" Evan placed his card on the table next to her food.

Lily nodded and picked up the card with the FBI emblem.

"You didn't kill her," Evan said, wanting to give the girl comfort.

"How do you know?"

"You were her friend. A good friend. I suspect from your description that you were drugged. Depending on what it was, sometimes drugs and alcohol don't mix, and some people have a reaction. Severe ones. We don't know yet. The coroner and pathologist will be able to tell us more, but let go of the guilt."

"Okay."

"I'm going to find who did this and bring them to justice. For Autumn." Evan knew he was making a dangerous promise, one that he might not be able to keep, but he had to. He had to do something. "For now, I'll get your parents. They love you too. When you're ready to talk to them, I'm sure they'll be there for you. Until then, get some rest and get better. All right?"

"I'll do my best," Lily agreed.

Evan tried not to appear like he was rushing out of the room, but he could only think about Mckenna. What had happened? Was she okay? He needed to see if there was another victim services person available for this case, but first he wanted to find Mckenna and check on her.

Seeing Lily's parents, he forced himself to stop. "She's doing well. She gave me good leads to go on, including looking for some buildings in the surrounding area where she was found. I'll let you know when I find out anything, but for now, don't pressure her. She'll talk to you when she's ready."

"Thank you, Agent Knox," Brenda said. Lily's father shook Evan's hand.

"You two didn't happen to see where Mckenna and Mocha went, did you?"

"That way." Lily's mother pointed down the hall.

"Thank you," Evan said. "I'll be in touch."

He power walked toward the end of the hall, wanting to sprint, but trying to have self-control. There was an exit sign and another sign pointing to the chapel. Would she have gone outside? Or would she have gone to the chapel? Evan decided to check the chapel first. It was easy to know if she was there or not. If she wasn't, he'd call her phone.

Taking the stairs down, Evan found the door to the chapel. He heard Mckenna's sobs before he saw her. Mocha was in the aisle, a paw resting on his handler's legs.

"Mckenna?" he said.

She sat up and turned to him, her eyes puffy and face red from crying. Evan fought the urge to go hold her. Console her. It was all he wanted to do, but that would be crossing a line. Mocha climbed halfway into Mckenna's lap and rested his head on her shoulder.

Evan never thought he'd be jealous of a dog, but he wanted to be the one to pull her closer. Have her rest her head on *his* shoulder. "What's wrong?"

"Nothing," Mckenna said. "I'm fine."

"Well, you don't look fine."

Mckenna rolled her eyes. "If you're just going to stand there and look at me like I'm a science experiment, then you can leave."

"A science experiment?"

"Yes, like I'm a freak or something."

"Hey, stop it," Evan said, striding closer. "You're not a freak."

"How do you know?"

Evan shrugged. "Because I'm an FBI agent? We're trained to know these things?"

Mckenna let out a laugh and then tears started flowing again.

"Can I sit down?" Evan asked.

Mckenna nodded and he sidestepped Mocha, giving the Lab a rub on the head, and sat down next to Mckenna. Before he could talk himself out of it, Evan picked up her hand. It seemed tiny, delicate. She had smooth skin—opposite of his rough hands full of calluses from the gym and his recent landscaping project that had been a stab at trying to make his house feel like a home.

"This case is tough. It must be bringing back a lot of memories for you. Hard memories."

Evan thought Mckenna wasn't going to answer, but she said, "It's not the memories. It's the case itself."

"What do you mean?"

Mckenna turned toward him again, and he wiped away some of her tears, letting his fingers linger on her cheek for a second too long. He tucked some of her dark hair back, wishing again that he could hold her close and somehow ease her pain.

"What I mean," Mckenna said, "is that Lily's kidnapping is the same as mine. I mean *exactly*."

Evan didn't know how to respond. "What are you saying? What do you mean by exactly the same?"

"I'm saying I think we had the same kidnapper."

"Seriously?"

"Yes. My kidnapper, Toby Hanson, has been out on parole. Everything that happened was the same. The party. The smell of rotten eggs. Being kept in an old building. The window where I sliced my side open and then running for my life while he was shooting at me. And that eerie tree Lily mentioned has been part of my nightmares since I was taken. Everything is the same."

He stared at Mckenna straight on, and took her other hand. Feeling her shake, he closed his fingers tighter around hers. "Then I'll find Toby Hanson and figure this out."

Mckenna hiccupped and took a deep breath. "You will?"

"Yes. I will."

"You believe me?" Mckenna asked.

"Why wouldn't I?"

Mckenna shrugged. "I'm used to having to convince people of what I'm saying, that's all." Tears began running down her face. "I should have gone to the parole hearing. Maybe if I had, Toby would still be in prison, Lily wouldn't be traumatized for the rest of her life and Autumn would still be alive."

"You don't know that," Evan said, leaning in closer. "You can't go there because even if you had gone to the parole hearing, Toby might have still been released. I'll find Toby. I'll investigate him. If he did this, he'll go back to prison and never get out. He'll never be able to hurt anyone again."

Good job, Evan, more promises you might not be able to keep.

But could they really have the same kidnapper? Or was Mckenna jumping to conclusions? But if what she said was true, so many of the facts were the same. Would Toby have gone back to doing this so soon? He would need to call his parole officer and find out where he was staying.

"Thank you for believing me," Mckenna said.

"You're welcome." Evan was relieved to see that Mckenna was calming down and shaking less.

Mocha seemed to come to the same conclusion as he stepped down off her lap and lay down on the floor. Evan found himself still wanting to hold her, make her feel better, be the one to help. Without thinking, he pulled her closer, wrapping his arms around her, smelling the sweet scent from her shampoo.

I'm overstepping here. I'm going to regret this. She's going to think I'm being pushy or even harassing her. She could tell my boss and get me in trouble.

Evan was about ready to talk himself into letting go when Mckenna leaned into him. Her arms tightened around his waist.

I guess she's okay with this. I'm not crossing any lines. Yet.

Mckenna tilted her head up. "Thank you for not only believing me, thank you for not making me feel like I'm some broken toy that needs to be glued back together."

Evan hesitated and then said what had been on his mind for the past couple of days. "You're one of the strongest people I know. Look what you're doing to help others. Not many people could do your job after what you've been through. I would never think you were weak or broken. I think you're amazing."

Mckenna came closer, her hands now resting on his chest. His heart pounded and he stopped thinking and trying to talk himself out of being with her. Taking her face in his hands, he leaned over and kissed her, starting out slow and tentatively, but she didn't pull away. Instead, she lifted one hand, placing it behind his head, bringing him closer, her soft lips crushing hard against his. The world stopped for a moment and a shock went through Evan as he explored the kiss deeper and deeper until they parted.

What the hell are you doing? But how amazing was that?

Evan searched Mckenna's eyes, wondering if he'd gone too far, but instead, she pulled him in again, this time with no hesitation.

Chapter Twelve

Mckenna lost track of time. For a brief second, she forgot about the moment in life that had defined the last nine years. Instead, she was lost in the kiss with Evan. Everything about him was perfect. He was sensitive yet, at the same time, strong. Not only was she able to forget the trauma, but she'd also felt safe with him in that moment. Like he would protect her no matter what.

And he believed her.

That meant more to her than anything. She'd been dreading talking with Evan about her kidnapping. Part of her emotion and tears were due to how, over the years, she'd feel something and friends and even her family would dismiss her because of her anxiety. It seemed like once Toby was behind bars, her family was able to continue with their lives, but she was secretly struggling to move forward.

She'd learned to put on a brave face, but inwardly, Mckenna still had a storm brewing—one that wasn't going away easily. It had been unleashed listening to Lily. What if Toby was the one who took her? What if he came after Mckenna? What if *he* was the one driving that Jeep this morning? What if no one believed her? What if she was crazy and making things up? Maybe it was just one big coincidence that Lily had a similar experience.

When Evan said he believed her, though, relief coursed through Mckenna. She forgave him for the things he had said earlier. For a short time, the storm subsided. Then they had kissed. She had never kissed anyone like him before. She found herself not wanting to leave, instead wishing to just stay in this moment forever.

There was another side to Agent Evan Knox, and she liked it. A lot.

They sat together for a while, Mckenna letting her head rest against his chest, Mocha down by her feet. She didn't want to leave, but she knew they both had to get back to work. Back to reality. Evan had a kidnapper to catch.

Mckenna sat back, her lips still tingling. Evan stood, giving her his hand, and helping her to her feet.

"I'll figure this out, Mckenna."

"I know. Thank you."

"Do you want me to walk you to your car?" Evan asked.

Mckenna thought about the blue Jeep following her that morning. Was that her imagination running wild? Or could Toby somehow have a vehicle and be following her? Or could it be someone else?

Stop it. Jeeps are one of the most popular vehicles in Colorado. When it comes to that, you're paranoid.

Despite her thoughts, Mckenna heard herself answer, "Yes."

She picked up Mocha's leash, giving him love and thanks for his help. His tail wagged happily as they walked out of the chapel and toward the parking garage. The heat of the August day hit her. Mckenna would be happy when fall rolled around and the days cooled off. It was the best time in Colorado with warm days and cool nights—her favorite time of year.

Opening the back hatch, Mckenna pulled out portable

stairs for Mocha and set them up. He expertly navigated them and went into his crate, turning a circle and then curling up and tucking his head so that he formed a ball. She knew he must be tired too. Even though being a therapy dog wasn't like a police K-9 tracking and expending lots of energy, Mocha would need time to recover. It was a different type of job, but it still took a toll on the dogs. She would fill the kiddie pool in the backyard and let him lounge in the cool water tonight.

Mckenna started the car and turned up the air-conditioning. She turned around wondering if Evan would give her another kiss, but instead he stood back, running his fingers through his dirty blond hair that had enough curl to make it wavy. He appeared distressed.

Was he regretting the kiss? Maybe it hadn't been as good for him as it had been for her. Mckenna's heart sank, and she stared down at the ground.

"I'm sorry," Evan said. "I uh…"

"For what?"

"What I did. Kissing you. It was unprofessional. I crossed the line. I shouldn't have."

"I wasn't complaining," Mckenna said, feeling her cheeks go warm. So, it wasn't as good for him. He looked like he was getting ready to say something else, but Mckenna beat him to the punch. If he was regretting the kiss, then she didn't want to repeat her mistake. Climbing in the front seat, Mckenna said, "I'm sorry too then. I also crossed a line and it'll never happen again. Thank you, though, for listening and thank you for investigating Toby Hanson."

She closed the door and backed out before any tears could start falling again. What a mess. Why had she kissed him? And why did she have to enjoy it so much?

EVAN STOOD WATCHING Mckenna drive out until she turned onto the street and her car disappeared down the road.

"You're an idiot," he said to himself.

He never should have kissed her, but oh man, what he'd give to do it again. But he couldn't. Evan hoped she didn't go to her sister and tell Cassidy what happened. The best-case scenario was office gossip would run rampant for the next couple of days. The worst-case scenario would be the FBI firing him due to another office scandal. Plus, he had sworn he'd never open himself up like this to anyone. Love never worked out.

Time to get back to this investigation. He had promises to keep.

Evan walked to his bu-car and slid into the front seat. He started up the vehicle and cranked the air-conditioning. Did he really think that Toby Hanson was responsible? It was a lead and he had to investigate it. What he hadn't told Mckenna, though, was that he had to follow other leads too. He couldn't have tunnel vision, but he didn't want her to think he didn't believe her. Whether the cases were connected or not, Lily's interview had been a trigger.

First thing first, he had to find Toby Hanson.

Making calls, Evan received the name of Toby's probation officer—Keith Warren. He dialed the number and heard, "Officer Warren."

"Hello, this is Agent Evan Knox with the FBI."

"What can I do for you?"

"I need to find one of your parolees, the sooner the better. I need to talk to him."

"Who do you need to find?" Keith asked.

"Toby Hanson."

There was a pause and then Keith said, "Funny you mention him. I'm heading to his brother's place now to do a home inspection. The judge said Hanson could stay with his brother Rex Hanson as long as the ankle monitor stayed on, and I deemed it okay. I want to do a follow-up inspection to make sure everything is good."

"Would you like some company on that inspection?" Evan asked.

"Sure. Is this a good number to text you the address?"

"It is, and one other question," Evan asked. "Has Toby's ankle monitor been in any unusual locations?"

"Not that I'm aware of, but I can look at that information and let you know. You know how it is—I have a big workload, so it's not like I sit and watch everyone's monitor."

"I understand," Evan said. "If you could look up where he's been, that would be great."

"Sure, I'll do that and then meet you at his brother's house."

"Thank you," Evan said, hanging up and waiting for Keith to text the address. He willed himself not to think about Mckenna. That kiss. Or how she felt that close to him and how he'd love to feel her even closer.

The text chime notification thankfully interrupted Evan's thoughts. He put the address in the GPS and a chill swept over him. Rex Hanson, Toby's brother, didn't live that far from where Lily was found.

Suddenly, Toby Hanson became a lot more interesting.

Chapter Thirteen

Evan found his way to Rex and Toby Hanson's house. The small, ranch-style home was nestled back in a remote neighborhood. As he put his bu-car in Park, the first thing Evan noticed was spray paint in bright red all over the garage that read, "Go back to jail."

Should be prison, not jail, he thought to himself, but he supposed correcting some vandal's graffiti wasn't what Toby and Rex wanted to hear. A short, stocky guy came around the corner, followed by a taller, lankier man. Evan recognized the taller man as Toby Hanson.

Another vehicle pulled in next to him. Evan assumed this was Keith Warren, but as always when going to question someone, he remained cautious. Stepping out of the vehicle, Evan turned to the man who had just parked.

"Officer Warren?" Evan checked to be sure.

"Yep, that's me."

Keith came over and the men shook hands. Evan considered himself strong, but Keith's grip crushed his fingers. He was glad when Keith let go. Evan also wanted to know what Keith had discovered about Toby's whereabouts. Any upper hand he had to question him would be helpful. "Were you able to check Toby's ankle monitor?"

"I did. He was at different locations that I want to ask him about."

Evan raised an eyebrow. He'd like to know more, but he'd get the information one way or another. Now he was curious. "Care to elaborate?"

"I'll send you the addresses and information. No problem. It does appear he went to the house of a Penny Gardner and spent the night."

Evan shrugged. "I think you're allowed to have a relationship if you're out on parole unless Penny is on the list of people he shouldn't be in contact with."

"No, I have no idea who she is, but I need to make sure he wasn't drinking or doing something more." Keith waved a package that contained a urine analysis or UA test. "I'll be double-checking it as much as I can. Care to tell me about your interest in him?"

Evan didn't care to share with Keith, but he decided he needed to give him something to help future cooperation. "I have questions about an ongoing investigation. I believe Toby may know something or have seen something. Let's go talk to him."

Before Keith could answer, Evan turned and strolled toward the house. Rex and Toby had turned around, watching them approach. Evan hoped they hadn't overheard much.

"Hello, Toby. Just doing a random check-in today. I need to make sure things are going well. And you need to take care of this," Keith said, waving the UA package at Toby.

"Sure," Toby said. "I can do that."

Evan was surprised. Most parolees dreaded the UAs for the obvious reason. Although some really did change their life in prison. Maybe Toby was one of those, minus the possibility of kidnapping of course. He pulled out his badge and identified himself.

Rex hadn't said anything yet and Evan wanted to get them a little more comfortable. Try to put them at ease. Tucking the badge back in his pocket, Evan pointed at the graffiti. "Looks like you have someone giving you some trouble."

Rex and Toby peered over their shoulders. Rex spoke first. "Yeah, the neighbors and town residents aren't too happy about my brother being home. We're trying to ignore it all."

"I'm sorry to hear that. If you need me to talk to anyone, let me know," Evan said. Not like the FBI worried much about parolees' homes getting tagged, but he was hoping to gain a little trust.

Rex shrugged and said, "Probably just some kids getting into summer trouble before they go back to school. We'll get it scrubbed and painted over."

Evan peered into the garage, where he saw a nice vehicle parked. He continued his small talk, hoping the brothers might relax a little bit and give Evan the upper hand. "I like your vehicle. Glad the vandals didn't tag that. Is it a Jeep?"

"Yeah," Toby said.

"I might be in the market for a new vehicle for myself. I'd like something comfortable that could also do off-roading. I'm between a Jeep and a 4Runner."

Rex and Toby stared at him like he was crazy. So much for small talk helping, but Evan waited for an answer. Keith had his arms crossed, but so far seemed patient. Evan was certain Keith had other things to do today and he knew that he needed to start asking the serious questions, but he waited out the brothers for an answer to his vehicle question.

"Both are great for off-roading. I don't think you can go wrong," Toby finally said.

"Well, I don't want to keep you from cleaning up that spray paint."

Rex shrugged. "It happened before. It'll probably happen again."

"Before?" Evan asked.

"Yeah, before Toby agreed to a guilty plea, many people in town decided that he was already guilty. I even lost my job," Rex said.

"Really?" Evan feigned interest. "Where were you working?"

"The Parker Ranch."

Trying to keep a straight face with no reaction, Evan repeated back, "The Parker Ranch?"

"Yes," Rex said.

"As in Mckenna Parker, the person you kidnapped?" Evan asked Toby. He could tell that Toby was reluctant to speak.

After a few seconds that seemed like an eternity, Toby spoke up. "Yes, as in that Mckenna Parker. Rex had nothing to do with it. They shouldn't have fired him, but I guess I understand."

"Did you know Mckenna Parker?" Evan asked Toby.

"No, I didn't work there."

Evan caught a quick glance between Toby and Rex. What were they hiding about Mckenna? "You knew her, then, Rex, right? Since you worked there?"

"I did," Rex said. "Saw her around a bit here and there."

"How well did you know her?" Evan asked, feeling a bit of jealousy. He pushed it away, but there was something about Mckenna that brought out emotions he didn't know what to do with. He tried not to think about the kiss earlier, but it was hard to forget that. He hoped he was keeping somewhat of a straight face.

"Well enough," Rex answered. "Why are you asking all these questions? My brother has served his time. I know why Keith is here, but why are you here?"

"Fair enough," Evan said. "I don't know if you heard, but there was another kidnapping. Two girls. One of them is deceased. I'm helping the sheriff's office investigate."

"And let me guess, you came here because I've been convicted of kidnapping," Toby said, an edge of sarcasm in his voice.

"Yes. I need to know where you were three nights ago. And don't lie to me. Officer Warren has the information about where your ankle monitor was." Evan decided to up his game and drop the "nice guy" act. It was time to get some information.

"I didn't do it," Toby said.

"That's not what I asked. I asked where you were three nights ago." Evan noticed Rex's face flush red. Toby didn't say a word. "You can answer me here. Or you can answer my questions down at the FBI office. Your choice."

Sighing heavily, Toby crossed his arms. "I was with a lady."

"This lady have a name?"

"Yeah. She does."

"Care to share it?" Evan asked, starting to feel annoyed. "Remember, we can do this here or at the FBI office. I'm sure your neighbors are watching right now. It won't help the vandalism situation if you leave in cuffs sitting in the back of my vehicle."

Toby and Evan locked eyes and then he finally said, "Penny Gardner."

Evan turned to Rex. "You know Penny Gardner?"

Rex shrugged and then nodded, his face still red, and he studied the mountains on the horizon instead of looking at Evan.

There's something off with these two, but what is it? Rex is upset. I wonder if Rex was investigated or just Toby?

What're the odds that Toby could have covered for Rex in Mckenna's kidnapping? Especially since Rex worked for Mckenna's parents.

Evan continued his questioning. "Where were you three nights ago, Rex?"

"I was at a party. Same location as my brother."

Evan perked up at the mention of a party. "You two go together?"

"We did."

Pulling out his phone, Evan brought up a picture of Lily and then Autumn, showing it to the brothers. "Did you see either of these girls there?"

"Nope," Rex said.

"Take a closer look," Evan said. "Just to make sure."

Rex and Toby looked at the pictures a little bit longer. Rex spoke first. "Still nope."

"Okay," Evan said. "I don't want to take any more of your time or Officer Warren's time. If you think of anything, please call me."

Handing the brothers his card, Evan said goodbye and went back to his car. He sat in the driver's seat waiting to start the vehicle. Toby went with Keith into the house to take care of business. Rex glared at Evan for a moment and then turned around and started scrubbing the paint on the garage.

Yes, something was off. They were hiding something. Was Toby covering for Rex? Did they work together and that was how two girls were abducted?

Evan knew one thing: he wanted more information from Mckenna, and he wanted to find Penny Gardner, because this case kept twisting and going in directions he wasn't expecting.

Chapter Fourteen

Confused, shaken and a bit hurt after Evan's apology for the kiss, Mckenna drove back to the FBI office, working to gather herself together. This was not the morning she had expected. She was thrilled Mocha had helped Lily come out of her shell, but shocked to hear about Lily's experience that was so eerily similar to her own.

Then there was the moment with Evan. He was right, he did cross a line…and she wouldn't mind doing it again. Maybe even going further. When her hands were on his chest, she could feel how muscular he was, and strong. His heart had been thudding. Didn't that mean he was into the kiss too? That only shook Mckenna up more. She'd never been this drawn to someone. It wasn't just his looks. Despite the office watercooler gossip, Agent Evan Knox had a soft side and he cared. Somehow, she felt safe with him. She wanted to get to know him better.

Or so she thought, because then he'd apologized for kissing her. Like he'd only done it because he felt sorry for her. Mckenna didn't know what to think. She just wanted this day to be done so she could go home, sit out on her porch that overlooked the mountains, sip on a glass of wine and forget about everything that had happened. She could start over tomorrow.

Mckenna parked, let Mocha out of the car and went inside, glad for the air-conditioning since the day had turned hot. Hopefully, the monsoon rains would start soon and then at least some clouds would move in along with some rain to cool things off. She wouldn't have to worry about Mocha in the car or his paws burning on the pavement. But she wasn't in any hurry to shovel snow.

She and Mocha turned a corner and ran into Cassidy, who immediately narrowed her eyes.

"What's up?" her sister asked. "You've been crying. I can tell."

"Nothing," Mckenna lied. She didn't even know where to start. The similarities between the kidnappings? Lily speaking again? Kissing Evan and liking it? Okay, not just liking it, loving it and desiring more, but then knowing that he would probably be cordial and on his best behavior since he believed he'd crossed a line. Yeah, she didn't even want to start discussing everything.

"I don't believe you."

"Well, then don't. I have work to do, Cass. I need to get going." Mckenna hated being that way with her sister, but she had to get to her office and away from everyone.

"Was he an asshole?" Cassidy asked, eyes narrowed again.

"Who? Evan?"

"Evan? Since when did you start calling him Evan? What's going on?"

"He told me to call him Evan and nothing is going on," Mckenna said. "Please, I need to get some work done and then go home and relax. It's been a long day. Don't you have work to do too? Aren't you working that big case with the serial bomber or something?"

Cassidy sighed. "Okay, but call me later. I can tell something's up and I'll get it out of you. I'm an FBI agent after all."

"I'll call," Mckenna promised. She and Mocha made it to her office and Mckenna closed the door, flopping down into her chair and taking a deep breath. She closed her eyes, thinking about her breathing and working on calming techniques she'd learned after her trauma. It was hard to focus, though, because all she could think about was him. When her phone pinged, interrupting her thoughts, Mckenna didn't mind.

Until she saw who the message was from—Evan.

Meet me for coffee? I have some questions.

At least he'd included a smiley face emoji.

Sure. Where?

How about your usual?

How do you know my usual? Mckenna typed back.

I see you almost every day with a cup from there. Plus, there's shade for Mocha.

He noticed? He was an FBI agent. Of course he noticed.

Okay, what time?

I'll be there in about twenty minutes. You want a mocha to go with your Mocha?

Mckenna laughed. Then she typed back I'm more of a latte girl, but don't tell Mocha that. See you in a bit.

Her stomach had butterflies. No one had made her laugh

like that in a long time. The thought of meeting him outside the office made her nervous, but not because he was gruff and a lone wolf like the office gossips discussed. Mckenna assumed Evan only wanted to see her to get information about the kidnapping. Nothing more. But she was falling hard for the good-looking agent—she just didn't want to fully admit it.

A FEW MINUTES LATER, Mckenna and Mocha pulled up to the coffee shop. She'd managed to avoid Cassidy on the way out. And her boss. If she didn't start getting her work done soon for her other cases, her boss wasn't going to be happy.

Mckenna's heart skipped a beat when she saw Evan sitting out front, coffees on the table in the shade and a bowl of water for Mocha along with a soft blanket for him to lie on instead of the concrete. Yes, there was another side to Evan. She was liking it more and more.

Evan stood when he saw her coming. He ran his hands through his hair trying to tame the waves that Mckenna had come to love. She'd love to run her fingers through his hair, but he only did this when he was nervous or stressed. She stopped in front of him but didn't get close enough for a hug...or another kiss.

Evan motioned with his hand for her to take a seat across from him and then he sat down. He had circles under his eyes and appeared tired. She knew he'd had a hard day too, from questioning Lily to comforting Mckenna.

"Thanks for meeting me," Evan said. "I'll get right to the point. I have more questions for you about your kidnapping to see if it could relate to Lily and Autumn's. Are you up for this? It's okay if you're not."

Mckenna felt a little embarrassed at her reaction that morning, but the shock was over. If Toby did this, then she would help put him back in prison where he belonged. "It's okay. I can answer your questions. I want to help."

"Good," Evan said, looking relieved. "Just let me know if you need a break at any point."

Mckenna took a sip of her latte, enjoying the bitterness of the coffee mixed with the creaminess of the milk. There was a part of her that had been hoping Evan just wanted to see her, but he had a job to do. So did she. "I'll let you know, but I'll be okay. I promise."

At that moment, Mocha took a big drink of water and then placed his head over Evan's lap, drooling water everywhere.

"I'm so sorry," Mckenna said, grabbing some napkins, leaning over the table and dabbing the spot where Mocha had drooled.

"It's okay, seriously," Evan said with a laugh. "Trust me, if you arrest enough people, you're going to get much worse on your pants, shirt, even face. I'll take dog drool over all of that."

Their hands touched as they both reached for more napkins. They both hesitated and Mckenna for a moment thought about leaning in closer and kissing him again, but then she thought about how he'd talked about crossing a line that morning. She handed him the napkins and sat back down. Mocha seemed quite pleased with himself.

"What questions can I answer?"

Chapter Fifteen

Evan filled in Mckenna about his visit to Toby and Rex's house as he finished cleaning up the drool spots. He threw away the napkins and then sat back down trying to forget that when Mckenna had leaned over to help clean up Mocha's drool, he'd seen down her shirt. What he wouldn't give to take that shirt off and kiss her everywhere—even down lower.

Stop it, Evan. You need to focus. Find out more about her background with Rex and Toby.

As Evan kept talking, Mckenna's face dropped when he mentioned Rex's name. He had to ask and find out more, not just about how she knew Toby, but Rex as well. One thing at a time.

"Toby claims he was at a party and spent the night with a lady friend. A Penny Gardner. I looked her up and she's a high school teacher. Do you know her?"

Mckenna clasped her hands together, but they weren't shaking. Evan desperately wanted to reach out and hold them again while he talked to her, but that wasn't the FBI way. At no time during his training at Quantico did the instructors recommend holding hands with someone they were interviewing. They'd never met Mckenna Parker.

Mckenna peered back up at him and then said, "Yes. I

had her as a teacher and I've kept a terrible secret. I know it's wrong, but I kept telling myself it wasn't that bad."

"What's your secret?" Evan leaned in closer, catching a whiff of her shampoo again. The sweet, flowery scent made him want to take her out of here right now and find somewhere private where they could be alone. For a long time.

"I should have said something sooner."

"Mckenna, it's okay. I promise. I won't judge you." Evan could only hope she believed him, because it was the truth. He wouldn't judge her. If anything, he wanted to ask her so many more questions. Nothing to do with the case. What was her favorite food? Did she like to hike? Camp? Did she have a boyfriend? He worked to remain focused on this case.

"Penny Gardner threw the parties. I'd bet money that it was her house and party that Lily and Autumn went to that night. That's where I was the night I was taken."

"Were Rex and Toby there that night?"

"Yes, they were. Ms. Gardner only invited students who had graduated. Rex was the oldest and Toby was in Cassidy's class. It's a small town. Everyone knows everyone. Rex was already working for my parents, so that's how I knew him. We all swore we wouldn't say anything because Gardner was the 'cool' teacher, and we didn't want her to get into trouble. Now I know how stupid that was. Maybe if I had told the sheriff everything, we wouldn't be here today."

"We can't change the past," Evan said.

"I wish we could."

"I think everyone has something in their past they'd like to change."

"But how many people want to go back in time to turn in a teacher throwing a party so that they don't get kidnapped, and another girl doesn't die years later?" Mckenna asked.

"Good point," Evan said. "But still, we can change the

future. I'm going to find out more about Penny Gardner. I'll leave you out of it, though, okay?"

"No, you don't have to leave me out of anything. I'm an adult and I'm a different person now. It's time for me to take a stand. Do you think Toby did this to Autumn and Lily?"

"I'm not sure yet. He was at the party, but so was Rex. Did anyone question him that you know of?"

"I'm not sure, to be honest," Mckenna answered.

"Tell me more about Rex. I heard he worked for your parents."

"He did." Mckenna looked away and then started petting Mocha.

Evan could tell she was uncomfortable again. Maybe more secrets? "Do you think there's any chance he was the kidnapper and Toby was covering for him?"

"I really don't know. I don't think so, but I didn't know either of them that well. Although I knew Rex better."

"Did you and Rex have a...relationship?" Evan didn't know how to put it.

"You're finding out all my dirty little secrets today," Mckenna said. Evan could tell she was trying to joke, but he could see stress.

"We don't have to talk about all of this if you don't want to."

"No, I want to. It actually feels good." Mckenna took a deep breath. "Rex started working for my parents when he graduated from high school. He was good on the ranch and my dad liked him. My dad had two girls, so I think Rex was like a son to him. When I was a senior in high school, Rex had been working on the ranch for a couple of years. I started flirting and one thing led to another. We had a fling going. He was my teenage crush. I was eighteen, so it didn't seem wrong, but eventually he broke it off. I think he knew that even though we were only a few years apart, at that time in our lives, we were in very different stages. He insisted we couldn't see each other anymore. I was heartbroken, but a few months later, I was kidnapped, and then, honestly, I didn't care anymore. My world was upside down. Once Toby was arrested, my parents fired Rex and that was that."

Evan leaned back in his chair with lots of thoughts going through his head. Would a younger brother cover for an older brother? Did Toby take Mckenna because he was jealous? How did this connect with Lily and Autumn if at all?

"Since I'm spilling my deepest, darkest secrets, there's something else," Mckenna said.

Sitting forward again, Evan broke his FBI interviewing rule and took Mckenna's hands. "What is it?"

Mckenna leaned forward too, bringing back memories of that morning. The way she tasted and how her lips felt. How he would need a cold shower every time he thought of her hands pressing against his chest.

"I've always doubted that Toby was my kidnapper. There. I said it."

Evan didn't know how to respond, but the look on Mckenna's face told him that she was hoping he'd believe her. "Why do you say that?"

"I mean, I told other people that and no one ever listened…until you. You didn't know the sheriff at the time. He was almost excited about my experience because it put him in the limelight. He also knew that the whole area was on edge. People wanted the kidnapper found so that they could feel safe again. I don't even know how they decided to question Toby or search his vehicle to find my stuff, but something always felt off about it. There's something else too."

"You can tell me," Evan said, running his thumb over her fingers.

"I ran into Toby. Recently."

"He shouldn't have any contact with you." Anger surged through Evan. He'd call Keith immediately and let him know. The sheriff too.

"No, no, it wasn't like that. We were both in town at the hardware store. My house is old. It's always needing something. We happened to run into each other out in the parking lot. He came over and said he knew he wasn't supposed to talk to me, but he was sorry about what happened. Not what he did to me, but what happened. The way he said it made me think that he wasn't apologizing for himself, but rather he was just sorry that I'd had that experience. Doesn't it make you wonder? What if someone planted the evidence? What if Toby took the fall for someone else? A friend? And there's one last thing."

"What's that?" Evan asked.

"I think I'm being followed. I mean over the years there were times that I thought I was being watched. Everyone told me it was anxiety. Toby was in prison, so I was safe. Recently I've had a vehicle following me. I've seen it a couple times now. I wasn't certain, but I saw it again this morning."

"Do you have a make? Model? License plate?"

"It was a blue Jeep. Colorado plates. The next time I see it, I'm going to see if there's a way I can get the license plate."

"When was the last time it followed you?" Evan asked, thinking about the blue Jeep he'd just seen in Toby and Rex's garage.

"This morning. On my way to the hospital. Although when I turned in, it went straight. Maybe it's a coincidence."

"I don't think it is." Evan desperately wanted to tell Mckenna, but he didn't want to scare her either. Maybe he could get video off the hospital security cameras that faced the street and make sure it was the same vehicle owned by Rex before he told her anything. She was safer not knowing. "Do you mind if I ask the sheriff for the files on your case?"

"No, not at all." Mckenna leaned closer and gave him a quick kiss. "Thank you for listening. You're the first person who believed me and didn't think I was crazy. I need to get back to work before my boss wonders if I'm quitting my job."

Evan watched Mckenna and Mocha head back to their vehicle. He needed to talk with Penny Gardner and find out why she was throwing these parties. But the thing was, even he was beginning to wonder if an innocent man had spent eight years in prison. And if that were the case, who was the real kidnapper, and could he keep Lily and Mckenna safe?

For now, Mckenna would be safe working at the office. He called the sheriff and asked if he could come and read through the files of Mckenna's case, explaining the connection. Plus, internally he thought that if he had to go back to the office and see Mckenna, he'd want to find an excuse to be with her—especially after her quick kiss that had taken him off guard. He needed separation to sort out his feelings. The sheriff agreed and as he headed out, the reality sank in that it was going to be another long night.

Chapter Sixteen

As he drove up I-70 to the mountains, the traffic was heavy. Friday night. Of course it was heavy. What was he thinking? Working for the FBI, he often forgot what day it was because they all tended to run together. Normal people headed out of town for the mountains on the weekend. It didn't matter what time of year it was. Summertime they went camping. Wintertime was all about skiing.

For Evan, he preferred finding spots to get away where he could think, but he hadn't had a chance to take a vacation in a long time. Until he was back on track for his career promotion, he would work seven days a week, 365 days a year, if it meant he could keep his job. The FBI had always been his dream. He didn't know what he'd do without it.

Cars crept along in gridlock, heading up the first big hill to the mountains. Semis were in the right lane, hazards flashing, signaling that until they got to the first point where there was a downhill, they would be crawling up the mountain with their heavy loads. At this rate he'd be there by midnight, but it gave him time to think about the case, Mckenna and even Mocha.

Thinking about the kiss she'd given him at the coffee shop made him need a cold shower again. A long one. He turned up the AC on his bu-car. That would have to do for now.

He loved seeing her laugh, which didn't happen often, but when she did, he was rewarded with the shy smile on her face. He could feel her inner strength. That of a survivor. She had fought for her life back and had it. That made him want to be with her even more and close this case. What if she wasn't safe?

At least she had Mocha. Sure, he was a typical Lab who was sweet and goofy, but Evan thought if someone really threatened Mckenna, Mocha would at least bark and growl. That might be enough to deter someone from harming her.

Traffic finally opened up after he passed a stalled semi. It didn't take Evan long to get to the sheriff's office. He went through the front door and the sheriff was waiting behind the front desk. She hit a button to let him in and waved him to the back.

"Late night for you," the sheriff commented.

"It is. Thanks for letting me come."

"No problem. It's a late night for me too. I'll be catching up on paperwork. I think that's all I do anymore since I became sheriff."

Evan laughed. "Being the top dog isn't always what it's cracked up to be."

"No, it's not, but I like it too. Here's an empty room you can work in. I had everything brought here, including the evidence if you want to go through it. You know all the protocols."

"Thank you," Evan said.

"I'm ordering some pizza soon, want some?"

"I'd love it."

The sheriff nodded and headed out of the room, leaving Evan with a bunch of evidence. Was this a wild-goose chase? One he was on because of Mckenna and the way she made him feel? Or were these cases really connected and was there more than one kidnapper? He hoped he would find the answers somewhere in these boxes.

EVAN WIPED HIS fingers on a napkin after eating a greasy piece of pizza, grateful for the sheriff sharing with him. He'd been going through files for a while now and the next set was labeled as photographs of Mckenna after she escaped. He threw away his paper plate and napkin, not sure if he was ready to see what she'd looked like after being found.

Over his career, including some time as a police officer before coming to the FBI, Evan had seen plenty of grisly things both in real life and in pictures. But this would be the first time he'd see someone he cared about in a report, and that changed things.

Sitting back down, Evan opened the file and started flipping through pictures. The pizza suddenly wasn't setting well. Several pictures were of Mckenna at the hospital. There were before-photos of huge gashes on her side. Then after-pictures with stitches. He couldn't tell how many stitches she had, but it was a lot. She probably still had scars. Would he ever get to see them? See what they looked like now? Run his fingers over them and kiss them? Tell her nothing bad would ever happen to her again.

He sat back and rubbed his face. *Get a grip*, he told himself. But he was starting to wonder what it would be like to be with her. Maybe just one night. How much trouble would he be in if they had a relationship? It wasn't like other agents didn't get married. The little bit of time he'd spent with her had been fantastic even though they'd been brought together because of a horrific case. It wasn't only her looks, although she was beautiful. But he also loved how strong she was and how hard she'd worked to overcome her past. She was vulnerable too, but somehow that added to her strength. She was someone he wanted to be with. Get to know more. He'd never felt this way about anyone before and it was getting to the point he didn't want to ignore those feelings anymore.

Okay, back to work. Think about this case and forget your personal life. You don't have one and for all you know, she doesn't feel the same way. Although she did kiss you back...

A knock on the door startled him out of his thoughts. The sheriff came in holding CDs that contained all the interviews.

"Here you go," she said. "Nothing like a Friday night watching a criminal confess. You really think there's a connection between this case and our current one?"

Evan had filled in the sheriff about Mckenna's memories and Penny Gardner. They had agreed they should go talk to Penny. The sheriff had been ready to arrest her at that moment, but Evan said to give it time. They needed to gather more evidence so that they could talk to her and get more information out of her. They also needed more proof that she was having these parties so that she could be convicted for serving minors. The sheriff had reluctantly agreed.

"I think there may be a connection, but I'm not one hundred percent sure yet. It's the best lead so far," Evan answered. "When do you need me to leave tonight?"

"You can stay the whole night as far as I'm concerned. I still have a big stack of paperwork and one of my dispatchers is sick. Since it's a Friday night, I might be filling in."

"Okay, thanks," Evan said.

"I'm down the hall in my office. Let me know if you find the smoking gun as they say."

Evan laughed. "I'll do that."

The sheriff closed the door as she left. He'd laughed several times now. He hadn't done that in forever. Ever since the incident at his previous office, he'd become serious, and he knew that most of his coworkers appreciated his work ethic but not his personality. He'd forgotten how to laugh—until he met Mckenna.

Evan popped the first CD into the computer and started watching. The interview started with the sheriff and another deputy or detective coming into the room. Toby sat hunched on a chair staring at the floor as the sheriff read his Miranda Rights. He already appeared defeated.

Evan listened intently, trying to catch anything in Toby's interview that made him think he was guilty, but as it went on, he had to agree with Mckenna. The sheriff back then, a large man with a big belly who was obviously quite full of himself, was relentless. Toby told him over and over he didn't know anything. He didn't do it. It was so repetitive that Evan decided to skip ahead a little bit. That was when he realized that the interview was over twelve hours long.

People might say they would never confess to a crime they didn't commit, but be interviewed—no, battered—for long enough and soon, you'd admit to anything just to make it stop. To go home. To get away. At one point Toby asked if he needed a lawyer. The sheriff never really answered, and anger boiled inside Evan.

Technically, Toby had never *asked* for a lawyer. He'd only asked if he needed one. So, they didn't have to stop the interview, but it would have been the right thing to do. Of course, any cop or agent knew that once a defense attorney was present all interviews were probably over, and they'd never get this opportunity again. He understood that side of it, but he still felt like it was wrong.

Evan continued watching until he couldn't stand it anymore. Then he went back to the file with notes about Mckenna's condition at the hospital. Not only did Mckenna have gashes on her side, but she was bruised. She'd told them that the kidnapper never touched her—that she had the bruises from running blindly while he was chasing and shooting at her. He'd never tried anything sexual either, which was amazing. That was usually the motive for taking someone. That or money. But she had said what Lily had—he'd wanted the thrill of catching them and then releasing them. He got off on the power and control. Whatever the reason, the more Evan went through the files the more he believed that Toby might have been framed.

By whom? Law enforcement? Would the sheriff have been so desperate to solve a crime that he'd plant evidence? Did the sheriff know about these parties? The current sheriff certainly had no clue this was going on in her area.

The more Evan read, the more he realized that Toby had never had a chance. Other leads weren't followed up. His vehicle was never processed for DNA to see if Mckenna had been in it at some point. Even that wouldn't prove anything necessarily. A good defense attorney could work with that and say that Toby had only given her a ride.

Evan stood and started pacing, trying to think better. If Toby didn't do this, then who did? He needed to get Mckenna and Lily together and question Lily again to see if their stories continued to match up. If either of them could think of anything more, that might lead him to the real kidnapper. It was still a possibility that Rex was the culprit, but would Toby take the fall for his older brother? Evan had seen stranger things in his career, but this was a big one. Serving eight years in prison wasn't something a person just did to help their sibling.

Wondering what the current sheriff knew about her predecessor, Evan went to her office, hoping she wouldn't mind an interruption. He knocked on the door and she waved him in.

"Question for you," Evan said.

"Go for it."

"I'd love to chat with the detective and sheriff who questioned Toby. Do they live around here?"

"No, unfortunately, the previous sheriff died from a heart attack and the detective lives in Florida now. I've lost track of him. I could work on that if you need me to."

"Not yet, but I'll keep that in mind."

"What're your thoughts?"

Evan hesitated. How much should he share? He'd been burned at his other field office when he shared too much with the jealous agent, not realizing what was going on. He still mostly had working theories. But he liked the sheriff and trusted her, so he decided to run Mckenna's theory by her. "Toby Hanson was forced into confessing. I'm not sure he's our guy now or back then."

"Holy…" The sheriff trailed off.

"Yeah. And if that's the case, I have to wonder if this is the same person who took Mckenna? Or are there two different kidnappers out there? I'm going to go home for the night, but if I need those files and evidence again, would it be okay?"

"Of course, anytime. Just let me know."

"Thank you," Evan said, standing and realizing how much he needed some sleep. "I'll keep you posted on anything I find out."

"And vice versa," said the sheriff.

As Evan headed out into the night that was starting to cool off, he had to wonder why the previous sheriff had gone after Toby so hard and had such tunnel vision. Thanks to him, a kidnapper could have been on the loose for a long time and there could be many more victims out there. He'd reach out to surrounding states and departments because he didn't think someone with this compulsion could stop for nine years.

Another thought crossed his mind. If Toby really was framed and Mckenna had told others her theory, was she safe? Evan didn't know what he'd do if something happened to her.

Chapter Seventeen

The next morning, Evan was out early for a run. He'd slept fitfully, which he blamed on not working out the past few days. Plus, a run gave him time to think. The more he thought about Toby's confession, the more he was certain that there was a kidnapper out there who hadn't been caught.

But he had to prove it.

Arriving back home, he showered and was about ready to leave when his cell phone rang. The caller ID said it was the lab. Maybe with the tox results?

"Knox," he said, picking up the call.

"Morning, Agent," said a person who sounded way too happy for this early in the morning. "This is Allison from the medical examiner's office and I have some results for you on the case you're working. Is this a good time?"

"It is." Evan started to pace around his living room. What type of drug would the results show?

"Both victims had alcohol in their systems. I know that's no surprise. They had enough to be slightly impaired, but not enough to be intoxicated—at least at the time this blood was drawn. On a side note, the coroner found a .45 caliber bullet in Autumn, but he doesn't think it killed her."

"If the alcohol and gunshot didn't kill her, then do you know what did?" Evan asked.

"I think so. There's more. Let me bring up the second test."

Evan was trying to remain patient but was having a hard time.

"Okay, they both tested positive for GHB or gamma hydroxybutyrate. It's a party drug, although it's sometimes prescribed for narcolepsy. When it's given to someone it can create euphoria or even heighten sex drive. It will definitely make it easy to get someone to do what you want, and the victim will have amnesia. I think it could also be the cause of death in Autumn's case."

"Why do you think that?" Evan asked.

"Because when it's mixed with alcohol it can be deadly. It can cause a coma and death. Everyone reacts to drugs differently. I found out that Autumn was also taking meds for depression and anxiety. She was taking Xanax, which is a benzodiazepine. The alcohol mixed with the benzos and GHB was a lethal combo for her. I'm shocked that she made it as far as she did before she collapsed. Adrenaline helped. Who knows? Of course, the pathologist and coroner will determine final cause of death, but I believe this is what killed this young lady. Very tragic."

"It is tragic," Evan said, "but at least we have some answers. Thank you."

Allison hung up and Evan headed out the door. He'd learned that Lily had gone home from the hospital, but he needed to talk to her. See if there was anything else she could remember and discuss the party. He called Lily's parents and received permission to come over. Then he opened Mckenna's contact on his phone.

He wanted to talk to her, but he wished it weren't for work. Right now, though, his priority was finding the sicko who took Lily and killed Autumn. If Mckenna had a connection to the case and was taken by the same person, he needed to figure that out too. Especially if it meant Mckenna was in danger. Evan hit the call button and heard the phone ring.

"Morning, Agent Knox."

His stomach was in knots. "I thought I told you to call me Evan."

He heard her laugh. "I know. You did. I was just teasing you."

"I like your teasing."

"Yeah? Good. What's up?"

"I uh…" Evan hesitated. How did he tell her that he went through her files? Saw the pictures. Knew intimate things about her that she'd never told him?

"Spit it out, whatever you have to say is fine."

"Okay. I went through the files last night and watched some of the interviews with Toby Hanson. I didn't have time to watch all of them. They kept him for hours."

Silence.

"You okay?" Evan asked.

"I'm good. What's your thought on my gut feeling that Toby didn't take me? That he might be innocent?"

"I agree with you," Evan said. "I mean, as an agent I need to investigate more. I can't say for sure that he's not guilty, but the techniques used to get him to confess could get anyone to confess to a crime."

"What's next, then? What do we need to do?"

"I need you to be careful. If there is a kidnapper out there who's never been caught and he starts to believe that Toby isn't being investigated for this case, then he could come after you." Evan hesitated again, thinking about Rex's vehicle. "If you see that Jeep following you again, you need to let me know. Right away, okay?"

"Okay, I can do that. What can I do to help? I'll tell you anything that I can remember."

"I want to be careful about how involved you are in this case, but I'd like to chat with Lily, and I think it would help to have you and Mocha there. I want to learn more about the party and then I'm going to speak with Penny Gardner. Not only is it time for her parties to stop, but she has information. She could even be withholding something, who knows."

"I can meet you at Lily's in about thirty minutes. Mocha and I were getting ready to head out the door," Mckenna said.

"I'll see you there. And Mckenna?"

"Yeah?"

"Be careful." Evan hung up. He'd wanted to say more than that. He couldn't wait to see her. He wondered if she would want to have dinner sometime. For now, though, he needed to figure out what was going on and keep her safe.

Mckenna loaded Mocha into her vehicle, and they made their way toward Lily's parents' house. She worked to not be overly excited to see Evan, but it was hard not to want to be with him. Or just around him. Sleep had eluded her last night as she kept waking up thinking about the kiss and how she wouldn't mind doing that again. But today was about work.

"We have to stay professional, don't we, Mocha?" Mckenna said. Talking to her dog helped her feel better sometimes. And focus. She heard Mocha emit a deep, contented sigh. "Plus, what makes me think he's even interested? Who apologizes for crossing a line after kissing a girl? A good guy who knows that we work together, that's who. What do you think, Mocha? Is this a mistake? According to Cassidy it's a mistake."

There was no answer except for snoring sounds.

"You're not much help."

Mckenna thought about the conversation with her sister the previous night. Cassidy had called after hearing a rumor that one of the secretaries in the office had seen Mckenna kiss Evan at the coffee shop.

"Why did I do that in public? Huh, Mocha?"

Cassidy had warned Mckenna that Evan was only out for himself. All he wanted was a promotion, no matter whom it hurt along the way. Evan was using her to solve this case and when it was over, he'd be done with Mckenna. Gone. Maybe even transferred again if by some chance the FBI did decide to promote him. Cassidy didn't want to see her get hurt.

But the fact was, Mckenna was beginning to think it was worth the risk. Evan was everything that Cassidy said— driven, wanting a promotion, "work first, didn't matter who it hurt" kind of guy—but she'd seen another side to him. One that she really liked and wanted to get to know better. He was the first guy she'd ever been with who seemed to want to get to know *her*. Not the kidnapped girl who was famous, but Mckenna for who she was.

Deep in her thoughts, Mckenna glanced in her rearview mirror. Her heart thudded quicker as she gripped the steering wheel. There it was. The blue Jeep following her. Again. She couldn't make out the driver. How could she manage to get the license plate and see the driver better? At a stoplight? Mckenna got off at the next exit and pretended to be going to a gas station. For once, she was hoping for a red light, but it stayed green, and she had to keep going. There was a gas station and small food mart up the hill.

Mckenna turned in and slowed down, making the Jeep also slow down. The driver was male, but he had on a hat and sunglasses. He sped up and she couldn't identify him, but there was something familiar. She managed to write down the plate number to give to Evan. This was too much of a coincidence. She was being followed and she didn't like it.

Turning back out of the gas station, Mckenna continued onto Lily's house, keeping an eye on who was behind her, but the vehicle never appeared again. The person had to know she'd seen him. But what scared her more was that the driver was bold and didn't seem to care.

Mckenna found the driveway for Lily's house, and as she wound her way down the hill to the residence, was glad she didn't have to clear this driveway in the wintertime. Evan was leaning against his vehicle. She saw him before he saw her. His arms were crossed, accentuating his muscles, and he was gazing off toward the mountain peaks, seemingly content. Even happy. She'd never seen him like that at the office. Ever. It only made him more appealing and attractive.

She parked and stepped out of the vehicle. When Evan turned in her direction, Mckenna's heart pounded a little faster. Was it her imagination or was he admiring her? Before she did something she regretted, like kissing Evan with witnesses again, Mckenna went to get Mocha out of the vehicle.

"Morning," Evan said behind her. "You need help getting Mocha out?"

He'd come over and was standing behind her, a slight grin on his face that made his blue eyes twinkle. His hair was still wet from a shower.

I'd love to shower with him.

The thought crossed Mckenna's mind before she could stop it and her face flushed red. "No, I got him. Thanks, though."

"You okay?" Evan asked.

Although thoughts of being with Evan had distracted her briefly, she was still feeling the anxiety from the Jeep following her. She stopped opening Mocha's crate. "I saw it again."

"It?"

"The blue Jeep. This time I saw the driver. He was a white male, but he was wearing a hat and sunglasses, so I couldn't make out more than that. I pulled into a gas station, and he kept going. I was able to get the license plate information."

"I can run the plates."

"That would be great. Thank you," Mckenna said. "I'll give you the information after we talk to Lily."

Mckenna went back to unloading Mocha. She set up the stairs for him to go down and when he touched the ground, Mocha started wagging his tail at Evan, a big doggy grin on his face. Evan crouched down and encouraged Mocha to come and say hello.

"Morning, buddy," Evan said. "No drooling on me today, okay?"

Mocha wagged his tail in response and leaned up against Evan, almost pushing him over.

"Looks like you need some love this morning," Mckenna said, instantly regretting her choice of words.

"I do," Evan said, standing. "Ready to go to work?"

"I am." Mckenna and Mocha followed Evan. This time she was mentally prepared for their talk with Lily. Whatever Lily shared wouldn't be such a shock.

Mckenna wanted nothing more than to find the person who did this so she could quit being followed and they could all move on with their lives.

Chapter Eighteen

Evan dreaded questioning Lily again, mostly because he knew that it wasn't just one person that his questions would trigger, but rather two. And one of those two he now had strong, protective feelings for—seeing Mckenna this morning, he knew for sure. When this case was over, he wanted to be with her. He wanted to know her in a way that only he could.

Mocha strode past him, seeing Lily on the couch. The sweet Lab went over and climbed up next to Lily and then rested his head on her lap.

"Is that okay?" Mckenna asked Lily's mother. "He doesn't need to be on the couch."

"It's fine. If it makes her happy then I'd let ten Labs sit on the couch."

Ten Labs might eat the couch, Evan mused, his mind going back to the dogs his dad had when he was growing up. Of course, those were high-energy dogs meant for tracking and odor detection. Mocha was the opposite and the epitome of a couch potato. But he was still a Lab, Evan thought, recalling the stolen, snarfed-down sandwich.

Mckenna took a seat not far from Mocha. Evan pulled up a chair in the living room.

"Do you mind if I record this?" he asked.

Lily shook her head no. Evan was relieved. If allowed, a recording of the interview would help in court. Especially if Lily didn't want to testify. Some victims did, some didn't. He knew Mckenna had turned down testifying, but she had given a victim impact statement at Toby's sentencing.

Evan said the time and date for the recording. "Lily, some of my questions may be difficult. Take your time answering and let me know if at any time you need a break. Okay?"

Lily nodded and he caught Mckenna giving him an appreciative look. He gave her a quick smile, trying to let Mckenna know that he was going to be as gentle as he could, but this was going to be difficult. For everyone. Even him.

"Tell me about this party again," Evan started. "How did you find out about it?"

Lily stroked Mocha's head and the dog gave a content sigh, reached up and gave the girl a lick on her cheek and then rested his head back in her lap. Mocha's encouragement helped Lily.

"Some of us had kept in touch with Ms. Gardner. She had a fake profile on Facebook that we all knew about, and she'd send out messages. There was never any pressure or anything. I don't want to get her into trouble," Lily said, a worried expression crossing her face.

"You won't get her into trouble." Evan knew he was lying, but he needed to keep Lily talking. He ignored the stare Mckenna gave him. She'd have something to say about it later because Mckenna knew Penny Gardner should be in trouble, but right now Evan needed information to close this case and keep Mckenna safe. Did he really know she was in danger? He'd be less worried if he didn't think that Rex Hanson was following her.

He wanted to talk to him again later. Right now, he needed to gather more evidence to help with an arrest. If he took what he had to a prosecutor, they'd laugh at him and tell him to come back when he had more.

Lily had quit talking and was peering out the big window that framed Mount Blue Sky.

"Lily?" Evan gently said. "What else can you tell me about these parties? Are there ever drugs there?"

"Mostly we just drank. I guess occasionally Ms. Gardner would have a marijuana vape, but it seemed like it was more for her and none of us ever took a hit off it or anything."

Evan nodded. He needed to know how the girls ingested the GHB. If they were doing drugs along with drinking, he hoped Lily would tell him the truth, but his guess was that somehow their drinks were spiked. "You ever hear of a drug called GHB? Some of the street names you might know it by are 'Liquid E,' 'Georgia Home Boy,' or 'Grievous Bodily Harm.'"

"No, I haven't heard of that," Lily said continuing to snuggle with Mocha. "Why?"

"I received the tox screen reports for you and Autumn. You had alcohol in your system as we know, but you also tested positive for GHB."

Lily's mother, Brenda, gasped behind them. Evan gave her a look and she backed away. Her husband took her to the kitchen, which relieved Evan. If he was going to get the truth out of Lily, he needed her to feel comfortable.

"But we didn't do any drugs," Lily said. "I swear."

"I believe you." Evan took a quick peek at Mckenna. She appeared calm. No hand clasping. He was glad she was doing okay with all this questioning. "I'm wondering, though, did you drink from unopened containers or was someone serving the alcohol?"

"There was someone serving the alcohol. He made margaritas. Said they were his specialty."

Now we're getting somewhere. "Do you remember what he looked like?"

"Not really. Older. About Ms. Gardner's age. Your age."

Evan didn't know how he felt about being called older, but he figured he was about the same age as Penny Gardner and all her "friends." Maybe the "cool" teacher was knowingly providing a spot where a predator could pick his prey. Evan took two pictures out of a folder he'd brought. One was Toby's mugshot; the other was a picture of Rex that he'd obtained from the DMV. "Was it either of these guys?"

Lily stared at the pictures and then quickly pointed to Rex's picture. "I think it was him."

Excitement and adrenaline started coursing through Evan's body. Maybe Toby had covered for his brother all those years. "Did he serve you two the entire night?"

"I don't totally remember, but I think he traded off with some other guy I didn't know." Tears began to run down Lily's face. "I wish I'd never gone to the party. I wish I had agreed with Autumn that we should stay at her place and watch movies."

"Listen to me," Evan said, hoping to bring Lily some comfort. "We all do things that we regret, especially when we're teenagers. It's normal. It's part of growing up."

"But did you kill your best friend?"

"No," Evan answered. "And neither did you."

"How do you know that?" Lily asked as Mocha climbed a little more into her lap, giving her a few licks.

"Because I know that the drug you two were slipped, GHB, had a bad reaction for Autumn. She was on medications that should never be mixed with GHB, and it was lethal. The drugs killed her. Whoever gave you two the drugs killed her, and they'll pay for it when I catch them,"

Evan said. He hoped his words would help. If not now, then maybe down the road.

He was also already thinking about how he wanted to figure out who the other guy serving drinks at the party was. When he visited the "cool" Penny Gardner, he'd have a chat with her about her guest list. For now, though, he'd put Lily through enough for the day.

Standing, Evan said, "Thank you, Lily. I know this is hard. You're being very brave. I appreciate you talking to me. If you remember anything else, call me. You still have my card?"

"Yes."

"Good, you can call me anytime. If it's after hours, you'll get an operator at the FBI switchboard, but she'll put you through. If you need anything, let me know." Evan took another look at Mckenna, relieved that she seemed like she was doing okay.

"Okay, I'll call if I think of anything," Lily said, then turned to Mckenna. "Can I pet Mocha a little bit longer?"

"Sure," Mckenna said.

"I'll wait for you outside," Evan said. He was ready to call the sheriff and get to Penny Gardner's house right now, but he wanted the license plate number of the blue Jeep Mckenna kept seeing. Then he could verify it was Rex and have a talk with him too.

Although, if Rex was threatening Mckenna, it would be hard to stay professional during that interview.

Chapter Nineteen

Mckenna and Mocha stayed with Lily for a little bit longer, Lily clinging to Mocha's neck. Part of Mckenna wanted to tell Lily about the connection she thought they had—the same kidnapper. But she knew for now, she needed to stay quiet and let Evan do his job. When the right time came, she'd tell her more.

On her way out, Lily's father stopped her and Mocha. "Do you think it was him?" he asked.

"Him? You mean Toby Hanson?"

"Yes."

"I really don't know," Mckenna said truthfully. "I'm sorry. I wish I had more answers for you."

"If it was, I swear, I'll kill that son of a bitch."

Mckenna took a deep breath. "I can't understand how you feel, but I do know how Lily feels and right now. She needs you to just be there for her, rather than plotting the death of someone who may or may not be the suspect. She wants you by her side through the good and the bad. And trust me, there will be a lot of bad ahead, but in some ways the saying that time heals is true. I've given you resources including some great family therapists. I suggest you reach out to them for Lily, and for you."

Mckenna gave his arm a soft squeeze, hoping he would

take her advice. She remembered her father saying a similar thing and it was one of the hardest things Mckenna had ever listened to. He had been venting to her mom, not knowing that she could hear, but she'd heard.

I felt like I made him into someone he wasn't. I felt like it was all my fault. Now I know better.

Mckenna and Mocha stepped outside, closing the door behind her. Evan was waiting, pacing back and forth, running one hand through his hair. Mckenna was beginning to understand this was Evan's tell for stress and thinking. She didn't want to interrupt his thoughts, so she headed to her car to get it started, Mocha loaded in his crate and the AC blasting.

She started her car, turning up the cool air as the sun beat down. Even though they were at altitude, which was cooler at night, they were literally closer to the sun, which made the heat feel more intense. Like the intense look she knew she was receiving from Evan.

Mckenna turned toward him. "I'm going to Penny Gardner's house with you."

"No, you're not. It's too dangerous. I need to go there with the sheriff." Evan had stopped pacing and now had his hands in his pockets. "But I would like to get the license plate number from you."

"Why do you think it's dangerous? Penny gave minors liquor and was stupid, but she's not going to hurt anyone."

"You don't know that."

"I do. I mean, I had her as a teacher," Mckenna said, her stubborn side kicking in. Evan was *not* going to leave her behind. Sure, her job was completely different, but this was also her chance to get answers.

Evan didn't answer for a while, and then he said, "Before I went to Quantico, my first job was as a patrol officer for the city I grew up in."

Mckenna wondered where he was going with this.

"I saw a man pulled over to the side of the road. I called it in and stopped to help. He said he was out of gas. I helped him push the car to the gas station. He seemed nice. Thanked me and I went on my way. Later that evening he shot a rival gang member, and it turns out that the car was stolen. I learned my lesson. You never, ever assume anything. He could have been a normal guy out of gas. But it turns out he was a murderer, thief and was also found guilty in a rape once his DNA was processed. I'm sure he had a good laugh over the stupid cop that helped him out. You might think you know Penny Gardner, but she's not only provided alcohol and marijuana to minors, but she's also had two parties now where you and two other girls were taken. I don't know that you'd be safe. For all I know she's in on all this, getting her kicks out of helping her man kidnap someone. There're sick people out there."

Mckenna crossed her arms. She understood what Evan was saying, but in her heart, she felt like Penny Gardner was just a teacher who never left her high school days and this was her way of trying to stay popular.

"Can I have that license plate number now? I'd like to see who's following you," Evan asked, holding out his hand.

A sly grin spread across Mckenna's face. She understood where he was coming from, but she also wanted to see the look on Penny's face when she showed up on the doorstep with the sheriff and the FBI. "I'll give it to you."

"Thanks."

"After you allow me to go with you to see Penny. I want to hear what she has to say. I need to hear what she has to say."

"No. I'll get the information from you later then," Evan said opening his car door.

"You're forgetting that I know where she lives. I grew up around here. I'll see you there," Mckenna said.

Evan shook his head. "Will you make me one promise and keep it?"

"It depends on what it is."

"If I ask you to leave because something feels off or to wait in your car, will you do it?"

Part of Mckenna wanted to argue, but she could see he was serious. And that he cared. She grabbed the piece of paper with the license plate information, took it over to him and held it out. "Of course. I promise I will do that. I'll see you there."

As Evan took the paper from her hand, Mckenna stood on her tippy toes and kissed him. She couldn't help herself. "Just so you know, I'm okay with the line we crossed."

Then she turned, walked to her car, got in and drove away, leaving a stunned Evan in the dust.

MCKENNA HAD SPUNK, Evan had to give her that. He was going to regret letting her come, but when she had pointed out that she knew where Penny Gardner lived, he knew he was beaten. She was going to be there whether he wanted her to or not. And to be honest, if that were the case, he felt better having her there when he was around. He hated the thought of her going on her own. And he had a bad feeling she would. Mckenna Parker was a complex person—she might still have nightmares from being kidnapped, but in other areas of her life, she was fearless. Like when it came to kissing him. He had only wished it had lasted longer. She had completely taken him by surprise once again before they left.

Evan wound his way through the back roads enjoying the scenery. He still hadn't explored Colorado much. Mount

Blue Sky loomed in the distance. While you could drive up there, Evan wanted to hike to the top. He'd made a list of fourteeners that he'd love to hike. The peak seemed both moody and mysterious sometimes. How and when he'd have time, he didn't know, but he would like that. There were fifty-eight fourteener peaks to choose from and this one was practically in his backyard. Maybe Mckenna would be willing to join him…after the case was over of course.

Forcing himself to focus, Evan found the turnoff to Penny's driveway and saw Mckenna's car right in front of him. Large pine trees lined the drive and seemed to close in around him. The trees cut out the sun, casting eerie, dark shadows on the road. The drive opened to a small, quaint, nice mountain home that was the opposite of the creepy driveway—it was almost cheery.

Evan parked, taking in his surroundings. Not only was he determining if there was anyone outside and taking note of any dangers, he was also assessing how thick the forest was. This part of the woods had old, mature trees, which meant the forest was quite dense. Someone could easily get two girls drugged, convince them to leave with them and disappear into the trees. There was a good chance no one would see them.

Mckenna parked nearby in the shade, rolling down the windows for Mocha. With the way the sun was blocked by the trees, Evan figured Mocha would be okay for a while. He knew Mckenna would never put him at risk. Mocha could also be a good way to get her to leave if Evan felt like she should. He might be able to use that to his advantage. He still didn't feel good about having her along with them.

The sheriff pulled up as Evan stepped out of his vehicle. She glanced at Mckenna and gave him a questioning look.

"Long story," Evan said as Mckenna approached them.

"But I told Mckenna that if we asked her to leave, she would. Right?"

"Right," Mckenna said. "I promised, but sheriff, I feel like you might actually get more out of Penny Gardner if I'm here."

"Okay for now," Sheriff Stewart said.

Evan could tell the sheriff had similar misgivings but was going along with it for the moment. They approached the front door, or fatal funnel, as most in law enforcement called it. Front doors earned that title for a reason—they were extremely dangerous. You never knew who or what was behind them. It could be a harmless kid or someone packing a 12-gauge shotgun ready to blow a big hole in everyone.

"Stay to the side of the door with us," Evan advised Mckenna. "And stay behind me."

Much to his relief, she listened. The sheriff rang the doorbell and stood off to the side with Evan and Mckenna. Mckenna seemed squished behind them on the front porch since there was a railing limiting room. Evan was glad to have her there although he wished there were a little more space in case something didn't go as planned. Footsteps approached and then the front door opened.

"Sheriff?" a lady asked. She was average height and build. Since it was summer, she was wearing shorts and a tank top, her hair braided back. He didn't see any sign of her having a weapon and her hands were where he could see them.

"Hi, Penny," the sheriff answered. "This is FBI Agent Evan Knox, and I think you know Mckenna Parker, who's with the FBI victim services response team. Do you mind if we come in and chat?"

"No, not at all," Penny said, opening the door wider. "Good to see you, Mckenna. I didn't know you were working for the FBI."

"Good to see you too," Mckenna said.

Evan figured that once they started talking, the "good to see you" stuff would go away.

"What can I help you with?" Penny asked.

"Please," the sheriff said, pointing to a chair. "We have some questions for you."

The sheriff, Evan and Mckenna remained standing. Evan could see the change in Penny's face—the moment when someone realized you were here to ruin their day. Of course, someone like Penny always earned that honor.

Chapter Twenty

"We're going to get straight to the point," Evan started out. There were times where he made small talk with suspects to get them more comfortable, but he suspected Penny might take advantage of the time and think about how to manipulate them. He went with the tactic of hitting her hard while she was still surprised and off guard. "I need to know everything about the parties you're throwing. And I mean everything. Including a list of attendees."

"I don't know what you're talking about," Penny said, smoothly.

Evan's tactic hadn't worked. Penny was going to play games no matter what. He had an answer for that. "You don't have parties at your house where there's underage drinking and sometimes some of the attendees don't make it home?"

"No," Penny answered, but Evan caught her glimpse toward Mckenna. Maybe having Mckenna here was good after all. He was about ready to launch into his favorite spiel of they could do this here or down at the FBI when Mckenna spoke up.

"Ms. Gardner. Penny. Whatever I should call you now, I'm going to stop you there. We both know about these parties. We both know I attended them, and we both know that I was abducted from your party. I protected you all these years and acted like the party was at someone's house I didn't know, but I'm a different person now. Getting kidnapped will do that to you. Answer his questions. Now."

Evan raised an eyebrow at Mckenna. She was good. She'd missed her calling and should apply to Quantico, instead of remaining a victim specialist. He thought Penny might continue to deny everything. Her eyes darted back and forth between him and the sheriff. He was about ready to tell her to stand and turn around so he could cuff her when she spoke up.

"Okay, I'll tell you what you want to know."

"Thank you," Evan said. He flashed a grateful look at Mckenna. Why did he have a feeling there was going to be another "I told you so" coming his way? "How do you decide who's coming to these parties?"

Penny sighed. "I can tell at school which kids need to let go, let off some steam, you know?"

Evan didn't know, but he stayed quiet. Sometimes, not answering made people feel like they had to talk more.

"I know what it's like to be that kid. But I never served alcohol or supplied drugs. I know better than that. If the kids brought something, I didn't know about it. You know how kids are."

"That's not what I remember," Mckenna said. "I remember you having alcohol."

"I may have had some drinks in the fridge, but I didn't supply them and I certainly didn't let any of you drink it. You probably snuck it," Penny answered.

"Keep going," Evan said before she and Mckenna could start pointing fingers. He wanted to keep Penny talking. That way she might slip up and contradict herself. He had no doubt that she had supplied alcohol to minors, but for now, he wanted more information. "So, you decide at school which kids should be invited? How do you approach them?"

"It just kind of happens. It started my first year of teaching. Just out of college, I was practically the same age as the seniors. I mean I was twenty-two, they were eighteen. I figured it would be fun and decided to throw a bash. Some of the kids found out and I invited them. I didn't see that it was any problem."

Only that they're underage and you're putting them in danger. Evan kept his thought to himself. "Who else comes? Are there people your age?"

"Yeah. I know some of the guys from around town. I met a lot of them hanging out at the bar, playing pool and stuff. I invite them too."

"Do you encourage them to hit on or sleep with any of your students?"

"What? No. This is just a fun time." Penny's face started to show panic as she shot quick glances at Evan and the sheriff. The sheriff remained quiet, allowing Evan to take the lead like they'd discussed.

"Were there drugs at your party?"

"No."

"Marijuana?"

"I have a vape pen, but again, I don't share it."

"Oh? How do you know someone else hasn't used it?" Evan asked.

Penny shrugged. "I take a hit and leave it in my room. I guess if someone finds it there, they might use it, but again, I'm not supplying it. If they did take a hit, then that means they're snooping around where they shouldn't be. I know better than to give alcohol or marijuana to a person under twenty-one."

"Are you sure you never intentionally supplied marijuana or alcohol to minors?" Evan asked. "Or something else?"

"No."

"You ever hear of GHB?"

"GH what?" Penny asked.

"GHB. Liquid E, Georgia Home Boy? Ringing any bells?"

"No, I've never heard of that, why?"

"We believe someone used it on Lily and Autumn at your party. Spiked their drinks. Any idea who might have done that? Who might have a drug like that?"

Penny's face went from belligerent to scared. "No. No idea. Am I in trouble?"

"That depends," Evan said. "You cooperate and tell us everything, mostly I need a list of everyone who attended the previous party, and I'll put in a good word with the prosecutor. Sheriff will too."

"I'll make the list, but I didn't do anything wrong. I would never want to see anyone get hurt."

"Good, then help me out because you have a big problem—over the past years, three kids have been abducted from your party. Two of them had a tox screen and tested positive for drugs and alcohol. Pretty funny thing if you didn't serve any alcohol at your party or supply drugs. If you're holding anything back, I'll make sure you're charged with obstruction of justice. If I find out you helped provide alcohol to specific kids so they could be taken, I will make sure I charge you with accessory to kidnapping too," Evan said. "Understand? But cooperate and that will help you out a lot."

"There were no drugs and alcohol at the party. After I write down the list, I want my lawyer."

"Deal," Evan said, handing her a notebook. He knew that

even if Penny didn't admit to it now, he had enough witnesses that would allow them to arrest and charge her with giving alcohol and marijuana to minors. The other charges would unfold as he investigated more. Evan didn't trust Penny Gardner one bit. She was a good liar, but even good liars were caught. "Start jotting down names. Tell the sheriff who your attorney is, and she'll call them. She'll also let you know that I'm going to get a search warrant for this place and have our evidence team tear it apart. If they so much as find a trace of GHB around here, any good word with the prosecutor is off. Got it?"

"Yeah, I got it," Penny said in a defeated tone, taking the notebook and Evan's pen.

"One last question, if you're willing to answer without a lawyer."

"Depends," said Penny.

"Do you know Rex and Toby Hanson?"

Penny's face flushed red with embarrassment. *Interesting reaction*, Evan thought.

"I know them."

"Toby says he was here and you're his alibi. Was he here?"

"Yes, he and Rex were both here."

"Can you account for their whereabouts during the party?" Evan asked, thinking about how being around drugs and alcohol was a violation of Toby's parole even if he didn't consume anything.

"I can account for Toby's, but not Rex."

"Why is that?"

Penny stopped writing and stared at Evan. "Because we were having sex. All night long. The party got going and I knew that Toby probably needed some companionship after being in prison, so we went to my bedroom and spent time together. I know he didn't do anything. And that's further proof I didn't have alcohol or drugs out in the open. That would get Toby in trouble."

"Yes, it would. Toby might go back to prison because of you and your party. What about Rex?" Evan asked.

"Rex knew what was up and he was pissed. I lost track of Rex at the party."

"Why would Rex be pissed?"

Penny sighed. "Because we'd been dating, and he thought we were a couple. I'd always told him I wanted an open relationship. It's not like I want to be tied down to one person."

Evan saw the look of disgust on Mckenna's face. He agreed, but he had to stay neutral. Even play sympathetic if it called for it. Whatever it took to get information from this lady. For now, with Mckenna's statement and Lily's, he had enough to arrest her. Then she could go sit in the slammer over the weekend and think about her next career, because she was done teaching. When Evan was done investigating and finding more witnesses to prove Penny had provided alcohol and drugs to minors, she would never teach again. But she didn't need to know that until he had enough information to get her to admit to her crimes. Had she helped the kidnapper? Evan would figure it out—one way or another.

"Rex was mad, but he got over it. I'm sure. I mean, he understands."

Maybe by kidnapping two girls and taking his frustration out on them. From what Mckenna and Lily had told Evan, the person who took them, and he was getting more and more convinced it was the same person, wanted control. Penny sleeping with his brother could certainly be a trigger. Evan had known people who had shot others for less. "Then you don't know if Rex was here all night or not?"

"No, I suppose not. Sorry." Penny continued writing down names.

Evan stayed quiet. He was certain the blue Jeep following Mckenna was Rex's. Now Rex had no alibi, and he could have easily framed his brother back when Mckenna was abducted. Or Toby could have realized it was Rex who committed the crime and taken the fall. But based on the interview tapes, Evan would bet on the first scenario of Rex framing his brother. He had to find Toby, which would be easy. One call to Keith Warren and he could get the info, but Rex might be harder.

He glanced at Mckenna. Was she in danger? Was Rex coming after her or following her to see what the FBI was investigating? Evan thought about how both Mckenna and Lily said the kidnapper talked about catch and release. Like they were trout and he was fishing. If it was Rex and he released Mckenna, would he be ready to start a new game of catch again?

He didn't know what he would do if something happened to her. He'd never felt this way about anyone, and he didn't know if she'd want to be in a relationship with him once she found out about his family and his past at the other field office, but he wanted to try. He wanted to be with her. No one had ever driven him this crazy and made him laugh at the same time like Mckenna.

Evan would do anything to keep her safe.

Chapter Twenty-One

Mckenna sat in shock after listening to what her former teacher was saying. Why did any of her students ever think she was cool? Now, as an adult, Mckenna realized that they were young and impressionable, and Penny Gardner took advantage of that. All sorts of feelings hit Mckenna from anger to sadness to hurt. She was taken advantage of by someone at the party and years later, Penny didn't even care. She hadn't even apologized. And she'd never come to visit Mckenna after her kidnapping.

She felt Evan's gaze and peered up at him. His expression was inquisitive, and she figured he was probably wondering if Mckenna was okay. She forced a smile toward him but had the feeling that he could already read her better than most. Even better than Cassidy.

The sheriff had an earpiece linked to her shoulder radio and Mckenna could tell she had a call coming in. Then the sheriff stood and opened the door as a deputy came inside. Penny glanced up from her list.

"I want my lawyer," Penny said.

"You'll be able to get in touch with him, but no matter what, you're going to jail and going to spend a couple nights there," the sheriff said.

"A couple nights?" Penny asked.

"That's correct," the sheriff said. "It's the weekend. You can't post bail until you get your first hearing, and a judge won't be available until Monday."

Mckenna thought the sheriff was suppressing a vindictive smile and she heard Penny mutter some choice words under her breath. *It serves her right for what she did to us. Spending a weekend in jail barely seems fitting.*

After Penny handed Evan the pad of paper with the names, the deputy who had arrived asked her to stand and turn around. He put cuffs on her and guided her out the door, taking her away. Mckenna let her breath out. She didn't realize how much she'd been holding it.

"At least she can't hurt anyone else," the sheriff said, breaking the silence. "Her teaching days will be over and I'm sure she'll be serving some time."

"I'm going to stop by Toby and Rex's house and see if they're home. I have more questions for them," Evan said, facing Mckenna. "And no, you're not coming to that interview."

Mckenna was fine with that. Listening in on Penny's interview had shaken her a bit. Realizing that Penny didn't seem to care what Mckenna went through or that she'd protected Penny all these years had hit her hard. She needed to process that and coming face-to-face with Toby or Rex wouldn't help. "I'm okay with that. I need to get to the office and make follow-up calls on other cases. Plus, Mocha is in the car and it'll soon be too hot for him. Even in the shade. Thanks for letting me come to this interview."

"I'll walk you out," said Evan.

Mckenna trudged to her car. Her feet felt heavy, and some anxiety stirred up inside her.

"Are you okay?" Evan asked.

"Honestly, no," Mckenna said. She liked that she could be

straightforward with him. With her family it had gotten to the point where she couldn't really share her true feelings. It would trigger anger toward Toby from her father, guilt in her mother for not being a better parent and overprotectiveness in her sister. Evan seemed to accept her for who she was and how she felt in the moment. "I thought coming with you would be good. That it would make me feel better hearing Penny confess to what she was doing... But hearing her deny everything didn't really help."

Evan pulled her into a hug, his strong arms making her feel safe. She trusted him like no one else she'd ever known in her life.

"I understand," he said.

"You do?"

"I do."

Evan continued to hold her. Mckenna was in no hurry to break away. His cologne smelled wonderful, and she could feel his strength.

The sheriff came over and cleared her throat. Mckenna and Evan pulled apart as the sheriff glared at her.

"Why didn't you come forward with the information about the party when you were kidnapped?" the sheriff asked.

Mckenna didn't know what to say at first. Evan glanced between the two women and was about to say something when Mckenna spoke up. "I was young, and I thought I should protect her. I know now that was wrong. But I was only eighteen."

"But Penny Gardner wouldn't have thrown those parties if you'd said something. Lily wouldn't be traumatized and Autumn would still be alive."

Mckenna scowled at Evan. The statement about her guilt when it came to Lily and Autumn was remarkably similar to what she'd said to him in the chapel when she'd first told him about the parties.

"Let's not go down this road. Mckenna knows she made a mistake," Evan said, trying to get between the two women. "What's happened has happened."

"But if your girlfriend had spoken up, then maybe we wouldn't be here now."

Now Mckenna's hurt had turned to fury. "Do you think that I don't know that? That I don't wish I'd done something different? I wish I had and now there's nothing I can do. I can't go back in time. So lay off. I'm willing to be a witness and help gather other witnesses so this doesn't happen to anyone ever again. I'm going back to the office. Call me if you need something. And I'm *not* his girlfriend."

Mckenna turned around and stomped off, ready to get out of there. Evan jogged up behind her.

"Mckenna, stop. Please?" he said.

"I have nothing to say to you," she said, getting in her vehicle. "You could have stood up for me a little bit more instead of saying I made a mistake."

To Mckenna's surprise he leaned in, pulled her close and kissed her. "I'm sorry the sheriff said all that. She's frustrated and she took it out on you, which isn't right. I'll talk to her. I promise. And I shouldn't have said that you made a mistake. That came out wrong. I'm sorry."

"I wanted to come with today because I thought it would help me feel better about not saying anything. Instead, I feel worse. I wish I could go back in time and say something, but I can't. And the sheriff is right—Autumn is dead now because of me. Because I didn't tell the truth about Penny."

"Autumn's death is not your fault. You were eighteen and trying to protect someone you looked up to. Autumn's death is the fault of a sick person that we're going to catch. Not you. Not Lily. Call me if you want, okay?"

"Okay." Mckenna knew there was a part of her that wanted to call him and another part that was mad and ready to never speak to him again. She had both the urge to invite him to her house and spend the evening with him and to slap him for saying what he did. Now her anxiety was really flaring up, but for different reasons.

MCKENNA AND MOCHA spent the rest of the day at the office. Mocha crashed on his plush dog bed, happy snores coming from him as Mckenna worked through her to-do list. She glanced down at her dog, glad he could rest. He'd been working hard, and while she knew he enjoyed his job, it was tough on him too. Everyone in this line of work needed their rest and downtime.

Hanging up the phone from her last call of the day, Mckenna leaned forward and put her elbows on her desk. Coming back to work had helped her and been a good distraction, but now it was time to go home, and somehow, even the home she loved for its charm and coziness seemed like it was going to be empty. Thank goodness for Mocha. But Mckenna knew what she was really thinking—she wouldn't mind another person being in her house and that person was Evan. Darn him for making everything so complicated.

"Hey, there."

Mckenna glanced up and saw Cassidy standing in the doorway.

"You doing okay?" Cassidy asked, coming in and taking a seat. Mocha lifted his head, saw it was his former handler, and after a few stretches, strode over to say hello. He put his head in Cassidy's lap, and she started petting him and scratching his ears. Mocha wagged his tail and leaned more into Cassidy's leg.

"He likes that," Mckenna said, avoiding Cassidy's question.

"Yeah, he does."

They sat in silence and Mckenna knew that Cassidy really was wondering if she was okay. Was it so bad to be honest? "It was a tough day."

Cassidy continued petting Mocha. "I bet. This case with the two girls must be rough on you. You know you can ask to not be on it anymore."

Mckenna shrugged. "I could, but I also understand it better than anyone."

"How's Agent Knox treating you? Is he being nice or still taking advantage of you?"

Mckenna laughed and shook her head. "He's being nice and the kiss you heard about was not him taking advantage of me. In fact, it might be the other way around, but at the same time he's so infuriating. I don't know what to think of him. One minute I think he's nice and the next minute he makes me mad."

"Oh, really?"

"Really. He's not so bad. There's a nice side to him, but then there's the side everyone here knows. I don't know who he really is."

"Be careful with him," Cassidy warned.

"I know what you said, but I can figure this out for myself." Now Mckenna was back to being annoyed with her overprotective older sister. "I'll be careful, but maybe everyone should get to know him better and give him a chance. Or maybe I should give him another chance. I mean he has apologized when I've been upset."

Cassidy stopped petting Mocha for a moment. "I know his type, that's all."

"What's his type?"

"He'll pretend to care, get you into bed because he's a guy with needs, but when the time comes and he's offered a promotion, he'll be out of here. I don't want to see your heart broken."

Mckenna stared down at her desk as if it would give her answers. "That's my chance to take."

"Then what are you going to do? Go with him? You that serious about this guy?"

"I don't know. We kissed. That's it for now, so it's not like I'm going to worry about moving in with him, getting married or even relocating. It was a kiss. Nothing more. It'll be okay. It wouldn't be the first time a guy broke my heart."

"I know," Cassidy said. "It's just hard to watch."

Mckenna thought about the couple of guys she'd been with over the years. She had been upset to realize that they weren't into her—they were just attracted by the limelight that came with dating her. At least the media had left her alone. She'd half expected to find them camped out at her house again when this case started, but for now, they were hounding Lily and Autumn's families. At some point, though, there would be a knock on the door and a reporter standing there. Mckenna wouldn't mind Evan answering the door and telling them to go away. That would be just fine with her.

"I'll be okay," Mckenna finally said. "Life is not easy, but to be honest, Cass, I really like him. You're right, though. He's only going to break my heart."

"Well, don't say I didn't warn you. I'm here for you, okay?"

"I know. I'm lucky to have such a great sister. I think

I'm going to get home. It's been a long day and I'm ready to crash."

"All right." Cassidy stood, came around the desk and pulled Mckenna up into a big hug. "Take care of yourself, sis. Call me if you need anything, okay?"

Chapter Twenty-Two

Parking in her driveway, Mckenna leaned back against her seat and took another deep breath. Maybe Cassidy was right about Evan. Maybe he was out for himself and was only hoping to get her into bed to fulfill his needs, as her sister had so eloquently put it.

But there was something about him that seemed so right.

She sighed. She needed dinner, a glass of wine and snuggle time with her dog. Mckenna helped Mocha out of the vehicle, and they entered her house through the side door. She left the front door for formal occasions or things like Halloween. She loved her little home that had been built in 1885 by the early settlers and miners. There was a rich history in this area and when she'd decided to buy the charming house, she'd found everything about it perfect.

Although sometimes she wouldn't mind not having the repairs that went with an old house. Last winter, the cold temperatures had made the plumbing succumb to its age. That had been a mess and cost a small fortune. What would this winter bring?

As soon as they stepped into the kitchen, Mocha sprang ahead of her and raised his hackles. He air-scented a little bit, nose up and twitching, and then let out a low growl.

Mckenna's heart pounded. She'd never seen her dog act like this.

Ever.

In fact, she'd always joked that Mocha didn't have a protective bone in his body and if someone broke in, all they'd have to do was give him a treat and a ball and he'd let them do anything they wanted. Cassidy had disagreed with Mckenna, saying that Mocha would bond with her and protect her. He might not be like a German shepherd, but he would do his best. Goose bumps lined Mckenna's arms, and her heart pounded as her chest tightened.

Who was here? Could it be the person driving the Jeep? But she hadn't seen anyone behind her. She'd been careful. Of course, whoever it was could have switched cars. She was about ready to bolt out the door when Mocha calmed down. His hackles dropped and he quit growling. If she didn't know better, he had a sheepish look on his face.

"Are you trying to scare me?" Mckenna asked. "You're doing a great job of it."

Mocha wagged his tail and headed over to his favorite spot—the couch. He climbed up and flopped down, peering at her with his brown eyes and a little wag of his tail as if asking for forgiveness.

"Okay, I guess there's nothing wrong. The stress of this case is getting to you too. I'll get changed and get us dinner."

Mckenna took off her work clothes and put on shorts and a T-shirt, but she still felt on edge. She decided to walk through the house and see if there was anything out of place or signs that someone had been there. She was probably overreacting, but she'd feel better knowing that her house was secure.

Mocha jumped off the couch and joined Mckenna on her

tour of the house. Everything was in place—including the pile of laundry.

"I wish someone would break in here and fold my laundry. Maybe vacuum too," Mckenna said to Mocha. He stuck by her side, which was also unusual for him. He was always there to comfort her, but once they were home, Mocha usually liked to hang out on the couch until dinnertime.

Mckenna had herself convinced she was paranoid when she arrived at her back door. The porch overlooked a beautiful view of mountain peaks. They were coming into her favorite time of year when the aspen trees changed to a gorgeous golden color and the hills were dotted with groves of yellow and red among the dark green of the evergreens. Mckenna was about ready to turn around when something caught her eye.

Some sort of book was open on her porch table. There were objects on top of it. Mocha stepped in front of her again, his hackles raised. She opened the back door, and the screen door gave a groan as she stepped out onto the porch, hands shaking and heart racing.

A low growl rumbled in Mocha's throat.

Mckenna forced herself to go over to the table, and when she stepped closer, she started crying. Fear coursed through her. The book was her journal. No one knew about her journal. Not even Cassidy or her therapist. Her therapist had suggested that she keep one to help process her trauma, but she'd never told anyone that she was doing it. Normally, it was tucked into the top drawer of her bedside table.

As she took another step closer, the old porch creaked. Mocha stayed in front of her and sniffed the journal, then he started growling.

She should run. Get out of here. Why was she still standing there? But fear paralyzed her. How often had she told victims about fight-or-flight? Now her feet were stuck in place. She wanted to see what was left on the journal.

Regret immediately flowed through her.

Close enough now to the table, Mckenna could see the object. A black diamond tennis bracelet in sterling silver. Her mother had given it to her for her sixteenth birthday. She'd been devastated that she lost it when she'd been abducted, but her mother kept telling Mckenna she didn't care. It was more important to have Mckenna back. Bracelets could be replaced.

Run, Mckenna kept telling herself. *Get out of here. He could be watching you. How dare he ruin your safe place?*

Then she saw the message. There was a scribble next to the bracelet that she could barely read. Mckenna lightly touched the journal, tipping it toward her. The words were hard to read, but Mckenna was able to decipher his handwriting and the message.

I'm so disappointed. I didn't release you so you could fall in love with an FBI agent. Remember, I love the game of catch and release. What made you think that you wouldn't be caught again? You were the best. There's no one else like you. I know, I've tried out plenty.

Now her flight instincts kicked in. Was he in the house? In the yard? Waiting to grab her? She turned and ran back inside, Mocha by her side. He seemed scared too. Mckenna grabbed her keys and phone, then the pair sprinted out to her car.

"Screw your crate," Mckenna said to Mocha. Getting him in his travel crate would only give someone time to grab her. She opened the driver-side door and Mocha hopped in. Mckenna waited for him to go to the passenger's seat and then she jumped in the driver's seat. She locked the doors and attempted to put her keys in the ignition, but her hands shook so violently she was having a tough time starting the car. Next car would have a key fob. That would be a much quicker getaway.

She managed to start the car and drove down the street to a coffee shop near a gas station. It was a busy area with tourists stopping to fill up and get their caffeine fix for the mountain drive ahead of them.

Her whole body shook as Mckenna managed to unlock her cell phone and dial 911.

Chapter Twenty-Three

Mckenna couldn't even remember what she said. It was like an out-of-body experience as hysteria took over. The operator was saying something in a calm tone about staying on the line. Officers were on their way, but Mckenna didn't hear a word. The dispatcher was only adding to her panic. She knew they were trained to keep her on the line, but Mckenna hung up. She needed quiet.

Mocha climbed over the center console and flopped on her lap while licking her face. She hugged him tightly, his soft black fur up against her cheek.

"You're such a good boy. You knew something was wrong. We should have left then. I'm sorry, boy. I need to do a better job of listening to you."

Holding Mocha, Mckenna could feel her heart rate slow a bit, some of the frenzy leaving her body. As she calmed down, clearer thinking came back, and she pulled up her security camera through her phone app. *I hope I have a clear shot of this person. I can't wait to see who it is.* Would it be Toby? Rex? Someone else? When the footage came up, disappointment hit. Somehow the person had seen the camera or knew about it. The intruder was an adult male, but he had his face covered and made sure to keep his back to the device. *So much for security cameras helping.*

She took deep breaths and saw that 911 was calling her back, but she didn't know that person. She needed to talk with someone she knew. A person who understood her. Mckenna rejected the call from the dispatcher and opened the contacts to Cassidy's number.

But she didn't want to talk to her sister either. Cassidy meant well but she was so overprotective that it felt like Mckenna was being smothered by her older sister. There was someone who listened to her, though. Who understood her.

Evan.

Yes, he'd made her mad, but she'd overreacted too. She had to admit that he was the one person who made her feel safe but allowed her to be herself at the same time. She wanted him now. Mckenna dialed his number, listening to it ring. *Please answer, please.* He'd been going to find Toby and Rex and she didn't know if he'd have cell signal up at their house.

"Pick up. Please answer," she said out loud. Just when Mckenna thought the call would go to voice mail, Evan answered. He sounded a little out of breath.

"Mckenna? Are you okay?"

Hearing his voice and his concern made her start crying again. "No. I'm not."

"What's going on?"

Mckenna filled Evan in about Mocha, the journal and her bracelet.

"Where are you now?" Evan asked.

"I'm in my car with Mocha at the gas station near the local coffee shop."

"Stay where you are. Lock your doors and don't open your window for anyone. Not even a police officer. I'll be there in twenty minutes. Stay put, you hear me?"

"Yes." Mckenna started crying again. She was so tired

of the tears, but so many emotions were hitting her at once, she didn't know what to do with them.

"I'll try to stay on the line with you, but I might lose signal."

The sound of sirens echoed off the mountains as several patrol vehicles flew by toward Mckenna's place.

Evan must have heard them too, because he said, "I'm glad you called 911 and that the cavalry is on its way."

Mckenna nodded and then realized he couldn't see her. "I did call 911."

"Good, let them get there and clear your house. I'm driving as fast as I can."

"Thank you," Mckenna managed to stutter out. "I can see my house from where I'm parked. They're going inside. Their guns are drawn."

"Good," Evan said. "If there's someone in there, they'll find him."

Mckenna thought she heard Evan mutter something about a sick bastard under his breath. There was movement near the side of her house, right by the door she'd entered. Someone in a hat and sunglasses took off. "There was someone in the bushes, by my house. They took off on foot."

"What?" Evan said. "Let me call that in. Stay on the line. I'm getting close."

There was silence as Evan must have switched calls. Evidently, he was able to get through quickly because the cops came sprinting out her side door, guns drawn, and they started clearing around her house.

The man had vanished. Mckenna knew he'd run up the street toward the west and disappeared out of sight. Where was Evan? Mocha leaned on her and licked her face again, working to soothe her.

In answer to her question, Evan's bu-car barreled around

the corner and pulled up next to her. Mckenna leaped out of her vehicle and Evan wrapped his arms around her, holding her tight. Mocha stuck his head out of the car and Evan rubbed his floppy ears. Mocha jumped out, put his front paws up on Evan's body and licked his face and then Mckenna's.

"I'm sorry. For earlier," Mckenna started to say.

"Stop," Evan interrupted. "You had every right to be upset. Tell me what happened."

"Mocha warned me. I didn't listen, but Mocha growled when we got home. He let me know something was wrong."

"You're a good boy," Evan said to the Lab, who had hopped back into the car.

"Are you okay?" Evan asked Mckenna again. "Did you see him? Did he try to hurt you? Grab you?"

"No. None of that. I'm fine. In fact, now that I'm calming down, I'm getting more and more mad. I have a security camera, but he knew it. I don't have good video of the intruder, which is even more frustrating." Evan pulled her closer and Mckenna could hear his heart pounding as she laid her head against his chest. "Did they find him? The person hiding in the bush?"

"I don't know," Evan said. "I'll find out more, but I'm not leaving you until there's an officer I trust who can stay with you. I'll have you send the security camera footage to me too. There's still important information we can figure out from it, like his height and weight. Anything helps."

"Thanks," Mckenna said gratefully. She didn't want to extract herself from his hug, but she also knew he had to do his job. And the sooner they caught this guy the better. Anger seethed through Mckenna as her tears dried up. How dare he do this. But who was "he?" Toby? Someone else? Who was driving the Jeep? Was it that person? Mckenna wanted to start peppering Evan with questions, but he was on his phone.

He hung up and said, "There's an officer coming here. Once she arrives, I'll go bag the journal and bracelet for evidence. I'll make sure it's a rush in the lab. Let's hope he did something stupid and left a fingerprint or DNA."

"Okay," Mckenna said.

A female cop from the local department drove their way and pulled in next to Evan. Evan went over and spoke with her and then came back with the officer. "This is Officer Taryn Ash. She's going to stay with you."

"Thank you," Mckenna said to the officer, who didn't look much older than her.

"I'll be back," Evan said.

Mckenna watched him drive to her house, making small talk with the policewoman and petting Mocha. Luckily some afternoon clouds rolled over, so Mocha wasn't too warm. Mckenna had to admit, it was nice to see Evan go into her house.

Too bad he was here under these circumstances.

Chapter Twenty-Four

He didn't want to leave Mckenna, but Evan also didn't want her to see how shaken he was. She was too involved in this investigation, and it was putting her in danger. Why had the kidnapper reached out now, after all these years?

Taking steps two at a time, Evan went to the door and showed the officer his badge. He went through the house to the back porch, with an evidence bag he'd pulled from his car. Everything about this house was so Mckenna. She had decorated the place in her own style, from pillows on the couch to pictures of her and Mocha together.

He wanted to stop and take everything in, learn more about her, be a bigger part of her life, but right now, he had to keep her safe. Following an officer to the porch, he saw the journal on the table with the bracelet, like Mckenna had said.

Putting on gloves, Evan went over and photographed everything. He'd call the ERT to have them process the house. Idaho Springs had a small department, and when he'd called, they said they didn't mind. Once he was done taking pictures, Evan bagged the bracelet. He could see the threat the kidnapper had scribbled into Mckenna's journal. Evan couldn't imagine how she felt.

He flipped through the pages to make sure there weren't

any other "souvenirs" or messages left, but everything else was in Mckenna's neat, perfect handwriting. A few pages before the threat, his eye caught a recent entry. It was about him. *Don't read it,* he told himself. *Don't do it. It's personal. You wouldn't even know about it if you weren't here.*

Evan went to shut the book, but he did catch one sentence that made him stop. He didn't allow himself to read anymore. This was her journal. Her personal reflections. He was violating her thoughts, but his heart pounded as he read the words: *I think I'm falling in love with Evan. He makes me feel safe.*

The thing was, he was falling in love with her too. He just didn't want to make her feel safe. He wanted to be with her and keep her safe. But could he do that?

And he hadn't told anyone in the office yet, but he'd put in for an ASAC or assistant special agent in charge opening in Oregon. If he got the position, in a month or so he could be gone. Then what?

That was why love would never work for him. He wouldn't only be breaking Mckenna's heart, he'd be breaking his own too.

EVAN WALKED THROUGH the rest of the house, careful not to disturb anything. The evidence response team would be here soon and process everything, but it would take them the rest of the night. Even if Mckenna wanted to wait for them to finish, he didn't want her staying alone. Not until they caught this guy.

Not knowing if the kidnapper was only targeting Mckenna, Evan had called Lily's parents and the sheriff. A deputy would drive by a couple of times while on duty. Lily's father had promised they would call if there was anything suspicious and keep everything locked including the windows.

Evan had one more room to walk through—Mckenna's bedroom. He opened the door and smiled at the pillows on her bed that had Mocha's picture. Her pajamas were hanging on the closet door—they were soft silk shorts with a lace-trim tank top. What he would give to see her in that.

Or nothing.

Get back to work. This is completely unprofessional. You think you crossed a line kissing her, this is worse.

But the words Mckenna wrote in her journal kept echoing through his head: *I think I'm falling in love with Evan.*

He wanted to be the one to keep her safe, but was he capable of loving her back? Or only breaking her heart like he'd been accused of many times? Nothing seemed out of place in her bedroom and there were no obvious notes. He didn't want to touch anything or go through much until the evidence team had their chance.

There was no way Mckenna was staying here tonight. As he made his way back into the living room, Evan decided that he should try to find a safe house and other agents to protect her. Seeing what she wrote rattled him. Maybe it would be best to have some space.

Because what he really wanted was for her to stay with him, but he knew where that would lead. It would *definitely* cross a line. Right now, he might hurt her if he transferred to Oregon, but it would be worse if they took this further.

His relationships in the past had always ended badly. Prior girlfriends had accused him of loving his job more than them. They'd been right. This was the first time he thought things might be different. He may have found someone he loved more than his work, but he didn't want to stop with the promotion. That was also his dream.

Right now, he had a kidnapper to catch, and he needed to keep Mckenna out of danger. Yes, a safe house. That would be the way to go. She could stay there and be escorted to the office until he found Toby and Rex.

Neither one had been home when he'd stopped by. He'd called Officer Warren to see if he could look up Toby's ankle monitor location even though it was Rex Evan had become really interested in. He hadn't told Mckenna yet, but he'd confirmed the Jeep he saw in Rex's garage was the one following her. He wanted to find both guys and bring them in for questioning. Unfortunately, Officer Warren hadn't answered, and Evan had left a voice mail.

Mckenna had to stay somewhere safe tonight. He wouldn't take no for an answer. Evan left the house and stepped under the crime scene tape that the police had strung up. Curious neighbors had come out and were standing on their porches, watching and gossiping. Evan ignored them and went over to one of the evidence team members.

"Let's go all out here," he told the man. "Fingerprints. DNA. And anything else you see that you think should be collected. I have the journal and the bracelet."

"That might take a while," the man said. "Is this person willing to stay out of their house?"

"It won't be a problem. I'll be moving her to a safe house. Call me immediately if you find anything."

"You got it," said the man.

Evan thanked him and then climbed in his vehicle. That was the easy part. The hard part would be convincing Mckenna to stay somewhere else for the night. Unless she was really scared, then maybe she'd be okay with it.

The officer was petting Mocha when Evan parked back down by the gas station. Mckenna appeared more at ease, which made him happy. He thought about the words she'd written. Love. What was love anyway? His parents certainly couldn't figure it out. He remembered the day his mother had walked out, and they'd never heard from her again. His father had found her, but she had handed him divorce papers and said she didn't want anything to do with them. His dad had an on-again, off-again girlfriend, but had never committed to her. Not that Evan could blame him after what had happened. Even though he'd read what Mckenna wrote about falling in love with him, Evan didn't know if he could handle it if Mckenna walked out on him. She hadn't called him until she was scared and needed him. What happened when she didn't need him anymore?

It was yet another reason that he should step away while he could—he didn't want to hurt Mckenna. That would be terrible. But the longer he let this go, the more hurt he'd inflict on both of them when the time came to leave.

Evan stepped out of his vehicle and Mckenna's face lit up seeing him. This was going to be tough. But he couldn't let this go any further. It struck him that he'd never really worried about hurting the other women he'd been with— not that there'd been a lot. Those relationships were different. Mckenna was special.

"Did you find anything?" Mckenna asked him.

"No, not anything obvious," Evan answered. "I had the ERT go through your place with a fine-tooth comb. If there's something there, they'll find it, but the bad news is it's going to take them a while. Your house is a crime scene. You may not be able to go back until tomorrow at the earliest, maybe even longer."

"I'll get a hotel, then," Mckenna said. "I'm sure I can find one that will take Mocha."

"What about your sister?" Evan asked, the thought coming to him as a good solution where he didn't look like a jerk.

"I don't want to put her out. I'll just get a hotel."

"Would you consider a safe house? Or asking your sister if she'd mind?"

"No. A hotel is fine," Mckenna said, eyes narrowing a bit.

Evan recognized the stubborn look coming on. Another reason he'd fallen for her—she said what was on her mind and stuck with it no matter what. But this time, it was her life at stake. "Look, I want you in some sort of protective custody. Your sister, a safe house, something. You can't be on your own until we catch this guy. It's too dangerous."

"Would you be the agent at the safe house?"

"No," Evan said.

"Then no. I'd rather be on my own. I know I can trust you. I'd call Cassidy, but she's working on a major case, and I don't know when she'll be home. I don't want to make her stop what she's doing to babysit me. Plus, she'll be the older sister pain in the butt and fret over me like she did after I came home. Staying at a safe house or with her feels like I'm giving up a piece of myself that I've worked hard to find."

Evan sighed and ran his fingers through his hair. *Don't do it. You'll regret this. You can behave yourself. You have three bedrooms. She can have one. You can stay in yours.*

"You're not going to change your mind on this, are you?" he asked.

"Nope," Mckenna said, crossing her arms and locking eyes with him.

"Then you're going to stay with me tonight."

Chapter Twenty-Five

Shock went through Mckenna with Evan's offer. No, he'd made it sound more like a statement. She wanted to say yes, but there was another side of her that wanted to say no, she could take care of herself. After her kidnapping she'd hit a point where she realized everyone, mostly her family, was treating her like she was something fragile that was going to break.

She had to constantly check in with her parents. Cassidy wanted to go with Mckenna everywhere and Mckenna's friends started acting differently. It was then that she realized she had to rebuild her life her own way, one step at a time. Even though the fear haunted her, Mckenna didn't want it to stop her.

Having a guy, even Evan, protect her seemed like she was giving up that freedom and independence she'd regained. On the other hand, the desire to spend time with him was difficult to ignore and before she could stop herself, she heard herself say, "Okay. I'll stay with you."

"Uh, good," Evan said, running his fingers through his hair. "I have extra bedrooms and a guest bathroom."

"Good," Mckenna said, holding up her phone. "Text me your address and I'll GPS it."

"Here, give me your phone. I'll add myself to your contacts. That way you won't lose it in a text thread."

Evan held his hand out and Mckenna hesitated before handing it over. What was she thinking? Why was she staying with him? She should get a hotel or call Cassidy. Even go stay with her parents at their ranch. But it was like someone else was controlling her and she had to admit, she *wanted* to go stay with him. Evan gave Mckenna her phone back.

"There you go," he said. "Pull it up on your maps and I'll follow you. That way I don't lose you and if anyone tries anything, I'll be in a better position to help you."

Mckenna took her phone back, her fingertips brushing his. Electricity went through her body from his touch. Like nothing she'd ever felt. "Thanks."

She pulled up the address and said, "You live near Red Rocks."

"I do," Evan said with a smile. "And at some point, when I'm not hunting down a kidnapper, I'll finally make it to a concert there."

"I've never been either," said Mckenna. The famous amphitheater and park was often a destination for tourists. Famous bands from the Rolling Stones to the Grateful Dead and even the Beatles had played there. Even though Mckenna didn't love crowds and preferred the mountains, she'd always wanted to see a concert there. Just for the experience. "We'll have to check out the concert schedule for the fall. See who's coming into town. I mean, you're the great Agent Evan Knox. You'll find this kidnapper in no time and then what will we do?"

"You're teasing me again, right?" Evan said.

Mckenna didn't want to hurt his feelings, but she did love giving him a hard time. "I am. Sorry, can't help myself."

"No, it's okay. I like it. Shall we head out?"

Mckenna nodded. She woke up Mocha and convinced him to give up the driver's seat and go back to his travel crate. While she'd been in a hurry and let him ride shotgun, it was safer for the Lab to be in a crate. He hesitated, liking his newfound spot in the car, but eventually cooperated.

Starting the car, Mckenna noted that her hands weren't shaking as much. Being with Evan calmed her down.

I wonder what kind of effect I have on him.

The drive was smooth, and about twenty minutes later, Mckenna pulled up to Evan's house on the outskirts of Morrison. The view was spectacular, and she could see the sharp edges of the large boulders that surrounded Red Rocks in the horizon. She let Mocha out of his crate as Evan pulled in the driveway and parked.

Mckenna waited for him to get out and then said, "You don't need tickets for a concert, you could sit on your front patio and listen to each one."

"I've done that a couple of nights. I can hear the music pretty well, but I still think it could be a fun experience."

"I agree," Mckenna said.

They went inside and she gazed around. The place was neat and clean, but it seemed like no one lived there. It had the basics, but nothing more.

"I love what you've done with the place," she said.

"Sarcasm again, right?" Evan laughed. "Well, when you're not home much, you don't do much decorating."

"I don't have clothes or Mocha's food or anything," Mckenna said, suddenly feeling anxiety. What *was* she thinking?

"I realized that too. What does Mocha eat? I can run to the store and pick something up. Get dinner too."

Mckenna told Evan the type of food but left out the part that she was worried about being on her own in someone else's house.

"As for clothes, I have some things you can wear."

"I'm going to look like a little kid in your clothes," Mckenna said.

"You can roll up the sleeves. As soon as the evidence team is done, I'll go with you to get some clothes."

"When they're done, I'd like to go home."

"When I find Rex and Toby Hanson, you can go home."

Mckenna grimaced at the thought of the kidnapper waiting for her. "You drive a hard bargain."

"I do. Let me give you the tour, show you your room and then I'll go to the store and be back before you know it."

Mckenna followed Evan around with Mocha stuck to her side. The tour didn't take long.

"Do you want to let Mocha out before I go?" Evan asked. "If he needs to go, I have a fenced backyard."

"I can let him out," Mckenna answered.

"I think it's better if I'm with you," Evan said. "Just in case."

Mckenna hated that she was being treated like someone who was fragile, but on the other hand, the note that was left in her journal was disturbing. She'd taken self-defense classes and done things to take care of herself, but the fact was, she wasn't a big person. She could easily be overpowered. She gave in to the fact part of her reasoning. "Okay. That's probably a good idea."

Mckenna thought Evan seemed relieved. He'd probably figured she was going to argue with him. They went to the back sliding door and the yard surprised her. A deck with two Adirondack chairs, grill and pergola spread out to a perfectly mowed and manicured yard. There were flower beds and xeriscaping around the edges.

"It's beautiful out here," Mckenna said. "I'm a little worried about what Mocha might do to ruin your landscaping."

"I don't care," Evan said. "I'm more worried about him stealing a sandwich or other food."

Mckenna giggled. That moment seemed like a million years ago now. "That's a legitimate concern. I'll keep a close eye on him."

They opened the door and Mocha bounded out happily in front of them. He ran around the yard sniffing and taking care of business when he suddenly stopped. His front leg was raised to a ninety-degree angle and he posed in a perfect point.

"What the heck?" Mckenna said. Then she heard the culprit at the same time she saw it—a squirrel was up in a tree and began chattering at Mocha. "Uh-oh… Mocha, come!"

While Mckenna prided herself on how well her dog listened, she knew the desire to chase the squirrel would override any obedience. Launching off the deck, Mckenna lunged to catch her dog, but missed. Evan cut him off before he could run through the flower beds and managed to grab Mocha's collar. Mckenna came over and snapped on the leash.

"Thank you," she said, a little out of breath.

"Remember what I said when he ate my sandwich?" Evan asked.

Great, here comes the lecture. "That I need to work on training my dog."

"That's it," Evan said, face serious.

Mckenna was getting ready to stand her ground and defend Mocha, even though she knew Evan was right. She did need to work on training Mocha more.

Suddenly Evan laughed. "I can tease you too. Don't break him of the squirrel habit. I might need to hire him because they keep trying to get into my garage and nest."

Surprised, Mckenna didn't know what to say. Evan did have a sense of humor and she liked it.

"I'll be back from the store soon. Keep the doors locked and make yourself at home," Evan said as they all went back inside. Mocha grunted and lay down on a blanket Evan had provided for him in the living room area. "I'm glad to see Mocha is settling in. Be back soon."

As the door closed behind him, Mckenna was suddenly overwhelmed. What was she doing here? She should have stayed on her own. He didn't even try to kiss her when he left.

Then a horrid thought crossed her mind. *I hope he didn't read my journal. I hope he didn't see what I wrote about falling in love with him.*

Chapter Twenty-Six

Evan drove to the grocery store and picked up dog food for Mocha, happy to find the brand that Mckenna had written down. The last thing they needed was for Mocha to get an upset tummy because of a food switch. Evan added steaks and potatoes for them and headed back out. When he turned onto his street, he stopped and took a moment to observe the area.

The officer he had asked to come watch the house while Evan was gone was sitting in his car. He'd parked in the cul-de-sac turnaround like Evan requested. He hadn't told Mckenna he had called in an officer, a buddy of his that was off duty. He figured she might not be comfortable with that, but he couldn't take any chances. Mckenna wouldn't be hurt on his watch.

Nothing seemed out of place or wrong. His neighbor was out mowing. Another lady, his nosy neighbor, was walking her small poodle and taking note of a different car parked in Evan's driveway. Evan was certain she had talked to his buddy. But the nice thing was there was nothing out of the ordinary. Everything seemed fine.

He drove down to the end of the street and pulled up "cop style" to his friend's car.

Evan rolled down his window. "Thanks for watching the place. Anything unusual?"

"Nope, boring as can be. The way we like it."

Evan nodded, glad his friend hadn't used the Q-word. That would be a jinx.

"Only action was your lady neighbor trying to figure out why there was a cop parked here. She was hitting on me too," his friend continued.

"Give her your phone number?"

"Nope, gave her yours." His friend laughed and then added. "You have some hot chick stashed away in your house?"

"What makes you say that?" Evan asked, willing himself to keep a straight face.

"Because you actually look happy for once in your life."

"Gee, thanks," Evan said with a laugh. "Am I that serious?"

"Do you really want me to answer that? Have a good night."

His friend waved and drove off. Evan parked in his driveway, got things out of the car and took them inside. Mckenna was good for him, but he had put in for the job in Oregon. If he was promoted, it didn't matter how he felt about her. He'd be gone.

THE DOOR MADE a clicking sound and Mckenna was on her feet, ready to run if it wasn't Evan. Mocha trotted over and sat in the hall, tail wagging. It had to be Evan. She had peeked out the front curtain and saw a cop sitting at the turnaround, adding to her worry about staying by herself. She'd figured that Evan had called him in and that both annoyed her and scared her at the same time.

Evan wouldn't have called in an officer unless he really

thought someone was after her. Mckenna was determined to find out more. What did Evan know that he was keeping from her? She had a right to know about her case.

Footsteps echoed in the hallway and Mckenna heard Evan say hello to Mocha. Despite her determination to find out more, she also had a smile on her face, happy to see Evan and spend time with him.

"Let me help you with those bags," Mckenna said, reaching out.

Evan handed her a couple and said, "There's dog food for Mocha and some steaks for us. Considering Mocha's history of stealing food, I'd put the steaks in the fridge where he can't get them."

Mckenna laughed as she put the steaks away. "He can be a thief, although the sandwich was a pretty brazen move."

"You can say that again. He's like a criminal who's escalating."

"Maybe," Mckenna said, taking the bag of dog food and realizing that Evan had bought a food bowl too. Mckenna had a bowl for water in her vehicle that she'd brought in, but Mocha's food bowl was still at the house. The thoughtfulness touched her. "I studied a map while you were gone."

"Oh?" Evan turned around and grabbed the steaks back out of the fridge, leaning in close to Mckenna. She wanted to reach out and pull him into a hug but refrained.

Behave yourself. He has you here to protect you, nothing else.

"What were you studying?"

"Your aspen grove out back triggered a memory. Of the night I was taken. I remember aspen trees. They were weird-looking, but maybe that was from the drugs. Anyway, there's a ghost town not far from where Lily, Autumn and I were found."

Evan had seasoned the steaks, and they all went out on his deck, waiting for the grill to heat. "I saw a ghost town mentioned in the reports," he said. "I don't think they found anything. No signs of a broken window or any signs of where you could have been held. We went to the same ghost town after Lily was found. Same thing."

"I know," Mckenna said. "It's just, I swear we had to be held around there somewhere."

"We'll figure this out," Evan said, the steaks making a sizzling sound as he threw them on the grill. "I'll go back there myself and look again. I wasn't the one who checked out the place, it was some of the deputies from the sheriff's department. But I think if they'd seen something, they would have said it. Tell me more about the aspen trees."

"I can only vaguely remember them," Mckenna said, frustrated. If she could remember more, then she could help the investigation. It would lead them to the person who'd done this. The Colorado mountains quickly became remote and even though the ghost town was near there, she didn't see anything else on the map but forest and rugged country. If there was a cabin or some other type of building, it could remain hidden.

Evan turned around and leaned against the deck, arms folded, staring at her. "It's okay, Mckenna. You were probably drugged too. I didn't see that they did a tox screen on you, which is too bad, but if you, Lily and Autumn have the same kidnapper, then there's a good chance you were drugged with GHB as well and remembering can be tough. That drug creates amnesia. We can look at the map together tonight. There's something we're missing."

"The aspen trees, though, they had a strange shape to them, like I told you. But maybe I hallucinated that from being drugged."

"What kind of shape?"

"It was like they were dancing."

She closed her eyes, fighting to bring back the memory, but it was fuzzy and unclear in her mind.

"Mckenna?"

Evan had stepped closer and was peering down at her. Before she could stop herself, she wrapped her arms around him, wanting him to hold her, to help these memories come back. She may have been angry earlier, but Mckenna appreciated him listening to her. To her relief, he returned her hug.

"I'm sorry for earlier," Evan said. "With the sheriff. I shouldn't have said you made a mistake. She didn't have any right to blame you either."

"I already blame myself."

"I know, and you shouldn't. Who doesn't make mistakes? Especially as a kid? I'm sorry."

"Thank you," Mckenna said, hoping the hug would last forever.

To her disappointment, he stepped back and took the steaks off the grill. Mckenna followed him inside, a little worried that she didn't see Mocha. Peeking around, she spotted him on Evan's exceptionally clean and light-colored couch, napping. There was going to be black hair everywhere. Evan might regret inviting them over. Maybe she should have taken him up on the safe house. Sensing Evan behind her, Mckenna said, "Sorry. I'll vacuum your couch."

"Doesn't bother me. Sometimes I think this place is too clean. Dog hair might be a nice change. Make it seem like a more lived-in home. Let's eat."

Chapter Twenty-Seven

"That was delicious," Mckenna said, taking their plates from the table to the sink. She rinsed them off, put them in the dishwasher and turned around to find Evan behind her, bringing some more dishes over. He placed them in the sink and their hands touched. Mckenna turned around and did something she'd wanted to all evening—pulled him closer and kissed him. This time there was no one around to see them.

She started out tentatively, not sure that he wanted this. She did, but it seemed like he'd avoided coming close all evening. She was about ready to pull back when Evan wrapped his arms around her and pulled her closer. He picked her up and sat her on the counter. Mckenna wrapped her legs around him, feeling him even closer and happy that he was enjoying this too.

Running her hands down his chest, she began to slowly unbutton his shirt, enjoying what she saw underneath. Evan trailed a finger down her leg and back up, eventually reaching under her shirt toward her scars.

Her scars. And what was hiding them. What would he think of what she'd done to cover them? Some apprehension washed over her, and Evan paused.

"Are you okay?" he asked.

Colorado K-9 Rescue

"Yes," Mckenna said, partially lying. What was she doing? She wanted to be with him. She could tell he didn't want to stop either, but what would he think of her when he saw everything? Before she could say more, Evan kissed her again, tracing the scars under her shirt. Her body responded in ways she'd never felt and suddenly Mckenna didn't care anymore. She wanted to be with him more than anything.

His hands traced her scars, then down her belly until he had a hand on each hip. Mckenna continued unbuttoning his shirt and pulled it back, running her hands up and down his chest, until she was brave enough to go a little lower and undo the top button of his pants.

"Let's take this somewhere else," Evan whispered in her ear, as he kissed her on the neck and nipped at her ear lobes.

She stepped down from the counter and they headed toward the bedroom. Mocha was off the couch, staring at them, and then lay down and covered his eyes with his paws. Mckenna and Evan laughed together.

"Don't worry, big guy, we'll close the door," Evan said.

Mckenna giggled and then went into Evan's room, turning around and becoming serious. His shirt was unbuttoned, but still on. Mckenna took care of that, then moving to his pants and unbuttoning them as Evan picked her up and laid her on the bed. Her shirt was still on, and Evan began to pull it over her head. What would he think of her scars and her tattoo? Would it turn him off?

Nerves swept through Mckenna as Evan got his first look at the red and orange phoenix she'd had tattooed to cover the nasty scars from *that* night. He stopped and stared, and she was instantly self-conscious, grabbing her shirt, ready to put it back on.

"Mckenna?" Evan asked, a questioning look as she went to cover herself up. "Are you okay?"

"I'm more than okay, but I saw the way you were staring at my tattoo. I should have warned you. Told you about the scars and how I made them my own."

"I love your tattoo," he said, gently stopping her from putting her shirt back on. "I love your scars because they're a part of you. I don't want you to do anything you're not comfortable with, though."

Mckenna hesitated. Did he really appreciate her tattoo? She cherished everything about it, the bird in flight, ready to take off out of the fire. A sign of rebirth, renewal and, most important for her, hope. "You love it?"

"I do."

Mckenna stopped redressing herself, staring at Evan. She could tell he was serious, telling her the truth. She threw her shirt on the floor and turned her side toward him so he could see everything better. "I wanted something to cover the scars. I loved the symbolism of the phoenix because it shows I can overcome my past."

"God, you're amazing," Evan said, tracing the outline of the mythical bird with a finger. "It's an amazing tattoo. It fits. You're so strong and beautiful. You have overcome your past."

Mckenna didn't know what to say at first. Most guys she'd been with didn't like the bird wrapping itself around her rib cage. They made comments and hadn't seen it for what it was. Evan was different. "You are the first person who's looked at it and understood it."

His finger continued tracing the outline and then found one of her scars. He traced that too, his face questioning as if he wanted permission. Mckenna pulled him closer and kissed him. Hard. He broke away and kissed down her side, making her want him more. His hands moved behind her and undid her bra and then moved back down to her shorts

and underwear, taking them off. She undid his pants, and
he kicked them off on the floor, kissing between her thighs,
his tongue probing and making her moan in ecstasy.

Kissing back up her belly, he stopped, tracing the tattoo
again with his fingers, and then kissing and caressing her
breasts. Mckenna tightened her arms around him, wanting
him as her hips rose up toward him. He understood, put on
a condom and entered her, making her gasp. Everything
about him was perfect and they started a slow rhythm that
increased with desire until they came together.

She'd never been with anyone like him. No one had made
her feel like this. Ever. She opened her eyes and saw Evan
staring down at her, taking her all in and then he said, "You
are so beautiful."

Mckenna woke up in a tangle of sheets, forgetting for a
moment where she was. Slight panic hit her and then she remembered everything that had happened. Evan. The amazing way he made her feel. How they would take a break and
then find themselves together again.

And how much Evan loved her tattoo. No, not just loved
it. Understood it.

Where was Evan? His side of the bed was empty.

She rolled over and realized that she'd fallen asleep, and
it was dark outside. What about Mocha? Was he still asleep
on the couch? He needed to go out. Mckenna untangled
herself from the covers, found her clothes scattered on the
floor, and dressed.

Everything seemed quiet, which was a good sign that
Mocha wasn't eating something he shouldn't. She trotted
down the stairs, but there was no sign of Evan. Mocha was
still asleep on the couch.

"You poor guy. You're exhausted from today too, aren't you?" Mckenna asked. "Come on, big guy, I'll take you out."

Mocha stretched, and then, one paw at a time, lumbered off the couch. They went to the back door and Mckenna let him out, happy that there were no squirrels this time for him to chase. They came back inside, and she heard Evan talking on the phone.

Following the sound of his voice, Mckenna found him in his office. He didn't realize she was there and was pacing back and forth, running his fingers through his hair again. Was it about the break-in to her house?

"I want them found. Now. Both of them. Use your app, find the ankle monitor and let me know when you have them. I need to speak with them immediately." Evan hung up and dropped his phone on the desk, back still turned to Mckenna.

"Hey, there," she said softly, hoping she wasn't startling him.

He turned around and his face went from serious to happy. "Hi."

They stood staring awkwardly at each other until Mckenna couldn't stand it. She walked up to Evan and gave him a long, slow kiss, her hands exploring and caressing his chest. She didn't think she'd ever get tired of him. Pulling back and wondering about his phone call, she asked, "Any news on my house? Did the evidence team find anything?"

"No, nothing yet," Evan said, a little out of breath after their kiss. His fingertips rubbed underneath her shirt, massaging her back and then finding their way down her legs. "I put a rush on processing the journal, but I don't think the lab will get to it until tomorrow at the earliest. I'll keep bugging them, though. And I asked one of the evidence team members to bring some of your clothes. I hope that's okay, but I figured you didn't want to go into the office tomorrow with what you were wearing."

Mckenna glanced down at her shorts and top that she'd changed into when she'd returned home earlier. At the time, she'd thought she'd have a relaxing evening. Despite the scare in her home, she didn't mind that she had ended up here at Evan's house. "It would be better to wear something more professional. Who were you talking to just now?"

"What? Oh, that was nothing. Just another case I'm working."

Over the past few days, Mckenna had learned many things about Evan. She could understand his body language and had a feeling he wasn't telling her the truth about the phone call, but she didn't push. It wasn't like she was telling him everything she was working on. "I let Mocha out. I think he's back on your couch. Do you want me to tell him he needs to sleep somewhere else tonight?"

A sly grin crossed Evan's face, and as he leaned closer to Mckenna, her back was up against the wall. "I think he's just fine. I think we should let sleeping dogs lie, as the saying goes. You, however, I have other ideas for."

Mckenna's heart pounded as Evan tucked some of her hair behind her ear and kissed her gently. Her body responded.

"You make me feel safe. Thank you," Mckenna said when they parted.

"I will always keep you safe. I'm going to figure out who this kidnapper is and make sure this time he's not out in eight years."

"Can you really promise that?" Mckenna asked.

"I don't know, but know that I'd do anything for you," Evan said, picking her up and carrying her upstairs. "First, though, I want to see that tattoo again."

Chapter Twenty-Eight

Early morning sunlight filtered through the slat blinds in Evan's room. He woke to Mckenna's soft breathing next to him. She was perfect in every way, and the night before had been like nothing he'd ever experienced. He wanted to call in sick to work and not leave the house, but the phone call he'd had with Keith Warren last night ran through his mind. That was enough to get him out of bed and heading to the shower.

Keith had told him that Toby's ankle monitor must be malfunctioning—he couldn't bring up a location and neither Toby nor Rex was at their house.

Evan had been furious, but he knew that sometimes malfunctions happened with monitors. The person might not even realize it until their probation officer showed up on their doorstep, but the fact that no one seemed to know where they were bothered Evan. Maybe one of them had broken into Mckenna's house. Maybe Toby never did cover for Rex because they were working together.

There were so many maybes.

He heard Mckenna stir, and he knew he had to admit it—he was in love. He'd do anything to protect her—even give up his own life for her. There were too many unknowns with this investigation, and he wanted answers.

Now.

If something happened to her, he would never be able to live with himself. *And how are you going to live with yourself if you get the promotion and move? Are you willing to break her heart for your career?*

Evan sighed and started the water for the shower. Right now, the less she knew the better, and not only about his promotion, but the case as well. That might be a way to keep her safe. What she didn't know wouldn't hurt her. He knew she wanted this resolved—probably even more than he did—and he would do anything to help find the kidnappers. He never should have let her come with him to Penny Gardner's home, which was a big mistake. It had brought her too close to the investigation and could be what prompted the break-in and taunting by the kidnapper.

For now, he had to separate her from the case. Maybe even talk to her boss about assigning someone else as Lily's victim specialist, although that would make Mckenna furious. However, it would be worth it if it meant she wasn't harmed. He could beg forgiveness later.

And he wanted her to stay with him until he could find Toby and Rex. As he waited for the water to warm up, and watched her sleeping, he realized he wouldn't mind if she wanted to stay with him *after* Toby and Rex were caught.

STRETCHING, MCKENNA WOKE up to Evan's side of the bed empty again and the shower running. She smiled and hugged a pillow to her chest. She was in love. She was certain. There was no one else like Evan. No one made her feel the way he did. But what if Cassidy was right... What if he was using her and was going to break her heart by leaving? What if once this case was over, he would move on and not want to be with her? What-if after what-if kept running through Mckenna's mind until she wanted to scream into the pillow.

But Cassidy couldn't be right. Everything with Evan seemed real. Perfect. Or maybe she wanted it to be that way. Maybe she was setting herself up for a heartbreak but, for now, she'd take that risk.

She thought about last night, when she'd asked Evan about his phone call. Was he talking about Toby and Rex? He'd said no, but she knew he wasn't being honest and that bothered her. Was he holding back to protect her? Or was he really working on another case?

Getting out of bed, Mckenna decided there was one way to get her mind off all these thoughts—she went and joined Evan in the shower.

EVAN HAD BEEN surprised when the shower door opened and Mckenna had stepped in with him. They might be a little late for work, but he didn't care. It was worth it to explore her body more and have her do the same back. He had to stop thinking about the things she'd done that morning or else he'd end up back in bed with her and they'd never make it to the office.

He heard her footsteps going down the stairs and knew she was going to let Mocha out. He'd told her to wait and not do it alone, but Mckenna was worried that Mocha might have an accident. Finishing his tie, Evan went downstairs and joined her. Luckily, she'd waited, but Mocha sat at the door looking desperate.

"Go ahead and let him out," Evan said as he opened the gun safe near the back door and pulled out his service weapon.

As soon as Mckenna slid the door back, Mocha took off.

Evan thought he really had to go, but then he heard barking and growling. "Get back inside," Evan told Mckenna.

"But…"

"Mckenna, please. I'll make sure Mocha's okay," Evan said, drawing his gun and holding it in a low ready position. He made sure Mckenna wasn't in view of any window and then he cleared the deck. His father had been the first person to teach him how to clear a room and he thought about the advice of breaking an area up into slivers like a pizza or a pie. No one was on the deck.

Evan listened. Mocha was still growling near his neighbor's fence. His neighbor had a big, poofy orange cat. Hopefully, Mocha didn't have the animal cornered. Evan cleared each area before heading toward Mocha, who'd gone back to barking. Just because Mocha was barking in one direction didn't mean that there wasn't someone else waiting to ambush him. Especially if Toby and Rex were working together.

Gun still in ready low, Evan went over to where Mocha was now pacing and whining. He'd recently put in landscaping and added in daylilies as a good flower for xeriscaping. In the dirt around the daylilies, there was a boot print—right where someone could see in the window. Evan glanced inside. The blind was down, but the slats open.

Someone had watched them last night.

Chapter Twenty-Nine

Feeling violated and sick along with anger at whoever this was, Evan didn't want to tell Mckenna. He finished checking his yard, and when he was satisfied no one was there, he whistled and got Mocha to follow him back toward the deck.

Mckenna stepped out. "Are either of you hurt? Was there anyone there?"

The urge to protect her surged through Evan. He didn't like to withhold information, but he couldn't bring himself to tell her what he'd seen either. When the evidence guy dropped off Mckenna's work clothes in a little bit, he'd pull him aside and ask him to cast the footprint. Maybe if he knew the size and type of boot, he could narrow down who was stalking her. Evan forced a smile. "Squirrel. Again. They're cute, but obnoxious little creatures. Everything's fine."

"Okay." Mckenna tilted her head slightly and shrugged. She went back inside with Mocha, telling the Lab she had a great breakfast ready for him—the same thing he had every day—dog food.

Evan stopped the fake smile he'd put on for Mckenna after she and Mocha were inside. He stared around his yard again. Someone had seriously crossed a line. You didn't come to an FBI agent's house, sit outside the bedroom window to be a Peeping Tom, and expect to get away with it. The kidnapper was growing bolder and more reckless.

Mckenna telling him about the "catch and release" phrase went through his mind.

"I'm going to catch you first, you bastard," Evan muttered. "And you'll never be released."

EVAN INSISTED ON following Mckenna again when they drove to the office. Ever since he'd gone outside when Mocha was barking, he'd been different. Mckenna knew he was holding something back. But what? And why? Cassidy's words went through her head again and Mckenna cursed her sister for saying anything. And then herself for listening.

They parked next to each other, and Evan was out of his vehicle first. Mckenna caught him looking around the garage, like he was clearing a room trying to find a suspect. Yes, something more had happened this morning and he wasn't telling her anything. Mckenna didn't know if she should be relieved or angry.

He could be protecting me, but it's better if I know what's going on. Then I'm not surprised by anything.

Mocha happily walked down his portable car stairs from his crate and wagging his tail, greeted Evan and then went and leaned against Mckenna. She rubbed his ears.

At least this guy will always be honest. I wish he could talk and tell me what was really making him bark. Or who...

The journal message from her former kidnapper ran through her mind. He, whoever he was—because she wasn't convinced it was Toby—knew about Evan. What if it was him there this morning? That would explain why Evan was on such high alert.

To say she was tired of being kept in the dark was an understatement. While she appreciated Evan wanting to keep her safe, she also craved honesty—even if it did make her afraid.

Evan put a hand on the small of her back and they headed inside, Mocha taking the lead. They entered the office and several people stopped what they were doing, obviously wondering why Mckenna, Mocha and Evan were coming in together. Mckenna couldn't help the heat that she felt rise on her cheeks. She was certain they were turning a bright red.

Glancing back over her shoulder, she saw Evan had his "office" expression on. Gone was the easy smile and the guy who had been nothing but tender and loving with her. Back was the intense agent that no one wanted to work with—the lone wolf, as Cassidy had called him.

Mckenna wanted to stop, kiss Evan in front of everyone and say, "There! Gossip about that today." Whichever secretary had talked to Cassidy about the kiss outside the coffee shop was gleefully thrilled to see them together.

Good grief, it's like high school or maybe even middle school, all over again.

They exchanged glances and Evan walked Mckenna to her office. "Stay here today. Work from here where you'll be safe. Okay? I'll touch base throughout the day and update you if I have anything."

"You promise you'll keep me in the loop?" Mckenna asked, still having that gut feeling that he wasn't being quite truthful which bothered her a little bit. Although after their night together, she did believe he wanted to protect her. This could be his way of doing that.

"I promise. Okay, better get to work." Evan gave her a quick wink and his shy smile, then straightened up and became serious again.

Mckenna watched him walk to his office while Mocha

leaned against her leg and gave a little whine. She scratched his ears and whispered, "You like him too, boy, don't you?"

She'd just booted up her computer and was organizing her day when someone strode in, and her door clicked shut. Cassidy stood glaring at Mckenna, hands on her hips.

"Why didn't you call?" she demanded. "Oh, wait, I think I know why."

Mckenna sighed and rubbed her forehead. This was not what she needed right now. It was time to see about a job opening somewhere other than Colorado or in a field office on the other side of the state. "Well? Why?"

Cassidy grabbed a chair, put her elbows on the desk and leaned toward Mckenna. "You spent the night with him, didn't you?"

The blunt truth seemed the best. "Yes."

"I heard that someone broke into your house and threatened you."

"Yes," Mckenna said.

"Why didn't you call me?" Cassidy sat back and crossed her arms with a hurt expression.

Mckenna instantly felt bad. Cassidy wasn't that upset about her staying with Evan, it was more the hurt of her little sister no longer asking for her or needing Cassidy's help. It had to be hard to be an older sibling and feel protective. Growing up, they were close, and Cassidy often took the blame when her mischievous little sister got into trouble. Mckenna suspected their mother knew the truth. But once she was kidnapped, everything changed. Mckenna realized now that maybe Cassidy blamed herself for what happened.

"I'm sorry I didn't call you," Mckenna said. "I know you're working hard on the serial bomber case and it's not going well. How's Cooper doing?"

"Yeah, that's one way to put it when it comes to this case. But Cooper is doing well. He's been great at locating odors. Much better than that mutt," Cassidy said with an affectionate glance toward Mocha. Mocha opened an eye, gave a squeaky yawn and then went back to sleep.

"Look, Cass, I appreciate your love and how much you want to be there for me and to help me overcome my own fears, but at some point, I have to live my life. Working this kidnapping case has brought back so many memories and emotions. It's been tough. There's a good side to Evan. He's been there for me. Helped me. Listened to me. He's a good guy and he was there for me last night."

"I'm sure he was probably there for you in more ways than one," Cassidy said with her arms still crossed. Her fingers dug into her upper arm, leaving white marks.

Mckenna's face flushed. "Yes, in more ways than one. I've always been honest with you. You're my sister and I'll be honest now. I like Evan. A lot. I know you're worried about him, but this is my deal. If he breaks my heart, then he does, but I want to take this chance. I think he does too. You can't always be there to protect me. You have your own life to live too."

"Okay, but I'm hearing rumors that Agent Knox, sorry, Evan, is investigating the possibility that your kidnapping is connected to this recent one. You really believe that's true?"

Mckenna stayed quiet. Her sister had never believed her when she said she thought the wrong person was in prison, but considering the recent kidnappings happened when Toby got out, that could mean the right person was in prison all these years. "I do believe they're connected. Lily's story was almost exactly like mine."

"Then I'll help find Toby Hanson and haul his ass back to prison."

"That's the thing, Cass. I'm not sure it was him."

"Then who?"

Mckenna thought about the Jeep following her. She suspected Evan knew who it was. Something else he was keeping from her? Was she desperate to have someone love her for herself and was overlooking things like the fact Evan hadn't been exactly forthcoming? "I don't know."

Uncrossing her arms, Cassidy reached out and took Mckenna's hand. "I'm sorry. I wish I'd gone with you to that party. I wish I hadn't covered for you when you snuck out of the house. I wish I could change the past."

"Don't we all?" Mckenna said. She saw Evan leaving his office in a hurry and wondered what was up. His face appeared strained, and he was typing something on his phone. Her cell phone pinged, and she saw the message that came through.

Promise me you'll stay in the office today. Don't go anywhere without me or Cassidy.

Why? Mckenna texted back.

A precaution, that's all. Just playing it safe.

"I can't go back in time and change all my wishes, but I can tell you that while Evan will probably do a great job solving this case and keeping you safe, which I appreciate, he's also not telling you everything. And if he does that, what else is he keeping from you?" Cassidy asked.

Mckenna wanted to fire back a strong response, but Cassidy did have a point.

"I'll see if I can find out what's going on," Cassidy said.

"No. Work on your case. I'll be fine."

"Okay—" Cassidy stood and went to the door "—but promise me you'll call me if you need anything or decide to go anywhere. If Evan is worried, there's a reason."

Chapter Thirty

The call came in as Evan was watching Cassidy and Mckenna have a heated conversation. He could barely see it since Mckenna's office was down the hall, but he had a bad feeling it was about him. Cassidy was warning Mckenna to be careful with him. He'd break her heart, and this was a fling. He'd earned that with what had happened in his previous office.

He hadn't been in a relationship with his partner like he was accused, but he did have a reputation for dating and dumping others he'd met. He'd realized this morning, when he saw that footprint in the dirt, that Mckenna was different. He couldn't imagine going home and not having her there with him. His house had always seemed cold and lonely, but with her there last night, there was a warmth, and he didn't want to lose it.

He was pulled out of his thoughts by his phone vibrating on his desk. The caller ID showed it was Officer Keith Warren.

"About time," Evan muttered, picking up. "This is Agent Knox, have you found them?"

"Morning to you too," Keith said. "Toby's ankle monitor came back on. I don't know where he was last night or why the monitor went down, but I finally had a ping on it this morning. I thought you'd want to come with me since you want him brought in. I figured you might want to take him to your office rather than mine."

"Where is he now?" Evan asked.

"A picnic area in the national forest not far from his house. Close to the Clear Creek Ranger District. I'm going to go pick him up. I can bring him back to the probation office."

"No, I want to meet you there," Evan said. "I want to know where Rex is. Once we have Toby, you can take him to the jail for holding and I'll go find Rex."

"Okay, whatever you want."

"Text me the address," Evan said, hanging up.

Mckenna and Cassidy were still deep in conversation. He didn't want to interrupt. Girl talk was always something he avoided. Having three sisters, he'd learned that the hard way. Instead, Evan texted Mckenna, hoping she'd follow his instructions and not question him.

As he rushed to his vehicle, he received a text from one of the evidence team members. They were done with Mckenna's house, she could go back, and he had the type and size of boot that matched the print in his flower bed—Ariat. A men's size 10. Unfortunately, they were common work boots and a popular size, which was why they were able to get him the information so quickly.

Evan put the boot size and type in his mental Rolodex and then hopped in the front seat of his bu-car and headed toward the mountains. If he could bring in Toby and Rex, this would all be over and Mckenna would be safe.

As he drove, Evan continued thinking about who could be coming after Mckenna. Who took Lily? He was more convinced that it was the same person, but he had nothing to prove it other than a hunch. Rex had obviously had feelings for Mckenna when he worked for her parents. It hadn't been as innocent as Mckenna thought. Maybe it was more than a fling to Rex even though he'd been the one to break it off. Evan understood—Mckenna had gotten to him too and cast her spell. He'd never imagined that he would feel this way about anyone.

Maybe Toby was jealous of Rex's relationship and he really did take her all those years ago and liked it. Or Rex and Toby worked together in some sick, twisted family deal.

Parking in the picnic area, Evan saw Keith outside his vehicle, staring around. The blue Jeep was also parked there. Could they both be up here? If they had decided to escape, they could hike deep into these mountains. Based on what Evan knew after reading through the sheriff's files on the case, both brothers had grown up camping, hunting, fishing and living off the land. They could easily disappear for as long as they wanted.

"I see the vehicle," Evan said. "Where's the ankle monitor pinging?"

"I was waiting for you to arrive before I looked around, you know, just in case they're both here. I don't know what's going on, but I don't feel like being ambushed. The ankle monitor is pinging around that little gulch over there."

Evan started traipsing toward the area that Keith had pointed. He pulled out his gun, just in case. He didn't like anything about this. The mountains weren't like clearing a room. The brothers could be hiding behind a tree or a boulder, with a high-powered rifle waiting for them. This could be a trap since Toby would know that having his ankle monitor go off the grid would start a search for him. Then having it suddenly start pinging again? That was too convenient.

Of course, if this were a trap and they did have a rifle,

Evan and his Glock wouldn't have a chance. He and Keith walked side by side, staying close to each other. Evan kept an eye to the northwest while Keith was making sure no one surprised them on the other side. They topped the hill and Evan glanced down below. There was a tree on the other side of the gulch and a man was sitting there. From this distance, he couldn't tell if it was Toby, Rex or someone else.

"Think this is a trap?" Keith asked him.

"Your guess is as good as mine." Evan started looking around, trying to see where someone might be if they were waiting to shoot them. That would be the most likely scenario. "Let's go and see who that is."

"We don't have anything to use for cover."

"I know," Evan said, "but I'm going anyway."

He started down the hill, working not to slide on the loose rocks that dotted the hillside. This was when he didn't appreciate the FBI suit and dress code. He'd rather have hiking boots and jeans on, not only for the traction on the boots, but also in case a snake was napping. He'd heard there were fewer snakes at altitude. But fewer didn't mean none.

Continuing down, he kept an eye on the man sitting against the tree. There was no movement.

"FBI, put your hands up," Evan called out, making sure to announce himself.

No response.

"I said, this is the FBI, put your hands up."

No movement.

He and Keith continued toward the tree, watchful of their surroundings. The man sat perfectly still, not moving.

"Stay here in case this is a trap of some kind," Evan told Keith. He figured that if someone were there with a rifle, they would have fired by this point, when he was on the hillside. He and Keith would have been dead by now. But there were other ways to set a booby trap, including a bomb by the body or some kind of trip wire. Evan stepped forward one foot at a time. Slowly. Carefully. His gun stayed pointed down, finger off the trigger, but he was ready to change that at any second.

"FBI," Evan said again. "Can you hear me? Are you okay?"

Still no answer.

Evan checked to make sure Keith was still covering him and then glanced down at the man against the tree. Evan crept around the front, still wary, although he was certain he knew why there was no compliance or movement from this individual. Getting to the front side of the man, he learned he was right. The person sitting against the tree was deceased. A single gunshot to the head.

And it was Toby Hanson.

Chapter Thirty-One

This was not what Evan was expecting. Did Rex do this? He waved to Keith. If someone wanted them dead, they would have done it by now. There was no need for Keith to continue to cover him. Keith made his way over as Evan crouched down and inspected Toby's boots. Wrong type. Wrong size. It wasn't Toby at his house this morning. Plus, based on rigor, he'd guess that Toby had died the previous evening.

Mckenna might be right. Toby could have been framed for her kidnapping. If he'd figured out who it really was and confronted them, then the kidnapper was desperate and had killed him to keep him quiet. So that left the possibility that Rex was the kidnapper, or there was still an unknown suspect. The unknown suspect could even be working with Rex.

Evan didn't believe in coincidences. The fact that Rex had been following Mckenna made him the number one suspect in Evan's mind. Mckenna. He pulled out his phone to text her and tell her to stay put and not go anywhere until he came back to the office. Of course that was now going to be late tonight. Maybe he could get her to go home with Cassidy.

His main priority, besides taping off a crime scene and

waiting for the coroner and evidence team to arrive, was finding Rex. Then he might feel like Mckenna was safe. The Jeep was parked at the picnic area. But he knew Toby had an old truck that Rex had kept for him. It was in the truck that Mckenna's jacket and some of her other belongings were found.

"Why were you staring at his boots?" Keith asked.

Evan didn't feel like answering and giving out much information to Keith. Technically, Keith's job here was done. As a probation officer, he didn't have to worry about Toby anymore. "Just curious about some stuff, that's all. I need to radio the sheriff. See if they can get a deputy to Rex and Toby's house on the off chance he's there."

"I can go look if you want."

"Don't you have other things to do?" Evan asked. "I mean I figure you have a list of parolees to check on. I don't want to put you behind schedule."

"I have a little bit of time before my next appointment and it's on the way back to my office. If you want me to swing in quick, I'd be happy to do it."

"Okay, thanks," Evan said. "If you think Rex is there, call the sheriff's office and ask them to send a deputy. Wait for backup so you don't approach him on your own. If Rex is there, the deputy will bring him in for questioning."

"Will do. I'll be careful," Keith said. He turned to leave and paused. "You know, I know Toby did a nasty thing taking that girl and maybe those other girls too, but I felt like he was trying to make it. Stay out of trouble, you know?"

Evan nodded, not sure where Keith was going with this.

"You didn't ask me, but if you did, I would say his brother, Rex, was really the guilty one. Anyway, I'll see if he's at their house and let you know."

"I appreciate it," Evan said, not sure what else to say.

He hadn't asked Keith, but they had come to the same conclusion.

Once on his own, Evan took a deep breath. This case kept getting stranger and stranger and the woman he loved was in the middle of it. He hoped Rex would be at the house, but he also doubted it. That would be too easy. The only thing he didn't doubt was that Rex may have shot Toby in cold blood. Being in law enforcement, he'd seen what families could do to each other. Often the most unspeakable acts came from those the victims loved the most.

His cell phone didn't work in this area, so Evan trudged back to his car and pulled out his satellite phone. He was able to get ahold of the sheriff's office and the local Forest Service officer. Luckily, since it was federal land as part of the Forest Service, he had jurisdiction and the sheriff could also be involved. The Forest Service officer was working on the other side of the forest several districts away. Evan told her she didn't need to come right now, but he'd keep her posted.

When he talked to the sheriff, she agreed to put out a BOLO —Be on the Lookout—for Rex. After she called that in, Evan asked her about Penny. Penny Gardner seemed to be a big key to this case whether she was involved intentionally or not.

"She was released on bond," the sheriff said. "Despite what I told her to scare her, a judge fit her into his schedule. She did a PR bond."

"Can you have a deputy check the house? On the off chance Rex is there?"

"I'll send one out right away. You need someone at the Hanson residence?"

"No," Evan said. "The probation officer, Keith Warren, said he'd stop and check on his way home."

"That was nice," the sheriff said. "Helps me out since I only have a couple deputies on duty right now."

"We'll stay in touch," Evan said, hanging up and grabbing crime scene tape out of his vehicle. Where the heck did one start taping out in the wilderness? He walked to the gate and closed the picnic area. The last thing he needed was tourists showing up and taking selfies with a dead body. Then he started running tape around the parking lot. He wanted everything around the Jeep processed and would get the vehicle towed to their garage for the forensic team to go through.

Then he ran tape in a large area around where Toby still sat. If Evan didn't know better, it appeared as if Toby was out enjoying the Colorado day, getting some sun. Arriving back to the parking lot, Evan found a spot where he had just enough signal to text Mckenna.

Are you okay?

Within seconds he had a message back with heart emojis, saying she was good. Then another message—What's going on?

She had a sixth sense, as if she knew that he wasn't only saying hello.

Not much. I'm thinking of you and miss you. I may be working late. Maybe think about going home with Cassidy. Tomorrow, I can pick you up and we can swing by your house and get your things. I'd love for you and Mocha to stay with me again. Tell Mocha he can have the couch. I don't mind.

The response was a little slower, but then, What aren't you telling me?

Evan didn't know how to answer. Tell her the truth? But if she knew Toby was dead, she might think she was safe. She could walk straight into a trap because Evan was certain that she was next in the kidnapper's plan. The game was catch and release, after all. He had to convince her to trust him and not ask questions. The less she knew, the better. He finally texted; I'll fill you in later. Just go home with Cassidy, I'm having a long day and it's going to be a long night. I'll meet up with you tomorrow.

He really hoped she'd listen.

Chapter Thirty-Two

Mckenna stared at her phone, willing it to give her answers, but she knew Evan wasn't going to tell her more. Why wasn't he being honest? She had a right to know what was going on. She'd defended him to Cassidy, but now she wasn't so certain. Had she really been swayed by his good looks and brooding personality? Cassidy was a good judge of character, why was she doubting her?

Because I'm completely in love, that's why. As the saying goes, love is blind.

Staring at her computer screen, she shut down the document on which she'd been working. This kidnapper wanted her, and while it scared her, she was so tired of this. Her life from eighteen years old on had been consumed with the kidnapping. She wanted to catch whoever it was. If she could lure him out somehow or figure out his identity, then this case could be over. After that, she and Evan could figure out if they were meant to be together or if it was adrenaline from the case that had made them cross a line.

What if she could figure out where she and Lily were taken? The aspen trees with the bent trunks were so unusual. If this really and truly was the same kidnapper, then Lily might remember the trees too. If they could talk, they could come up with the location. Wherever it was, it couldn't be far from the ghost town. It had to be nearby.

Why hadn't anyone been able to find it? How hard had they looked? This was what irritated Mckenna with law enforcement. They'd brought Toby in and said there was enough evidence that they didn't need to figure out where they'd been held. She remembered the other sheriff saying it would be nice, but the prosecutor had a strong enough case.

But if Mckenna could figure out where they were taken, then maybe the FBI and sheriff could determine for sure if it was Toby. This needed to be over. For Autumn. For Lily. And for Mckenna. She wanted freedom from this case. She'd take Mocha along. He'd warn her if there was someone coming after her. He'd done that at her house and at Evan's. She had more faith in Mocha protecting her than any human— especially if the human wasn't going to share information.

She was tired of being afraid. Today she was going to face her fears so that she could move on. Sitting in her office made her feel weak and useless. That wasn't why she'd become a victim specialist.

"Come on, Mocha," Mckenna said. "Let's go talk with Lily. Together we can figure out where this sick jerk held us. No more of this stupid catch and release stuff. I want our life back…with or without Evan."

Mocha's tail made a thumping sound as he wagged it against the floor. They stood and Mckenna attached his leash and headed out of the office. She hoped to avoid Cassidy, but she ran into her sister as they headed toward the exit.

"Where are you going?" Cassidy asked.

Be brave, Mckenna told herself. *You don't need Cassidy to protect you. You can take care of yourself.*

"We're headed to Lily's house. I have some things I need to follow up on with her and her parents."

Cassidy nodded and then said, "Did you hear the news?"

"What news?"

"Toby Hanson is dead. Someone shot him in the head. Got what he deserved, if you ask me."

Mckenna was speechless. Why hadn't Evan told her this? Why was he still concerned about her? What wasn't he telling her? She was done with everyone protecting her. Even Evan.

"I take it Evan didn't tell you," Cassidy said.

"No," Mckenna answered, trying to hide the hurt, but aware that her sister knew better. "Maybe he doesn't know."

"Evan's the one who found him," Cassidy said, wrapping Mckenna in a hug. "Sorry, I know you want to believe that he's this special guy, but he is who he is—someone who's difficult to work with and keeps to himself."

"Well, thanks for letting me know," Mckenna said. She would not cry in front of everyone in the office. And especially not with her sister right now. "I better get going."

"Okay, call me later. Let me know that you're good. But at least you don't have to worry about Toby anymore."

"Yeah, that's true," Mckenna said, pretending she was relieved.

She and Mocha got to her vehicle and then she leaned back against the driver's seat, holding in the tears. She was hurt, but the tears were there more from anger. Anger at still being the one who everyone thought was weak. The one who was broken or damaged. But she wasn't, anymore. Like the bird on her side that was taking flight, so was she. She would figure out where she and Lily were kept.

If Toby really was the one who took her, then at least she'd have the closure of figuring out where they were kept. But if, like she suspected, Toby had been framed, then maybe she could help bring a kidnapper to justice.

THE SOUND OF his phone ringing made Evan startle. He was waiting for a deputy to arrive to watch the scene until the coroner and evidence team could come. Even though Keith had offered to check on Rex, Evan was the one who wanted to find him. Mckenna would be safe once Evan slapped cuffs on Rex and booked him for kidnapping and at least a double homicide. Keith was calling and Evan hoped he had some news.

"Agent Knox," Evan answered, pacing back and forth.

"Keith here. I checked the house. Sorry, but no one is home. No sign of Rex at all. In fact, I peered in through his bedroom window because the shade is up and I think he may have left town."

"What makes you say that?" Evan asked.

"I can see the safe is open and there's nothing in it. Looks like he packed all his belongings, because the bedroom closet is empty."

"You don't by any chance see any boots around the house, do you?" Evan asked.

"Let me look around."

There was only the sound of Keith breathing as he looked in the windows. "I do see some boots outside the back door."

"Any chance you can tell the brand? Size?"

"Sure, hang on a second." Silence again and then, "Ariats. I'd say around size 9 or 10. I don't see the size label and I don't have gloves to handle them. But they are men's boots."

"Okay, thanks. I appreciate your help."

"My pleasure. I'm heading back to my office for some appointments. If you need anything, just call."

"Yeah. Okay." Evan hung up. If Toby had covered for

Rex, then maybe they'd had a confrontation that ended out here at the National Forest. But why out here? Why not at home? Or maybe this had turned into a testosterone battle since both the brothers had been with Penny Gardner. Rex might not have appreciated the "open" relationship Penny wanted—especially with his own sibling.

On a whim, he decided to dial Rex's phone. You never knew if someone would be dumb enough to answer a call from the FBI. Stranger things had happened in the past. To his surprise, he heard a faint ringing. Peering around the parking lot, he realized the sound was coming from the Jeep. Nobody was in it—he'd already cleared the vehicle, but he hadn't seen a cell phone. The ringing stopped as the call switched to voice mail.

Evan grabbed gloves from his bu-car and then jogged over to the Jeep. He dialed Rex's number again and pulled on the gloves. Would he get lucky and find the car open? Luck was on his side as the driver's-side door was unlocked. Evan carefully peered around. He didn't want to disturb much so that the evidence team could do their job, but he finally found the phone between the seat and console.

Now Evan was puzzled. There was no sign of Rex in the area, but he'd have the sheriff send more deputies so they could search a larger area. Maybe Rex was out here somewhere. Maybe this was turning into a murder-suicide. Or Rex had taken off like Keith thought and left his phone behind to stay off the grid. A headache was starting to form, and Evan went back to his vehicle to get water and ibuprofen.

His phone rang again. "Hello, Sheriff. I was getting ready to call you."

"What about?"

"You first," Evan said.

"My deputy who went by Penny Gardner's place found her dead. Single gunshot wound to the head, just like Toby. We found the bullet. It's a .45 like Toby and Autumn. We'll send it to ballistics to see if it's a match."

"You're kidding me."

"I wish I was," she said. "I'll get our crime scene team out there to start processing things. Guess the coroner is going to be busy today."

"You can say that again."

"So why were you calling?"

Evan gripped his phone. "I tried calling Rex's phone."

"Good idea."

"I heard it ringing," Evan told her. "In the vehicle. I found it. I don't know the code, but I'll bag it for evidence and maybe our tech guys can crack it. Long shot getting into these phones, but you never know. I thought that we needed more deputies to come and help look for Rex in this area, but if Penny is dead, then I don't know where we need to be looking. Everywhere, I guess."

"I'll see if I can call in extra deputies. Some of the younger ones will love the overtime and they still think cases like this are fun."

"I remember those days," Evan said with a laugh.

"You're not that old. Neither am I."

"I guess this job can make you jaded pretty quick. Thanks for your help, Sheriff. I'll keep working leads on my end and keep you posted."

"Over and out," she said.

As Evan put his phone back in the belt clip, he had to wonder, did Rex kill Toby and then go kill Penny? Was he trying to cover up all the loose ends? There was still a couple and one of them was Mckenna. He had to make sure she was okay.

Evan dialed her number and heard it ringing, but she didn't pick up. "Hey, there, it's me. Evan. Call me, okay?"

Hanging up, he sent her a text as worry started to build. Maybe she was in a meeting or something. Evan called Cassidy, but it went to her voicemail too. He tried the office next and asked if Mckenna was there. His heart sank when he heard that she'd left.

And no one seemed to know where she'd gone.

Chapter Thirty-Three

The mountains stood out against the light blue sky—a color that reminded Mckenna of Evan's eyes. There was a part of her that was still angry and hurt that he hadn't told her about Toby. She had a right to know as a victim, and he'd lied. Well, not exactly lied, but he'd kept the information from her.

If Mckenna was going to be in a relationship, it had to be honest. After everything that had happened in her life, that was the one requirement she had. Sighing heavily, she made it to the driveway of Lily's house and turned in. Mocha stood in his crate and shook, the tags on his collar creating a jingling noise.

She had a call and text from Evan, but for now she ignored it. She'd call him back after she talked to Lily. Right now, her only focus was seeing if together she and Lily would be able to recall more details about where they were kept. It was the best lead to find this bastard and end this all. No more kidnappings. No more deaths.

The last thing Mckenna wanted to hear was Evan ordering her back to the office without telling her why.

She knocked on the door and Lily answered. Mckenna thought she looked better than the last time she'd seen the young woman. Her face had more color and today she had on some light makeup and her hair pulled back into a ponytail. She looked like a kid again and that made Mckenna happy. Their experiences had made them both grow up too fast.

"Thanks for letting me swing by," Mckenna said, as Mocha went in front of her and greeted Lily.

"Oh! Mocha," Lily said, kneeling and saying hello. The Lab responded by leaning into her and licking her face. "Come on in."

Mckenna followed Lily to the living room area, where Mocha made himself at home on the couch. "Are you sure your mom doesn't mind him up there? He knows better. I can tell him to get off."

"No, it's okay," Lily said, taking a seat next to Mocha and snuggling in with him. Mocha rolled to his side and stuck a paw up in the air, indicating he wanted his belly rubbed. Lily obliged. "He's such a great dog."

"He is," Mckenna agreed with a smile. Mocha made a big difference in her life too. "Do you mind if I ask you some questions? Not as a victim specialist or in any type of investigative capacity."

"Sure. As long as I can pet Mocha."

"You bet," Mckenna said. Where did she start? She didn't want to bring up bad memories, but she needed to see what Lily remembered. Sometimes it was best to start slow, but Lily seemed like she was doing well today. Mckenna decided to go for it and get right to the point. "I don't know if you had heard, but when I was about your age, I was kidnapped too."

Lily paused petting Mocha for a second and glanced up. Then she went back to the belly rub. "No, I didn't realize that."

"It was a similar case to yours. In fact—" Mckenna took a deep breath "—I think there's a chance the same person took us. I went to a party at Ms. Gardner's house. I don't remember much, and I didn't see the person who took me."

Mckenna watched Lily to make sure she was handling what she was saying okay. Mckenna knew how shocking it had been for her personally when she'd listened to Lily tell Evan her story. Lily's eyes were big, but otherwise she seemed fine.

"I woke up in a room and I wasn't tied up either. I was able to start looking around for an escape, but the man was there. I never saw him, but he talked about how much he enjoyed catch and release fishing, but it had become boring to him. He wanted to try it with humans. I was his first. Talk about a sick person."

"Did they catch him? I mean, if they did, then how did he kidnap me? Wouldn't he still be in prison?"

"They did catch him. His name was Toby Hanson," Mckenna answered. "He was released a couple weeks ago."

"Then can't that agent go arrest him? He promised justice for Autumn."

"He wants to," Mckenna said. Should she tell Lily that Toby was dead? She didn't want to scare her, so she'd keep a few details out. This was what Evan was doing for her. In a way, it was protecting someone by omission. She was still annoyed with Evan, though. Shoving that thought aside, Mckenna continued. "The thing is, now we're not sure Toby was my kidnapper. He may have been falsely convicted."

"Oh. I've heard about things like that on TV and stuff."

"It happens. I want to ask you a few questions because no one has been able to find where we were taken and held captive. Maybe if we could figure that out, we'd know who the kidnapper was. It could be as simple as he owns the property."

"Okay," Lily said. "What do you want to know?"

"Do you remember seeing a grove of aspen trees with funky, curved trunks?"

Lily's eyes widened. "I do. I thought I was seeing things."

"I did too, but I researched it." Mckenna brought up some pictures on her phone and showed Lily. "I thought the drugs made them seem weird or something, but it turns out there are aspen groves like this due to avalanches. When an avalanche happens, the soil can shift the trees. Those trees still need sunlight, so they get a curve in their trunks. It doesn't happen often, so I think this could help narrow things down."

"There was a smell too," Lily said. "Like rotten eggs."

Mckenna nodded. She remembered the distinct odor as well. "Yes. I remember that too. I thought at first that it was a sick joke. Like the man was leaving bad eggs for me to eat."

"It was so gross."

"It was."

"What do you think that was from?" Lily asked.

"I think wherever we were kept was near a mine. Sometimes fool's gold or pyrite can smell like that. If there was an old mine and we were kept in an old mining building, then we might catch whiffs of rotten eggs."

"I know about the ghost town, but that agent said he'd checked it out."

"I know," Mckenna said. "I've been doing research today and I found a second ghost town. One that's not on a map and very few people know about. It's on Forest Service land and there's no easy vehicle access to it. And because of the mines, the Forest Service tries to keep the area closed. But doing that in the mountains is impossible. Someone can always find a way in. And the other thing about this mine is that there's a creek. I think that's the one you followed."

"So now what?" Lily asked.

"I'm going to go there. I want to see it for myself. If it's the right location, then I'll call Evan."

"Evan?"

"The agent," Mckenna answered.

"Oh, are you two like, you know? A thing?"

"I'm not sure. It's complicated."

"Always is," Lily said.

"You're wise for your age."

"Thanks. You should have Evan go with you."

Mckenna heaved a deep sigh. Lily was right. But for some reason, Mckenna wanted to do this on her own. She doubted anyone would be up there now and it was part of facing her fears. "I'll see if I can find it first. Could be that it's so old, there's nothing there."

"How will you get to it?"

"The same way I think our kidnapper did. If you drive to the edge of the ghost town, you can hike in. It's a short hike although there's rough terrain in the area, at least based on the map. Driving a vehicle in would be harder," Mckenna said, standing. "Thanks, Lily. I appreciate your help."

Mocha saw Mckenna on her feet and hopped off the couch, ready to get back in the car and go on with his next adventure. They said their goodbyes and headed out to the car, where, after loading Mocha, Mckenna sat in deep thought. She was certain she'd found the place. Lily was right, she should have called Evan, but to be honest with herself, that scared her too. What if he was just a one-night stand? Or wanted a quick fling before he headed on to his next assignment, wherever that was. Mckenna had fallen for him, and she didn't want to be hurt. But she also believed what she'd told Cassidy—that it was worth it and her decision to be with Evan. It wasn't like she hadn't wanted last night or had not played a willing role. If it was a fling, she'd be crushed, but she would also learn from giving in to her feelings.

"SHALL WE CALL HIM?" Mckenna asked Mocha. She heard a little snore in response. Mocha was also tired from all the excitement. Mckenna dialed Evan, but it went to voice mail. She almost hung up and then decided to leave a quick message about what she'd figured out.

Relaying all the details about the ghost town and the location of the old mining camp, Mckenna finished with, "I'm going there to check it out. I'll let you know what I find."

She hung up, now wishing he had answered. But Mckenna needed to know if the mining camp was where they were kept. Then she could tell Evan or the sheriff and feel like she'd done her part to help solve the kidnappings and sort of make up for keeping the secret about Penny's party all these years. She'd drive there, hike back and take a quick peek, see if there were curvy-trunked aspen trees and a bad smell and then leave. It wasn't like a kidnapper would be waiting there for her. It would be fine.

Mckenna wanted, no, she *needed* some answers. She needed closure so she could move on with her life in whatever way she was meant to—with or without Evan.

Chapter Thirty-Four

Once the evidence response team arrived and the coroner showed up, Evan decided to head to Toby and Rex's house. Climbing in his car, he checked his phone. Nothing from Mckenna. Then he realized that he didn't have service again.

He'd had a learning curve with cell phones in the mountains. One minute you could have service and the next minute it could be gone. Even law enforcement had times when there was no radio service. Although due to the fires in recent years and the need for emergency response, more repeaters had been put in. Still there were spots in the mountains where nothing would get through. Maybe a text if you were lucky, which was why you could text 911. If you had enough bars, it might go through.

Sighing, Evan put his phone down and headed toward Toby and Rex's house. At one point his phone dinged, telling him he had a voice mail from Mckenna.

"She's okay," he muttered to himself, finding a spot to pull off on the shoulder of the road. There weren't many good areas as roads around here often had trees lining the road or a large drop-off with a guardrail and very little room. He found an area for slow vehicles to get over and stopped. He played the voice mail, but Mckenna must have also been in the mountains. Her message cut in and out, sounding garbled. He caught something about a mining camp.

There wasn't enough cell service to get back to her, so he pulled out the satellite phone. That had better reception. Evan dialed her number and heard it ring and ring until her voice mail picked up.

"Mckenna, it's Evan. I couldn't understand your message. Look, I know I haven't filled you in and I'm sorry. I shouldn't have tried to protect you that way. I don't know what's going on, but Toby is dead. I'm worried that someone might be coming after you. Go back to the office. Please. Do this for me—" Evan stopped and then added "—I'm in love with you. I don't know what I'd do if anything happened to you. Call me when you can."

He hung up and put the car back in Drive, navigating back onto the road. There. He'd said it. Admitted it. He was in love with her. She was more than someone to only spend the night with. Evan wanted to know everything about Mckenna, and that time he'd been telling the truth; he didn't know what he'd do if anything happened to her.

If he knew where she was going, he'd try to find her right now, but his best bet was to find Rex and arrest him. Then it wouldn't matter where Mckenna was. She'd be safe. He hoped there were answers at Rex and Toby's house. A clue, something that would give him an idea of where Rex was going. Maybe Keith would have some ideas of where Rex would go.

His experience with probation officers was limited—most of his interactions with them happened when he needed to find an informant or a suspect. He could call their PO if nothing else was panning out. He hoped Keith could provide some direction.

Finally arriving at the property, Evan decided he'd do a

quick walkthrough. Although Evan had filed for a warrant, he told the sheriff of his plan to search the house based on exigent circumstances. Since Rex was his top suspect and a threat to Mckenna, he had to make sure Rex wasn't hiding and that Mckenna wasn't being held.

Checking his phone again, he found there was at least a decent signal here. Evan dialed Mckenna, but it went to voice mail again. He called the office and asked for one of his tech guys.

"Hey, there, Knox. What's up?" the guy asked.

"I have a favor to ask. Would you mind seeing where Mckenna's phone is located?"

"Sure, give me just a second."

Evan could hear typing and then the guy said, "I think her phone is here in the office."

"Have you seen her?" Evan asked.

"No, but you know me, I'm in my room all day staring at screens. Hey, I heard you two are together now. That true?"

"Thanks for your help," Evan said, hanging up. Was she back at the office? Then it hit him. She had a personal phone and a work phone. The tech guy had probably pinged the work phone. He called back.

"Hey, again. Now what's up?"

"Can you find the location of Mckenna's personal phone?"

"Why? Did you two have a quarrel?"

A quarrel? Evan glanced at his phone. Who called a disagreement a quarrel? A tech guy, that's who. "No, it's a work deal. I'm trying to find her. It's for a case. No quarrels."

"That's going to be harder. I need a warrant for her personal phone and I'll have to contact the carrier, so it might take a while."

"If I can get a warrant, can you find her pretty quick?" Evan asked.

"I think it's true. I think you two have a thing."

Evan wanted to strangle him through the phone, but he needed to play along. "Okay, we have a thing going, but I'm also worried about her and a case we're working together. I'll see if I can get a quick warrant and then, can you find her?"

"I can try, but it's going to take some time. I'll be in touch."

"Thanks. I appreciate it," Evan said, hanging up before the tech guy could ask more questions that he wasn't ready to answer yet. At least not until he talked with Mckenna and made sure she was safe and then told her he was completely in love with her. He hoped what she'd written in her journal was true and she still felt the same way.

Getting out of his car, Evan headed in the direction of the deputy watching the scene. He signed in on the sheet to keep track of who was at the crime scene. Then he headed inside, hoping to find some answers and not more questions.

THE FIRST BUILDINGS of the ghost town appeared as Mckenna's vehicle reached the top of a hill, bouncing on a gravel road. Clouds had rolled in, threatening an afternoon thunderstorm and what Mckenna called a five-inch rain—one drop every five inches. Some of the buildings had broken windows, boards falling off and signs hanging half down. There were some dead trees around what used to be an old church, their branches like ancient, gnarled fingers waiting to grab you.

Stepping out of the vehicle, Mckenna checked her phone, but there was no signal at all. It didn't matter. She just wanted to find the location of the mining camp and then see if she could find the trees with the curved trunks. After that, she'd leave.

Her stubbornness kept her driving here, but the closer she came, the more she realized that this was only her reaction to all the emotions hitting her at once. She couldn't let it go even though she knew it should. All that talk about moving on and being so strong was often something she said to make herself believe that.

The truth was, she still struggled, but she knew part of being strong was continuing. She would see what she could see and then leave. Mckenna was going to get Mocha out of the vehicle, but with the clouds and cool breeze, she decided she could open all her windows and the back hatch. The temperature had dropped at least ten degrees, with the storms threatening to roll in. Another reason she needed to find the trees quickly.

Mocha thumped his tail, but he was curled up on his crate bed, so she figured he was happy to stay and sleep here anyway. "I'll be back in a few minutes, buddy."

She pulled out her map and studied it again. So many people had become used to using GPS on their phones, but her father had taught her how to read a map, use a compass and not rely on technology. She was grateful for that now. Based on what she could tell, she needed to walk to the west side of the town and then down a hill to the south. She should be getting close to the location once she navigated down the hill.

Map and water bottle in hand, Mckenna grabbed her phone too. Just in case she managed to get a signal. Plus, she felt naked without it.

Another small gust whipped up, picking up dirt in its path and shaking the dead tree by the church. The debris hit her eyes and Mckenna had to turn her head to avoid it. The wind died down as fast as it had started. More clouds blew in, and the sky darkened. If there was lightning, then she really needed to get out of here. Lightning strikes happened often in the mountains. As a child, she'd been knocked down by a bolt that had struck near her house. She'd never forgotten the power and fury of Mother Nature.

Mckenna picked up her pace, almost jogging, feeling her chest tighten. Was it from anxiety? Altitude? Both. For a moment, the sun came out from behind the clouds. A shadow appeared to her side and she whipped around.

No one was there.

Then she heard it. The cry of a hawk circling and hunting. A predator stalking its prey—although a hawk didn't play catch and release. A hawk struck hard and fast, its prey rarely knowing what hit them. Mckenna shuddered and broke into a run, ignoring the shallow breaths that plagued her.

Just find these trees, see if there's a mining camp and then get out of here.

Finally on the edge of town, she found the hill that went down toward the creek. There wasn't a clear path, but there also wasn't a lot of vegetation or trees in her way. The hill was steep enough that she almost had to sit back on her butt and slide, but she managed to get down. Looking back over her shoulder, she realized that had been the easy part—going back up was going to be the hard part. Maybe she could find an easier spot to get back uphill.

She continued toward the location she'd found on the map. It was still about a quarter mile's hike and the terrain was rough. Rocks jutted out and dead trees had fallen over, making her journey more difficult. Slipping a couple of times, Mckenna scraped her knee, ripping her pants, blood trickling out.

Great. Good job. This is the dumbest thing you've ever done. Well, maybe not the dumbest.

Being the wild child of the family, she'd tried plenty of

stupid things, but this was right up there with the best of them. The old mine and camp buildings had to be close by. Mckenna stopped and checked the map again. It had to be right over that hill.

Thunder rumbled in the distance.

She better hurry up. As the thunder died down, Mckenna had an uneasy feeling. The one she had when she was followed. As she was about to scrap her plan and run back up the hill to her vehicle and leave, the wind started again.

This time it brought a faint odor of rotten eggs with it.

She was close. The answers were so close. Just a little bit further. That was all she needed.

Forcing herself to not chicken out, Mckenna continued. Her legs burned, and she kept gasping for air as she navigated the rough terrain. Stopping again to catch her breath, she heard a loose rock roll down the hill until it landed in the creek with a soft plop. Then there was another noise. Human. Cries for help.

Someone else was here.

Chapter Thirty-Five

The smell in the house made Evan gag and cough. It wasn't decomp. More like dirty dishes and old food that had sat in the sink for several days. Walking into the kitchen, he found exactly that—dishes piled in the sink, not even rinsed. Flies buzzed around the mess.

Through the kitchen and down the hall was the back door area where Keith had seen the boots sitting outside. Sure enough, there were a pair of Ariat boots. Evan had put on gloves before he even came into the house. He also had on shoe booties to try not to disturb the scene. He wanted to find Rex, but he also wanted to convict him. If Evan messed up anything, a good defense lawyer would manage to get a "not guilty" charge for their client.

Pulling out his phone, Evan stepped out the back door and took pictures of the boots. He didn't want to touch anything, but he wanted everything documented. The boots were a key to this. If they matched the prints outside his window, then he would know that Rex was the one there watching them.

But they wouldn't tell him where Rex was now.

Even put his own shoe next to the boots. He was a size eleven. These were probably about size ten which would be a perfect match. There was some dirt on the outside of the boots. Dark soil. Just like the expensive soil Evan had been talked into buying by the landscapers. They had said it contained sheep manure and his plants would grow well in it. Colorado's soil was not meant to grow flowers. He had agreed. Reluctantly, because that increased his budget, but now he was glad he had. It would make the soil easier to match because sheep manure couldn't be found in many places in Colorado other than farms and potting beds.

Evan made a note to ask the evidence team if the imprints also matched the ones outside his window.

The boots had him convinced now. Rex was his guy. But had Rex fled the state? Or was he up in the mountains somewhere, hiding out, camping and hunting? He might have to see if his boss would allow the chopper to fly over some areas around the picnic area where Toby was found and the forest close to the house. He might have great areas to hide out in the remote mountains, but he couldn't get far on foot. And from what Evan knew, there were no missing vehicles, and the ATV was still in the garage.

He headed back inside and toward the bedrooms, wanting to see how much Rex had packed. The carpet down the hall was old and worn. Dirt stains and other stains showed through what was a light color at some point. The first bedroom belonged to Toby.

It was small and didn't take long to go through. It also wasn't the room he was interested in. The next room was Rex's, and sure enough, like Keith said, the closet was empty. Could he take all his clothes and still escape on foot? Backpacks could fit a lot, but it was strange to Evan that he would take everything and hike into the mountains.

He'd called Denver International Airport and asked them to keep an eye out for Rex, sending his driver's license photo and telling TSA that Rex was considered dangerous.

Be careful and call the Denver police on duty at the airport if he was spotted.

There wasn't much else of interest in the room. In fact, the room was bare. The last bedroom was sort of an office, or maybe more of a man cave. On one side there were shell casings with gunpowder and the equipment to load and make their own ammo. While that was interesting, Evan knew the brothers hunted and many hunters did that. But the big thing was, Toby wasn't supposed to be around any weapons while on parole.

There was also the little fact that the casings, .45 caliber, matched the size of the bullet used to shoot Autumn, Toby and Penny. But why leave this out in the open?

If Keith had seen this on a walkthrough, he wouldn't have approved of Toby staying here. There was a good chance that Rex had hidden all of this. Maybe even Toby didn't know about it.

Across the tiny room was a desk with a photo album. It was flipped open to the middle. Rex and Toby didn't seem like family-photo-album kind of guys, but who was Evan to say? He went over and peered at the pictures.

They must've been taken about the time Mckenna was abducted. Rex would have been working at her parents' ranch. Toby would have been around the same age as Mckenna.

They were having fun, drinking beers. With about six pictures per page, Evan stared at each one closely. Why was this open to this page? It was just a bunch of party pictures. The kind that most people forgot and stuffed away into a closet once they were adults. He leaned closer. Then it hit him—it was one of the infamous parties at Penny's house.

He was about ready to leave when the last picture caught his eye. He stared at it, taking in everyone in the photo.

"You've got to be kidding me," Evan muttered.

THE ROCKS ROLLED down the hillside because Mckenna had knocked them loose. Maybe the wind had blown hard enough to move them. Mckenna ran different scenarios through her mind, hoping she was right.

There couldn't be anyone there. She'd made sure she wasn't followed. But she wasn't a trained agent. She was a victim specialist. Why was she doing this? About ready to scramble back up the hill and get back to her car, Mckenna turned and then she saw them—the aspen trees.

Their trunks curved in the same direction like dancers, frozen in time. It was beautiful.

And frightening.

Her breathing became short and ragged. Fear gripped and paralyzed her. She needed to get out of here. Now. But her feet wouldn't move. Trying to get control over her constricting chest, she gazed around and spotted the mining camp building on the other side of the aspen trees.

There was a window, broken out. Parts of the glass were jagged. Other parts were smooth where Autumn had taken her shirt and being the smart girl she was, smoothed down the glass and protected them so she and Lily could escape. Her shirt was still on the edge of the window, flapping in the breeze. It was like a ghost waving to her, letting someone know that this was the spot where a horrible crime had happened.

She'd found it. Mckenna had done what law enforcement hadn't been able to by figuring out where they were all kept. And she'd faced her fear. Pulling out her phone, Mckenna snapped pictures of the trees, the building and then zoomed in on the shirt. She wanted to make sure she could show Evan.

Now it was time to leave.

Her breathing was still short, sharp gasps. Mckenna

worked on inhaling deeply, calming down. She had turned and was pushing herself as fast as she could go when she once more thought she heard a cry for help.

Was she imagining things?

Maybe Autumn's ghost was here with the shirt. *No.* She heard it again.

"Help!"

That was a human, and it wasn't her imagination.

Was it a trap? She should get to her vehicle and get out of here. Call 911. That was what any normal person would do. But Mckenna couldn't do that. She remembered being huddled in that room. Afraid she wouldn't ever see her family again.

Hoping. Praying. Making promises with God and the Universe. If they saved her, she would give back. She'd quit partying. She'd help others.

When she escaped through the window and the lady found her, she knew she had to keep her promise. Mckenna turned around. She couldn't see anyone, but she remembered the layout of the building.

She would see who was inside.

Chapter Thirty-Six

Evan's phone chirped. He had the warrant. Blowing out a breath, he flipped through the photo album, searching for more pictures. The one he'd found had been a little bit blurry. He wanted to be one hundred percent certain that he'd seen the person he thought he had in the pictures. Because if it was him, that complicated things. A lot.

He'd come to the last of the photos, all of them documenting teenagers partying the night away before real life came and made them grow up. Among them was one who would go to prison for the next eight years of his life, but what Evan was looking for was a clearer picture of someone else, someone who was in the background. Then he found it. This picture was better. It was him all right. Young and awkward. Pimples all over his face.

But it was undoubtedly him—Probation Officer Keith Warren.

"You weren't completely honest, were you, Keith? Neither was Penny. She didn't mention you on the guest list," Evan said out loud. It helped him think. This didn't necessarily mean anything. The fact that Keith never revealed growing up around here or knowing Toby and Rex was odd. In fact, he should never have been assigned to Toby as his

PO. That meant that the judge didn't know, and even Toby hadn't said anything. But why?

Could all three of these guys be in on this sick and twisted catch and release deal? Evan needed information, quickly. He tried Mckenna again, but she didn't answer, making him worry more. Then he called Cassidy. She answered on the first ring.

"Knox? Is everything okay?"

"I don't know," he answered truthfully. "Have you heard from your sister?"

"No. She told me she had to go to talk to Lily. Have you tried calling her?"

"Yes," Evan said, trying to keep his frustration in check. "If you hear from her, will you tell her to call me?"

"I'll do that. I can call Lily's parents too."

"I'll be honest, I'm worried," Evan said. "We need to find out if she's still at Lily's house. There's something else too. Do you know a probation officer by the name of Keith Warren?"

"Sort of. He grew up in our town, but moved away when we were in middle school."

"Did he move back?"

"Sometimes he'd visit. He was nice when Mckenna was taken. Helped look for her and stuff," Cassidy said.

"Did you know he was Toby Hanson's PO?"

"I'd heard that."

"You didn't think that was a conflict of interest?" Evan asked.

"No. I mean Keith and Toby never hung around each other. I thought they barely knew each other."

Evan closed his eyes and took a deep breath. "I think Keith knew them better than he ever said. Cassidy, I'm worried he's one of the kidnappers and that he's after Mckenna again."

"Do you have proof? Where are you? I'll meet you and help you out."

"I'm at Rex and Toby's house, but nothing here is leading me to Mckenna. Can you ask around the office and see if she checked in with anyone?"

"I'll do that. I'll let you know what I learn," Cassidy said. "And Knox?"

"What?"

"I know this isn't the time, but I need to know one thing, right now."

"What?" Evan said.

"Did you do anything to hurt my sister? Break up with her? Anything like that?"

"No. I would never do that." Evan stopped for a moment. He'd rather tell Mckenna first, but right now, if it helped Cassidy get going with looking for her sister, then he'd break the news to her. "I'm in love with her. I'd never do anything to deliberately hurt her. I need to start from here, but call me if you find out anything."

Cassidy hung up and Evan grabbed the photo album, bagging the photos with Keith in an evidence bag. Keith had been playing him. The boots and the missing clothes now seemed too convenient. Evan went back to Rex's room and found tennis shoes stuffed under the bed. Size nine and a half.

Just to double-check, he went to Toby's room and found shoes. Also nine and a half. The boots at the back door were too big for both men. Keith probably planted the boots he'd been wearing when he'd spied on Evan and Mckenna at Evan's house. No wonder he had offered to come check on Rex.

It gave him the perfect opportunity to plant evidence. Only this time he'd become sloppy, leaving the wrong size boot.

Evan thought about the scribbled handwriting in Mckenna's journal. He strode back out to the kitchen. There had to be a grocery list or something with Rex and Toby's handwriting. He finally found a list of supplies for the hardware store.

The handwriting wasn't exactly the neatest in the world, but it was much better than the scribbles in the journal. He needed a sample of Keith's handwriting. If it matched, then not only did he need to find Rex, but he also had to find Keith.

He called Keith.

Mckenna could be in more trouble than he thought.

Supposedly, Keith had been heading back to the office for appointments. Evan dialed the number for Keith's boss. Thankfully, he answered.

"This is Agent Evan Knox. I've been working with one of your probation officers, Keith Warren. Is he still at the office? I need to get in touch with him and he's not answering."

"No, sorry, he left early for the day. Took some personal time. I'm not sure what's going on, but he said something about needing to take care of business."

"Great," Evan muttered. "Can you do me a favor? I know this sounds odd, but I need to see Keith's handwriting. Can you find something that you can legally send without a warrant and shoot me an email with an image?"

"That is an odd request."

"It's important. It could make or break a case I'm working. I can get a warrant, but I don't have time."

"Let me see what I can find. Maybe there's something in his office."

Evan waited, pacing. Time seemed to stand still until finally, the man came back on the phone.

"I found notes he made that have nothing to do with any of his parolees. I'll send you a picture."

"Thank you," Evan said, hanging up.

He couldn't leave right now. He had signal at this house. Just then, Cassidy sent him a text.

I called Lily's parents. Mckenna left and no one knows where she is. I'll drive there and see what she wanted with Lily. Maybe that will help us find her.

I'll meet you there, Evan wrote back.

As he rushed out the door, the evidence team was pulling up. Evan handed them the pictures and mentioned the boots. "These are important items. Can you start by dusting for prints in the back room where they were making bullets? If you find a print, run it through the database to see if it matches Probation Officer Keith Warren. Call me if there's a match."

The evidence gal had a confused look on her face but agreed.

Evan had a bad feeling that Keith and Rex were in on this together. Rex had been following Mckenna. Two guys would make it easier to kidnap two girls.

And certainly, quite easy to kidnap one woman.

Chapter Thirty-Seven

Part of Mckenna still wanted to run. She could get help. Come back with law enforcement, but she'd have to drive a good distance away and if someone was in trouble, then she was leaving them. She made herself stop. Listen. Look around. There didn't seem to be anyone else nearby.

The cry of help shattered the air again.

Mckenna remembered calling for help too. Once she came out of the haze of the drugs and realized what a remote location she was being held in, she'd stopped yelling and started looking for a way out. That memory hit her clearly. Mckenna couldn't bring herself to leave someone, but the voice sounded like a male and that concerned her. Although, this far away, she couldn't hear for sure. Gazing around, Mckenna realized she could use the aspens with the curvy trunks to help conceal her. If she approached the mining camp cabin from that direction, then maybe she could see in a window and discover who was inside.

Telling herself that after this, she would never investigate things on her own, Mckenna forced herself to move and follow her plan. The hillside was steep leading to the aspen trees. Probably why an avalanche happened. It was incredible that the mining camp building itself hadn't been destroyed by an avalanche years ago. Of course, that could be why this part of the ghost town was hidden. Plus, the smell of rotten eggs meant that gold had never been found, or if it had, it would have been in very little quantities. That explained why not many people knew of the place.

The trees waved in a breeze that picked up, making rustling noises with their leaves. The edges were starting to turn a slight gold color. It wouldn't be long before this grove of trees would be part of the fall beauty. Unfortunately, the trees were also witnesses to horrible crimes.

Mckenna leaned up against a trunk and listened again. The cries for help had died down. She hadn't heard or sensed the presence of anyone else here other than the person inside the building.

Just take a quick peek in the window, see who's there and then get the heck out of here. You can do this.

Mckenna took a deep breath and continued down the path that led to the old building. The window Lily, Autumn and she had escaped out of was on the other side. There were a couple of old windows at the front of the building. Where had she been kept? The room she remembered was dark. She didn't remember windows, but maybe the kidnapper had boarded them up.

Stepping up to the old window, she glanced inside. What she saw made her catch her breath. The old glass made things distorted, sort of like looking through a bad kaleidoscope.

Mckenna went over to the other window to get a better view, but she still couldn't see well. All she could make out was that there was a person in a chair and they were tied up.

She pulled her phone out and, to her amazement, it had one bar. Enough to get a message out. Hitting Evan's contact, she typed in a message and hit Send, hoping that she had enough reception to send a message to him. Then she stepped inside, the door creaking as she took in a room that had been a part of her nightmares for years.

Her body shook, but now that she was inside, the shaking wasn't just from fear—anger and rage also filled her. How dare someone do this to her? To other girls? To anyone at all? They'd taken away her innocence as well as Lily's and the worst act of all was taking Autumn's life. She surveyed the room, turning around slowly, peering into the shadows when she heard a moan.

Walking through a narrow hall, she found a closed door. Open it? If it was a trap, this would be the time she'd be the most vulnerable. But the anger and determination to face her fear now pushed her forward. Mckenna turned the knob and let the door swing back, the hinges creaking. She remembered how Evan had her stand to the side at Penny Gardner's house, so she did the same thing.

Waiting.

Nothing.

Her breathing was short and fast. Her heart pounded. Fear was creeping in, ready to take over. Slowly, she peered around the corner and saw the man tied to a chair. Blood trailed down his face and his head lolled to the side. The part of his face Mckenna could see revealed a black eye almost swollen shut.

Sensing Mckenna, the man turned his head the other way and stared at her with his better eye. "Mckenna? What are you doing here? Help me. We have to get out of here. He'll be back any minute."

"Rex?"

"Yeah, it's me."

Mckenna strode forward and, finding the ropes that tied Rex's hands, began to undo them first. "Who did this?"

Rex screwed up his face. He was in serious pain. "Keith Warren."

"Toby's PO?"

"The one and only."

"I don't understand," Mckenna said, stopping her work on the ropes. She barely knew Keith Warren, but would a probation officer do this? Or was Rex setting her up? Should she trust him?

"Keith moved away from this area when we were kids, but he'd come back to visit. He's a sick and twisted person. Please, untie me and I'll explain it all."

"Okay," Mckenna said, still uncertain. She needed to change tactics. She didn't know whom to believe anymore. Why would Keith kidnap her? And Lily and Autumn? He didn't know anyone around here *that* well. What made him come back and target this community? Her fingers were shaking as Mckenna went back to undoing the ropes that tied Rex's hands behind his back.

The knots were beginning to loosen when Mckenna realized Rex had a terrified expression. He was about ready to say something when a jolt of electricity shocked Mckenna. She fell back, her body thumping to the dusty floor.

"Hello, Mckenna. I missed you."

Keith.

She struggled to get to her feet, but her body wasn't responding. Keith hit her with another jolt from a stun gun and she dropped again. He wouldn't get the best of her. Ever. Mckenna refused to give in as she worked to move again, but he nailed her with electricity once more.

"This is what I don't like about stun guns," Keith said. "They really don't incapacitate people well enough."

Mckenna didn't answer. She had to stay calm. She'd escaped once and she could do it again. For now, she'd pretend like she couldn't move. If nothing else, it was so he wouldn't shock her again. Why hadn't she left when she had the chance? What about Mocha?

What about Evan? She'd never told him how much she cared…or loved him. Would she get the chance? Who knew, but she'd fight hard to see him again. She had to be smart for now and play Keith's game. But would he release her now that she knew his identity? More likely he'd never let her go.

Keith crouched down, putting his face close to hers. His breath reeked of cigarettes mixed with a stench of body odor, but Mckenna refused to turn away. She wouldn't give him the pleasure of intimidating her. He started tying her hands together.

"What's wrong? Nothing to say? Where's your FBI boyfriend now? You two had a great night last night. I enjoyed watching."

Mckenna's stomach churned. Had he really seen them? Was that why Mocha was barking? Evan probably didn't want to tell her if he'd noticed anything in the yard. Why hadn't he told her? Or maybe he didn't see anything.

Keith continued. "I don't know if I like that tattoo or not, though." He pulled her shirt up a little, staring at her side. "Too bad you covered up your scars. I rather liked them."

It was hard not to answer him. To tell him there was a special place in hell for people like him, but for now, Mckenna stayed quiet, biding her time. He was having so much fun goading her, she could tell he wasn't making the knots as tight as he should.

"Well," Keith said, standing, "that should hold you for now. I need a little time to get my plan in action. I'll have to be careful, but if I do this right, Rex over there will take the blame."

Mckenna wondered how he was going to do that.

As if reading her thoughts, Keith said, "He's a bit beat up, but after we play our game of catch and release over and over, I think you might be a little beat up too. I'm thinking through a scenario where you fought him, so he has defensive wounds all over him. And you almost escaped. Almost. But then he caught you and killed you. I'll make sure your FBI lover finds Rex with the murder weapon. Meanwhile, I have a job offer in Wyoming. I hear it can be a remote place to live. Not many people up there. Just the way I like it."

Keith walked out the door. "Don't go anywhere. Not yet."

Chapter Thirty-Eight

Flooring the bu-car, Evan cursed the winding road with the switchbacks that forced him to slow down as he drove to Lily's house. He would accelerate on the straightaways. After what seemed like an eternity, he arrived at the entrance to Lily's house.

Cassidy's vehicle was already parked there, and she wasn't in it. She must be inside. Evan leaped out of his car and up the steps where the door opened for him. Brenda, Lily's mother, invited him in.

"Agent Knox," she said. "The other agent is in the living room with Lily."

"Thanks," he said. "Were you here when Mckenna was?"

"No, I was out grocery shopping. When Mckenna called I thought it would be great for her to come by and check on Lily so that she didn't have to be alone."

"Okay," Evan said, heading into the living room where Cassidy was already seated. Lily was holding a pillow against her chest and appeared worried.

"You're not in any trouble," Cassidy was saying to her. "We just need some information. Okay?"

Lily nodded and clutched her pillow tighter.

"When Mckenna came here today, what did she want?" Cassidy asked.

"She wanted to see if we had similar memories."

"Similar memories?" Cassidy asked.

"Yes, she thought we'd been taken by the same person," Lily answered.

Evan could tell Cassidy was trying to wrap her head around that thought. Mckenna had told him that her older sister doubted her feeling that Toby was innocent. He spoke before Cassidy could question the idea. "What specifically did she ask you?"

Lily glanced back and forth and said, "We talked about the bad smell and dancing trees."

Evan didn't know what to make of dancing trees. He'd start with one thing at a time. "I remember you talking about the smell before. Mckenna too."

"Yeah, like rotten eggs. Mckenna said it could be from a mine that was near where we were kept. From fool's gold or something like that."

Evan thought about the ghost town Mckenna had mentioned. He hadn't made it there yet himself, with everything else going on. A sheriff's deputy had gone there and wasn't able to find signs of anyone being kept in any of the old buildings, but Evan didn't know if the deputy had searched the whole area. Evan had googled pictures of the town. There were no obvious mining areas in the pictures, but like so many Colorado ghost towns, it had been built during the gold rush. If the mine was nearby, but no longer in any kind of use, trees and shrubs may have overgrown the area or any surrounding buildings. That might be why the previous sheriff couldn't find where Mckenna was held.

"Tell me about the dancing trees," Evan said.

"Well, they're not really dancing, you know, but they look cool because the trunks are all curved in the same direction. Mckenna and I both thought they seemed like they were dancing."

"I've seen pictures of trees like that. Aspen trees," Cassidy said.

"They were aspens," Lily said. "We both thought maybe we were seeing things because we were drugged."

The ghost town had to be the key. If there was an old mine in the area, then maybe that was where Mckenna had been held. And maybe where she had gone looking for answers. It was Evan's best lead. Should he go out there himself? See if a deputy could go? It was Mckenna. For any other case, he might send a deputy, but this was different. Mckenna was different. She'd changed his life in ways he hadn't expected. He couldn't imagine a life without her.

"What else did she ask you?" Evan said. The more information the better. Cassidy was watching him but allowing him to take the lead now in the questioning.

"That was it," Lily said, then whispered, "Is Mckenna going to be okay?"

"She'll be fine," Evan said, making yet another promise that he didn't know if he could keep. By the looks on their faces, Cassidy and Lily knew he was only saying Mckenna would be fine to make everyone feel better. "Thanks for your time."

Cassidy and Evan stood and thanked Lily's parents and then headed out the front door. Cassidy was about to say something when Evan's phone rang. With hope, he pulled it out, wanting the caller ID to say "Mckenna" but instead it was a sheriff's office in Wyoming. One of the ones he'd sent memos to in case they'd had similar kidnappings.

He answered the phone.

"Is this Agent Knox?" a man asked.

"It is."

"Son, this is Sheriff Alan Lewis of Fremont County. You asked about kidnappings fitting a certain MO?"

"Yes." Evan gripped the phone. "Do you have cases like the one I sent you?"

"We do, as a matter of fact. Some of them include missing Indigenous women. We've helped with two of the cases, although the Bureau of Indian Affairs has worked on most of those. I could give you my contact there."

Evan had never worked with the BIA, but he welcomed anyone who had information. "That would be great. Thank you."

He wrote down the contact's information and then on a whim asked, "Do you know a man by the name of Rex Hanson?"

"Nope, doesn't ring a bell."

"What about a probation officer named Keith Warren?" Evan asked.

"Oh, yeah, I know Keith. Good guy. He came here about seven years ago to take a course and have a little vacation. We connected then. I think he just accepted an opening up here in the probation office. In fact, one of the cases I was talking about happened around one of the times Keith was in town. He offered to help us search for the girl. Volunteered a lot of time and stayed an extra week. He said he hated the way Indigenous women went missing without anyone helping."

"Did he?" Evan asked.

"He did."

"Did you find the girl?"

"We did, but unfortunately, it was too late," the sheriff said. "Same for the other girl. They were both found deceased and shot. The bullet was a .45, and based on what you entered in the system, I think we have a match."

"That would be a huge break in this case. Will you send me the information on the ballistics?"

"I'd be happy to."

"I'm curious, was Keith ever with anyone?" Evan asked, thinking about Rex being a partner in the crimes.

"Not that I knew of. Seemed like kind of a loner. Nice guy. Liked to go fishing. He said it was relaxing and he liked doing catch and release since he was staying at a hotel. Can't cook a fish over a campfire there."

"No, you can't do that," Evan answered, his stomach dropping at the mention of catch and release. "Thank you, sir, for your time. I appreciate it."

"You want me to send the files?"

"Yes, please do."

The sheriff paused. "Son, I've been in law enforcement my whole life. This isn't my first rodeo. Keith Warren murdered those girls, didn't he? Or at least you're suspecting it."

"That's right. I think he did a similar thing here, only this time he screwed up."

The sheriff muttered some choice words about how people never were who they seemed.

"If you see him in your area, for any reason," Evan said, "arrest him right away. There's going to be a warrant out for him soon."

"You got it. I still can't believe this. Can't trust anyone."

"No, you can't. I'll let you know if we get him in custody." Evan hung up the phone. Cassidy was over by her vehicle, leaning up against it. Evan filled her in about Keith and the area up in Wyoming near the Wind River Reservation.

"I can't believe it," Cassidy said. "I didn't know him well when he did live around here, but now that I think about it, he was a loner then too."

"I'll let the sheriff know," Evan said. "I'm going to find this ghost town. Maybe Mckenna is there."

"Be careful. Get a deputy to go with you for backup," Cassidy said. "I'll get a memo out to all field offices in Colorado, Wyoming and maybe Utah and New Mexico too. Who knows where Keith could be."

"Thank you," Evan said. "I'll take someone with me and search the area surrounding the ghost town. I'll let you know if we find anything."

They started getting in their vehicles and then Cassidy stopped and said, "Hey, Knox."

"What?" Evan asked.

"You're not so bad after all. I can see what my sister sees in you."

Chapter Thirty-Nine

Mckenna lay quietly, the only sounds her shallow breaths and Rex's moans every now and then. When she was certain that Keith had left, Mckenna rolled over and sat. He'd tied her hands behind her back, but while she was trying to free Rex, she'd seen a sharp edge of glass and grabbed it.

She'd managed to hang on to it even through the stun gun. Her neck ached where he had connected with her, but she ignored the pain and focused on the task at hand—escaping. Again.

The ties loosened as the sharp piece of glass started sawing its way through. That and the idiot hadn't done a very good job of securing her. He should have used cuffs if he really wanted to keep her captive.

Footsteps echoed on the front boards outside the building. Mckenna paused, wrapping her fingers around the glass, careful not to cut herself. She had to pretend like she was still tied and unconscious. The door opened, hinges creaking again. Footsteps came closer and closer. Mckenna closed her eyes and hoped he would be fooled.

The stench of body odor and cigarettes wafted toward her again. Then she heard him say, "I know you're not asleep. Or knocked out. Sit up."

Keith grabbed her by the shirt and hoisted Mckenna to a sitting position. She worked hard to pretend like she was still tied. That was her advantage, and she knew from previous experience that she needed to bide her time. Wait it out. There would be a moment when she could attack him. Maybe she could even hit his jugular with the piece of glass.

Staring at her with dark eyes, Keith said, "I saw your dog up there. Sorry, but when this is all over, I'll have to dispatch him. You know what I mean by that?"

Mckenna wouldn't give him the satisfaction of answering, but she did. The term dispatch was one that wildlife officers used instead of euthanize. *If anything happens to Mocha, I'll kill this guy.* Mckenna wanted to say that out loud, but she knew that he'd enjoy it. It would only make him happy.

"I want to see that tattoo again," Keith said, lifting her shirt. Now Mckenna was furious. That was her tattoo. Her phoenix. And there was only one other person who was allowed to touch it.

Keith tilted his head and then said, "I guess it's growing on me. I'm not usually into tattoos."

Taking his finger, he was about to touch it, when Mckenna kicked her foot and nailed him in the groin. It wasn't enough to give her a chance to get to her feet, but it got him away from her. No one touched her without consent. Anger flashed through Keith's eyes, and he took his fist and punched her in the jaw.

Pain exploded and she saw stars for a moment. It was hard to breathe as she gasped in surprise.

"That's what you get for that," Keith said, standing.

At least he had backed away from her. Mckenna couldn't stand it anymore.

"I'm not a teenager. I'm much stronger and you should be careful," Mckenna said, breaking her silence.

At Mckenna's threat, Keith started laughing and shaking his head. "I'm so scared."

He thought so highly of himself that maybe if she got him talking, she could find the moment to lunge for him. "Why are doing this? What are you, some sort of loser?"

His laughter stopped and Keith balled his fist again. Mckenna was certain he was going to hit her, and she closed her eyes and braced for the impact.

"I'm not a loser," Keith said.

"Then what are you? Why are you doing this?" Mckenna felt behind her. She gripped the piece of glass and slowly scooted back, trying to put some distance between them.

"What? You trying to psychoanalyze me now? Figure me out?"

"I guess," Mckenna said, deciding to try a direct approach. If it made him mad, she might be able to get him close enough to swing the board around and nail him in the head as hard as she could. "I mean, if you're going to kill me, then the least you could do is explain why you take people. This whole stupid catch and release thing."

"You know…" Keith came closer, but not quite close enough. "You women and all your manipulation."

"What do you mean?" Mckenna asked. "Who's manipulating you? I'm the one tied up."

"Exactly, you're the one tied up and I have complete control over you. There's nothing you can do."

Keep him talking. He's just about in the right spot to hit with the board.

"Control? Why do you want control?"

"Why do you have so many questions?" Keith asked.

Now he took a step back, in the wrong direction. Mckenna needed him close enough to hit him while she was sitting down. If she tried to stand, he would grab her or hit her with the stun gun again. She'd only have one chance at this, and it better be perfect. He'd caught her again, but there was no way he was going to release her. This game would end today—one way or another. "I figure if you're going to kill me, I have a right to know."

"No, you don't."

"You said I was your first. Why me?"

"Because you were that whore's favorite student. At least for that year," Keith said. "Of course, now I know that she tells everyone they're her favorite. Right, Rex?"

Rex groaned. Mckenna wondered what part he had to play in this. "Whore? Who are you talking about?"

"Seriously? You don't know?"

Mckenna thought about it. "Are you talking about Penny Gardner?"

"Now see, you know more than you realize."

"But I don't understand," Mckenna said.

"You're not meant to understand," Keith said, hitting Mckenna again before she could react.

Everything went black.

Chapter Forty

Pushing the accelerator, Evan drove as fast as he dared to the old ghost town. He had a map, and while it wasn't necessarily difficult to get to the old town, it wasn't a fast drive. Currently, he was on pavement, but the next road would be gravel.

He'd called the sheriff before leaving and she knew exactly where Evan was headed. She'd told him she was short on deputies with all the crime scenes and manpower this case was taking. She'd promised to call in extra deputies and then head up to the ghost town to back Evan up herself. She also warned him that there'd be just enough cell service to maybe send a text. Maybe. It was enough to tease you and then not go through. But radios worked up there at least.

Evan spotted the green county road sign; it was the correct one. He turned and the road quickly went to gravel. It wasn't smooth. Washboards made his vehicle fishtail and kept his speed down.

"Hold on, Mckenna," he muttered. Although he didn't even know if she had gone to the ghost town. If she wasn't there…he couldn't think about it. Nothing could happen to her. He'd pushed away love his whole life, not wanting to be like his parents with four kids, a divorce and one parent walking out. He and his sisters had ended up being more like parents to each other and their father.

Every relationship Evan had tried was a failure, but it wasn't anyone's fault but his. He didn't think he could ever love one person so much that he'd give up anything for them, but then along came Mckenna.

He'd been intrigued with her from the start. There was a time that Evan would have just had a fling with Mckenna, like Cassidy said, love her and leave. But he'd known when she spent the night that she was different. This was no fling. The thought of losing her was a punch in the gut.

Please, please be here. You're tough. You're a survivor.

Evan rounded another corner and his vehicle continued to bounce all over the road. A bull moose stood out in a meadow grazing. Not a care in the world. No idea that a serial kidnapper was in his territory.

After what seemed like an eternity, Evan spotted old buildings in the distance. The road's ruts became deeper. He'd be lucky to have any suspension left by the time he arrived. Explaining that bill to his boss would be fun, but he didn't care. He'd pay for it himself if he had to. All he cared about was finding Mckenna.

The road ended where the old town began. He could envision the settlers moving up here with high hopes of striking it rich. Instead, they endured a harsh environment where it was hard to grow anything in the summer and winters were long and cold with deep snow. No wonder it had been abandoned. They had no idea that over a hundred years later, a sick kidnapper would bring teenage girls here for his own twisted game.

Evan drove down what used to be the street and his heart rate increased. Mckenna's vehicle was parked in front of the old church. The windows and back hatch were open. Mocha was standing in his crate, nose pressed against the metal.

Evan parked and got out of his vehicle, and heard Mocha's tail thumping in excitement. "Hey, there, buddy. Where's your mom? She'd never leave you in the car like this."

Hands on his hips, Evan stared around. Where was she? If anything happened to her, he'd never forgive himself. How long had Mocha been in his crate? He unfolded the portable stairs he'd seen Mckenna use to make it easy on Mocha to get in and out. He needed to find her, but if he didn't take care of Mocha, Mckenna would never forgive him.

The dog was happy to see the stairs come out and bounded down, rushing for a dead tree to take care of business. Once he was done, Evan gave Mocha some water and petted him, letting him lean against his leg. As much as Evan wanted to put Mocha away and start searching for Mckenna, he knew he better wait for the sheriff to arrive.

He might need backup.

Crouching down, Evan continued scratching and petting Mocha. "I'm glad you're okay. But your mom. Where is she? Is she always this stubborn and impulsive?"

Mocha gave him some licks and turned in a circle, then came over and leaned against Evan again. Wrapping his arms around the dog, he thought about his childhood dog and how his dad had taught him to track and hunt with his Lab.

Track.

An idea began to form.

"How bad *did* you flunk out?" he asked Mocha.

The Lab gave a little whine and flopped to the ground, rolling upside down for Evan to pet his belly.

"That bad, huh? What do you think, do you think you could do one track? It would only be once, and it would save us time. I haven't done this in years, so we're the perfect pair, an FBI K-9 flunky and someone who hasn't worked a dog since he told his dad he was joining the FBI and not the K-9 unit. But I think we could at least try, don't you?"

Mocha sat back up.

"Okay, let me find your leash."

Chapter Forty-One

Head pounding, Mckenna tried to sit up. Nausea hit her and she paused, her eyes having trouble opening. That bastard had hit her hard, but as far as she could tell, he wasn't here now. Was he close by? Or had he left so that he could come back at night to finish his plan?

Luckily, he hadn't noticed that her hands weren't tied. That she was just pretending by holding her arms behind her back. There was a bottle of water sitting close to her with a straw to help her drink if her arms were still bound. Mckenna was tempted. Her lips were dry and cracking from the heat. Sweat dripped down her face as the old building had very little airflow. She could feel that she was dehydrated, but she didn't dare take a drink.

Who knew what Keith had laced the water with this time.

GHB again, or even something worse. Reaching for the bottle, Mckenna poured about half out. It wouldn't hurt to make him think she'd drank some.

She managed to sit up all the way, cursing herself for her moment of stubbornness and deciding that *she* would be the one to find the cabin. As if Evan or anyone in law enforcement with a brain couldn't have found it.

Stop being hard on yourself and think about how you're

going to get out of here. You escaped once, you can do it again.

Closing her eyes, she waited for the feeling of nausea to go away. What she wouldn't give right now to have Evan wrap his arms around her. Tell her everything was okay. And then spend another night with him. And another and another.

She had to keep going. This time it wasn't only for her or her family—it was for Evan too. With her eyes closed, she'd listened for footsteps, the door creaking, something to let her know that Keith was around. She hadn't heard anything, so she took a chance and put her arms in front of her, massaging her forearms that were sore from her holding them behind her back, pretending to be tied.

A groan made her pause. Was Keith here? Was he back?

She stared around the room and spotted Rex. Keith hadn't taken him yet to enact his plan, so maybe she had time. His face looked like a raw hamburger. While Mckenna had been knocked out, Keith had probably taken his frustration out on Rex. She had to get out of here and get help, but the room was closed tight. Lily had talked about a small opening they had managed to squeeze through and get to the window from where Mckenna had escaped long ago. She remembered seeing Autumn's shirt still hanging there. It gave Mckenna strength to fight, get out of here and make sure Keith never harmed anyone again.

Mckenna worked her way around the room, dark from a lack of windows, but some bits of sun shining in through slats in the wood. She had to find the spot Lily had told her about. Mckenna's fingertips were becoming raw from trying to find an opening. Some wood slivers poked her, and one even went under a fingernail, but she didn't care. She didn't let the pain stop her.

Finally, after thinking that they were in another room in this mining camp building, she found a spot that was loose. The board was hanging by one nail but had been propped back up. Too easy? Another trap? Part of the crazy catch and release thing? She gently pried it back. The hole would be tight, but Mckenna thought she could fit. Lily and Autumn had been a little smaller than her. She was about ready to slide through when a noise stopped her.

A wheezing sound came from Rex. Was he even conscious? His chin was resting on his chest. Mckenna went over to him. She gently untied his ropes. She was still uncertain if he was Keith's partner, but there was no way he could harm her now. He probably wouldn't even be able to walk. Even if she made it through the hole in the side and out the window and was able to open the door from the outside, she couldn't help him out. Mckenna knew she was strong, but not strong enough to help him up the hillside and back to her vehicle. She would at least untie him to see if she could make him a little more comfortable and then see if she could get back to her vehicle.

I'll release you again and catch you, over and over. His words echoed in her mind. There was a good chance Keith was waiting. He'd enjoy the chase, but this time she had an advantage—she wasn't drugged. Now she was even more certain that the water contained GHB and Keith was trying to make it easy to catch her again.

As she took one rope off, Rex stirred.

He couldn't really control his head, but he managed to open one eye and stare at Mckenna. "Forget about me. Save yourself."

If Mckenna hadn't been so close to Rex, she might not have been able to hear him. "Don't waste your energy. I'm going to get out of here. I'll get help. I promise."

"It's…a…trap." Rex wheezed harder.

"How do you know? Are you working with him?"

"No, I'm not working with him," Rex answered. "He killed Toby and then tased me. I tried fighting back, but he got the upper hand while I was down from the shock."

"Save your energy," Mckenna said, but then she realized this could be her one chance to get some answers. "I do have one more question."

"What?" he asked, this time a little more clearly.

"If you're not working with Keith, then why have you been following me? It was you, wasn't it?"

Rex nodded his head yes. "I didn't mean to scare you."

Mckenna could tell it was hard for him to talk, but she wanted answers. She *needed* answers. "You did scare me, why did you do it?"

"I always knew Toby was set up. My brother wouldn't have done that to you. He wouldn't have hurt a fly, but I didn't know who had taken you." Rex stopped, catching his breath, and then continued. "We just wanted to clear Toby's name. He might have been out on probation, but he'd lost his life too in a sense. Those years in prison changed him. When he first went in, he thought someone would figure it out. He asked his lawyer to get a PI and keep working on his case, but his lawyer dropped him and told him to serve his time. He'd get out on good behavior. So that's what he did."

"So why follow me?"

"Because the day Toby ran into you and spoke with you, we watched you leave. Toby started freaking out. He'd just seen Keith. He knew if Keith had spotted him talking to you, he'd be in big trouble. Maybe even have to go back to prison. I told him that Keith hadn't seen him, but we watched you leave and then Keith started following you…"

Rex stopped speaking, gasping for air. Mckenna figured

he wouldn't be able to continue talking, but then he took a deep breath and spoke up again.

"We started wondering if there was any way Keith had done this. I mean it was a leap, I suppose, but it was the first lead we'd had. Then the next day those girls were taken, and I heard about the one dying. I knew that Toby would be the number one suspect." Rex attempted to inhale and groaned in pain, but then continued.

"When the FBI agent showed up with Keith to question us, I knew I had to catch Keith following you. I had to do something because this time, with the death involved, Toby would go to prison much longer. Maybe even life. I didn't think he'd survive. I had to do something. I was desperate. Especially because Keith would be happy to lock Toby up again. He's that kind of person. Vindictive. That's probably why he took those girls after Toby was released. He wanted payback."

"For what?"

"He sometimes hung out with Penny Gardner. I think he had a major crush on her. The little prick even barged in once during a, uh, you know, a moment. Flew into a jealous rage. I'd always suspected him of setting up Toby but could never prove it."

"What else do you remember about him? When he lived here?" Mckenna asked.

"He was a weird, loner type. I thought if I kept following you, I'd see him again. Find a pattern of sorts and start gathering evidence against him. I know, you don't have to say it, dumb idea, but we were desperate. We were tired of people harassing us and Toby wanted a life. He wanted to move away, which would be difficult due to his probation. I still couldn't believe that the judge made Keith the PO for

Toby. Toby even told the judge there was a conflict of interest, but I guess the probation office is short-staffed, so it didn't matter."

Rex took short, ragged breaths. Mckenna felt bad asking him to talk, but she needed to know the truth. The next time Keith returned, he'd probably kill them.

Mckenna could tell talking was taking a toll on Rex. She was able to undo the ropes around his hands and started working on the ones around his feet that tied him to the chair. "When did you know for sure that it was Keith?"

"First, I found old pictures from one of the parties at Penny's house. It was the night you went missing. I didn't remember him being there. I don't think Penny knew he was there, but then again, I didn't remember much from that night. We were all drinking a good amount. But when I found the pictures with Keith in the background, I called him. I told him what I had and that we needed to meet. I wanted to hear his version of the story. Toby and I had planned on secretly recording the conversation. Keith wanted those pictures. I could tell. I figured I would try to get him to confess to what he did and give him the photos. I had better ones at home, but I didn't tell him about those. I was keeping those for evidence. But my plan backfired on us. He met us down by a tree, out of sight of the parking lot. That should have been our first clue that he wasn't going to talk. He shot Toby and before I could get away, he nailed me with the Taser."

"You didn't go armed?" Mckenna asked.

"I did, but everything happened so fast I couldn't pull my gun."

"I'm so sorry, Rex. I'm sorry about Toby and everything. I know it's been hard and I'm going to make it up to you by helping you escape."

"Get out of here," Rex said again, through harsh breaths.

"I'll leave once I get these off. It gives you more of a chance if Keith comes back."

Rex gave a laugh that created a little bit of a coughing fit. Mckenna thought he might have a punctured lung. "I don't have a chance. Save yourself. It looks like you found an opening in the side of the wall or something. Go. It's what Toby would want too."

"I think Toby would want me to try to save you too," Mckenna said, changing her mind about leaving Rex behind. He had tried to stop Keith. He'd done what he could and Mckenna didn't know how, but she'd get him to a safe place where he could hide until she could get help. If she left him here, Keith would certainly kill him since he'd already killed Autumn and Toby. She'd heard an agent say once that when someone killed, it became easier to do it again.

Mckenna believed that statement—especially with Keith. She had to get Rex out of here. The final rope came undone, Mckenna's fingers were raw and bleeding from both searching for the hole in the wall and undoing the rope. She was about to go back to the loose board, slide it back and slip through, when she heard the front door creak, its hinges giving a warning.

"I told you. You should have left," Rex said.

Mckenna knew he was right, but she'd made her decision. And she was done with this. Done with the nightmare and feeling afraid. If she was going to see Evan again, she had to be brave, face her fears and make Keith pay for everything. Instead of slipping through the hole, Mckenna pulled and pried the piece of wood. The rotten board popped off, a nail still stuck in it.

"Perfect," Mckenna said.

"What are you doing?" Rex asked. "Get out of here."

Mckenna ignored him, gripping the board behind her. Keith Warren was going to pay for everything he'd done.

Chapter Forty-Two

Evan continued to convince himself that his idea would work. Mckenna had told him about Mocha's history of flunking out. The dog would find only Mckenna, not others, when Cassidy had tried some tracking training with him. Maybe Mocha would track Mckenna, maybe not, but if the dog could follow her scent, it was the best way to find her quickly.

He had a bad feeling that she was in serious trouble.

Sheriff Stewart pulled up and parked. She came over with a questioning look on her face, glancing at Mocha and then Evan.

"I don't know where Mckenna is," Evan said. "But her dog, Mocha, has had some tracking training. I want to try to use him to find her."

"Some tracking training?"

"He was supposed to work for the FBI as an explosives detection and tracking dog. He failed out of both and so now he's a crisis K-9."

"What makes you think that he'll track Mckenna?"

"Because in his training, Mckenna would hide. She volunteered to do it so he could get extra tracking training. He would only find her. If anyone else hid, he would start tracking and then flop down and refuse to move. He could be quite stubborn, but since it's Mckenna we're searching for, maybe he'll do it."

"Okay," the sheriff said. "I'm game to try it. Do you have any experience working dogs?"

"I do. My dad was a K-9 handler. My sisters and I grew up working dogs."

"Okay, then let's do it. I will be your backup officer. Tell me what you need as I don't have a ton of experience backing up a K-9 handler."

"Just let the dog work, stay behind me, and shoot anyone who tries to shoot us. I won't be able to pull my weapon or observe our surroundings. I'll be watching Mocha and his body language."

"You got it. Anything to help find Mckenna and see if we can nail this guy."

"Thanks," Evan said as he went to Mckenna's front seat and grabbed her jacket. Normally there was a whole protocol for tracking. He should have gloved up and put her jacket in a plastic bag to preserve the odor, but at this point, he was hoping that Mocha would entertain the idea and do this. Forget the usual operating procedures.

Raising his voice to heighten Mocha's interest, Evan let Mocha sniff Mckenna's jacket. He didn't know what command had been used for Mocha to track, so he went with a standard one. "Find her. Go find her. Seek. Come on, let's go find her."

At first, Mocha tilted his head at the sound of Evan's higher voice. His tail wagged and he gave a short couple of barks. Doubting his plan, Evan gave it another shot.

"Go find her, Mocha. Where is she? Where's Mckenna?"

At the sound of Mckenna's name, Mocha turned and sniffed the ground. He glanced back at Evan asking if this was what Evan wanted.

"That's it, boy," Evan said. He used his arm to cast Mocha out in different directions. Now the Lab appeared to be more focused. Using Mckenna's name had helped.

"Find Mckenna," Evan repeated a few more times.

Evan was about to let Mocha sniff the jacket again when he noticed a shift in Mocha's body language. The Lab's tail poked straight in the air and his breathing changed. Evan's dad had taught him to listen to the sound of a dog breathing. When they were in odor or had caught an odor they were trained to find, their sniffing would change along with the body language. Mocha continued to make snorting sounds as he pushed his nose to the ground. The dry hot day was making it harder for him to pick up Mckenna's scent, but suddenly the dog took off in a trot toward the other end of the ghost town.

Weaving back and forth, with his tail remaining straight up, every now and then Mocha would pause. Evan would be about ready to let him sniff the jacket and cast him out again when Mocha would resume his search, intent on his mission and appearing to remain in odor.

When they reached the edge of town, he saw a deep slope that went down at a sharp angle. Evan knew it would be hard to keep his balance downhill and there wasn't anything past this area. Mocha didn't hesitate and pulled on the leash.

"You think he's on her scent?" the sheriff asked behind him, her gun drawn and ready.

Evan knew she'd have a hard time holding the gun and backing them up going down the incline. Mocha continued to pull on the leash and whine. "I think he is."

"Then, let's do this," the sheriff said. "I'll be okay."

"So will I." Evan gave some slack in the leash and worked to not lose his footing. Just when he was thinking that

Mocha was taking them on a wild-goose chase, he saw a grove of aspens.

They had curved trunks and appeared to be dancing.

FOOTSTEPS ECHOED AS Keith came down the hall toward them. Mckenna prayed her plan would work. If it didn't, there wasn't a plan B. She forced herself to slow her breathing, to concentrate. Her timing would have to be just right. Rex's breathing remained haggard and harsh. She'd made him talk too much, but she had to know the truth. Now that she did, she knew Keith was ready to end his game of catch and release. After killing Autumn and shooting Toby in cold blood, there was no going back.

But if she was successful with her plan, he might not be able to ever hurt anyone again. If she hit him hard enough, other young women wouldn't lose their lives. Other women wouldn't feel the terror that had possessed her for so long.

She would swing as hard as she could. For her. For them. And for Evan. She wanted to see Evan again so she could tell him her feelings.

Even if Evan decided to leave, like Cassidy said he might, Mckenna didn't care. They were meant to be together. She was certain. She could only hope he felt the same way.

The door hinges creaked and groaned as Keith peered inside. Mckenna sat huddled in the corner just like he'd left her. The board was behind her. Rex hadn't tried to move. Mckenna didn't even know if he could move. The only good part was that Keith hadn't noticed that they were both untied.

A sly smile spread across his face. There was something different about his expression and it made Mckenna's heart pound. Keith came over.

Crouch down, you bastard. Go ahead, get close to me again.

Keeping her head down, Mckenna had her eyes open, but with the darkness of the room and the fact that Keith thought she'd had some of his "special" water, he wasn't paying attention. She was glad she had poured some out. Hopefully, the spot where she'd dumped the water had dried.

He stood there for a minute, Mckenna staring at his boots. If she concentrated on them, she could still pretend that she was sleepy from the water. She had to make him think she was groggy and unable to fight. Taking the toe of his boot, he nudged her.

Trying to see how asleep I am? Just wait until you find out.

Mckenna kept an eye on his boots as they stepped back. She didn't dare look up and give away that she was fully awake, but she waited and watched until his feet turned around.

Now, she thought, leaping to her feet, and before Keith could realize what was going on, Mckenna took the board and swung as hard as she could. The board connected with Keith's head, giving a satisfying crack as it connected. He dropped to the ground and Mckenna rushed forward, hitting him again and again until she drew blood.

Horrified at what she'd done, even though she knew he deserved every bit of the beating, Mckenna rushed for the open door. She was about ready to step out when Keith's hand grabbed her ankle, his fingers wrapping around her and then pulling with such strength that Mckenna smacked the ground, falling hard.

She had the wind knocked out of her for a second, but her flight instinct continued to kick in. She was a survivor. She was strong. She was no longer a victim, and he would not get the best of her.

Mckenna took her free leg and began striking his face

with as much force as she could. For a moment, his hand tightened, but then she connected with his nose, hearing another satisfying crack. She hoped she'd broken it, her horror at hurting this man long gone.

His fingers loosened and Mckenna took the opportunity to pull her leg away and scramble to her feet. Pushing with all her might and forcing her legs to work, Mckenna bolted out the door. Despite the head injuries, Keith was right behind her and gaining fast.

Mckenna glanced over her shoulder, stumbling and tripping. She fell to the ground and was scrambling to her feet when Keith grabbed her again by the ankle. This time Keith was full of rage and fury, and Mckenna knew it wasn't going to be easy to get away.

Chapter Forty-Three

Mckenna kicked hard again, but Keith was ready for her move and ducked to the side. She hadn't noticed until now that he had grabbed the board Mckenna had hit him with. Raising it above his head he slammed the board down, but Mckenna managed to roll out of the way.

The board split in two as it hit the hard, rocky ground. Mckenna tried to free herself from his grip, but he was too strong, his fury-fed adrenaline making her no match for him. When the board split, it had created a sharp, spear-like side, and fear coursed through Mckenna as Keith pulled his arm back, ready to stab her.

"No," Mckenna screamed, trying again to get away. "No!"

She writhed on the ground and saw that same sly smile cross his face.

"You're mine. You thought you got away, but I've been waiting to catch you again. This time, there is no release."

Mckenna was about to scream when she heard a female voice.

"Put that down or I'll shoot."

Mckenna managed to turn and wiggle, escaping Keith's grip as he was distracted. Coming toward her was Mocha, Evan and the sheriff with her gun pointed straight at Keith.

She was going to get up and run, when Evan yelled, "Mckenna, stay down. Stay down."

Every part of her wanted to spring away, to flee, but she trusted Evan. Mocha took off, racing toward her, and Evan let go of the leash. Mckenna stayed down, but scooted away from Keith as the sheriff kept her gun trained on him.

Keith appeared to be deciding if he was still going to stab her. Unsure what he would do, Mckenna shoved Mocha behind her, trying to keep him safe.

"I said, put the weapon down," the sheriff said again.

Evan repeated her command. As the sheriff and Evan continued to pressure Keith into dropping the board, Mckenna kept slowly scooting away, trying to stay down, but gain distance from this monster.

Keith's words, "This time there is no release," kept going through her mind. He wasn't going to let her go, even if it meant the sheriff and Evan shot him. Rearing back, Keith gripped the sharp stake in both hands now. He lunged toward Mckenna.

A couple of gunshots echoed off the surrounding hills. Screaming, Mckenna rolled away as the stake shattered against the rocky ground. Keith's body landed with a thump next to her and then Evan was there, kneeling on Keith's back and cuffing his hands.

The sheriff was there too, helping Evan roll Keith over so they could start administering first aid.

"You're one lucky bastard," the sheriff said. "We hit you in the shoulder and it's nothing vital. Looks like you're going to get to the big house and stay there for a while. I don't think you'll get a warm welcome considering you're a PO. Just as bad as being a cop in prison."

The only response from Keith was a groan. Mckenna was shaking and Mocha lay on her, draping himself across her lap, trying to comfort her. Mckenna started petting his head. Realizing that the sheriff had Keith and was patting him down for weapons, Evan came over to Mckenna, his face serious.

"Oh my God, I'm calling an ambulance. I thought I'd lost you. Forever," Evan said.

"I didn't know if I'd see you again," Mckenna said, pulling Evan closer. He sat down next to her and hugged her, Mocha grunting a little since he was caught in the middle on Mckenna's lap. "I don't need an ambulance, but Rex is in the mining building. He's hurt, bad."

"Are you sure you don't need an ambulance?"

"I'm sure," Mckenna said.

"I'm still taking you to the hospital. Just to make sure you're okay. You have a nasty bump on your head and your eye is starting to turn black."

"Keith caught me a couple times, but I think I managed to get some payback," Mckenna said. She glanced over at Keith, who still had blood running out of his nose.

Evan followed her gaze. "That was you? You broke his nose."

"Good," Mckenna said. She stopped petting Mocha and ran her fingers across Evan's cheek. "I love you, Evan Knox. I don't know if you feel the same, but you should know that I am totally in love with you."

"I thought I'd lost you. I never want to feel that way again. I love you too, Mckenna Parker," Evan said, leaning in and kissing her, his lips gentle and caressing.

Mckenna wrapped her arms around Evan and pulled him in, never wanting to let go.

A BIT ANNOYED at Evan's persistence that she needed medical attention, Mckenna lay on a bed in the ER. The doctors had done all their poking and prodding and thought she might have a mild concussion and be slightly dehydrated, but otherwise she was fine. She had agreed to IV fluids and then Mckenna would be released. She was ready to go home.

Mocha was lying on the bed with her at her insistence. The hospital didn't really want the dog in the ER, but since he was technically a therapy dog and had hospital clearance from visiting Lily, they'd given in. There was only one other guy she'd like to be here with her, but she knew he was down the hall, interviewing Keith.

Evan had popped in once to check on her and said that the shot to Keith's shoulder wasn't bad. He'd be transferred soon to jail, where a medical team would take over his care. That way they didn't have to have a deputy guard him. Until then, Evan was going to get all the information out of Keith that he could. Amazingly, Keith hadn't lawyered up yet. Evan had also told her that Rex was in stable condition and would be staying a few nights at the hospital.

Voices echoed down the hall and Mckenna groaned. She could tell it was her family. Not that she wasn't happy to see them, but she didn't want to be fussed over right now. She wanted to get the fluids and go home—with both Mocha and Evan.

The door opened and Cassidy peeked from behind the curtain. Seeing Mckenna in the bed, she said over her shoulder, "She's dressed. You're good to come in."

"Why don't you announce that to the whole hospital?" Mckenna said, with a sarcastic tone.

"Good idea, let me go to the nurses station and see if I can get on the intercom."

Mckenna laughed. Her sister could always rival her sarcasm. Their parents came into the room with concerned looks. Her mom started crying when she saw her.

"Oh, my baby," her mom said, coming over. "Hi, Mocha."

Mocha lifted his head and thumped his tail on the bed.

"He's tired," Mckenna said. "He worked hard to find me. And I'm fine, Mom, really."

"You're the best dog," her mom said, rubbing Mocha's face. "I'll buy you your favorite dog cookies forever."

Mocha wagged his tail even harder. Mckenna didn't know what to say to her family. She finally said, "This is all over. Evan says Keith is going away for a long time."

"Evan?" her mom asked.

"Agent Evan Knox," Cassidy interjected. "He's been the agent assigned to this case."

"Oh! That's the man who had the idea to let Mocha track. We'll have to find him and thank him too."

Mckenna knew that her sister was getting ready to cover for her. The last thing her parents wanted to know was that she'd spent the night at Evan's house, but Mckenna did want them to know one thing—Evan was now a part of her life. Her mother had worried that Mckenna's experience would mean she would never have a normal life, which Mckenna translated to her mother fretting about not having grand-children. Neither she nor Cassidy had been in a serious re-lationship, and their mother was constantly worrying that she'd be the only person at her bridge club without grand-children or even a son-in-law.

"Yes," she said. "Agent Evan Knox was not only assigned to this case, and he did have Mocha track, but there's some-thing else you should know…"

"Yes?" her mother said.

"I'm in love with him too."

"Does he know this?" her mother asked.

"Yes. He does," said Evan, standing in the doorway.

Her mother turned and scanned Evan from head to toe. "Very nice, dear. Very nice."

"Oh geez, mom," Mckenna said, her face flushing red.

Evan shook hands with her father. Mckenna could tell by her father's expression that he already liked Evan. Then to her surprise, Evan gave Cassidy a hug. That made her happy as well.

Her mother was getting ready to launch into more questions when Cassidy saved Mckenna. "Well, we can all see that she's fine," Cassidy said. "Let's go get something to eat and then I need to get back to work. Plus, Cooper is hanging out with another handler, and I need to pick him up soon. Let's leave these two alone."

Mckenna thought her mom was going to argue, but she ended up following Cassidy out the door. Her father came over and gave Mckenna a kiss on the cheek and squeezed her hand. He turned to Evan and said, "Take good care of her."

"I will," Evan promised.

Mckenna could hear her mother still talking about Evan as they all walked down the hall. Then they stepped on the elevator and there was quiet. "Well, now you met my family," she said.

"I like them." Evan leaned over and gently kissed her, taking his fingers and caressing the bump on the side of her head where Keith had punched her.

"How did it go? With him…"

"It went well. I guess getting shot and being caught red-handed helps a person confess."

"To everything? Even my kidnapping nine years ago?"

"Even your kidnapping," Evan said. "And others, including a couple in Wyoming where he ended up killing his victims."

"Others? Besides Lily and Autumn? And he killed them?"

Evan filled Mckenna in about how Keith went to the Wind River Reservation in Wyoming to go "fishing."

"He was smart enough to know that he couldn't do that same thing here, not while Toby was serving time. At some point he went to a probation officer training up there and realized that so many of the Indigenous women had gone missing he didn't think anyone would miss another one. Plus, there're so many cases, the Bureau of Indian Affairs and FBI can't keep up. It was the perfect hunting ground for him."

The story made her sick. "If only I'd stood my ground more when I thought Toby was innocent. Those young women wouldn't have had to endure that torture and they might be alive."

"You can't blame yourself."

"I know," Mckenna said. "But I know what they went through, and I want to make sure their families get the help they need."

"I have all the cold cases from the local sheriff and BIA. With Keith's confessions, they can now give the families closure. I know that won't bring their loved ones back, but at least they can get some justice," Evan said. "Once this went across state lines and involved a reservation, it became federal. Keith will be prosecuted in federal court. He'll serve time in a federal prison, and you know what?"

"What?"

"Federal prisons don't like to release their inmates early. I'll make sure he doesn't get out until he's an old man or not at all. He's never going to hurt anyone again."

"Thank you," Mckenna said, pulling Evan down and kissing him again.

When they parted, Evan smiled and said, "I can't wait to get you home. Alone. All to myself."

Mckenna's heart rate monitor increased, and she laughed. "I guess I can't hide that I can't wait either. At least not while I'm hooked up to this thing."

Evan smiled. "I'm on administrative duty since I shot Keith. They have to investigate. Instead of sitting at my desk and doing paperwork, I am taking a couple personal days. I have some ideas of things we can do."

"I look forward to discovering what those things are, Agent Knox."

Evan kissed her and then came up for air. Mocha groaned and slid off the bed, walked over to the corner and sat, sulking. The Lab glanced over his shoulder at Mckenna and Evan, and they laughed.

"Come here, buddy," Evan said. Mocha ambled back over. "You're a part of my life now too. My couch is your couch."

Mckenna giggled at that and said, "Or, we can always stay at my place too. That way your couch stays pristine."

"I don't care where we go or where we stay, as long as I'm with you. There's one more thing, though, before I break you out of here."

"Oh yeah? What's that?" Mckenna asked.

"I hope you don't mind, but there was someone who wanted to visit you. And Mocha. She wants to see him too."

Evan signaled for someone to come in. Lily walked through the door with a bouquet of flowers.

"Oh my gosh," Mckenna said. "It's good to see you."

Mocha perked up when he saw Lily and after she gave Mckenna the flowers, he leaned up against her leg. "It's good to see you too," Lily said. Then she added, "You really found him? It's him?"

"Yes," Mckenna and Evan said in unison.

"He admitted to everything, Lily. Plus, we have plenty of evidence even if he didn't confess to the kidnappings,"

Evan added. "The fingerprints on Mckenna's bracelet and journal matched Keith. He kept the bracelet as a souvenir. It seems he liked to keep trinkets to remind him of his victims. He took a necklace from Autumn. The evidence team found that in his house along with other items probably belonging to the girls in Wyoming. After I interviewed him, the prosecutor offered a plea deal. I think he'll take it. If he does, you won't have to testify or anything."

Lily nodded. "I would, though. Testify, that is. If it meant doing it for Autumn."

"You're a good friend," Mckenna told her. "Keith will never hurt anyone again. We'll all make sure of that."

Lily turned to Evan and said, "Why? Did he ever say why?"

"You mean why Keith started kidnapping girls?" Evan asked.

Lily nodded. Mckenna wondered how much Evan could say, but she also knew that Lily had rights as a victim to learn things about the investigation. Evan would know what he could and couldn't tell her.

"Sort of," Evan answered. "I asked him about why he took Mckenna. He'd come back to surprise Penny. She'd visited him a couple times and he thought they were in a serious relationship. When he got to Penny's, the party was going on and he caught Penny with another man. He was furious and wanted to prove that he could get any girl. He had Liquid E that he was going to offer Penny, but he drugged Mckenna instead. He said he liked the thrill. He loved having control. It kicked off some sick fantasies for him. He's going to go through a mental competency evaluation before anything moves forward in the court system."

"How did he frame Toby?" Mckenna asked.

"He said he saw Toby's truck and once he had you, he

knew from taking his criminal justice courses that if he threw your jacket and some other personal items in Toby's truck, there was a good chance it would be found. Especially if he called in an anonymous tip."

"Can I ask *you* a question," Lily said, turning to Mckenna.

"Sure," Mckenna said.

"The fear. Are you still afraid?"

Mckenna nodded. "Yes. Although my fear is different now. It's something I can face better, learn to manage, but it's a part of me. It makes up who I am. Have you gone to the support group I suggested?"

"Yes, last night was the first one," Lily said.

"What did you think?"

"I liked it."

"What did you like?" Mckenna asked.

"To realize that even though all our experiences are slightly different, there are other victims out there like us. That they've been able to move forward and that they feel the same fear and have the same emotions and it's okay."

"I liked it for the same reason," Mckenna said. "I go every week, so I'll see you next time. Maybe we can grab coffee afterward."

"I'd like that," Lily said. "I'm going to head home now, but I wanted to thank you. For finding him. For Autumn. For me."

"You helped too, Lily," Mckenna said. "Being brave and remembering things to tell us was important and helped a lot."

The young lady smiled and then headed out.

"You want me to walk you to your car?" Evan asked Lily.

Mckenna loved his offer. She understood that something so simple as going to your car in a parking garage might feel like a huge achievement and was scary at the same time once you'd had an experience like they had. She loved that Evan knew that too.

"Yes, please," Lily said.

"I'll be back," Evan said, leaning over and giving Mckenna a quick kiss.

"I knew it," Lily said, with a big smile.

"What?" Evan asked.

"That it's not complicated like you said, Mckenna. You two are a thing."

Chapter Forty-Four

A couple of days later

Mckenna snuggled closer to Evan, the sheets tangled between them. They'd ended up back at Mckenna's after Mocha started chewing on Evan's couch. The Lab was happily snoring on his bed, content to be home.

The sun went behind some clouds making the room darken. Mckenna couldn't remember ever being this happy. Once she had been released from the hospital, Evan had taken the personal days he mentioned. Originally, they were going to hike to the summit of Mount Blue Sky before it closed for the winter and try to get tickets to a concert at Red Rocks, but so far, they hadn't made it very far out of the house.

She closed her eyes, for once feeling safe and secure. Protected.

"There's something I need to tell you," Evan said.

"What's that?" Mckenna asked, opening her eyes, and propping herself up on one elbow so she could see Evan and trail a finger down his chest.

Evan swallowed hard, his face turning serious. Now Mckenna was really wondering what he had to say. "You have a girlfriend? Wife?"

"What? No. You really think that?"

Mckenna laughed. "No. Of course not. I'm teasing you and now, whatever you have to say, it'll be fine."

Evan sighed. "I've been offered a promotion. To ASAC."

"What? Evan, that's great. It's what you wanted. Why do you look so upset?"

"Because it's in Oregon. But I think I'll turn it down."

"Why would you do that?" Mckenna asked. "This is your dream. You want to keep moving up the chain, don't you?"

"Well, yeah. I told them I would think about it."

"Why?" Mckenna asked. "You should pursue this. Opportunities like this don't come along all the time. What's the problem?"

Evan ran his fingers down Mckenna's side, trailing along her phoenix tattoo. "The problem is I don't want to lose you. My job isn't the most important thing in my life. Not anymore. Plus, I'd miss Mocha. I haven't had another guy to watch TV with in a long time."

Mckenna giggled. "Have you thought about the possibility that there might be options? Like I could see if there was a transfer available for me too. And Mocha. Maybe there's an opening in the Oregon office."

"You'd do that?"

"Yes, I would. Just like I know you'd give up this offer for me. We'll figure this out." She leaned in and kissed Evan, her fingers trailing from his chest down lower. "But for now, let's not worry about it."

"Works for me," Evan said, responding to her touch. "Maybe we can hike Mount Blue Sky tomorrow."

* * * * *

COMING SOON!

We really hope you enjoyed reading this book.
If you're looking for more romance
be sure to head to the shops when
new books are available on

Thursday 23rd October

To see which titles are coming soon, please visit

millsandboon.co.uk/nextmonth

MILLS & BOON

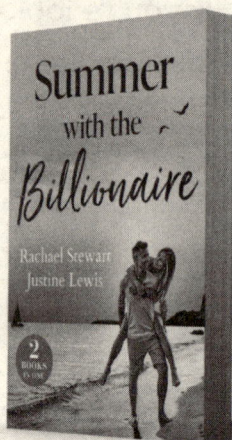

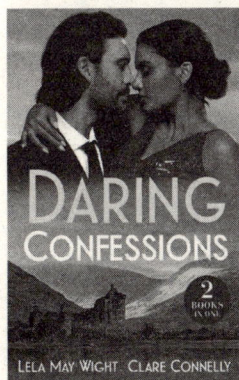

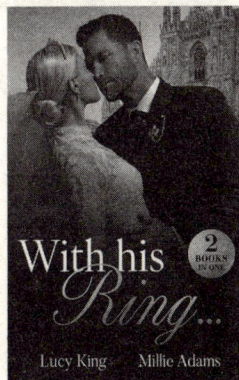

LET'S TALK

Romance

For exclusive extracts, competitions
and special offers, find us online:

f MillsandBoon

X @MillsandBoon

@MillsandBoonUK

@MillsandBoonUK

Get in touch on 01413 063 232